THE PERFUME
WOMAN'S DIARIES

Pran Joshi

Leadstart
INKSTATE

ISBN: 978-93-5458-588-3

First published in India 2022 by Leadstart Inkstate
A brand of One Point Six Technologies Pvt. Ltd.

123, Building J2, Shram Seva Premises,
Wadala Truck Terminal,
Mumbai 400022, Maharashtra, INDIA
Phone: +91 96999 33000
Email: info@leadstartcorp.com
www.leadstartcorp.com

Disclaimer: This is a work of fiction. All the names, characters, businesses, places, events and incidents in this book are either the product of the author's imagination or used in a fictitious manner. Any resemblance to actual persons, living or dead, or actual events is purely coincidental.

Editor: Vaibhav Pathare
Cover: Chinmayee Samant
Layouts: Ashwini Rane

Dedication

For my grandchildren…

Jeyven, Leiya and Jhasin…all Chhina's

Iyla Joshi Moylan

PRAN JOSHI comes from a family of teachers. He earned a Bachelor's and Master's degrees in English Literature from Mumbai University. His destiny took him to Kenya and soon in 1969 he was in Toronto. After getting Canadian certifications, he was hired by Moira Secondary in Belleville, ON. With success came meeting and dating an exceptional young nurse, Ramani. Ramani worked as a nurse in a newborn nursery in Belleville General Hospital. Pran and Ramani got married in 1970 and have three children. Their eldest daughter Supriya married Tejinder and has three children. Their second-born Aarty married Adam in North Carolina and they have a vivacious daughter.

Teaching brought Pran many accolades and awards. But nothing makes him happier than receiving messages from his former students or meeting them in person. After retiring, Ramani and Pran travelled the winters in warm and sun-kissed Southern Europe. However, he missed teaching and he needed that spark again. To douse that spark, Pran applied for a teaching position in South Carolina and Dr Kathie Greer hired him. Under her leadership, Pran thrived and Dr

Greer encouraged him to be a teacher trainer.

He enjoyed the phase of teaching again, but soon his first grandchild's arrival meant he and Ramani would come home, and enjoy proximity to their grandchildren in Toronto and participate in their growing and education. They enjoy travelling, reading, walking and spending time meeting their friends.

Acknowledgements

I am gladly indebted to Selina Bickrum, a peripatetic teacher, and my bespoke sister, shining paths for students in South Africa, the USA, and China; and now continuing with the same vigour and love for students in New Zealand. When I asked her, she readily agreed to read the first version of the Perfume Woman's Diaries. She amended, suggested new and different angles, and then went through the rewrites with unflagging love and respect for my novel. Then Joan Dunn and I met at Tim Horton's Coffee once a week to discuss what I had written. Joan guided the manuscript to its final shape that included a re-imagined ending.

My family members were a part of the project from the get-go. Supriya and Tejinder Chhina and Aarty and Adam Moylan supported my ambitious plans and Rahul answered all the questions on high tech issues. Ramani, my better half in every respect, supported me in all the steps that I went through to bring this novel to its published form. Words just don't reflect to what length she went to in this journey. So, family, accept my thanks. And finally, I would like to thank Pooja Dutt and her support team at the Leadstart for their due diligence and professionalism to make sure that 'The Perfume Woman' was ready to meet the world.

I must also thank my innumerable students and faculty colleagues, especially in Belleville, Ontario, Canada, and the USA, who listened to my stories while I taught, or during teacher training seminars. Some of them goaded, cajoled me to write a book. This is for you, my dear students and teachers for your love and respect that you showered on me and continue to remain in contact with me.

Having taught in India, Kenya, Canada, and the USA, I have come across many students and teachers in life. I am certain that some of you will be happy that your former teacher, colleague, wrote this novel. If you, a book lover, stumbled upon the Perfume Woman and would like to comment, please do let me know. Nothing will make me smile more than receiving a quick email from you telling if you enjoyed The Perfume Woman.

You can write to me at: Theperfumewomansdiaries@gmail.com

Contents

Chapter One

Daughters Come Home

As the sweet smell of flowers wafted through the house, for the first time in his life, Ayush realized that Somi was beyond his reach. Though he'd been aware of this fact for most of their married life, it hit him only today as he watched her standing in the garden arrange and rearrange flowers in a long-stemmed vase. He liked staying out of people's matters for most part, including those of his wife's. However, for some reason, today, the way Somi's thoughts unfurled all over her face as her fingers traced out the shape of each Hydrangea, awoke in her husband, a sudden concern.

He sighed deeply, deciding it was better if at least one of their daughters could come visit them for a few days, rather than confronting his wife directly. Throughout the day, the couple was normally enveloped in silence, their house seeming less and less of a home after all their daughters had moved out.

They'll find a way to know what was going on in her head, he figured.

Making sure not to sound too worrisome, he casually dropped an email to their two eldest daughters. Then he returned to his work on interest rates and currency values, but thoughts of Somi lingered in his mind with certain unease. It seemed that she had his undivided attention today; his gaze going back to her repeatedly, something that she would've wanted him to do all their married years. He tried to wave the thoughts aside but found himself reclined on his chair, and without making much effort, observed her.

She was now standing before a row of white, dark purple and pink- all lilacs that she had raised with much affection and care, in meditation. She plucked them along with a spike of lavender and wove the bunch into her hair. He knew just how proud she was of her garden- as much, if not more, as she was of their four young and beautiful daughters. Somi had raised them with utmost love and care and now that they were away; her attention was consumed by the plants in their garden. She had made sure that they got it all, without any compromises, and the results could not have made her prouder. The compliments that she received from neighbours for the hard work made it worth all her time and efforts, the same way their friends and relatives gushed about their daughters. The basics, for her, remained invariable between off-springs and flowers: tending to matters with love and care, not being afraid of any weeds or dirt that came in the way and always being there when required. And after a while, you could see them bloom and blossom into their own beautiful selves.

Whenever Ayush was in a snit, introspective or nostalgic mood, Somi would sit on either a bench or the swing in the backyard listening to chirping chickadees, starlings, goldfinches, Cardinals, and robins. She would see her favourite squirrels, chasing, climbing and nibbling. The outside filled her life with sweet sounds, aromatic presence and feelings that transported her back to the glorious time of friendship.

Ayush had retired a while ago from his distinguished career with the International Monetary Fund, but he was not one to sit idle. He knew that the quietness of retirement eventually got to him, and so he began doing some consulting work alongside writing for finance journals and a subscription-based newsletter. He wasn't one to have frequent mood swings or give in to his temper easily. In fact, he seldom got angry, but the only thing about him that irked Somi was his habit of looking into spaces so closely that more often than not he would completely dissolve into them, totally absent from reality. If she asked him, upon noticing, where his mind was, he would mechanically reply with, "Oh, I'm just putting things into perspective." To her, he always appeared to be putting his ideas, trends or history in a "perspective" of his own. If she prodded further, he would dismiss it unapprovingly, as though she had entered a restricted territory of his universe.

Contrastingly, Somi too had recently felt that Ayush was behaving differently. His demeanour was peppered with frequent nostalgic mood swings, very unlike him. She tried to steer clear as she knew he'd like her to, but something about the way he was lost within himself intrigued her even more. *My husband has a good income and a great life. So, what is it, then, that he has to put into perspective?* She wondered.

It wasn't long, before she concluded that there wasn't much that could be done. He had no faults as such; he was a dedicated father and a sincere husband. He had provided them with a decent lifestyle, a good house and together, they had built what they could call a home. Over the course of all these years, Somi had come to terms with his silence of "putting things into perspective" as a character aberration. Moreover, she had realised that she too, preferred her own space. In all these years that they had been together, she couldn't categorize a single incident as a fight, nor misunderstanding. In essence, no one could ever suspect anything to be wrong or amiss between the couple as such, though only their hearts knew better. When by herself, she contemplated whether she had been quiet for too long, that maybe she should be the one to end the stagnant silence that lived between her husband and her. However, something stopped her every time.

For Somi, Ayush had been the one ever since she could remember. However, this feeling was not reciprocal, since he'd had his own following. Girls had always sought him out, though he was never intrigued, until the one time, he fell hard for a girl, and Somi knew all too well about it. In fact, until today, this silence that she had come to terms with had grown from the fact that Somi knew her husband was still in love with another woman.

Her daughters were her escape all this while. She was their mother but only by relation. She had always been like a friend, and they had reciprocated with equal respect. Late-night conversations, Tuesdays reserved for movies, lunches and shopping- they did everything together. However, all this changed once they were old enough to move out and into their own respective lives, leaving their mother alone with her thoughts. She missed them, needless to say, despising the separations that distance caused. And so, she thought of them frequently, and today, as she tended to her beautiful garden, her thoughts were of her daughters.

From inside the house, Ayush shouted out to her, "Som, Zara is calling."

However, when he saw Somi still lost in thought among the flowers; he sighed into the phone, "Zara, your mom is busy talking to her lilacs and fixing them onto her hair and not that I want to scare you, but she has been quieter than the usual. She seems lost and immersed in her thoughts. Talk to her and see if she needs anything, would you? Okay? Alright. Let me call her again."

This time, his voice rose through the house and into the garden, "Somi! Zara is waiting on the line." Somi looked up from her trance to see Ayush peering out of his office window, waving the phone in his hand.

"I think she heard me this time. Don't tell her I asked you to call. Here she comes. Take care, be forever young. Love you."

Somi almost tripped as she snatched the phone from Ayush.

"Hey, how is my baby doing?"

"Mom, in case you forgot, there are two who succeeded me. And I'm doing well."

"Oh! Of course, baby. How are you doing? How is your hubby, Shaan doing?"

Zara snickered on the other side. She knew arguing with her mother over this was a lost cause. "Shaan is fine, Mom, we both are doing well. It's been so long. I was thinking all of us could do with a little get together. What do you think? We could have our usual lunches, movies and goes without saying, the late-night chats. We could also try a little something different and go hiking if you'd like?"

Ayush was startled to see Somi speak with excitement over the phone, "Oh Zara, what are the odds?! I was just thinking about calling you girls to come over some time soon. This couldn't have been more perfect. I'll call the other girls too..."

"Not to worry Mom, I've already done that! Anya and Bijli will come over with me. I also have an announcement to make but let's save that for when we meet. No, we are not expecting a baby yet. I will check with the little one too. However, you know how busy she is with her NASA program. It's going to keep her away for a few months. But I'll check if she's doing fine. Even among just us, I know we'll cook up a storm! I'll message you with the details soon! Meanwhile, you take care, okay? Ti amo!"

When Somi slowly put down phone, Ayush saw her genuinely smiling after a long time.

Somi and Ayush were blessed with four vivacious and talented daughters. Because of Ayush's work, the family had been transferred from place to place and as a result, the girls were born in different countries all over the world, their respective cities contributing to a certain personality trait in each of them.

Lavanya, the eldest, was born in Buenos Aires and was called Anya by all. Likewise, Nirjara or Zara, as she preferred, the second one in the line, was born in Milan where the family stayed for seven years. With the Italian help in their home, both Anya and Zara picked up everything Italian- language, arts and a taste for Italian foods and flavour. Since they were only a year apart, they were remarkably close and emotionally bonded. Anya became an international business and trade attorney, while Zara specialized as a forensic expert in illegal money transfer, after graduating as a chartered accountant and financial auditor. Whenever they both met their father, they would have non-stop conversations on world economy, finances, taxation and investments. Their meetings seemed like a mini seminar to everyone around them.

The next two girls, Anoushka and Bijli, were born one year apart as well, six years after Zara. Ayush and Somi decided to make Toronto their permanent home at the time. After their holiday trip to the Canadian Rockies, Niagara Falls and Toronto, Somi and both the daughters expressed a strong desire to live in Canada. With the right job opportunity at IMF, they moved to Toronto.

Anoushka, a fanatic of science fiction and space exploration was identified as a gifted student in her primary years. After graduating from high school as an Ontario scholar, she finished her undergrad degree in Physics at the University of Toronto. Her interests took her to MIT, and soon she became a researcher at Carnegie Mellon University in Pittsburgh, her work eventually bringing her to the attention of NASA's Mars Programme.

The youngest Bijli, like her name, was a lightning rod. Intellectually, she was sharp, but her moral dimensions were even more profound. She was at the forefront of fighting for social justice for women, children, immigrants and the indigenous people of The First Nations. Her organizational skills were outstanding; her knowledge of the issues was impressive and widely accepted.

Somi's friends often used to say that god had placed the fountain of learning in the Vyas household, something that the couple always took great pride in hearing. And now, they were both eager for Friday to come. Still holding onto the receiver of the phone, Somi reminisced on how quickly her girls had grown up, from sweet young children into independent and confident women. However, most of all, she smiled wide at the prospect of them all being together; their house would be a home again, filled with laughter, yelling, singing, music, conversations and the aroma of food, all the things that she held dear.

It didn't take long for Somi to get started with her preparations. Owing to her love for cooking, by Wednesday, she began by preparing dishes that she knew would need more time and effort with than the rest: marinating lamb (fondly known by her girls as 'chewy meat'), butter chicken, chicken *tikka* and meat for kebabs in their respective spices. Alongside this, she also began preparing a slew of vegetarian delights and platters of various cookies and Indian sweets. She knew just how much all of them enjoyed munching over light snacks while watching movies or during conversations. There were also times when they'd linger into the kitchen either early afternoon or late night relying on the fact that their mother had their sudden pangs covered too. The refrigerator, therefore, was well-stocked with delicacies. Her girls were coming home after quite some time, and she wanted to give them a feast! As she moved around the kitchen, all this preparation made it seem as though she was organizing for a party, and she felt herself smiling in anticipation.

On Thursday afternoon, Somi cut red onions, peeled and sliced garlic cloves, chopped cilantro, crushed freshly roasted cumin seeds and put on her cooking apron that proclaimed her to proudly be the '*Queen of the Kitchen Dominion*'. She poured cooking oil in a copper-bottomed pot on the stove. When she heard a slight sizzle of the boiling oil, she dropped in it black mustard seeds. The seeds cracked as though fireworks on show inside the pot. She then sliced garlic alongside whole cumin seeds. Her hands were used to this familiar rhythm. She felt like a maestro leading all her ingredients into a delicious harmony. Almost instinctively, she placed in the marinated lamb and lowered the heat. She knew the crackling of mustard and roasting of cayenne peppers would soon make Ayush sneeze, leading him into the kitchen, his nose following the exquisite aroma.

The fragrance of garlic, mustard, and cumin, mixed with a touch of sugar, lemon and yogurt that Somi used for the marinades, began to usurp the empty house. And just as she had predicted, Ayush abandoned his perch in the home office shadowing the delectable fragrances, found himself in the kitchen. The combined smells of all the different spices had created a heavenly atmosphere, and just for a moment, the husband and wife were enveloped in this seductive dance of food and love, forgetting all the distances between them.

Later in the afternoon, she kept busy, making the Indian savoury snacks that her girls loved: *madhi, theplas, dhokla, handvo* and *muthia*. She made various kinds of chutneys to go with it: chilly, garlic, cilantro, tamarind, mint, and peanuts. Yet again, the aroma of heat, tart and sweetness brought Ayush to the dance floor. This time he touched the curve of her back, gingerly as though, after years of marriage, it was still an alien touch. He inhaled from her all the aromas that hung around the kitchen. For a brief moment, it seemed to the two of them, that time had frozen, and they had broken their barriers to let the other one in. Somi smiled nervously, onion and knife still in hand, pleased yet unsure of how to react to Ayush's sudden affections. *All this house needs now*, she thought to herself, *are the girls.*

Anya and Bijli, both of whom lived in Toronto itself, drove to the airport to pick up Zara, and the three of them came home together. Keeping up with her dramatic persona, Zara entered the home and comically declared with open arms, "We are all here, so, let the party begin."

After an exchange of long hugs, the wine bottles were opened, and the food was laid out. Even though Anoushka was being missed by all, the house finally shook itself out of its slumberous lethargy. It indeed felt alive again and Somi felt herself basking in this warm energy. It was only after dinner that calm returned to the house. Ayush, Somi and the girls were all lazing around in the living room with desserts and cups of coffee being passed to others. Everyone found themselves a comfortable spot and settled in.

Picking up the day's newspaper, which had the horoscope section open, Bijli laughed and asked, "Hey Zara, did you read your horoscope today?"

"It's not like I read it ever, but no, not today. Why? Does it have anything interesting to say?"

Making sure she had everyone's attention, Bijli straightened up and cleared her throat, "This week your attention turns to your parents as well as your own heartaches. Conversation with a sibling could be worthwhile. You will have to tread carefully." She read it with such drama that everyone chuckled as she read out the last line.

"Very funny," Zara replied, fake frowning.

"Now that we are on it, Bij, why don't you read Dad and Mom's?" Anya prompted from the other side of the room where she lay on the floor, flipping through the pages of a book.

Before Bij could read even fold the pages to the other side of the column, Ayush dismissed the action. "Don't bother, Bij. I don't believe in this mumbo-jumbo, hocus-pocus crap."

"I agree with your father on this. Don't bother with mine either." Somi added quickly.

The girls turned their heads to their mother. "Mom, stop following Dad's wishes so readily. You are your own person, you know," said Bijli, closing the paper finally and sitting up straight. "By the way, Mom, didn't you learn the art of horoscope reading from Grandpa?"

"Yes, she did, and like him, she was good at it too." Ayush said. "But, anyway, my Zara, tell us about this big news that you didn't want to disclose over the phone the other day. What is it that you wanted to surprise us with?"

As smoothly as he did it, Somi didn't like Ayu's prompt dismissal of her presence from the conversation. She knew that Ayush often sent new jobs advertised by IMF, World Bank and the UN to their daughters. If he found decent positions advertised in the Economist, he would let them know as well. He did it even though he knew his daughters followed the same sources. This was one of his ways of looking out for them. If there was one thing, he shared with them, especially with the elder two, it was a love for economies and banking. At times like these, she felt left out, but showed no displeasure; just sighed and looked away.

Noticing her mother moved a little sideways, Anya almost whispered, "You are okay, Mom?"

Somi smiled and nodded appreciatively at her.

"Well, Mom, Dad, it's a new job offer. To be honest, it came completely out of the blue. One day, somebody called me up to tell me that I had been referred by one of my clients for a position, and that they wanted to see me in person. After an exchange of quite a few emails, when we met, they offered me a high-profile job in the National Treasury."

The other two girls almost clapped and high-five in appreciation while Somi smiled from one ear to the other.

Sensing the sudden excitement in the room, Ayush sat up straight. Zara sat up straight too. She knew she would have to answer the upcoming questions that her father had for her.

"Did you have your first orientation?" Ayush asked lowering his glasses.

"I did, Dad. And though the job is with the Treasury, my position will be liaised with the Justice and Homeland teams. I even met with all the power-brokers there."

"So, what will be your primary work there?"

"I'll look after the local transactions as well as the international money transfers going to certain destinations. Since Mumbai is one of their largest contacts for India, I will also get to interact with the people dealing with illegal money matters there. It'll be kind of a detour from what I am doing presently but the span of knowledge seems luscious, and I think I'm going to enjoy this job a lot."

"I hear you. However, when you say learning, what exactly do you think you would be gaining from the experience?" Ayush was curious. Somi and the other two girls were intrigued by this to and fro of questions. And even though Bij quietly slipped between them and like a referee, offered a mock mike from Ayush to Zara, everyone knew who would have the final word in the conversation.

"Well, just how the system is organized from top to bottom," Zara continued. "I'm interested in knowing how far exactly the web for illegal money laundering extends. It is only an extension of what

I have been doing until this time albeit now I get to do some field work alongside. "

"Hmm," said Ayush stroking his chin. Zara was right; it would be an interesting new post for her. He was pretty confident; she had always proven her stance in whatever she had been involved with. "It makes sense," he said finally, "Though the travel might be a little stressful, I'm very sure you will cope with that change in the system as well. If you want my help getting set up in Mumbai or the local travel there, let me know. Your mom and I know the place inside out."

Hearing the name of the place of her birth stirred something in Somi. She listened with rapture as Ayush outlined the areas and neighbourhoods popular with tourists visiting Mumbai, and those that the girls could be safe getting around by themselves too. As always, he missed no detail, let go of no nuance to paint an accurate and brilliant landscape of a city that sat deep within Somi's heart. Their Mumbai! As he described to the girls the streets, the sounds and the sights, she thanked yet again, her husband's sharp and photographic memory, which hardly let go of a single detail from its crevasse. He was well known to remember every minute detail- no date was forgotten; no meeting left unrecorded, no colour, smell or spectacle, no matter how mundane, was consigned to oblivion, regardless of how much time had passed. This was Ayush's gift.

Thinking his work, for the time being, was done, Ayush placed both hands on his knees and stood up to leave. He also felt that it would be best to leave the girls to have some quality time with their mother. He knew that until he was around, Somi would not get a chance to open up and speak her mind. He kissed goodnight to each of his girls. As he headed toward his bedroom immersed in an unfinished crossword puzzle, Zara shouted, "Hey, Dad, is it okay if I use your laptop for a few days? I don't want to miss out any work emails while I'm here."

"Of course, you can. But where's yours? I thought you were always on work mode and traveled with your own."

She made way to the laptop and laughed, "I do. But I had to return mine to Accenture when I quit this week. Anyway, I was thinking of buying a new one since the old one's too slow now. Carrying it would have made no sense. So, could I? It's only a matter of a few days."

"Anything my forever young Zara desires. I've another one I can use." He smiled.

"Why does Dad say *'forever young'* whenever he speaks to Zara?" However, amidst all the movement, Anya's question went unnoticed and unanswered.

As he turned to leaving again, Anya said, "Hey Dad, I ran into your old friend, Professor Divecha. She says hello."

Ayush nodded in response and climbed up the stairs to the bedroom.

Once he was out of sight, Somi looked at Anya, who suddenly felt her mother's bone-chilling glare piercing through her. "What did you and Prof Divecha talk about?" She asked, enunciating every word with clenched teeth.

Anya answered in a soft tone, "Ma, we've been over this before. When I met her for the first time at Osgoode Hall a few years ago, and you had the same question. She just said hi, and we didn't talk about anyone in particular."

Somi nodded meekly, fidgeting in her seat.

"Do we have anything to nibble on, to go with all the spicy gossip we all have got to share?" Piped Bijli. Though they had barely finished dinner an hour ago, the smell of food still wafted through the house, and Bijli's stomach growled in response.

Relieved by the distraction, Anya quickly got up to bring the Indian savouries that their Mom had prepared the day before. However, Zara seemed to be the only one who noticed her mother's sharp change of tone and demeanour. She wondered why the mention of Professor Divecha had shaken Somi up so much and why she was overly concerned about the conversation. She had reacted the same way when the name had been mentioned a year ago and Zara was now curious as to whether there was some link between the two, whether there was anything in Somi's past or present that could be traced back to the professor. The only thing, however, she could not understand was why it couldn't be shared with her and her sisters since their mother had always treated them more like friends rather than daughters.

The rest of the weekend passed rather quickly. The girls remained in their pajamas for the entire two days until early Sunday evening when Anya and Bijli left for their condos to get back to work on Monday morning. And now that she was off work for some time, Zara stayed with her parents. The house returned to its usual calm, peppered with the sweet murmurs of Zara and Somi's chats.

Monday morning, as were their habit, Ayush and Somi went for a long walk in their neighbourhood lined with trees and picket fences across both sides of the street. As they walked side by side, they admired the lawns, gardens and garden decorations. This was one of the very few interests that they shared and Somi looked forward to it each day.

"You could almost describe the owners of these homes and gardens," Ayush said, amused. She nodded in agreement. "Yes, for instance, I can tell this couple is the one for minute details, and that couple for sure loves simplicity and symmetry; and yes, this one is for naturalness, freedom of will." Somi chuckled at the way Ayu pointed at various lawns like a child.

Then they came across another house, almost overrun with the wild flora growing around it, and Somi exclaimed, "This particular one, frankly, doesn't give a damn about their surroundings." They both burst out laughing as they made way back home.

On their return, they found Zara in a pensive mood, curled up on the sofa, reading her daily horoscope in the Globe and Mail.

"Your inquisitiveness has taken you to places and people. Get ready for more excitement this week but do remember that ultimately curiosity ended up killing the cat," she read it aloud. She mulled over the statement for a moment, and then recalled her horoscope from the day before. *No matter what you do today, do not jump to conclusions.* She shrugged and dismissed the predictions. She folded the newspaper shut as she saw her parents looking at her mischievously.

Before either of them could begin pulling her leg, she jumped up, "Today the breakfast is on me! I'll go and start preparing for it."

The day passed the same way as the weekend had, with neither much work nor much effort. With Zara in the house, Somi and Ayush had something else to focus on rather than the silence between them. At least for now, neither of them would be alone mulling over their thoughts.

That evening, after dinner, dessert and a little conversation, her parents went to bed looking really happy after a long while. Zara felt proud to see things getting back to normal again.

She took Ayush's laptop to do a little work before bed. She changed into pajamas, fixed her bed and fluffed the pillows all around her to get herself comfortable before settling under the covers with the laptop. She fired the computer up and looked at the numerous icons on the screen, overwhelmed at the number of files saved on the desktop. She had never thought that her prim and proper Dad would be thoroughly disorganized in maintaining his laptop, so she started clearing the clutter. She arranged the all scattered files into one folder on the desktop and smiled at the finally clean screen. Then momentarily forgetting that this was Ayush's computer and not hers, she instinctively clicked on the 'Mail' icon, and waited for new messages to download. It was only when she couldn't recognize any of the names on the list that she remembered this wasn't her computer. The entire folder was full of just one name: Mrin. For as long as she had known her parents, neither of them had ever mentioned this name. Before she could log out, or even ask her dad about Mrin, her subconscious self asserted itself. She found her eyes scanning the message; curiosity, naturally, taking the better of her.

From: Mrin@*****.com

To: Ayush@*****.com

Subject: Knock Knock.

Ayush,

Hi, I'm looking for a long-lost friend who I knew in Bombay many years ago when I was taking some elective courses at the graduate level.

Some common friends that we had were Megh Dalal, Simi Shah, Nikhil Desai and RK Kapoor among others. I think Kapoor was your closest of friends. Some of my friends in Bombay told me that you now lived in Canada. I felt we could connect again. If you are the Ayush, I am looking for, please respond to this email. If not, forgive my intrusion.

Thank you.

Mrin

Zara felt confused. The names mentioned by this woman in her email claimed them to be good friends of her father's; but in reality, she had never heard of any of them before. Or it could also be someone by the same name. However, then again, the inbox was full of emails repeating her name and this was only the first, meaning that they had had further conversation. She felt her conscience knocking in her head to logout of the email account. She did not need to get involved in the personal matters concerning her father. However, somehow, she couldn't. She had never known the college life, or any of the younger years for that matter, of her father and maybe this was a way she finally could. She remembered her father dismissing the topic of his life before marriage with a gentle nod and lack of interest. Below that email lay her father's response, and before she could think, she found herself already reading it.

From: Ayush@*****.com

To: Mrin@*****.com

Subject: Re: Knock Knock.

Mrin,

Yes. YES! Oh, Mrin! Thank you for your email. Yes, I am, in fact, the Ayush you are looking for. I'm so happy to receive your email; you have no idea how improved my day feels already. I have a lot of questions but let us just start by asking who shared my email address with you? I would like to, personally thank them for this. Next, I'm eager to know anything and everything about you. I know this might sound as if it's moving too fast too soon, but I cannot control my excitement. For me, the gap of all these years seems vanished with this one email of yours. I've missed you so much, Mrin.

Oh, Mrin, I cannot stop smiling!

All this while, the time and the distance that had been between us had created mysteries surrounding you. And let me add that they were not pleasant ones. I had thought that something dreadful had happened to you. Nevertheless, obviously, I was misinformed. I don't know if you know just how many attempts, I made to locate you, but to no avail. Thank you for taking the first step, like always.

Looking forward to hearing back from you soon,

Ayush

Zara was now more confused than ever. She had never seen her Dad talk in an effortless flow and get personal with anyone. She could hardly ever recall her parents, for that matter, get so intimate! She fidgeted with the keyboard for long before her curiosity, again, got the better of her, and she decided to read further.

From: Mrin@*****.com

To: Ayush@*****.com

Subject: Re: Knock Knock.

Oh Ayush, I am so thrilled to receive your answer. I didn't believe that I would actually find you again, after so many years having passed. Though I'd wished and imagined it repeatedly, I now find myself at a loss for words to express myself! Before we continue, however, I have some requests to make.

First, I'm *not* going to ask you questions about your present-day life. If you would like to discuss something, it would be up to you. But I do not want to talk about my life. You may learn about me in dribs and drabs, but it would never be a definite answer. Would you please respect this wish?

Second, I've questions about my own past and in particular, the three years of college, which you were most familiar with. Would you answer my questions without shying away from the intimate details? I'm having a difficult time piecing together some things.

I cannot thank you enough for getting back to me and with such warmth. I tender my sincere apologies, in advance, for these rules that sound arbitrary and even selfish. I know my reasons are not good enough to even pen them down.

I'm looking forward to your email too,

Mrin

Zara had never felt more guilty; reading her Dad's personal emails seemed like crossing a line she had rarely thought she would, but she also felt irate that her father would write emails to some woman from his past who came knocking on his Internet portal! What was more unbelievable was the camaraderie with which they talked. She couldn't remember a single event where her father *"could not stop smiling."* She also didn't like her Dad writing, *"I've missed you so much, Mrin."* She chewed on her lip wondering, "Why did Dad say that he thought something dreadful had happened to her? What was the mystery that had surrounded this woman? And most of all, who is *this* woman?" She was alarmed to read that her Dad shared intimate knowledge of her life. Their fondness for each other seemed evident. Zara didn't like the tone of this email one bit since it showed a new side to her Dad, one that she didn't know had ever existed. Since this information was brand new and rather overwhelming for her, she decided she will share it tomorrow with Anya. And then, despite the guilt of invading her Dad's privacy, she found herself reading yet another email, the last one for the night.

From: Ayush@*****.com

To: Mrin@*****.com

Subject: Re: Knock Knock.

Mrin,

Haven't you always loved to surround yourself in an aura of mystery! Now I finally believe that it's you I'm speaking to! Although, it seems rather unfair that you appear here suddenly, after years of silence, and equally important I can believe it is really you that I'm talking to. However, what seems rather unfair is that you appear here suddenly and determine which doors are forbidden for me to enter. There is so much I wish to know, so much I want to ask, and so much I want to tell you- it has, after all been some forty plus years since we last met, talked or communicated. Nevertheless, I am just pulling your leg here, sorry if I offended you. However, it is funny how, once, every small detail of my tastes, wishes, whims and dreams were known to you. You prided yourself on being so adamantly nosy when it came to me or my habits. And why not? You knew me better than I, let alone anyone else.

Well, Mrin, that's fine. I know the past hurts both of us. But I hope it has worked out fairly for you as well as it has for me. Neither of us is heartless enough to remain immune from the inherent pain that nostalgia leaves behind. However, at times, this is what life is, and we have to move forward with it.

Mrin, correct me if I'm wrong, it might be the age catching up or the mere fact that we talked after so long, but there's something different about your emails. Not only are good-byes distant and impersonal, but they lack something uniquely Mrin, the closures. I remember vividly how brilliant you were in the closing of letters or saying good-byes, especially if they were dear to you. You used to close with poems, beautiful sayings or jokes. I remember everyone in our group gushing about the articulate letters they received from you on their birthdays or any special occasions. Even in our residential complex, if you might remember, you were the one who everyone approached for writing beautiful letters/greetings for them. Please pardon me if you think I am crossing the line here, but I would really want you to close our emails almost the same way, if not exactly, the way you did before.

Well, I don't think I have breached any of your rules you set for me until now.

Thank you again, Mrin. I hope you're doing well. It isn't a query but more of a hopeful wish from a friend.

Regards,

Ayush

Zara was in tears now. At the moment not only did she feel betrayed but also hurt. There was never an occasion when she could recall her father saying things half as sweet for her mother. It pinched her. It was all wrong. This woman, Mrin, or whoever she was; she had no right to come into their lives like this and complicate things. For the first time in a while, things seemed to be smoother between her parents. Despite the email from her father about Somi's behaviour, the past three days with Zara and her sisters seemed to rejuvenate their mother. Their laughter had given her new life; their visit had given her something to look forward to. Suddenly, all the effort seemed futile; the house seemed hollow. As the women had been bonding over food and memories, their father had been writing emails to a woman from his past. This realization opened the floodgates of her tears further. Any trace of sleep had now disappeared, as did the guilt with which she had hesitantly opened the last message, and irritated and determined, she scrolled to read more.

From: Mrin@*****.com

To: Ayush@*****.com

Subject: Re: Knock Knock.

Ayush,

I apologise for not answering you appropriately earlier. I have been busy with some personal health issues. Nothing to worry about but I would respect it if we do not talk about it any further. This should answer your statement, "I hope you are well..." albeit partly.

I'm glad that you remembered my "closures." I almost forgot them myself. Life has brought many changes, and some are not what I expected or turned out to be how I would have liked them to. They are pretty demanding and more often than not, don't leave much time for creativity and literary explorations. As far as the memory is concerned, with age, that is something that takes its own toll on a person. Some reach the stage earlier than the others and it seems I might be at the brink of age enveloping mine.

I had forgotten that we had lived in the same residential complex! How silly of me! Even so, in reality, I have fuzzy memories of our apartment in Matunga. I remember it was a great neighbourhood with plenty of young people; a happy community where almost everyone knew everyone by their names. I also, very faintly, remember our group of friends in college. What a group of people were we!

Now as my memory weakens and leeches my diaries from those days provide me clues to remember. They are full of entries, one of the earlier ones being about how I met you for the first-time during electives in our graduate program. I flip through its pages and am intrigued by all these entries that cover nearly all of those three years of college that we spent together. Below is perhaps the first time I mentioned you, though I have faint recollections of the pictorial landscape, would you mind writing them down the sequence in your next email? I would really appreciate if you could shed some light on it. This diary entry will be my closure for today.

A stranger turned and looked at me searchingly.

My eyes first averted.

Then, our eyes met and locked… as if forever.

His glimpse glazed with adoration.

Beckoned me to him.

And I, unaware, eyes transfixed, as if in a trance,

Rushed like a river to my ocean.

Thank you Ayush for being so patient with me. See if you could solve this puzzle for me. I hope it isn't too much to ask.

Take care,

Mrin

At this point, Zara felt honour-bound to turn her Dad's computer off, despite the feelings of hurt and jealousy. She looked at her watch, and saw it was barely eleven. It wasn't late to call her sister and talk about it; she thought, talking with her might calm her down, or some paths would open to resolve the dilemma.

She rang Anya and told her about the emails. With every word that left her mouth, coated with hurt, irritation and jealousy, she felt lighter. However, by the time she finished, she could only feel her heart sinking. Then she added, "And apart from all that, she wrote a poem for Dad."

On the other side of the line, however, things were different. Anya had never seen her sister so restless and fumbling with her words before. Zara was the last person to be intimidated by anything, let alone some random emails. She figured that the night would never end if she didn't talk to her.

After a brief silence, Anya said, "A poem makes the relationship romantic, to say the least. However, we do not know for a fact about the intimacies of their relationship. It could have been a college affair. But it is normal, right? Maybe they were good friends, and that is what Dad misses about her. Having said that, I also understand your fears but if there's one thing we know about our Dad, it would be just how much he has always and still loves us. Please stop worrying. Let's talk about this tomorrow in person, okay? Let's see all that we have and read through these messages. However, for now, stop prying into Dad's emails and get some sleep."

Talking to Anya made things better for Zara. She had always been the one who knew how to tame the storm inside of her and maybe that was the reason they bonded so well together. Although she was still slightly distraught for her mother but the reassurance that came from Anya made her feel relaxed. She wasn't sure how this turn of events would influence things in the future, but she was absolutely sure that her Dad had always done the right thing and wouldn't disappoint her.

She kept the laptop aside and pulled the covers of the sheets right up until her nose so that only her eyes would be visible, and looked outside. She knew that whatever she had read would come back to haunt her in her nightmares if she didn't think calmly about it, so she found herself thinking about the details more logically now.

Her dad had been the one to recollect the fact that Mrin, and he had shared a community space. She wondered how anyone could ever forget their childhood home. Why, she clearly remembered the house that she grew up and played in with Anya. Those were her first memories; she had always held them close to her heart. But the woman did say she had *"a fuzzy memory"* and had *"some health issues."* Keeping aside her own fears she thought more of this woman, Mrin. Did she have an accident? Did she experience some trauma-related amnesia? Did she have Alzheimer's? Maybe that would be a good thing. If the woman lost most of her memory, Mom would be safe. As the thought flashed through her mind, she felt guilty for her callousness; her parents taught her better. She instinctively sent her apologies out to the universe. Long before she could dwell further, she was asleep.

Tuesday morning was like any other day for Ayush and Somi. They woke up, went for their ritualistic morning walk, read the papers, enjoyed their breakfast on the backyard deck, savoured their garden and listened to the birds, squirrels and the occasional wind chime. The only difference was the presence of Zara. She spoke politely to both the parents, somehow feeling that no matter how hard she tried to push all that she read the previous night; she could not look at her Dad in the eye and talk. Needless to say, this didn't go unnoticed by Ayush. He asked if everything was okay with his for-ever-young daughter.

Zara decided to ignore answering the question verbally and nodded her head quietly.

Later in the afternoon, she readied to take the train to be with Anya. Zara took an overnighter along with the borrowed laptop. As she left the home, her parents came through the door, hugged and kissed and said, "Have a great time with your sister."

Chapter Two

Hearts in Turmoil

Zara met with Anya that evening at the Eaton Center, Toronto's fashion mall in one of the trendiest locales in the city. One could see the entire spectrum of the humanity represented on the longest street, Yonge Street alongside hearing almost every language and witnessing every culture. The intersection of Dundas and Yonge Streets was Toronto's answer to New York's Times Square where neon lights with their loudness mingle with the cacophonous beauty of humanity.

The two sisters hugged tightly, Zara more than Anya, and walked to a restaurant together. Taking a quiet seat that overlooked the brimming excitement outside, they placed their orders and began to talk.

Sensing the eagerness in her sister's voice, Anya interrupted, "Zara, I called Professor Divecha at Osgoode Hall to check if she could see us."

Distracted from what she was about to say, Zara asked, "Who is she?"

"You've already forgotten? Remember, the other night when a near blow up took place between Mom and me? When I'd mentioned how Professor Divecha sent her regards for Dad? After coming back to my condo, I had thought about how she had once mentioned that she was in the same university as Dad in Bombay…"

"Oh right! Did you get to talk to her again? What did she tell you about Dad?"

"Well, after our phone call last night, I traced her number to see if she could tell me anything about dad from his youth. We had a brief conversation this morning, but she didn't say anything we don't already know. That even in those days, he was intelligent, astute…."

"No unusual stuff?"

"Not anything in particular that stood out. She did mention something very strange though. Dad used to have a lot of female friends who all affectionately called him 'Ayu'. All except one. I don't know what that meant, but for some reason, the thought hasn't left me yet," said Anya, musing.

"Okay, let's go back to this weekend. What exactly happened that Mom flipped out so badly?"

"Well, after you asked Dad about using his laptop for a few days, I mentioned that I had happened to bump into Professor Divecha, one of his classmates from his college days, and that she had sent her regards. That was it. Dad didn't make any fuss; he only nodded quietly. But once he was gone; Mom wanted to know exactly what we had spoken about, whether the professor had mentioned any names, asking me to repeat every single word of the conversation. And now, that I think about it, this isn't the first-time Mom reacted that way to me meeting Professor Divecha. The first time, her prosecutorial questions were so tiring that eventually I had said, 'Okay, Mom, I give up. I'm going to invite the good professor here; she can meet Dad and you and tend to your inquisitions herself!' That was all I had said, but it was more than needed…"

"What do you mean?"

"Well, she was angry. She lashed out, *'Don't you ever dare do anything like that!' blah blah…"* said Anya rolling her eyes. Their orders for coffee arrived, and they sat there sipping quietly for some time.

Zara spoke, "So, when do we meet Professor Divecha? I think she might hold some important answers. I'm curious to understand these new sides of our parents- Mom so angry and restless while Dad so chirpy and eager."

"That's true. She's out of her office for a few days. However, as soon as she's back, she's going to see us. For God's sake, don't tell Mom. I'm scared she'll either hit the roof or us," said Anya sounding a bit horrified.

"Okay. However, Anya, the email exchanges between Dad and this strange woman, Mrin are still bothering me. I'm able to think of little else." Zara couldn't hold anything any longer.

"So, tell me more," said Anya.

"I hate the idea of Dad exchanging emails *now* with a woman he knew so many years ago. They might have been close or whatever, but it's been a long while, almost forty years. He has a family and responsibilities. And let's not even begin with the poem. It burns me up, to say the least." Zara said.

Anya lifted her palm and placed it across her sisters on the table. Zara's body language- closed fists, clenched teeth, sweaty hands- they were all so unlike her. She had never seen her sister act this way nor could she blame her, sensing that Zara both resented their father and was confused by his exchange of inappropriate emails. Though she said nothing more, Anya knew that the real conversation on this topic would happen only after she'd read the messages. So they paid their coffee bill and walked quietly along Yonge Street towards Lakeshore for a while, Anya continuing to study the storm of agitation growing in Zara's heart.

When she couldn't take it any longer, she held her sister's hand, "It seems, Zara, you have all the evidence. You prosecuted Dad, found him guilty and now are ready to pronounce your sentence too. Is that right?"

Zara didn't respond.

"Look, you're here for some time, anyway. Why don't you, Mom and I go away for a few days in the Caribbean, far from the noise, have time together and get rid of these demons? Away from these emails and suspicion... That was the initial plan, wasn't it? To talk to Mom about what it is, if there is anything at all, that is bothering her? Don't you think we should be thinking a little about that too? And as for Dad, he has never shied away from neither his family nor his responsibilities. Let us just cut him some slack before we know the entire story. He almost never goes for any friend's reunions or parties so maybe that is what is getting him excited with his replies. Meantime we don't want to put ourselves through the emotional wringer and judge him for something that we don't completely know. What do you say?"

Moments like these were when Zara couldn't be thankful enough to have a sibling like Anya. Once again, not only had she calmed her, but also given her mind the rest it needed.

"Anya, I don't know how you do it, but thanks for being so calm and assured. Maybe you're right. Maybe I have been fixating on these letters too much. My brain has been working on overtime unwrapping their meaning, and maybe that's because of all the free time I've had lately, being consumed by that anticipated job in D.C. Yes, let's go somewhere for a few days. I like the idea. I think even Mom needs to go out for a while; she's been living in a shell for too long."

"That's all that I needed from you. Worry not; I will make all the arrangement. How about we leave in ten days for St. Maarten? I would have wrapped up my cases and briefs by then, and I think I have some accumulated vacation time that I should be able to use."

"That's prefect! Let me know about all the details, and I will talk to Mom as soon as I get home. I'm sure it'll do us all some good, taking time off our mundane schedules and go do something new."

Anya could see an instant change in Zara's demeanour, breathing and speech. She was happy to have diverted her for a bit. But as far as she knew her sister, it wouldn't be too long for the storm to rise up again. However, she hoped to change that once they would get to spend some more time together.

After dinner, the sisters took a cab to Anya's home on Toronto's signature address at Lakeshore Boulevard. The view of the Lake was enchanting from her two-bedroom condo. Standing by the window, Zara could see the CN Tower, the Dome, the Air Canada Center and Toronto's Financial and Fashion Districts.

"So…did you read more of the email?" Anya asked hesitantly.

Breaking her gaze from the spectacular view, Zara answered almost hazily, "No, I was completely agitated, to be honest. It was too much information to take in one night's time, one hour to be precise. Even though talking to you had quietened me down, I was unable to sleep for a long time, awake by the thought of imagining to share our father with anyone else. And what's more is that I had an urge to send this Mrin-woman an angry email!"

Anya stared at her sister, her eyes wide and almost shouted, "Did you?"

Zara didn't answer but made a gesture of denial. At this point, Anya knew she had to do something. It wouldn't take long for her sister to lose her temper and then who knew what she would end up doing. She sat her down on the sofa and held her sister's hand in hers.

"Zara, you need to calm down. This is an emotional situation where our parents are involved. We cannot deal with it so hastily. We have to be rational, clinical and detached, put our head above our shoulders and think clearly. Most of all, we cannot do something in a matter that we aren't completely conversed with and end up giving our parents the hurt that they might not deserve. Before we make any move, all the options must be studied and weighed, okay?"

Zara lowered her eyes and sighed, "I'm sorry. I know I'm acting irrationally, but it's only because I'm trying to be protective, especially towards Mom. I don't want some woman to just come in and ruin a relationship our parents have worked so hard towards. But you're right. I will be more careful, and I will not do anything in a moment of weakness that might hurt either of them. I promise."

Anya smiled, "Great, so we need to lay down some situations that we don't want either to experience ourselves or our Dad. First of all, when we're with Dad, we have to treat him with respect. No effrontery, nor judgments. Remember- whatever happens, he will always be our Dad. We need to love him the same way we have all these years. Agreed?"

Zara shared the confidence in her sister's voice too. "Yes. Agreed." Then she stood up and hugged her sister for the sensible advice. As she broke from the embrace, her attention diverted to the wall behind her Anya. She looked at the pictures hung on it, two, in particular, that stood out for their light and elegance.

"I really like these pictures of Mom and Dad. They look great, don't they?" she said, almost dreamily.

Anya turned back to look at them too. "Yes, Mom's picture looks so soft, so gentle."

"And Dad's picture is so artistic, romantic and classic." Anya added, smiling widely. "You can make digital copies of them for yourself to keep if you'd like."

Beaming at the thought Zara exclaimed, "Yes! I was thinking about the same thing. Let me do that first thing tomorrow!"

With that, both the sisters went to freshen up and unload their thoughts from the day. By the time they had both showered and got into their pajamas, it was well past ten p.m. Making herself comfortable on the sofa, Anya asked Zara to fire up their father's laptop. Then she connected it to the larger TV screen in the living room so they could both read the messages at the same time. Zara read the first five emails, and as Anya read them, she scanned her sister's face for any trace of anger or hurt.

When Anya was done reading up to where her sister had finished, she turned to Zara. "I must say, I thought you were exaggerating, but you were actually very precise and correct with every single detail you told me both last night and today." Then with a sigh, she added,

"It seems like she either was very attracted to Dad or genuinely loves him. It takes some amount of serious infatuation to write verses as poetic as '*...she rushed like a river to her ocean*'. What do you think?"

Zara was one step ahead of Anya, having already dissected the poem in a complete literary analysis, perhaps even overcompensated with its metaphoric meanings. She had compared her Dad's name, *'Ayu'* and the 'ocean' part in the poem, knowing that his name literally meant life. It was said that life came from the ocean, and Mrin had rushed like a river to her ocean. Quite content with her in-depth analysis of the poem, she presented it to her sister. On getting no reply from Anya, she asked, her tone hurtful, "Doesn't that bother you?"

 But Anya didn't take the bait and carefully crafted her reply, "It would bother me if Dad were having a relationship with her *now*. If this happened thirty, forty years ago, then no, it honestly doesn't bother me. Remember, we've all had our crushes where we might have done things that look questionable now. However, going back to your question, what would you prefer? Dad living in misery or leading a life full of love? And by love, I do not mean having a relationship with this lady but reminiscing over those moments that he cannot share with anyone and maybe have a hearty laugh about them? And to be honest, I think we know our father well enough to judge on whether he might leave our mother or not, all because of a few flirtatious emails from a woman from the past."

"Anya, I don't know how you can rationalize everything so easily, but I just can't view life in those stark terms. I'm not afraid to admit that I might have thought, more than once since last night, how our Father might leave our Mother for this other woman. Have you read between the lines? Can't you see how comfortable he is with her, something that we have never felt him share with our Mom?" At this point, Zara's eyes stung with tears.

Anya held her close, "Zara; that's what life is all about- facing stark choices, filtering them through the prism of your psyche and then confronting them. To be honest, most of the choices are not good.

Someone always, eventually gets hurt. But I've said it before, let's not haste with our judgements. For all we know, we might only be hurting ourselves. Come, let's read the next one."

Knowing that the night was going to be long, they sat close and read on.

Chapter Three

The Beginning

From: Ayush@*****.com

To: Mrin@*****.com

Subject: Re: Knock, knock.

Mrin:

I hope you're feeling well, and whatever you have is not long-lasting. I don't mean to break your rules, but say it simply out of concern. As you know, I've always respected your wishes, even when they were thoroughly against our best interests.

We lived in a wonderful neighbourhood. As I mentioned it earlier, it was a compact space when it came to everyone knowing almost everyone by name. It included four apartment buildings with a vast playground in the center where the kids congregated to socialize, learn, play or indulge in some mischief, while the elders huddled up to discuss politics or household gossips each day. You lived in the building right across from us. I don't know if you know, but on a good day, I could peer right into your bedroom. Anyway, after high school ended, your family moved to a newer development near Worli.

The poem is terse but beautifully written. I can relate very much to it, and wonder if it celebrates our initial meeting as adults at the Bajaj Institute of Management. Yes, that's one instance I remember very vividly.

I walked in through the front entrance to go straight to my seminar.

Even though we were quite some distance apart, the smell of your lilac perfume couldn't help but seduce me, and as I turned to my left, following the scent, it led me out toward the coffee shop and straight to you. The way you walked, confident as if you knew the place inside out. So graceful you were, it was like seeing someone walking on a fashion ramp. Your hips were swaying, your purse twirling by your side. You looked like a dream. I could hear my heart thump at every step of yours, afraid that it might pop out if you moved any closer to me. You were a sight to behold! I only realised later, after you had walked toward the frozen mannequin of me, who you actually were.

In the five or six years since you had moved away from Matunga, you were no longer a teenage girl. You were taller, filled out, dressed fashionably and looked stunning. That day, you wore a light pastel *salwar kameez* with matching sandals and minimal colour and make-up. Your shoulder-length hair blew freely in the daytime breeze. A smile completed the look, and before I could stop, I heard myself say, '*Oh heavens above! She's stunning!*' more loudly than I would've actually wanted to. However, let me also add that it wasn't one sided. All through this, our eyes had locked and remained transfixed, even though you tried your best to avert them. After my unintentional outburst, we walked straight to each other with smiles on our faces, and you said, "Do I know you, stranger?"

"I don't know. But would you like to know me?" I flirted.

"Regardless of my wish, it seems *you* sure would like to know *me*." You had flirted back in the same tone.

"Yes, Mrin, tell me who you are."

My response shocked you, and even though we had both burst out laughing; your earlier confidence now seemed distant, giving way to a girlish vulnerability. I introduced myself, and the past came back to you with shyness in your body language. To lighten the moment, I suggested meeting in the coffee shop after our respective seminars to catch up after so many years.

So Mrin, perhaps the lovely poem is all about our first meeting. If you have a different memory, please let me know. I wish you had shared this poem with me in those years we were together. It would have been so different to hear you read it out to me while I could see your expressions, rather than read it forty years later trying to recreate the moment itself. Those were the best years of my life. Nothing has ever come closer.

Regards,

Ayu

Both the girls could sense the unease and tension brewing in the atmosphere, but neither of them dared to say a word. Even the ever-pragmatic Anya found herself unable to defend her father after this last email. In silence, Zara clicked to the next message, and the pair read on.

From: Mrin@*****.com

To: Ayush@*****.com

Subject: Re: Knock, Knock.

Dear Ayush,

One of my diary entries says that you've got an amazing photographic memory, which you just proved in your last email! I am happy that through our respective abilities, we are able to reminisce over the past together.

My next diary entry in prose is not that elaborate, but a poem that captured perhaps how your presence awed and unnerved me; powerful eyes that draw people, and my complete inability to assert myself. I did feel adored just like my poem says. However, that could have been the subtle way you approached me, how your wit and banter left my cheeks flushed a deep red.

 But as I re-read the entry, I noticed that it also said that 'a restlessness had descended on me…I wish my seminar ended sooner." Like you said, we met in the coffee shop the rebuilding of the old ties began. Now, something must have happened during our conversation that put me on guard. I'll post my diary poem for you and tell me if you can connect the dots. Here is my closing poem for this email.

Coffee shop conversation

so akin to game of chess

Every bit of conversation a positioning

Every gesture a camouflage

My stranger's a good strategist.

He moves his rook.

He smiles, but his eyes reveal.

The nature of his smile

Such intrigue excites and propels me.

I can smile as well.

And play his game.

Ayush, I will be going away for a few days, and I might not be able to respond to your emails. Forgive me in advance for my absence.

Take care and be merry. Regards,

Mrin

P.S. I loved it when you mentioned noticing the lilac scent on me… it had always been my favourite.

The silence grew denser as both the sisters didn't know what to say, their heads heavy with doubt and confusion. Anya walked out to get some water and sat down staring into the screen with her bottle. She offered it to Zara, whose eyes seemed transfixed onto the screen. Without a word, Anya clicked on the next message.

From: Ayush@*****.com

To: Mrin@*****.com

Subject: Re: Knock, knock.

Dear Mrin,

I hope that you were on a fun trip or visiting close friends, and that you feel much better. Even after all these years, you haven't grown out of your habit to surprise the other person. I'm amazed at your ability to encapsulate the entire conversation in one metaphor. And answering your questions, yes, the idea of reminiscing over those shared secret memories of ours using both our abilities is something that I have started looking forward to.

I was restless and lost, to say the least, in my seminar as well. Your image, so alluring and the smell of the lilac intoxicating, kept on overlapping with the on-going lecture. All I could feel was an urge to see you again soon. As a matter of fact, and don't laugh at this, I might have excused myself a few minutes before the seminar ended. I found the idea of waiting for you in the coffee shop, as promised, to be more comforting than daydreaming in a seminar. Having said that, let me also add that I was nervous that you might not turn up, but when I saw you enter, I lit up!!

I think the poem expresses your doubts or perhaps your cynicism. I think I may have behaved like a typical young man driven by his hormones a little. I recall I said something; you disputed and stood your ground. I reversed my position. Then I did something that's etched in my memory. As we were discussing something, you had leaned further, peered straight into my eyes and laid your palms open on the coffee-table. Reciprocating, I began to talk animatedly, leaned forward too, peered into your eyes and placed my palms in yours and held them for a few seconds. You remained nonchalant as if nothing untoward had happened. But in that brief moment, perhaps you felt something that I had not wanted to project? Mrin, do you recall anything that I'm saying? Does it somewhere in your mind reawaken or goad your recollection?

I'm not saying that I'm sorry for my unplanned "gesture." It was instinctual, spontaneous. However, as surprised as I was at my reflexes, your calm manoeuvre and mature response amazed me even more.

During the entire hour-long conversation, you yielded no ground. You remained my equal, as you would always be in the time we were to spend together. You kept your charm and sense of humour levelled at every point. Above all, you kept my dignity too, and at no time made me feel like a cad. The easiness with which our conversation flowed that day is something that had rarely happened with me before. Your poem shows your own self-confidence, that you can "play a game" as well as anybody else, the game being a playful volley of words.

I must add though, that you were always up-front and honest and never minced your words and maybe that is the reason why everyone wanted to be around you and why being in your good books was regarded as a privilege by most.

Well, Mrin, do you see what I see? Do you think I have done justice to solving our past puzzle a little for us? Please correct me if you think I stand in the wrong on any point.

Regards,

Take care of yourself.

Ayu

At this point, Zara snatched the remote from Anya and flung it sideways. A long silence ensued after which Anya figured that she would have to be the one to speak first. "I can't believe that Dad still remembers even the smallest gestures of casual flirting and the sexual attraction with this Mrin woman. Both have remained honest to themselves, neither of them regretting it."

Zara dug her face into one of the cushions and spoke, "That's because he's a man blessed with photographic memory, and he was seduced by her charm, and you know what…"

"In this case, photographic memory is not a blessing; it's a curse."

"I'm pretty sure the Mrin woman kept her palms open on purpose, inviting a mirror response from him. I'm certain the details are incomplete and there was more that happened. I'm sure she lured our father just like she's luring him now. In legalese, you call it 'entrapment'?"

Instead of quibbling with Zara, Anya walked over to the balcony overlooking the lake, the baggage of emotions too heavy for her to take. She was aware that instead of anger, she almost felt a twinge of jealously, wondering whether she would ever find a comparable man in her life; someone who respected and understood her as much her father did this woman from his past. She thought of the amounts of self-confidence that must have taken her father to admit that he had acted like a cad. But then, it seemed that Mrin had never let him feel like one. Contrary to what she knew her sister feels at the moment; Anya was totally smitten by the kind of love that for her had only existed in books and movies but now stood live in front of her, embedded within the words of personal emails she had no business reading. She turned around towards her sister.

"Zara, despite your strong views, I'm sure you'll agree that this woman does seem to have it all. From these letters, it's evident that she's a beauty, has a sense of humour, brains, charm and composure. She is unapologetic and does not mince her words, and still she has people longing to be in her good books. And she has a man who supports her and respects her for the same. What else would a woman want?"

"Really, Anya? I cannot believe you are saying these things because at this point I'm more concerned about us than her, to be honest. I feel fragile and agitated at what our father is doing- engaging in the writing of letters to an apparently long-lost lover!" Zara crossed her arms as she spoke. "And above it all, I'm now doubting your allegiances…"

Anya raised her eyebrows in confusion.

"Look at the way you are dealing with the situation. You rush to defend this woman and forget that you need to worry about our mother, the woman who has raised us with so much care and love. Who is she to you, and what will this do to her, if she were to find out, ever?"

Anya couldn't believe what she was hearing. All this while she had been trying to console her sister through pragmatism, and this was how her comments were being taken.

"Look, Zara, sisterhood has its privileges, and if I can't be honest with you, then what's the point? I will be there for you no matter what. However, I also know your anger, and annoyance is born from the responsibility to feel towards Mom, and trust me; I feel the same. I don't love her any less than you, but…"

Her voice trailed on, unable to comprehend the conflicting tides of loyalty to her mother and adoration for a stranger that clashed within her. So, without saying anything that might anger her younger sister further, Anya walked back inside the house with a meek, "Let's read on…"

Chapter Four

Tell Me about Our Typical Day

Though she didn't voice it, Zara could tell that Anya was deeply hurt by what the two sisters had read. She also knew that arguments wouldn't get her anywhere with the ever-impulsive Anya; she would only get further embroiled. This was a strange and difficult situation they were in, and Zara wondered what she could say to console her sister. However, like Zara, Anya too realized this and putting aside the bitter bile rising in her stomach, sweeping away the uneasiness from her tone, reached out to her sister.

 "I'm sorry, Zara, for being so aggressive. If I hurt you…"

And before she could even complete the sentence, Zara smiled widely, "Worry not, no offense taken and if your Highness agrees, let's read more."

From: Mrin@****.com

To: Ayush@*****.com

Subject: Knock, knock…

Ayush, thank you once again for a vivid and introspective recollection. My mind doesn't remember much, but my heart tells me that you're precise. You were always known for 'doing the right thing' and placing your palm in a girl's, unless she is yours, was a no-no. It shocks me now, but I must have somehow shown extraordinary restraint so that you might not feel offended. These are not my memories I speak from, but merely a logical observation. However, I should say that they reflect upon how I would have seen this "stranger," whose eyes shone with adoration for me.

Can you tell me something about the experiences we shared with other? Not us as a group, but just you and me. I wrote my diaries in cryptic notes to remain safe from my brother's clutches- these poems I attached to my emails are remnants of those notes. Secured we remained, but now my diaries elude me as I fail to decode them, years later. This annoys me and I feel a deep void inside me, despite having led a full life in my youth. I now sense emptiness. Time has not been as kind to me as it has to you and at this moment, you and your photographic memory are as if a lifeline for me. You're the only one who can remove the sense of loneliness by connecting me to significant events of my personal life.

Ayush, my diary says that we both spent much time at the Bombay University Library before and after classes. We became close seeing each other every day, sharing coffee and conversations. I am sure soon our lives became inseparable and intimate. Can you tell me what our typical day was like? Please, don't miss any details. Be a painter for me, Ayush.

Take care,

Mrin

Thou livest in my eyes when I'm awake.

Thou movest in my heart as I lie in bed.

Thou dwellest in my mind when I dream.

I whisper thy name so gently.

Then I moan thy name with desire.

Thou art the sole resident of my feverish being.

A House on fire.

When Zara presented an elaborate song-and dance explanation for the verses in the earlier letters, Anya had accepted them and had even understood them as words of youthful infatuation. However, this last verse had a different tone altogether, one that hinted at the blossoming of love and desire and even Anya didn't know what to make of it.

Finally, Zara broke the awkward silence permeating the suddenly vast room, making them both feel small and helpless, almost like children. "I wonder why Mrin's brother would be against her friendship with Dad. I don't understand."

"Perhaps it has more to do with the cultural difference than anything else," Anya speculated, "Here in the West, brothers often even support their sister's decisions to be with a certain boy. However, this was in India and life was different when Dad was young, I suppose. And it sounds like Mrin was just protecting them both by writing her journal in code."

Zara nodded a small, meek signal and sighed. "Okay, let's read the next one."

From: Ayush@*****.com

To: Mrin@****.com

Subject: Knock, knock…

Mrin,

I was happy that I saw you at the Bajaj Institute and soon as we both walked to each other, I knew who you were. I kept my silence and continued the game all young men and women play, full of tension, drama and flirtation. Soon you realized who I was and the common bonds of childhood we had shared helped us to continue where we had left off. You recalled to your amusement festival dances, picnics and walks to the library that we had shared with other kids until you went to private school in the hills.

My classes for most subjects were at Elphinstone College; yours at the Bajaj Institute, right across the lush green Oval Grounds from the University Library. I had two seminars at the Bajaj with you and whenever we found the time, we did spend it talking over cups of coffee. However, truth be told, I sought multiple opportunities just to be near you, see your smile, feast on your presence and of course, inhale your particular, intoxicating smell. To be honest, I experienced a new kind of sensuality whenever you were around. As if I was wrapped around in silk and satin made of lilac petals. I was disappointed that you didn't know the extent of my admiration, and if someone hinted at our relationship, you would pre-emptively tell them that we were just childhood friends and nothing else. It wrenched my gut for I wanted to be so much more than a friend.

Do you recall Mrs. Alvarez's incident? "Baba, you're in our program, but you sit with others. These girls are wondering…." I could hear giggles erupting from your friends, but all I saw was your face. It was lit up and maybe you were wondering how I was going to handle the situation and disentangle myself.

I remember myself saying, "Yes; these girls are wondering…" urging her to continue.

"Why don't you sit with us… we would like to talk with you, know you more and be your friend," said Mrs. Alvarez with a mischievous smile and a wink.

Perhaps you may recall that I was less outspoken at that time, but among the table of beautiful women in their twenties, all giggling and staring at me with mischief paramount in their minds, I saw your red face, flush with pride in me as if saying, "Let's see, how good you are, Ayush Vyas?"

"We are waiting," said Mr. Alvarez.

Emboldened, my stomach turning with impending embarrassment, I sat down on the offered chair.

"You see, "I began hesitantly, "I'm a shy and introverted man. Because of this flaw, I gravitate to women who take the lead. Now Mrs. Alvarez, please tell me, would there be any takers at this table?"

Mrs. Alvarez shushed the giggling girls and asked, "Where do you think you want these girls to lead you?"

"Hopefully into a conversation or path not ventured on before." I responded, more confidently this time, "So are there any takers?"

Your friends chirped, "Yes, yes."

"For a seemingly shy man, you're really good at selling yourself, Ayush," said Megh teasingly. Then you added mischievously as if to scare me, "Ayush, conversing with girls is dangerous. Before you know, you will lose your footing, sense of judgment and later *anything* can happen."

"*Anything…*," repeated Aruna, enunciating each syllable slowly.

"Before you know it, you will be dancing and prancing and emoting all over the place like Shammi Kapoor," said Megh, imitating the famed Bollywood actor's dance moves.

"Ah yes, this is exactly what I'm afraid of. Even though the term 'anything' is open-ended, it has limited connotations in this present situation of danger. So, what am I supposed to do?"

Allowing my pragmatism to take over the shyness, I laid my cards down that day. "Well ladies, this is a rare occasion for me as I am hardly ever in the presence of such beautiful and affluent company. And the truth is, I find myself at somewhat of a loss as I come from a different world altogether than your own. Full disclosure. I'm a simple man; my family doesn't own factories, businesses, properties or anything of the nature."

"Ayush, you've nothing to lose then," said Mrs. Alvarez. Her eyes revealed mischiefs that belied her age.

I smiled and nodded and then added my last words, "Everything I have to offer is in here." I placed my hand over my heart, keeping you in the corner of my eye.

I was shocked how words came out and formed themselves into coherent sentences. I was happy to realize that my supposed shyness was not a permanent fixture, but a young man's hesitancy to express opinions. I must confess that I wanted you to be proud of me. I felt in my heart that my silence or hesitation wouldn't impress you, and your friends might think I couldn't think under pressure and be good at witty exchanges.

Do you remember this incident with the girls in your class? After this, twice a week before and after lectures, I became a part of your elite crowd of the beautiful and popular. And though you were all fabulous in your right, albeit a little unapproachable at first, what you helped me do was change my perception of the young rich Bombay girls. Not all were seeking marital matches or wealthy boyfriends, most- your clique included- were serious about their careers as college lecturers and tutors.

I must admit that my middle-class upbringing contributed substantially to the narrow and unflattering view of the elite, especially the women. I presumed them to be ultra-busy, doing their own little things, highbrowish, self-engrossed class of women gravitating to their niche circle and accentuating their entitlements. Nevertheless, when I saw Lulu Divecha spend time to understand my views on the nature and fragility of beauty before she could critique, enhance and make it better, I began to understand the flaws in my presumptions. And then, as you already know, I eventually became friends with all of them and sometimes wonder what and how they are doing in their lives. Wouldn't it be wonderful to attend a class reunion if there ever was one?

I understand that Lulu Divecha is teaching here in Toronto now. I almost forgot that I met a young man called Anuraag at a workshop I was doing in New York. He came up to me, introduced himself and talked about his mother. Would you believe she's none other than your best friend, Megh Dalal? Give her regards when you have a chance to speak with her.

By the way, your poem reminds me of our lives, post-Kirti College, as you generously used the pronoun 'thou' whenever we were alone. In a way, your words echo the sentiments of Bollywood lyrics; and

Mrin, I must admit that, even after all this time, and they still make my heart soar with nostalgia!

Take care,

Ayu

"So, it appears that Dad had a great campus life…" Anya began.

"You are out of focus… go from the wide lens to portrait…"

Anya didn't like Zara's caustic remark, but she held her peace grudgingly. She understood that her sister would like her to take their mother's side. As a lawyer, she was more concerned with someone who was not getting justice, Mrin, but in her heart, she knew she was ready to go to the end of the universe to protect her mother. That she was absolutely sure of despite her penchant for not loudly pronouncing her sacred duties. On the other hand, Zara couldn't stand Anya's indifference to what was unfolding for her mother. She was angry that Somi's fate made little or no difference to Anya, but more than that, what infuriated her was their father's childish shenanigan.

Anya saw her sister's sulk written large all over her face. She kept calm and refused to be baited, until Zara was compelled to speak up again.

"Listen up, Anya, my hoity-toity big sister. I want you to refocus," and then suddenly raising her voice, she shouted, "Just for once. Think about our Mother."

No sooner than the words were out, Zara knew right away that her tone and words both were offensive and hurtful. She regretted that the proverbial arrow had left the bow. Her mouth wide agape, her face twitched and eyes pleaded for forgiveness. She could hear the echo of her last sentence reverberate in her ears, and with her hands tried to cushion the hammering sound the sentence had launched.

Anya looked up at the clock. It seemed to have stopped. The air within the room was suffocating and stifling. Her eyes stung; slowly, she walked to the fridge and poured herself a glass of cold water. She drank it and splashed some on her face. Then she inhaled and looked at Zara, who was flailing about her hands through the air, trying to explain herself. Nevertheless, Anya wanted to hear none of that. She grabbed her purse from the countertop and rushed out of the condo. Zara, now teary and upset ran after her sister, but lost her, just as she scrambled into the elevator and out of her sight.

For the next half hour, Zara peeked into every café, restaurant and bar that were still open until she found Anya sitting on a bench, sobbing with her head resting on her knees. There was a group of young men and women hovering around her, wondering if they should intervene. Unsure, yet they didn't want to leave a vulnerable woman alone for her safety.

Happy on finally having found Anya, Zara just grabbed her in her embrace with whimpering. Well-meaning bystanders sensing safety, walked away. Anya didn't resist her sister's gesture, though she didn't reciprocate. Zara too felt tears slowly spilling down her cheeks for a while; they sat there in silence and tears.

"Let's just go home."

They began to walk.

"Anya, if you don't mind, I'll go back to Mom and Dad's place tonight."

Anya, who had been keeping quiet all this time, snapped at her sister, "Yes; I mind it. You're not going anywhere until this is resolved, you understand? Our mother lives…and in this fight, either I die or Mrin dies. That's the way it's going to be here. Did you hear?" Her words boomed in Zara's psyche and soul and reverberated in ears until she said, "Yes."

Looking at heavenwards, Zara gave thanks for the horrible storm that had just passed between them. Arms interwoven; they reached their condo and Zara suggested perhaps they could call it a night.

"Alright, we will read one more message and then go to sleep."

The condo still seemed to hold the remnants of tension, and the sisters awkwardly settled on the couch, eager to have things go back to normal between them.

 "How come I didn't get the education you got, Anya?"

Anya, surprised at the strange question, asked, "What kind of education did I get that you didn't?"

 "Well, with the education you have, your mind does not get carried away as mine does. I am analytical, financial. For me, it's about the immediate assessment, quickest possible response and at times, that is not the best approach to everything. Especially unsuitable for situations like this. Nevertheless, you, you delay, defer your judgments, layering them with explanations from either side of the coin, but I don't. I know this comes from the field of work that you're in; a lawyer must assess without bias, and so you don't have problems in appreciating Mrin's personality, whereas I do, even if it is solely on a principle. When you stand up for her, for her independence, her fearlessness, it annoys me, and I consider it a verdict on our mother. And to be honest, it makes me feel bitter that our mother is not at the top of your concerns."

'Well, my little sister, this confessional is valuable, and I know it took a lot for you to say it. I just want you to know that though my style is different, I am concerned for our mother, the way you are. However, I don't jump to conclusions. You're right in saying that in me, there is an inherent conditioning to rationalize, but you will get there too. We will both get through this by understanding the complete story, not just one side of it. Even so, be assured that I will protect our mother at any cost. Come, let's read on…"

Zara smiled through her tears and knew that above all, despite their differences in the opinion, she trusted her sister completely.

From: Mrin@****.com

To: Ayush@*****.com

Subject: Knock, knock...

Ayush:

That was not the painting I had in mind, but it will do.

You said I echo Bollywood lyrics. Is that a compliment? I'm sorry that you had no idea about my affection for you, but it was difficult to display my feelings among all of my friends. Even now, though forty-odd years have passed, I find myself whispering thy name ever so softly before going to bed each night... Time has passed, but I still remember you with the same longing and desire.

I don't know what I did, or you did, or others did that we ended the way we did: separated, distant and never in contact. However, in time, I hope you'll open all the locks and give me access to the memories we created together. That is my only hope.

Now, do I recall the incident of Mrs. Alvarez? Yes, of course I do! This is what my diary said, and I have de-coded it in brackets for you with my answers in brackets. My brother used to peek into my diaries and then kind of blackmailed me for small favours. Instead of writing your name, I outmanoeuvred him by creating an imaginary friend representing you.

There's a man in my class, who is absolutely smart, but is ill at ease around women. There are girls in the class eyeing and craving for his attention. Despite his hesitation, I would like him to talk to me and be my friend, just only mine and nobody else's. (I just wanted him to fill my life and nobody else's) Intuition tells me we understand each other; know how the hearts feel without verbalizing anything. (We became pretty close) Mrs. Alvarez was encouraging the girls in the class to be friends with him and even pursue him because of his scholarship, handsomeness and oratorical abilities. (But she meant just pursue him for charm) My secret desire spilled out, and Megh and Simi know how I feel for him. (Fallen head over the heels). I call him, Sanj, my beautiful heartthrob Sanj!

My friends adored your good looks and charm, but it was your distance and aloofness that had won their hearts. They thought you were an Adonis. I felt so happy that they all liked you, but I wanted to keep you all for myself. I remember wishing time and time again, how wonderful life would have been it was just the two of us- away from friends, far from family from family, far even from our everyday lives.

Ayush, you were such a handsome man... tall, muscular, well

coiffed, and stylishly dressed. Your lips were forever tempting me. We used to joke and said that 'those lips were made for kissing.' I've forgotten many details, but your face is one I could never forget. It's all but engraved upon my mind and sometimes, as if in a trance, I find myself tracing with my fingers the imaginary contours of your face, your cheeks, eyes, nose, chin and lips, and finally bring that finger to my waiting lips for a kiss. Reading out loud what I just wrote makes it inappropriate, especially since there is the distance of so many years between us. However, then again, I never apologized for my feelings, behaviour, thoughts or language. And neither did you ever made me feel ashamed about things about the past. Now, due to our age, I find myself feeling guilty and embarrassed. Isn't it interesting that time, our age moulds us into self-surveillance. The things I really want to say to you, I find myself holding back, for fear of overstepping, and I wonder if you feel the same way…

I have wondered many times how you look now. I hope you are youthful, well-toned and muscular, just as I remember you to be, and not fat with a beer belly, balding head and wearing thick, dense and impenetrable glasses, hiding your eyes! If this has come to pass, please don't tell me. I want to preserve the image I have of you.

Kirti College and the following days occupy a central place in my journal, and I've read these pages repeatedly. However, though with the passing of time, I cannot grapple with the essence of emotional texture and passion, still, I feel moved, my skin turns red, and my heart misses a beat at every mention of you on the page. But then in no time it's all gray again! Age has been most unkind to me in this regard, and sometimes, when I read through the past, it's like my phone is ringing and regardless of how many times I say hello, no one is there on the other side. Pardon me for infusing this email with my emotions, but at times my medication takes the better of my thoughts and hormones. Such is my desolate hopelessness; my heart knows; my body remembers, but my brain cannot connect all the dots. The body knows there was electricity, and there was magic. In my diary, there are words, but you need to help me by imbuing them with life.

Ayush, our memories of the past make us unique. Without them, we are nothing. Memories define our wellness and health, and that's what I need the most. I am asking you today to give me those memories, the dreams, passion and physical urges that once filled me with exhilaration. Otherwise, I am just a lump of flesh waiting to rot. Ayush, I want you to know that I'm asking too much of your generosity. I know that this request might upset you, urging you to remember painful memories of my disappearance, but you are my last chance and recollecting my past. I realize full well that having you again in my life…or me in yours…is absurd and preposterous.

Please do accept my apologies for doing this to you, from taking away the time you could be spending with your family…but Ayush, as I am blindfolded, take my hand and walk me through the day spent at Kirti College, to the park in Dadar where we kissed for the first time. I need to know, need to feel it, need to remember it. I love you, Ayush, I've always loved you. Help me relive that love. Take care,

Mrin

Friends and foes alike ask me,

"Where do you dwell?"

They wonder if I'm okay.

They say my cheeks are rouge,

But eyes are hungry and searching.

 They know, but pass no judgment.

Their eyes tell, their smiles reveal.

I am found out.

I blush as I feel so lilac-naked.

Both the sisters sat quietly, digesting what they had read so far. However, little did Zara know that Anya had more sympathy for Mrin as she had known the same truth. That sometimes when love happens, life happens at just the same time and along with it, come events of unrest, often demolishing that love and romance. And despite her best efforts, she couldn't hide her own inner turmoil. Anya was teary at Mrin's loneliness and just thinking of it made her feel a sense of drowning. Zara sat silent too, not absorbing the heaviness of the words or emotions, but understanding the loss of memories that one might hold precious. However, it was the ending of the email that surprised them both.

"I'm glad she finally understands that their meeting or union is impossible, and that Dad has a family. That should soothe your nerves and mine too!"

However, Anya didn't answer. She simply walked to the wall that held the photographs of their parents and paced quietly in front of it.

"Is it Mrin's situation that has you so upset and agitated?" Zara asked, suddenly worried for her elder sister.

"Yes and no, I am upset for Mrin, but it's my own life as well. Often unrelated things make us reflect on the perplexing truths of our individual relationships… like right now."

"Do you mean your relationship is going sour right now?"

"No, Zara, I'm fine right now. Even so, you know the adage of "once burnt…" I am always on guard. And because of that perhaps I'm missing out on some great relationships. I need to teach my heart…"

Suddenly Zara felt both naïve and selfish for not having been perceptive of her sister's feelings. She walked over and held her with both arms, "Anya, are you okay?" Zara felt a sudden rush of tears.

"Zara, life is relentless and unmerciful to some. She, Mrin wants to know *now* why Dad and her relationship folded before its natural conclusion, why they had no future. And her description of utter hopelessness is chewing up my guts, for her question is very much also my petition," said Anya, looking through tears into her sibling's eyes.

"Don't be cryptic and elusive, Anya. I can sense you want to share something. I have also known failures and deceptions and experienced mind games. We all have. You've been a fantastic elder sister, but maybe I take you for granted at times and don't appreciate you enough. You can share anything you want with me…"

"I will; in due time, I will" Anya smiled, "You know; I recall so fondly how all four us used to talk about our troubles, our happiness, and our friends under the same quilt. And here we are, without Anoushka or Bijli, just half of a complete set, doing it again. Even so, this time it's about our Mom, and like you Zara, I wish that she emerges from this unscathed. She protected all of us; she's the biggest, most comfortable blanket in our lives, and though I feel for Mrin, I hope this doesn't end up being the unravelling of our parents' relationship."

"You're absolutely correct, Anya."

 "Zara, it's past midnight and I have a big day at the office tomorrow. How about we shut the computer and resume later?"

"That might be a good idea" Zara sighed, "I can't believe I am saying this, but our emotions have gotten too tangled up and given all that's happened tonight, Anya, if we read on I think I might not be able to handle it, and impulsively might end up hurting you again. Of all things, I don't want that."

Anya stroked her younger sister's cheek, "You could never truly hurt me, Zara, and you know that. As for tomorrow, you might still be asleep when I leave for work, so let's meet in the city for drinks in the evening, after I'm done for the day."

With that, they hugged each other goodnight.

Chapter Five

John Donne

Next day, Zara, sipping on strawberry lemonade, waited for Anya at Hard-Rock Café on Yonge Street. Right across from her seat, she could see the Eaton Centre. She could see a steel band playing Caribbean music, some toddlers running around the sprinklers getting soaked while their parents were keeping a close eye on them, teenagers roller-blading and a few homeless people sleeping under a shady canopy. She loved this side of Toronto, rich with humanity and its idiosyncrasies. There were Rastafarian, drug peddlers, hookers and fast food vendors. You could see suits, jeans, designer clothes as well as *Salwars*, *dhotis*, *hijabs* and *burkhas*. Cops didn't hassle anyone; they just sauntered around unobtrusively, but keeping vigilance on everything. Jehovah's Witnesses were handing out flyers; Muslims were giving away Qurans, all under a single blue sky.

"I love Toronto," she mused.

Anya arrived, hugged Zara and before she sat down, took a sip of the lemonade and asked the waitress for another. Shrugging off her stiff suit jacket, she pointed at a kiosk across the street. "I saw Prof Divecha at that ticket counter when I was here with some friends."

"Well, I'm really looking forward to seeing her and talking about Dad's life in Mumbai."

"Me too…I want to find out more about the campus there. It's such a rushed city, but even then people find the time to enjoy and savour life. I think that's why they call it The Maximum City. And it's a strange thing to say because we've never lived there, but I always felt like I could connect with Mumbai. Though, it's funny how we never got a chance to see it from a local's perspective, having visited it so many times!"

"That's true. Maybe we'll get invited to a family event or find a business excuse to go there someday? Anyway, tell me, how was your day? You're off work pretty early…"

"It was a good day at the office. I talked to my boss for taking a few days off. Other than that, it was a pretty mundane, routine day. You know how it is, as soon as the summer arrives, the firm's partners head for their golf clubs or cottages in the Muskokas and other areas leaving us to slog for even their share of work. Anyway, what about you? What did you do?"

"Saw some friends, it was nice. Most of them are married or pretty successful in their careers, and I'm happy to see them so settled. By the way, I was thinking let's eat here, if you don't mind? I skimmed through the menu and came across some favourites, plus it's been so long."

Anya nodded, and almost immediately Zara added, "And I am so sorry about last night, again. I just…."

"It's water under the bridge, so don't fret over it. Tell me, what you like to eat?" She waved at the waitress, and they ordered. While eating, Anya could see, intermittently, the ghosts of emails intruding on their dinner conversation, but she dismissed them with respect. She didn't want the extra baggage of guilt and regret that wasn't theirs to begin with crowding their evening. Plus, she knew what awaited them at home was a pile of unread emails, ready to be dissected.

And so the dinner was a light one, with the sisters catching up on life and friends, both careful not to mention the words such as Mom, Dad or Mrin. While walking back south towards the condo on Yonge Street, they talked about the men in their lives. Anya narrated amusing incidents from past dates with men in the legal trade, stressing deeply on how family life, which was primary to her, was often secondary to them. Zara gathered if her sister had an option, she would prefer a non-legal trade spouse, but before could get into nitty-gritty of the relationships past; they were at the condo. She decided to leave the topic for some other time. Once inside, they changed into pajamas and made themselves comfortable on the sofa.

"Zara, wait a minute. Don't start reading just yet. Let me talk to Mom; I always call her at this time."

Anya talked to Somi and then passed the phone to her sister. After a few minutes of greetings and small talk, Zara wished her mom adieu and hung up.

Zara said, "Well…let the heartache begin…"

From: Ayush@*****.com

To: Mrin@****.com

Subject: Knock, knock...

Mrin, Mrin, Mrin…

Let me begin this email with a confession. I would very much like to mirror the love and affection that you shower on me today. And it would, no doubt, be a natural response borne out of our history of reciprocity. However, I realize now that any declaration of affection from my end would eventually end up upsetting me. Perhaps not immediately, but certainly some time in the future when I think back to the words I might write. If you are wondering why that is so, then let me tell you it is because I'll be neglecting a principle, I hold very dear to my heart. When we were together, I had vowed that I would never do anything that would hurt you... That benchmark still holds true for me. In your place, today, I have my wife and four lovely daughters and such behavior on my part would both hurt them and undermine their importance to my life, neither of which I would ever intend to do.

So, despite some self-conscious reticence, I will be as much forthcoming as possible, albeit with guilt for the celebration of our beautiful past. My memory still calls your name out loud with love and then a cavalcade of sequences is unfurled; scene after scene your smiling face weaves magic that, despite its absence, makes my past reverently so rich. It's true that you're not in my life *now*, but certainly you have never been out of it either, mentally or emotionally. Who could ever regret the time I spent with you? I don't want to forget that at all. It's a significant part of my life, our life… And I am happily certain that you are making a family-load of your own people laugh, read, sing and live in a world of rich imagination. So nor do I want them to suspect anything undue transpiring between us now. I hope you take no offence at my hedging explanation.

Coming back to where we left off last, let me write about the celebrated Kirti M Doongursee College event. One of your classmates asked her brother, a professor, to give an overview lecture on Aestheticism to interested classmates on Saturday, January 22, 1972. Since I wanted to be around you, I volunteered to audit the lecture.

I met you at the college around eleven on that typical January morning in Mumbai. Not too hot, not too cold. And you looked as beautiful as ever. You were thrilled to see me, and on our way, we stopped at an ice cream booth, relishing the ice cream, a brand called 'Kwality', served in small cups. Since we still had some time left, I remember we sauntered to the sea in front of the college.

As you looked across the waves, you suddenly broke into an *impromptu* song, beautiful and romantic from a Bollywood movie. All the sweethearts, who had hidden themselves near the beach, perked up to see the siren out to enliven and encourage their hearts. We saw them snuggle up and even though their bodies couldn't get any closer, they still, with their caressing fingers, tried relentlessly to feel clinging to one another. Even though we were not lovers yet the setting, romantic pairs on the beach of the Arabian Sea brought about sudden changes in you and subsequently in me. The tsunami started. Body temperatures rose; hearts beat faster; swagger in our feet and lips began to sing.

You undid your bun, and in the soft breeze, your hair cascaded all over your face as well as mine. You twirled your head to fling your hair behind. I gasped. You were the sexiest woman I had ever seen. The sea sprayed your face in a fleeting moment. With droplets of water on your hair, glistening face, and out-stretched hands, you were a sight to behold! It was an unforgettable moment. You smiled and looked at me provocatively. I had never seen such a body language of temptation and invitation from you before. I was too young then to understand what was going on, but now I realize that the walls were coming down, and boundaries were disappearing. Your tongue was licking your lips; you were checking if your antics, looks, curves and the ambience of love and sexuality around us, and within us had seduced me. You brushed against my body repeatedly. Once you overstepped and tripped, your *dupatta* fell off, and for a fleeting moment, I could see the underneath of your blouse, but your eyes were glued to my face to see my reaction.

Your eyebrows lifted playfully into mischief and the neck slightly turned, and you stared at me.

 I said, 'looking good.' You thought that was funny.

However, in all honesty, that day at the beach, you were hot and frisky. When I didn't give in to your charm, you smacked me teasingly with your *dupatta* and hung on to my shoulders, grabbing me with passion. Honestly, I liked it a lot, Mrin; I loved it. I could feel the softness and fragrant warmth of your body. Your openness was refreshing and inviting. I would have never crossed that boundary of decency and probity without your consent. However, that day, what grew between us was an unspoken emotional understanding. You realized that it wasn't just your physical charm that had drawn me to you, and I realized also how deep of an effect you had on me. Before I knew it, my hands were around your waist, and soon I was holding your hands. Without saying a word, declaring our loyalties, we became lovers. Our bodies needed no approvals. They approved us.

We left the couple on the sea tetra pods behind and entered the college for the lecture. However, I have to say, our minds were on anything but what was being taught; our fingers brushed against each other's arms, our feet played footsie underneath the desk, and our bodies yearned for more. Out of respect to the professor, we stayed put but kept exchanging love notes throughout. 'Let's go to the 'Romeo Corner', you wrote finally, and I readily agreed, and we exited the hall.

Romeo Corner is a little park filled with aromatic shrubs and trees next to the college. It was visited more by young couples or gawkers than students needing rest. Believe me when I say, I had never seen your face this mellow, soft and tender, this vulnerable, this ready. I thought to myself then, 'how is it that a girl this beautiful, witty and talented has remained unasked or unsought.' I almost couldn't believe my luck.

Mrin, I know as you said you 'are blind-folded.' But am I giving you enough details and clues to goad your mind to awaken from slumber and say 'Yes, this might be the way it happened'? I want to hear from you. You need to read your diary one more time and see if what I described connects with your diary or not. Once I get the confirmation, however, rough, I will continue. Thus far what I narrated covers about until one-thirty of that day's afternoon. We have yet to visit the Romeo Corner, then take a long scenic walk through the streets of south Dadar, and reach the Dadar Circle by seven in the evening. There are still quite a few hours of the day left for us to unravel.

They know, but pass no judgment.

Their eyes tell, their smiles reveal. I'm found out.

I blush as I feel so lilac naked.

As your poem says, when one's in love, one's behavior exposes an internal transformation. In your case, it must have been your frequent pink blushes. I can still remember the rouge creeping up to your cheeks quite vividly.

Now, my wife calls me as my daughters have arrived for the weekend. Mrin, remember, I loved you once and have never forgotten you.

Ayush

Zara's fingers coiled tightly around her sister's hand. "I fully empathize with her, Anya. Love has turned her on. When this chemistry happens, one has no choice but to follow the instincts and surrender and that includes common sense too… It has happened to me, and I'm sure it has happened to you too. One has no control over speech, memories, actions; I understand what she must be feeling. However, this is our father, we are talking about."

"There you again Zara, hedging. I thought you'd changed…"

"Yes, but I cannot discount the fact that she acts like a shameless huckster… showing all her wares, getting the deal closed."

 "Zara, I was going to agree with you until you brought back your traditional quibbling…I think what you earlier said is more precise. All attempts at control just disappear when you meet someone you think is good for life, and you end up showing, as you characterized, all wares and assets… It may not happen that way in every case, but that's how it goes generally. Now, this is editorial, Zara; for you, the physical display of affection is too much, perhaps because the man you are reading about is our father. However, when a woman loves her man, she has to let her guard down to show that there are no walls between them, when all inhibitions are abandoned, Mrin and her man haven't reached that stage yet, but soon they will. And this is the beginning of that relationship."

"Anya, I don't like your analytical approach to this love affair, which is almost voyeuristic. Let me remind you again; our mother's life is at stake."

"But Zara, even Mrin knows that, do recall her assertion that her being with Dad in the future is absurd and preposterous. Not to mention the first part of Dad's email, how can you overlook that? Read it one more time."

Confused, Anya scrolled up and putting aside her anger, read the beginning of Ayush's email again. As she read, her eyes widened and for the first time, she registered the words their father had written.

"Anya, I can't believe it. How could I have missed this? I feel almost foolish and ashamed of myself of imagining horrible things our Dad was capable of committing. While all the while, he was trying hard not to cross that line, not to slip back into the past because of us, because he could never do anything to hurt us. I feel awful for judging him…" her voice trailed and her eyes moistened.

"You have an incomparable familial instinct to protect those you love. These are great qualities, my li'l sister, but we must always give people a chance to prove themselves before we pounce to judgement. As the legal adage says one is innocent until proven guilty."

Zara nodded, wiped her eyes dry and hugged her sister, grateful that she had shown the patience Zara could not. Still embracing her, Anya clicked onto the next email.

From: Mrin@****.com

To: Ayush@*****.com

Subject: Knock, knock.

Dear Ayush,

When I read your words now, I feel as though you are God's gracious gift to me. You have made me see and feel the days of the past, see myself as I looked then. Perhaps as a lover, you make me appear more attractive than I ever was, a youthful amorous girl, Ayush. From your narrative, I can say I was a mischievous woman…wasn't I?

Instead of my love throughout life, what you received was a wound that has pained you. Perversely, this pain is now sustaining you. In this, I am your mirror image. When you are not in my mind, my life is out of balance. Your words now give me poise. Even so, I must confess that I have learned to live with it and accepted my fate. I'm also sure that, likewise, you too have come to concur with life and moved on without me. Like water, life finds its grade too. What I'm saying is that the past informs the present and cultivates the future. Without your memory, I am in pain. However, thinking of you and how you are in life now, and reading your words and through them, reliving our past together, bring me peace and pleasure.

You might say now that life is full of ironies. When we no longer physically have someone in our life, they continue to thrive in our heart and mind, linger on and at times, make us neglect those that are materially present. However, this irony is like a coin. One side is the past, and the other is present taking into a future. Reading and writing these mails are making me seek the continuance of life. Again, this is your gift to me.

My diary is certainly not as graphic and pictorial as your narrative, but it was a momentous day in my life... our togetherness we shared at that time. It deserves more attention to detail. This is what I wrote in my diary. I have decoded the entry in brackets for you now, so the real message remained a riddle to my brother at the time.

One of the glorious days ever it was for me. I attended a lecture at Kirti College with my best friend. (that's you). I arrived a bit early at the college. So first, we had ice cream, and then sauntering on the beach, we found young people, engrossed in themselves, doing the things youthful people do. I felt some strange tingling sensation in my heart and a tightening in the belly. I am so happy that Sanj was with me. He has such a positive and powerful influence! My beloved friend made me realize that young folks ought to have trust and freedom for their growth and know their character. T diary, you've been patient with me in listening to my questions and feelings. I must confess that I'm under a magical spell. My soul wants to soar with Sanj and touch the heights and depths both wish to encounter.

The January sun is shining in my sky.
The light sea breeze brushes against my cheeks

The air's filled with luxuriant scents of the bower

There are dreams afloat everywhere I cast my eyes.

The universe is humming a happy tune.

Thou held my face twixt thy hands

Inaudibly whispered thy desire

Hold me there firmly for a millennium

See, what thou hast gifted to my life.

Ayush, indeed your account concurs with my diary entry. You have painted a perfect picture of that morning and early afternoon. Please finish the day for me. Lead me to Dadar Circle. Remember to give me every detail. Don't censor the memory; help me put the pieces of the puzzle together better!

I love you forever; that's what I used to say, isn't it? I know I have long lost the right to say that to you, but I certainly say it to all my friends as a mark of well wishing.

Mrin

P.S. Ayush, I do realize that I'm really unfair to ask you to write a vivid and pictorial narrative of rendezvous we had. Without knowing your family status, I am asking for details that may seem titillating and libidinous. You be the judge of how much you can tell me. However, be a graphic portrayer of whatever you see. May I ask for your forgiveness for the lapse? I understand that you have a wife and daughters. Perhaps they will forgive for the transgression. I never asked you for details of your family, nor do I intend to ask in the future. You have been kind to me in not asking as per my request. However, feel free to write me anything you wish to, as nothing would make me happier. And one more request…when you're looking at your daughters, do tell yourself, "Girls, I see your mother in you, but I also see in you a woman I had known once."

Yet again, there was silence as the sisters began to digest what they had read. Something had been troubling Anya and with her eyebrows knitted together, she turned to her sister, "Zara, I wonder why she isn't asking him about his family. Don't you think that's a little fishy? And then she doesn't want him to ask her about her life… why so secretive? What's she hiding? This is gnawing my innards. On the positive side though, she's becoming more aware of Dad's family, and that's a great sign. Maybe she'll eventually just leave him alone."

"I hope you're right about her leaving Dad alone. I'm concerned about Mom's reaction to this, if she were to find out. However, I have to admit, despite the disgust I feel on reading these emails where she is trying to get close to Dad, I do admire her philosophical interpretations of their time together. I thought I would never be saying this, but perhaps she's looking for a truce, some kind of understanding to decipher what life has dealt her. Maybe she's just trying to clear whatever issues drove her and Dad to separate in the first place…"

Anya stared at her sister, impressed at Zara's calm and logical reaction. Then suddenly, her thoughts went back to their mother. "Mom should never find out about this! I can't wait to see the last of these emails when I can breathe freely again, or look at Dad in the eye and be convinced that he's not a lying two-timer."

"To be honest, when I left the home the other day, I could barely talk to him or look at him. He even noticed and asked if something was the matter with me. I didn't wait to answer him, just dashed out of the house with a bag and his laptop."

Anya was not surprised and told Zara that she'd probably do the same thing. What a whirlwind of a situation they'd gotten themselves into. Part of her almost wished that her sister had never chanced upon the emails in the first place. Ignorance was bliss, after all, wasn't it? However, at the same time, this gave her a completely different outlook on her father. For the first time, she saw him freer, uninhibited, and youthful almost. And though her heart went out to

Mrin, she felt her pain and melancholy; she found herself wishing her father could be like that with their mother. Wouldn't it be lovely; she smiled to herself, and it was almost as if Zara could hear her thoughts, since she voiced the same wish.

"I hate to admit it," she began, but I sympathize with Mrin. What could be sadder than losing one's memory and relying on old lover to help put the pieces back together? But then I think of our mother, and everything goes for a spin, all the logic and the sympathies. Couldn't Dad have ignored her mails or discouraged her from writing questions to recoup her memory? If he had done that, this might have never happened."

Then she walked onto the balcony, looking at the island lights glowing, in the distance, Zara found herself pondering over the essence of Mrin's last email, "How ironic it is that we value what we have lost, and neglect what we still have." Her thoughts were with her husband, Shaan. They barely spoke since she'd arrived in Toronto. She knew he was busy, making money, spending money. That's what she liked about him too, that he was a go-getter. However, nothing in his life was long lasting. Friends came and left. Jobs came, got upgraded and soon new jobs arrived. His life shifted effortlessly from one city to another and then another. That was his style…without roots, peripatetic. If something was lost, his explanation was *'easy come, easy go.'* He never liked to be told, and never liked to be reminded. Though she had learnt to mould herself to this unpredictable lifestyle, what always remained in the back of her mind was how long her union was going to last.

Noticing Zara mumbling to herself, Anya came and stood next to her. "What's wrong?"

"I was just thinking about Mrin's comment that we value the lost ones and neglect the ones who are with us. I know she was referring to Dad, but to be honest; it made me think of Shaan. Anya, we have a good life together but sometimes, I just hope he would cherish it more, cherish me more. That something would give him a gentle reminder, like Mrin seems to be sending to Dad. In some strange way, she is warning him not to let what he has lost for something he desires. Shaan hasn't called me here in the last two days…"

"But Zara, neither have you. What stops you from doing so? Is it pride? Did you guys have a tiff?"

"Nothing of the kind… He is kind of slow in such gestures; that's all."

"And you're not?"

She smiled. "Yes, perhaps I am too, but not with you or Mom or Dad. Shaan is different. His attention seeking behaviour tires me out. He doesn't believe in making phone calls or spontaneous gestures. Perhaps like Mrin, he believes more in the past and less in the present. However, in some ways, he reminds me of Dad, actually, in that he takes for granted the people that populate his life because we will always be there, like Dad often does to Mom. And truth be told, reading Mrin's emails have filled my heart with fear. What if Shaan and I end up the same way as Mom and Dad? Maybe that's why I feel so defensive for Mom."

Anya hugged her, "Oh Zara; I'm sorry to hear this, but you are different than Mom, and Dad is distinct than Shaan. I'm sure it won't hurt for you to check up on him, make the effort."

"Yes, I will, but later. I won't be able to focus on Mom if Shaan shows up in the mix."

"Hmm, then let's finish the second part of that last email. I know it's going to tear us up; they haven't even kissed yet, and I'm dreading those details. If I were alone, it would have crippled and devastated me, but I am glad to face Mrin in your company…come, let's read further."

From: Ayush@*****.com

To: Mrin@****.com

Subject: Knock, knock.

Mrin,

I am glad to have had finally a peek into your personal diary. You were smart to use codes to create a secret world. I'm also touched by the moniker you gave me; the word *"Sanj"*, which I don't know if you realised then, that it's an abbreviated name for Sanjeev, literally meaning living and reviving. That's downright prescient, even though it didn't happen, or was at best, short-lived that our relationship was living and thriving. I must confess that I failed to grasp the intentional meaning of the nickname I read a few mails earlier.

However, I think that you didn't fully grasp the idea of diary writing. Yours is a log of events, places, and people. Diaries ought to have no bars to revelations and explorations of the self, others and issues affecting the person writing it. It's not to protect you from others' censure or disapproval. This is where you spill out your inner thoughts and scary, insecure or even perverse feelings.

Yours is not a gut-wrenching self-revelation where your emotional truth is littered on those inky pages. You hid your emotions, kept as many secrets as possible so others like your brother Nikunj being among them, did not have access to your innermost thoughts and feelings. I'm pretty sure that you're quite aware of the distinction now, but not then when you penned these entries. Despite my comments, I mean no harm. It just proves I too am distressed as you are for accessing these lapsed memories. But worry not, we will put this puzzle together no matter how shrouded the memories seem to be. These email exchanges are the key to get out of the house of horror that you inhabit now and I will help my friend get through.

This pain, I hope, makes you strong and not weak. The pain is definitely not sweet when it starts. First, it grinds, and then it grates, and finally pulverizes. The longer you rub it into your mind, the sweeter it eventually becomes. That's how pain inures you to get accustomed to it and relish it, Mrin. Sometimes one has to climb a mountain to prove that you're prepared to risk everything for what your heart aspires. Without it, your life will be empty. Perhaps we failed to see and climb this mountain, or chose a roundabout route to avoid the discomfort. But the good sign is that the river of life has pulled us along the smooth flow and we've survived. Despite the losses, we are kind of connecting to the river's topography, its bends, its heights and its precipitous falls. Breathe easy, Mrin, you'll be all right, easy flowing calm waters are ahead.

Now back to the afternoon of Saturday, January 22, 1972.

I wrote in my last email that 'I had never seen your face this mellow, this soft and tender, this vulnerable, this ready.' I felt that you were hot and aroused, and your note to me confirmed those feelings. At the end of the lecture, people tried to talk to you but you registered little, unaware of anyone else, except me. Some of your girlfriends were surprised and exchanged giggle and glances. And when they saw us entering the Romeo Corner they exchanged even more glances!

We sat on a bench in a secluded corner of the park, under a Jacaranda tree and overlooking the Lilac in front. You closed your eyes, taking in everything that the garden offered. Like the flowers, aromatic, blooming and beautiful, around us, I was with the woman who was equally intoxicating, inviting and ready to open up. Suddenly, and almost inaudibly, I heard the two words that seemed to stop my heartbeat. "Kiss me."

And I kissed your closed eyes ever so gently that whatever you imagined, remained undisturbed. You leaned your head on my chest and we sat there for a long time in complete silence. The electric sexual energy we had both felt before seemed to dissolve into the serenity of the park. The lustful desire in your eyes had been replaced with softness. No words were exchanged between us, there was no need to. Then just as quietly, you walked up to the lilac tree, plucked a few blue flowers and held them out. Almost instinctively, I took them from your palm and wove them into your hair. Hand in hand, we left the park.

Taking a slow, scenic route, we strolled three hours to reach Dadar Circle. We traveled by Dhruv Road, and then on to Savarkar Road to visit the Siddhivinayak Temple on the corner of Gadgil and Bole Roads in Prabhadevi and offered our prayers to *Ganesh*. After the worship, you asked the priest to bless you in Sanskrit. He looked at you quizzically, wondering why you had requested the Sanskrit blessings specifically, but blessed you nonetheless, saying *'Ayushya maan Bhavah'* I was elated inside.

At the sound of my name, you looked at me and accepted the blessings along with the two meanings of the word 'Ayush'. May you be blessed with 'long life' and may your life be filled with me. "Yes, you're a part of this blessing, Ayush. I'm blessed," you said, hanging on my left hand. You looked at me searchingly to know about my prayers, but I said that prayers must remain private. In retrospect, I have no idea if my prayer succeeded or not. Tell me how happy you are, and I'll know my answer.

Then we prayed at the Portuguese Church with candles. On the way, you bought pigeon feed and scattered the grains in the Kabutar Khana for the birds. We then went to the Hanuman Dattatrey Mandir to pay our homage.

"Our meandering looks like we're on a five-shrine pilgrimage. I've never been to so many shrines and holy places in one day," you said and I laughed.

At that point, we stopped at restaurant and as we sat sipping cold coffees, I remember us staring into each other's eyes with the utmost happiness and contentment.

You said, 'Ayush, in the park, I was all yours. You could have done anything with me, anything you wanted.'

'Yes, I know. But the day's not over yet,' I said tactfully, to lighten the subject.

By evening time, as we passed Tilak Bridge a cool burst of breeze hit our faces. You turned to avoid the gust and looking into my eyes asked, 'Ayush, tell me, why do I like you?'

Looking into your eyes I replied, 'I have often wondered about that too. It's almost as though we are opposites, but they say opposites attract each other. And to be honest, if I am able to make you happy, then that makes me happy."

We reached Dadar Circle and bought a box of mixed *mithai* from Joshi Buddhakaka Mahim Halwawala Store. You picked a piece of *ghari* from the box and commanded, "Open your mouth, Ayush," and then placing it in my mouth, mocked blessing me, "May your life be forever sweet." And then you pinched my cheek with your greasy fingers. The store clerk liked what he saw and refused to accept the money. Then you offered him a piece of sweet, which he readily accepted to witness our happiness.

We walked back past the Empress Building to sit in the little park in front. It was a perfect evening after a gorgeous day. There weren't many people in the park, some older folks, but mostly just the young couples. You led me to a secluded spot behind a bushy shrub. You were humming a melancholic song from a Bollywood movie *Ashli Naqli*. The song encapsulated the psychological state of our minds so brilliantly! It celebrated our love and our deepest anxieties....

Tera mera pyaar amar,

phir kyon mujhako lagata hai dar

Mere jivan saathi bata,

kyon dil dhadake rah-rah kar

Tera mera pyaar amar,

phir kyon mujhako lagata hai dar

Mere jivan saathi bata,

kyon dil dhadake rah-rah kar

"Ayush, I have no fear at all. I feel liberated. I am free and unshackled. I am blessed" Then you ran. arms spread wide as if to take to flight to the land of happiness. Everyone enjoyed your unadulterated euphoria and clapped their hands at your elation and excitement.

Your face beaming as you returned next to me at the bench. "Tell me, Ayush, why do you like me?" you asked, inverting the day's earlier question.

"Mrin, you have got a heart like a translucent shimmering pond reflecting God's glory. Whatever you touch turns into lyrical beauty. When you arise, the Sun comes out. When you smile, the seasons dazzle. When you speak, the words come to life in their dance. When you stretch your arms, I come running to embrace you. You're a spellbinder; you're a clown; you're a poet, and you're the model, Leonardo da Vinci looks for when…"

You were listening to me, seriously and intently. First like a child, your eyes were wide open, mouth agape and listening to everything I was saying. Then I saw that you were moved, tears started rolling down your cheeks and you remarked, "An economist turns romantic poet! Wonders never cease!"

Embarrassed, I chuckled.

You said my voice was thick, whisper-like, almost sonorous and subdued. It had a cadence that you had not heard before. Your eyes, glistening, slightly teary, were keenly focused on me. Then you kissed me on the left cheek, saying, 'Now I know why I love you.'

I extended my hands, and so did you. I held your hands, drew you closer to my heart in an embrace, and then you kissed my lips.

I said quietly, 'You like me because I love you. And I pray you never leave my side.' And I stared, into your eyes to see your answer reflected in your gorgeous eyes with a slight tinge of blue which I hadn't noticed before.

You replied, 'I love thee too and accept thee as thou art. Tell what price the world will put on thy head, that I may bring that ransom as part of my trousseau.'

I was dazzled by your beauty, lyrical utterances and eyes that showered sunlight and moon light. I was transported to another world where dreams live forever, pain is an outcast and friendship knows no end. My heart wanted to burst with extreme ecstasy, and I felt that my entire inside wanted to jump out of my body and dance.

You shook my shoulder and said, "Ayush, speak."

Incredulous, I kept staring at you and said, "Bring no dowry, just yourself."

Simultaneously, our faces drew closer, and we kissed as if forever. Our first kiss, infinite and sublime happiness! I heard a choir of angels celebrating our love. Then your eyes fixed and narrowed for keener focus on my face, lips slightly apart, head tilting to one side exposing your long and slender neck, eyes blinked again and a faint smile emerged. Then you said, 'Now kiss me like you're horny!' That cracked me up and the angels too. Only you, Mrin, could turn a romantically rife moment into a more provocative moment with a wisecrack!

But you were serious and meant what you said. 'Ayush, get ready for love bites', and you gently bit my fingers, hands, cheeks, and then grabbing my neck said, 'Here comes your first hickey!' and left your teeth marks for all to see. 'Ayush, dogs pee to mark their territory; the girls leave hickeys to lay claim on their men. Understood? You're out of bounds for other women. You're mine and mine only.'

Even in that moment, I kept laughing at your choice of metaphor.

Then you pulled my face to you, kissing me gently, and then slowly inserting your tongue in my mouth. You kissed my lips again for a few seconds, bit my lower lip and lightly chewed it, and somehow hooked up with my tongue and took it in your mouth. It was long; it was deliberate, and it was incredible. It was like sucking on a syrupy ice cone.

I was gasping for air. My heart skipped a beat… that kiss gave me a rush which I had never experienced in my life. I wanted it to go on… and on, forever.

You said, "Ayush, that's your first French kiss, man! Learn and enjoy something new every day. That's if you want me to climb the mountain with you!" We both laughed again.

"So, I should learn something new everyday… I'm glad that guys in Bombay left you alone."

'Correction: Many have chased me. Most left me after I opened my mouth. The rest left mid-way through their second encounter.'

'How many guys have you kissed to be so good, I mean great?' I recall asking you.

You said, "Lover, you are the first man my lips have locked with; *Numero Uno*. I'm sure you will be the last one forever to touch my lips with fingers, eyes or lips... But I must teach you a thing or two here. Good men never ask their women about their past encounters or indiscretions with other men."

"But how did you become so good that you took me to the gates of heaven?"

"Well, going to a girls' school in Shimla was a big help. There, practicing on arms, chocolate bars and ice cream cones certainly helped. An American classmate from San Diego was our instructor. These California girls know a lot about life. Her parents worked in Dharamshala with the Dalai Lama."

Right then, a municipal worker with a hooked rod turned up to nudge the gas on to light the street lamp pole.

It was time to depart. Alas! We took a cab and went to the Buddhist Temple on Gaffar Khan Road in Worli where you lived. We prayed standing at the gate of the temple. Then you showed me your apartment from the road, informing me of a sign that would become key in coming to see you. "If the kitchen lights are on, this means I'm alone and you can come up with no problem!"

I reminded you, "Mrin, I know your parents since childhood. We've got an excuse, don't worry."

Hugging me, you smiled and turned to walk towards your apartment. I don't know how long I waited before I let all facts and happenings of the day sink inside of me, dust myself and walk to my house.

Mrin, this is a long email. However, it was a pivotal day in our lives. I've given you all kinds of details, even those you might consider silly or inconsequential or lurid. According to your instructions, I have included everything I remember without being a censor.

Read the last one and this one together to see the whole picture. I hope your skin and blood goad your mind to yield to your soul.

Let me know if this picture breathes life into your memory. I fervently hope so.

Take care,

Ayush

Anya saw her sibling's eyebrows squeeze and eyelids tighten. Anger and repulsion were written all over her face, reflecting what was inside in her heart and soul. Anya knew this was not the time to have disputes and disagreements with a woman ready for a battle.

Calming her down by massaging her back, she said, "Zara, ask yourself this…what did our Dad have to offer this girl? He didn't come from a rich family nor have a parent with a great profession. He was not a popular athlete. His family owned no land, estates or assets. Tell me. If this woman just wanted physical intimacy, then why did she wait all those years until she was in her early twenties? You know how it is, most people think they're ready way before Mrin and Dad even kissed! Dad was the man on whom she lavished her love. Is that very unusual for a woman? I don't think so. As I said earlier, we need to be a little more rational, or empathetic. Don't feel angry or repulsed, but feel respect…for his sake, Dad's sake. Fine, forget for a moment that it's Dad and think of him as just a man, and Mrin as just another woman. Now, cut a little slack, will you?"

As she breathed in heavily, Anya words had a comforting effect on Zara. Her facial muscles now relaxed and her looks softened loosing hostility. She looked at Anya, smiled and softly said, "You're so right. Everything she has, she is ready to lose."

"You move my heart when I least expect, my precious Zara."

"No matter what I feel, I cannot discount the truth. I also like what Dad says about the value we attach to pain," said Zara with a little sadness.

"Yes, I like that so much too. He is always looking for relative values and this is not any different. In this case, Zara, your pain is greater than mine because you consider what this woman could do to our parents' marriage, more importantly to Mom's future. One more thing, without offending you, I must admit that I'm speechless at Mrin's ability to control and guide how she was going to love, or be loved. She was spontaneous, natural and erotic...not contrived."

To Anya's surprise, her sister nodded again, agreeing, not saying a single sour word.

 "And if you don't mind, Zara, when I visit Mumbai next, I am going to go see this college, walk on the Arabian Sea's tetra pods and enter the Romeo Corner. Reading their letters makes me feel like walking the same route they took, traverse every nook and cranny of the neighbourhood, savour street foods, visit the famous temple, the Joshi sweet shop at the Dadar circle and sit in the park. If I have a lover, I'll give him a hickey, a French kiss and lather his face with my love. That's what I'll do." She giggled on completing her sentence.

"You know, surprisingly that is what I thought too!" chimed Zara and both the sisters laughed for the first time that evening, momentarily forgetting their concerns and worries.

Chapter Six

A Suitor with Deep Pockets

Anya and Zara took a well-deserved walk before resuming the reading session. Then armed with large, steaming styrofoam cups of Tim Horton's coffee, they settled down into their favoured sofas.

"Okay, Anya. Start the torture."

"But you're getting used to it now."

"Less talk, more substance," said Zara.

Anya loved this new side of Zara's internals. She clicked on the next email.

From: Mrin@****.com

To: Ayush@*****.com

Subject: Knock, knock.

Dear Ayush,

You made me feel my naughtiness. Yes, you certainly did! Reading, thinking and then re-imagining about how I spent that day with you gives me millions of goose bumps. It was best time of my life, that's when my garden was in full bloom and my sky was full of scintillating stars. And you've a pretty good idea how and why it happened

I am so glad that I was unlike other girls. I now pride myself on my playful impishness then, which has through these emails, brought excitement and satisfaction that I didn't live in vain. I did have some satisfaction that I was my own person; I was spontaneous, and lived each moment to my best of capabilities. As you know, it didn't happen with any other man, just you. I was not immoral or unbridled. You had a magical aura about you, and I wanted to live in that aura. However, I need to explore my rebellious, maverick personality in detail to find out why I was unlike other women. I hope I've time for that.

Again, your narrative matches my diary. When I read how you have described our days and my habits, I see it becoming a picture. But you've made it come alive; it has transformed a one-sided picture into a three-dimensional beauty. It's no more a flat sepia picture, but a multi-coloured picture, full of motion and emotion. And for all this effort that you continue to put in, I will always remain in debt to.

Your evaluation of my diary, too, is right. Somehow, I feared then that some feelings and experiences were personal, and that's how they should be kept. Ayush, I was only in my early twenties! I was unaware that I could be open and honest in revelations and evaluation of my life. I don't know if you ever asked me if other men chased me or not. But I can understand if men my age pursued me, but I do have my diary telling me that grown men with families wanted liaison with me, which thoroughly disillusioned me about moral façade that people carried around their persona. My youngish adventurous spirit was fully misconstrued by many men and they thought I was foolish and naïve and an easy catch. In that period of heartache, you showed up and amazed me with the alarm. Alarm, you ask? Yes, that's when you placed your palm in my palm on our first meeting. But I have a feeling that what I felt for you on that day and onwards was real, strong and heartfelt.

Remember, I told you earlier that my diary was partially in codes when it comes to very personal issues. Now I don't even know this person I am writing about, let alone what my experience was! Here is some more coded snippet from my diary-

Despite being busy at the Reserve Bank of India, Sanj finds time to pamper me! My best friend ever, who fills my being with warmth, excitement and my soul with dreams! Without Sanj walking with me, I feel alone and lost... Without his comforting sound and gentle touch, I feel my lungs constricted, difficult to breathe. We walk together to Bombelli's to see Mantra Chamak Mahavir. No wonder my stomach is again in knots as I perhaps don't want to see him, but Sanj says I need to.

Ayush, do you recall anything about this person? Who was he? Why did I not want to see him? Why did you say I had to see him? And what transpired during the meeting? Did you accompany me and stay there with me?

Until your email arrives, I'll read your messages repeatedly, eager to grab that past and never let it go, just hold tightly like a precious piece of my life.

Take care,

Mrin

I close my eyes,

Hide in thy embrace.

Inhale deeply in thy musky chest

No one can see me anymore.

If I ever need to, I can just slip into thy heart

And weave melodies that echo thy heart.

I shall cleave here forever

And shall know no other home

My heart shall accept no trespassers

No one shall dwell here

That doesn't carry thy name.

If my heart is not Ayush-filled

It shall be boarded up, bolted and best forgotten

There shall be no songs, no merriment.

No dance, no jigs.

No spilling swigs and no chatter

There shall be no lust, no laughter.

If I must live, so I shall

Only to count my diminishing days

In the lease provided for His parlays

I shall know no despair

Keep in my heart this lovely affair.

I close my eyes,

Hide in thy embrace.

Inhale deeply in thy musky chest

No one can see me anymore.

Anya's eyes were teary and no longer did she try to hide them.

"I am touched by the dignity, love and caring between these two people. All her prayers came to naught," said Zara

They remained silent for some time. Zara coughed to shake Anya out of despair.

"I can sense a certain grimness of life in their encounters because of complete helplessness," said Zara.

"Yes, circumstances are gumming up…"

"But they still say the right things and wish the best things for the other."

"I know. Could it be out of the forlorn hope that at least one of them did well and found a certain measure of happiness?"

"Would either of them want it without the other having it too?"

"They're the definition of unselfish love."

Zara was honest, but wanted to know more about Mrin's competitive suitor, secretly hoping that her father would lose the competition. Her honesty won over as she spoke.

"I'm callous to even think such things. I say one thing, but in my heart, wish something else. I'm so sorry, Anya."

"No, you're actually great. Your heart knows what's right, but it's your mind, your concern for Mom and your own definition of family honour stops you from seeing the bigger picture," said Anya.

"Zara, she says at the end that she would like to pursue a little more about her character. Then she adds, 'I hope I've time for that.' What is she saying? Is she foreshadowing her death? Complete loss of memory? What do you think?"

"That's a very good point. Anya, both the guesses are pretty decent. I feel sorry for her, you know."

From: Ayush@*****.com

To: Mrin@****.com

Subject: Knock, knock.

Mrin:

I've tears in my eyes as I write this, reading repeatedly how your prayers for me have not been realized. Neither does your poem comfort me. We're two dignified humans with wounded and unhealed hearts.

I think Mr. Mahavir is unquestionably, the encrypted name for Mr. Jain. His first name, Mantra Chamak, is decoded as Om Prakash. So it is Om Prakash Jain. I remember his father was your dad's boss at one of his Jaipur factories.

Om adored you. You can't blame him for his impeccable taste. You were together at college in Jaipur where you both played tennis and badminton for the college doubles teams. He thought his old money, and his father's influential position would endear you to him. You never shut him down. At no time did you tell him that you had someone in your life. He never got anywhere with you, but he thought all he had to do was to wait, shadow you, offer you gifts and sing your praises.

Obviously, you didn't want to see him because of your liaison with me. Our hearts found their rhythm, our dreams a voice, and our lives a vision. Even then, you were annoyed that I was forcing you to see him. He needed to be told in a responsible and stern voice that he must move on for his own good. Reluctantly, I accompanied you and asked you to introduce me as your boyfriend.

We walked from the library, past the courts, went by the Parsee Kuwa, and past the Church Gate Train Station, and then we were at Bombelli's. Om was standing there, a half-burnt cigarette between his fingers of his hand, looking remarkably debonair in his designer clothes and well-coifed hair. He was disappointed to see a man with you. However, he remained composed as you made introductions.

"Om Prakash, meet Ayush, a very close and dear friend."

And then you said to me, "Ayush, this is Om Prakash. A very good friend from Jaipur College where we played tennis and badminton doubles for the college."

I kept waiting for you to declare our relationship, but I believe being in the moment left you stumped as to how you should respond. On seeing your confusion, I ventured forth, "Om, Mrin and I are really together. I'm her boyfriend. Perhaps she doesn't want others to know *now*."

 "Well, in that case, congratulations to both of you, Ayush and Mrina" Then he paused momentarily and added, "Well, Mrina, let me be your backup insurance." He winked.

Om called you Mrina, naturally out of affection, but he pronounced like Marina. Moreover, I thought that was a silly idea to have a 'backup'. Nonetheless, in a composed and civil way, I said, "Mrin's a rare fine gem. She ought to have insurance for sure."

But in my mind, I was wondering what was wrong with men who accepted being second choice, forever in the hopes of graduating to first. I was disgusted with the man's approach to life. More importantly, I was concerned that despite your flamboyance, you would tolerate such idiots. I just wondered how he had chased you as long as he did. I do recall you saying that your dates didn't last longer than two with such laughable dolts, but your wish of not offending your dad's boss may have played a role.

But you considered Om's offer terribly funny, and smiled. And after hearing your positive reaction, he ignored my snide comment altogether. Then the goofball sprung a surprise and said, "Ayush, is it okay with you if Marina and I talk in private?"

I said, "Sure" and flung a ten-rupee bill on the table for my coffee and walked away.

Seriously, in the first place, I should have picked a fight with him for suggesting my failure in pursuing you. Secondly, I should have refused to leave and reassert my boyfriend rights. I erred. But then I'm never happy being assertive. I'm decent at expressing my views, but I lack that killer instinct. No wonder I get bested by small minds and even smaller hearts.

"Hey, Ayush, my lover, wait up for me outside, okay? We won't take long... twenty minutes, tops. I absolutely need you. We've to go back to the library," you shouted. Now, that shout sure made me feel like a millionaire! I looked back at you, smiled and I raised my right-hand thumb in response. I hoped Om Prakash got the message loud and clear.

When you finally came out, you saw a young man selling flowers. We walked to him and you picked a bunch of lilacs. I fixed the flowers on your hair. Knowing well my clumsiness, you helped me put them up neatly. From there we went back to the university library, holding hands oblivious to the chaos around us.

Mrin, this pretty well covers your meeting with a beau who brought you an insurance plan. I honestly hope that you'd a better luck with your beau after me…After all these years, I wonder whatever happened to Mantra Chamak Mahavir aka Mr. Om Prakash Jain from Jaipur?

Also, once you came out, you did tell me the offer he made to you. Instead of narrating his offer, I rather wait for you to tell me. Look in your diary, perhaps there may be clues. I do recollect you came out of the restaurant in a huff; you looked rattled.

Mrin, please do take care and be well.

Ayu

Zara asked, "If Mrin loves Dad, then I wonder why she doesn't tell this other beau? Sounds like a two-timing opportunist, don't you think?"

"Perhaps you're right," said Anya, "but they let the Jain guy know, in no uncertain terms, that Mrin had a lover. There was no ambiguity there."

"But obviously, she didn't marry him either…."

Anya nodded, and then after a pause, she said, "I feel awful that Dad's not assertive."

"Yeah, even today, he's the same. I don't know if he's uncommonly principled, or genetically like that or negligent…"

"Zara, I do remember when we were teenagers, we were proud of his habit of being non-threatening."

"Yes, he gave us enough space to hang our heads in shame. However, I think this is more of a Shakespearean tragic flaw in his character."

"Perhaps his weakness has taught us to stand our ground."

"Agreed, but I never considered it to be a weakness. I thought it showed his inner calm and strength," said Zara yawning. Anya followed suit, which was evidence enough that it was time for bed.

Again, the pair decided they would speak tomorrow during the day, when Anya was at work, about where to meet for dinner in the evening.

Chapter Seven

A Wedding in the Family

Next day, Thursday, Anya told her sister that they would meet at the Shark Club in Eaton Center for a quick drink before dinner. Anya was there in time, but Zara was nowhere near. So, she went inside at at the bar, ordered a martini, sipping it slowly. Soon, a young man standing right behind her asked the bartender for a drink too. Recognising the voice, she turned around and said, "Hey stranger, how have you been?"

"Gosh, Anya, I'm sorry I didn't see you. What's going on with the firm? You been hiding or low profiling?"

"Jordan, the firm is firmly rooted and I am learning to swim with the sharks."

As she finished the sentence, Zara showed up and hugged Anya. Introductions were made and as the sisters were making their way out, Jordan forwarded his phone number to Anya and said, "Let's meet for a dinner someday, Anya."

"Sure. Call me later." And they walked out.

Barely seconds later, Zara said, "He's a hunk."

"Yeah, but he's the legal type. You know I avoid them."

Zara nodded but continued to look at her older sister teasingly. They decided to go to the Old Spaghetti Factory for dinner and despite the evening traffic, tourists, jostling through the commuter crowds, managed to reach their destination in ten minutes. Anya was a regular at the restaurant and a familiar waiter escorted them to her preferred corner table. Soon their table was laden with a basket of fresh Italian bread, olive oil infused with vinegar, garlic and a pitcher of fruity Sangria.

"I always enjoy this drink…" said Zara, relishing the taste.

Anya laughed, "Yes, it's thanks to Mom we acquired the taste… brandy, red wine and vermouth! Oh, speaking of which, did you ever suspect that there could be a fissure in Mom and Dad's relationship?"

"Well, they are not very communicative with each other… monosyllabic conversations. To the point answers, mostly," said Zara.

"Yes, exactly. And here I thought people married for a long time knew each other well enough to read their spouse's mind." Anya's eyebrows knit together as she waited for her sister to weigh in.

"We all strive for that kind of unspoken bond in matrimony, don't we?" she smiled, "But I always thought that Mom and Dad they behaved less like husband-wife and more like roommates."

"What do you mean?"

"Notice it next time you're around them. Usually, they stay out of the other's way, have their own private den, very business-like, congenial and non-threatening, never close, soft or intimate."

"I hope we are wrong," said Anya, as the waiter brought their dinner.

"I know that we visit them very infrequently now, but is it possible that what we see is filtered through the lenses of bias, Anya? We see what we want to?"

For a moment, Anya regretted bringing up the topic altogether, for she saw no merit in Zara's point. But always looking at the complete picture, she came to her parent's defence, "Well, they do yoga, go for long walks together, read books, listen to music, and take trips to see old friends…"

Zara laughed, "Yes, and they have their book clubs, temple visits once or twice a week and treks to library. I think they're doing enough things together. They're doing more things together than

Shaan and I do. But that's not what I'm talking about…"

"I know, I understand what you're saying. Their relationship has come to a lull. And I hate to say it like this, Zara, but sounds like so has yours and Shaan's. You two need to spice it up." She wiggled her eyebrows animatedly.

"Oh, we spice it up with arguments, silent stares, deep sighs and snorts," said Zara with a boisterous laugh.

"This is no laughing matter, Zara."

Once finished, they took a leisurely walk to Anya's condo. Once back at the condo, Anya checked her messages, snail mail, got the next day's office wear ready and came out to the living room, as did Zara. Content with their dinner, comfortable in their cozy pajamas, the two snuggled on the couch, as had become their routine.

"Going back to the Mom and Dad conversation, Anya…they connect, but seem a little at odds…like they're hesitant to reach out to one another. It seems like despite the years they've spent together, there is still a barrier of formality between them. I know they love one another, but their union seems more bound by duty than affection."

"Well said, you're right. I've been thinking the same thing for a while and this trip home just fermented that belief. But maybe we should stop looking at trees and look at the entire forest. Despite our observations, they're doing okay, I think. Relationships at their age are less about words or filling the air with noise. Even the silence matters. It's about knowing that the loved one is not too far."

"Yes, I hope you're right, Anya. Now, let's look at another tree."

From: Mrin@****.com

To: Ayush@*****.com

Subject: Knock, knock.

Dear Ayush,

So, you cried and joined my club, is it? Such is life. Even now, we don't understand why God separated us. And me, well, I'm still at crossroads, and haven't figured out which road to take. All I know that I will not walk the path that denies me your memories. And *now* having found you through these emails, my grief is lessened and the silence I live with is neither torment nor a burden. And if you do notice any sort of grief, please understand, as I said once earlier, that my medication and health issues often claim the better of me.

Despite your pictorial description, I can't recall anything about the Jain guy. It must have been either a trivial event or a traumatic one that my psyche doesn't want to remember. However, you're funny to pick out the poor man's difficulties with pronunciations! Yes, I thought that perhaps he had a lisp causing him to mispronounce. That being said, I find your account on Om Prakash Jain really funny. Did it happen like that? Going through the diaries in the last few hours, I found that my mother didn't like him pursuing me either, but mostly due to his speech impediment. She imitated his use of 'telling' as 'thelling'

I still have no recollection of me ever going out on a romantic date with him. All we did together was to play doubles tennis and badminton for the college team. Yes, I went with my parents to their various homes for dinners or picnics, but I never initiated anything and, in my memory, and nor did he. My diary does say that he found various excuses to be around me but it amounted to nothing. That day, when he asked you to leave us in private, he proposed to me with a diamond ring, but for me, that was just a sign of the ways in which he thought he could claim me…by buying expensive colour. Perhaps this explains my 'huff' or my being 'rattled' when I came out of Bombelli's. I think I was so pissed off and disgusted by him that I left him midway through his deal details.

But tell me, isn't it normal that in arranged marriages such things are commonplace? Or perhaps that was how it was when we were young. A girl just doesn't want diamonds, colour or palaces, she wants her man to love her, adore her, and respect her. With you, I saw heavens and stars and the universe and I felt only utmost happiness. In comparison, he had nothing, it seems.

Ayush, if you don't mind, I need to sort out another diary entry about the Matunga Residence Complex and your sister. Does this paint a picture to you?

Sanj took me to the Matunga residence. There were talks of Sona getting married. There was another girl Somi, I think, my age. I don't think she likes me. She was asking all kinds of questions in an oblique way about my friendship (relationship) with Sanj. Was there jealousy, competition or pure nosiness? These two girls kept on bringing Sanj's dad in the conversation. On my previous visit, the same thing had transpired.

Ayush, did your sister Sona (is that her name?) get married? Did I attend her wedding? It was a big event, wasn't it? Were Sona and Somi best friends? Who was Somi? Was she truly close to your dad, or were they just trying to one-up me and play mind games? What kind of women were they? In the back of my mind, I hear a keen lament these two girls were chanting, and the intoning keeps on echoing, repeatedly. The chant is on the same pattern as *"paddy cake, paddy cake"* but the Hindi words seem to be saying, *"Will leave, Will go, Will have no choice. We heave; we heave; up she goes... Has no poise. Will leave, Will go, she has no choice."* It is like a loop being played in my head ad nauseam.

It's an annoying droning that eats away at me whenever I think about the Matunga Residence Complex. Am I imagining this, or did it happen? I believe the complex was a friendly neighbourhood to live, learn and make life-long friends. Then what could have happened which led to this?

I look forward to your response, Ayush. Take care of yourself and be well.

Mrin

I stay awake to welcome dreams come my way

Dreams that cover thy face must stay at bay

I play with fire, throw snowballs, and chase the clouds

I hide my sorrows, conceal all cares, and indulge clowns

I look for you at the paradise gate

Thy arrival brings laughter and joy to my fate

"It has ceased to be a romantic saga between the soulmates. I'm also quite shocked to read Mom's name in this email. So, Mrin knew Mom and now I'm curious to know why her and Aunt Sona didn't like her. It pains me to say that my sympathies for her will have to be questioned," said Anya.

"Anya, to be honest I am bit surprised to hear that. I thought you were her pro bono attorney and defending her whether you believe it or not. As far as I'm concerned, unlike you, I am hedging, at least right now," said Zara.

"I would first like to know how the whole story unfolds, before I make up my mind about her. I've learned my lesson not to jump off the cliff without the parachute of due diligence."

"That's a good way of looking at it, Zara. Aren't you surprised at Mom's semi-blind following aunt Sona?"

"I do recall that Dad used to tell us about Aunt Sona's magisterial attitude demanding respect and even obedience from other girls. I think aunt Sona was the power broker here, I believe Mom may have picked up or finessed her controlling instinct from her. She was natural and Mom just a novice," Said Zara.

"That's a pretty astute insight in understanding characters, Zara. And Yes, I do remember Dad saying how Aunt Sona and Mom were so close. Didn't she play a role in their wedding too?"

"I think she did. Let's find out what Dad has to say about this…" and Anya brought up the next email.

From: Ayush@*****.com

To: Mrin@****.com

Subject: Knock, knock.

Oh Mrin,

Your diary is getting truly sad. Is it the nature of love and lovers, or is it indicative of our reality? Did we break up, or just drift away? I'm not sure which, but your poems seem to prepare us for that eventuality. I hope together, we discover why hearts so full of rapture did in the end, feel emptiness and grief.

Now to Sona and Somi! Yes, Sona is my younger sister. When I took you to my home one afternoon, Sona and Somi, both were there. They had been close friends since childhood and Somi even lived on the same floor as we did. She is as old as you are, but Sona is at least a couple of years younger.

The pair went to a women's college where they took courses not requiring intensive work. Nevertheless, their love of literature, poetry and psychology was sincere, although superficial as they refused to do rigorous work. They were both good with languages, written as well as spoken. They loved to annoy boys and girls who were competition in any way. In this respect, they demeanour was ferocious, absolutely ugly and relentless.

Since you were with me, they considered you a threat. Somehow in their cabal, they decided my marital future. They seemed to have agreed that I should be wedded to Somi, and unfortunately, they had co-opted my father in their grand scheme. Trust me when I said, you're not the only one who was at the receiving end of this strange game. Every girl in the complex who spoke, or even 'looked at' me with amorous affection was their target for vengeance.

That day, they were just probing to determine how close we were, and how often we met, if we attended the same classes the full day, or the entire week, or the whole year. They wanted to know the extent of your 'magic', 'power' and 'influence' over me.

But Mrin, you were absolutely great with them. You kept your cool, your sense of humour, but mainly your distance. You didn't show much interest in their conversation, hobbies or shenanigans. Instead of engaging and entangling with them, you ignored them most of the time. It proved to work out in your favour later as you were out of their suspicion list.

They both were close to my Dad. Somi was keen about following a career in palmistry, astrology and numerology and if you remember, my Dad was very good at these arts. He was well-known for it, as well. Since Somi was dedicated with her work and education she got, my Dad mentored her, allowing her to audit conversations with some of his clients. To be honest, my Dad thought she would make a name for herself in this pseudo-science.

I'm surprised that they tried to place some hex on you. But I think you're mistaking Sona and Somi for Rhim Jhim and Jhil Mil, the girls with unusual names. They were our neighbours who received attention because of their work as folklore entertainers. These two were relentless pursuers of my love and affection, as well. They were the other bookend!

Sona's arranged wedding took place in the summer of 1972. Yes, it was an elaborate affair that lasted three days, yet it was in my Dad's view a scaled-down affair to reflect the tough economic times we all were experiencing. Your family attended all three days of celebrations and feasts. You were involved in many aspects of the celebrations, functions and rituals.

Later, you confided that you would also like the same glamorous wedding. You had planned to co-ordinate wardrobe designs and colours for the entire wedding party for each ceremony for three days. You wanted a wedding full of colours, flowers, music, lights, aromas, foods and dances. You wanted energy, electricity and celebrations. It was going to be an absolute Mrin signature affair! When I mocked your enthusiasm, you said, 'In that case, let's elope and do a quick temple wedding. What do you say?' You seemed big on temple weddings to solve the problems. I'm surprised how we never resorted into doing it.

Yes, I've another recollection of the wedding in which I found my Dad having a very engrossed conversation with you on his right side and Somi on his left. When I asked you about it after the wedding, you shrugged it off, but I saw a subtle change in your attitude, and later a dwindled desire to visit my home and meet my Dad, Sona or Somi. I must add here that Somi is altogether a different person now, loving and self-composed, assertive, but never imposing. If anything, she could learn from you, how to let herself go, be instinctual and more expressive.

Mrin, I hope this narrative throws some light on your experiences with Sona and Somi. I hope that even if you can't recall the details, you're able to see what transpired. Your diary picked up all the strands very perceptively.

These passages from your diary make me miss you, Mrin. Please don't stop sharing them.

Take care,

Ayush

"Anya, before we get into nitty-gritty, do you see a contradiction in Dad saying Mom and aunt Sona loved literature, but that love was superficial?"

"No, he's not contradicting at all. He's saying that they loved literature but they never studied, researched or critically examined anything. It's like they had knowledge, but they refused to mature and take it to another level. You know that it happens all the time, Zara."

"These two were against Mrin, and then Grandpa finds a need to talk to *them* in a busy wedding function. Didn't he have others things to look after, Anya?"

"Yes, exactly. Something happened at the wedding when Mom, grandpa and Mrin were talking. According to Dad, Mrin was different with his family as the talk. So, something big did happen and we need to find out what." Zara said.

"I can't believe that such a strong love ended in such a whimper…." said Zara, much to her own surprise.

"Yes, it pains me to hear you say that. There's no rationale, excuse, pretence or even some drama. It's like something fell from the sky and crushed what seemed like a blossoming of something beautiful."

There was brooding silence. They stared at each another and looked at the ceiling.

"Our Dad is supposed to have a photographic memory and precocious intelligence, and he can't remember if they broke up or just drifted away?" Anya said almost in a whisper, incredulous, scratching her head.

"I'm upset that people closest to our hearts are maligned by none other than our father who called his sister and wife 'ferocious, ugly and relentless'," Anya continued.

"But it's true that aunt Sona knew how to put up a fight. Her spats could be ugly as she would refuse to yield any ground…She should have gone into politics instead of literature," said Anya.

Anya looked at Zara whose her eyes narrowing and focusing, her face saddened and taking a deep breath, her chest heaved as she exhaled.

"You know Anya, for the first time I feel for this woman and our Dad. I begin to have revulsion for my own playing God with the lives of other people. No one has a right to decide who falls in love with who other than the people involved themselves"

Anya said nothing, but was proud at her sister's sense of maturity and tact in creating a composed deduction of what they had read. Zara wasn't necessarily warming up to Mrin, she had just divorced herself from the situation, observing now detachedly, as if both their mother and Mrin were just two women who happened to be in their father's life... Anya smiled and squeezed her sister's hand, nodding in affirmation.

Chapter Eight

Vendettas

From: Mrin@****.com

To: Ayush@*****.com

Subject: Knock, knock.

Dear Ayush,

I thank you for your account. It explains how two women, my contemporaries, were small-minded and small hearted, very much like how you described Om Prakash Jain. You commented, "I get bested by puny minds and even smaller hearts." See, Ayush, the trouble is not with the small-minded and small hearted people because their success relies on those deplorable attributes. We lose because winning their way is an anathema to us. We fight with reason and ethics; they fight with emotion and selfishness"

I remember having jotted down in my diary about "the nature of people" seminar we once attended. However, my diary says good people do good deeds because it's in their nature. The idea of evil doesn't even cross their mind. I think it is how you are wired- personally, emotionally and genetically- that controls your conduct. Conversely, that's how "bad" people are wired. It seems they don't have any choice. So, forgive them. Ayush, just as through your explanation, I have done too. I say, be true to yourself and be good to yourself.

After I wrote about them, I found another item I need you to explain for me to understand my conversation with them. Here goes: *Sona's friend Somi keeps on talking about Avani, and how they succeeded in removing her from the picture. They were gleeful in saying, 'Papa was happy, but Sanj wasn't!' Now, let's see who is next…Were these two saying that I was going to disappear the same way?*

I am touched by your brutal honesty in portraying your own as you saw them then, without any defence, pretence or feigned ignorance. It tells me of the honesty with which you view people and how you are able to derive the very truths out of their characters.

I'm sorry for sadness or melancholia in my poems. Ayush, above all I miss your friendship that brought me the understanding of life. I do think of you with affection and gratitude, I feel so tired, better get some sleep now.

Mrin

I welcome pitch darkness of the night.

Therein thy face's luminous and bright

Conversation endless and revealing

Warmth of thy lips softly soothing

Thou knowest everything

What's unsaid, what hurts and is not healing

Tomorrow when I see you and yearn

My own favorite butterflies will return.

I welcome pitch darkness of the night.

Therein thy face is luminous and bright

Would thou know, my sweet lover

My own sweet butterflies

"So, there was another girl, Avani, in Dad's life before Mrin. Dad seemed to be quite the charmer!"

"Zara, how do you know that it was a romantic relationship?"

"Just an educated guess, Anya, based on what is written in Mrin's diary."

"I suppose you're right…"

Both sisters were impressed that despite Mrin's young age, she was quickly able to grasp the issues of genetics and psychology of behaviour. Moreover, their Dad's habit of calling things as they were, regardless of whether they were about his loved ones or not, had remained consistent. The sisters had always been appreciative for his honesty.

"If it's wrong, it's wrong no matter who does it. That's what he's always believed."

"That was the briefest email yet. Let's keep on going" Anya clicked onto the next mail.

From: Ayush@*****.com

To: Mrin@****.com

 Subject: Knock, knock.

Dear Mrin,

Even though I lead a life filled with memories, sweet yet caustic and burning, it's good that you're probing my psyche and allowing me to re-live those youthful days with a woman as genuine as you. Phoniness was never your style! You always had liked my brutal honesty, but Mrin, I observed and learned this habit from you. As I said, you were without pretence, and since I was starting to learn a great deal of life lessons from you, I too led my life mostly without pretence.

I would like to underline the word "mostly" as I've kept up the charade with my wife and my four sweet daughters who have given me love, respect and a good name. By telling them about ourselves, I fear that they'll feel immense pity for us both, and my partly wasted life. I hope you forgive me for this lapse, this pretence, this charade. As the one who taught me to love, you will appreciate my responsibilities to the people I now love.

I must add here that my wife, Somi is a wonderful spouse and a devoted mother. Without her standing next to me, I would have led an empty existence… After your departure, she salvaged my life… I cannot even tell her about us without hurting her. I spared her; rather I spared myself from inflicting pain on her.

Now to your email question! Yes, Sona and Somi's resume includes the expulsion of Avani from my life. Yes, it pains me to admit that my father was a part of the troika that played havoc in my early adulthood.

Avani and I were in the same high school and were very keen competitors in all school activities. We were both natural leaders and would often win competitions in dancing and acting, were well-informed in general knowledge, properly trained in elocution, debating and writing. She would win all the girls' awards, and I, the boys. She was a great girl who knew how to talk, present arguments, but did all this without being disputatious. As a teenager, I quite fancied her. We would walk home together with other kids, but when her apartment came, we would stop a while, chat a little more and then climb up to our respective homes.

Somi, in particular, didn't like Avani for two reasons. Firstly, I liked her. Secondly, Avani was talented in every respect. And if Somi didn't like another girl, how could my sister Sona? They kept at their rumor-mongering, insinuations and backbiting for a year. When Avani was within earshot, the girls would often compare her looks with mine with comments like, 'Oh my brother is fair and tall and handsome. She is so short, fat, and ugly. We can't imagine them together.' They'd attack her style of dressing and at times, even her social status. I'm ashamed to say that their comments were relentless and ferocious and most of all, uncalled for. It was truly unbearable for Avani to endure such undeserved nasty attacks at an early age in life. But she had a character of strength, and will power. She lasted as long as a young girl could bear without much support.

I spoke to my father, explaining to him what the girls were doing was not right. 'What would we do if some other kids spoke like this, all lies, about our Sona?"

My father went to Avani's home and saw her parents, asked for Avani's and their apologies for Sona's offenses. Avani told me much later after we split up that my father was very polite and conversed for some time. However, I don't know what happened after that meeting, but pretty soon, Avani moved from our school to another one a few kilometres from where we lived. Nobody knew which school she went to. It remained a secret. I understood the need for keeping it so.

Had it continued, I would have liked to see her more often and date her, but wasn't meant to be! It was an affair without any of the juicy details that transpire between two adolescents. But that girl left a permanent imprint on mind about how nourishing a friendship it could have been between us. There were no exchanges of gifts, letters, or any physical touches. It was a pure friendship, and there were no strings attached.

My life has been a mirage, chasing something I think is permanent, but turns out to be fleeting at best and at the worst nonexistent shadow. You came into my life; I think. Didn't you? Sometimes I think you were not in my life, but a huge capricious trick of my imagination. Tell me, were you really in my life? Is there a proof of your existence and presence in my life?

Mrin, I wasn't morose or maudlin like this before, but your emails have awakened all those questions, experiences and feelings that are now tearing me apart. I don't think that this troika would have succeeded to expel you from my universe as you lived in a far and different world, much immune from the toxic atmosphere of my own home. Any pretence of supernatural power, including my father's unshakable belief in astrological powers could have never even touched your aura. I know we could have survived any attack from them. But did we? Could we have?

These questions, Mrin, are very much like your questions. However, yours come from a different condition and dimension. Regardless, still they are akin to what I'm asking now.

We both need to find a sanctuary, believe me. My haven has been with Somi. I wish you have a husband as good as Somi has been a wife to me. And you, you were her childhood friend until you went to a private school in the Shimla hills. I do recall you, Sona, Somi and other kids walking to school together. Your going away to the Hills may have prompted some to dislike you for the class status. In your case, out of sight might have meant out of mind for many people in the complex. But going back to Somi, yes you, Sona and Somi did become good friends a little before Sona's wedding Away from my sister's influence, Somi is an exceptional woman. When you meet her, and I hope we all do, you will know what I mean.

Mrin, I'm sorry if I've saddened you or burdened you. Your problems are more serious and difficult than I could ever imagine mine to be. You don't need any more to trouble you. I hope that I'm answering all your questions. To you, real or imagined, I'll be honest. I wish you were here, not so far from where I can see you and hear you.

Remember that I love you, Mrin, and shall love you forever.

Take care,

Ayush.

Anya and Zara began to tear up when they read about their father, and wondered why people silently carry the grief of pain-burdened past that remains unspoken, festering inside. They had no doubt about their Dad's honour and integrity; they were touched by his generous and heartfelt affection for his four daughters. But more than believe, the sisters shared the collective feeling that an injustice had been done to their father and Mrin.

"Zara, you talk about injustice to Dad. I think it is that and also cruelty to him. Even in his adolescent years people tried to manipulate his life. The same people who he thought were near and dear. I don't know if I will ever forgive aunt Sona."

"We siblings fought as well, but we didn't run any one's life or choices. We complained about certain friends of theirs, but all we did was to keep an eye on them and if they needed our intervention we spoke with the sibs without anger, jealousy or threats."

Despite the heart-rending experience, they were proud that their father who loved their mom and treated her with respect, honour and dignity.

"Zara, at least your question about Mom's future is answered."

"Yes, but when you claim to love your wife, how can Dad write to Mrin that he loves and misses her too?" Anya didn't answer, but she felt her Dad had done nothing wrong in loving their mother and Mrin at the same time. They were, in fact, completely different kinds of loves. What made her most uneasy was that she couldn't explain or justify it. But she wanted to stand up for him and his deepest love.

"Zara, I agree with you to an extent. But there is something in my heart that's churning and I feel horrible that I can't explain it. I don't have the right words."

"You're conflicted."

"Exactly. Can a man, or a woman for that matter, love two people at the same time with equal passion without feeling guilt and regret? That's the question in my soul, which I just can't answer yet."

"Is it tearing you up to the extent you feel horrible for not defending Mom?

"Yes, I want to defend her. If I don't as you do, I feel I am a rotten daughter. I'm her first born; I should be leading the lynching crowd to throw the first stone in the pit... What stops me?"

"I understand your predicament, Anya. But there is power of ethics and responsibility in you that, instead of hurling you in a maelstrom, is pulling you back from the convulsion of self-destruction."

"If my belief's ethical, then why do I feel flawed, as if I've committed betrayal?"

"That's because you have conflicting opinions and reconciliation of those views is so difficult for you. We have believed that you can't love two people at the same time, and Dad is doing just that. Your love for Dad is so deep that you can't condemn him, and the worst is that your defence of Mom is weak. I think the soiled, dirty feeling is from that disconnect."

"How do I escape it?"

"If we see good proof that there's no lying and cheating on Dad's part and he's open with Mom about his love for Mrin as well as for her, then there's no duplicity, nor any secrecy about his relationship with Mrin…"

Anya pondered over what her sister said. "Yes, that makes sense. Secrecy leads to lying and eventually it becomes loathsome poison."

"Well, let's hope it doesn't come to that! I just really want the whole story to come out in open, so that we can finally breathe without our lungs constricting."

"Love is not unholy, provided it doesn't deprive or demote others. We should always follow our heart's desires for they do often prove to be true. But secrecy, yes, it can be seriously hurtful at times…" Anya's voice trailed off and for a moment she was quiet, as if in contemplation. Then suddenly, she turned to face her sister, and with wide eyes and a low-pitched voice, said, "I have never told this to anyone, but have felt it from time to time, and these days, it is stronger than ever. I have this urge to be a mother, to have a child, with or without a husband."

Zara looked at her sister in confusion, surprised at the turn this conversation about secrecy had led them too, and then her face softened, "Anya…" she began, still digesting what her sister had revealed. "That's wonderful!" and then laughing, she hugged her tightly, "Now I know all your secrets, Anya, we will work on this one!"

"I love you so dearly, Zara."

That night, the sisters went to bed smiling. For the first time in days, the taste they went to bed with was not that of Mrin and Ayush's past romance, but of the tender desire that Anya had revealed.

Chapter Nine

Graduation and After

Next afternoon roaming the Little India district on Gerard Street, Zara bought something for her mother. As she was paying the bill, Anya called her.

"Zara, I've booked a table for four for dinner at Donatello this evening, and I'm emailing you their address."

"But we're only two. Who are the third the fourth?"

"A surprise for you, go wreck your brain now." Anya said mischievously.

When Zara reached Donatello at six, she found Bijli waiting inside at the bar. Grinning ear to ear, she hugged her little sister lovingly. As they settled down at their table, Bijli said, "I am famished, and their prices are ridiculous. Looking at their fare, I could go on an instant diet."

"Bij, don't worry. Just enjoy the evening with your sister whom you love to hate." She teased her playfully.

"But you know why I dislike you. When you're around, I get mocked, insulted and pinched. No wonder I love you more from a distance."

When the waitress approached, Zara ordered bruschetta, Carpaccio and roasted peppers and a bottle of Spanish red-wine Monticillo Crianza Rioja. She asked the server to delay bringing the order until other two guests arrived.

As they waited, the sisters talked for a while about what had been going on in their lives since they'd seen each other recently. Suddenly, Bijli looked at the sidewalk through the window. "I can't believe it, Zara… Look who's joining us!"

Zara looked up to see Anya walking side by side with Somi, holding hands and smiling.

"Zara, how do you like the surprise? And even better, she is staying overnight," Anya said.

"I'm glad Mom is here too. I went to the Little India and bought a *chunni* for you to wear with a pair of jeans. Here," said Zara handing a shopping bag to Somi, who withdrew a beautiful traditional Indian scarf from it.

"This is gorgeous, Zara. This will really go well with even my khakis and chino capris. Thanks, sweetheart."

They spent nearly two hours talking and laughing about their family in Canada as well in the USA and India. After the dinner, Bijli took the subway home and other three rode a cab to Anya's. Somi was curious about what the sisters had been up to. "I was missing you all so much. I had to call Anya and get invited. I wasn't sure if you guys were busy doing something over the week so thought Saturday might be a good day to have fun in the city."

"I am glad you called, Mom. We were missing you too! I'll let the office know I won't come in tomorrow, and we will have fun, probably some shopping and lunch," Anya said.

"But tomorrow is Saturday, Anya, don't you have the day off anyway?"

"Ma, we lawyers are like doctors and fire fighters, always on call. Somebody's flying in from overseas, and we had to see her."

"Well, I hope, you get paid over-time," said Somi, her tone suddenly so maternal that the sisters burst out laughing.

Three women walked on the waterfront feeling the soft breeze touching their face and playing with their hair. They stopped by a street musician playing on a flute.

"I always enjoy flutes," said Somi as she opened her money purse to leave some for the musician. He smiled at her as saying 'thanks'.

When they returned home, they talked about things at home, her friends and Dad. When it came time for bed, Anya said, "Ma, Zara will sleep with me and you sleep in the other bedroom where you always do."

Once everyone was settled in their bed, Anya and Zara brushed their teeth, changed their clothes and talked for a while before they turned on the computer. At first, they had been hesitant, given that Somi was in the next room, but their recent findings on Mrin actually being friends with their mother tipped their curiosity over the edge.

From: Mrin@****.com

To: Ayush@*****.com

Subject: Knock, knock.

My dear Ayush,

In the light of what Somi means to you now, I thank you for your honest and introspective reading of Sona and her world when they were younger. Feuds, innuendos and character assassinations...do you ever wonder why a family that gives equal nurturing to all of their children, ends up with kids of opposing characters? It's more than a nature vs nurture dilemma. I believe that's where the previous incarnations and accumulated karmas come into play. What is it in our free will that doesn't allow the identical nurturing to produce the same results? Where does the free will find paths of divergence that are against the overall milieu of the family, Ayush? I think what we bring from our previous birth experiences explains the opposite divergence. Perhaps what I'm trying to say is that at that point in time, Somi and Sona both needed to work their Karma out.

 I can see you are experiencing an emotional trauma; I am sorry for causing it. My questions are taking you into the realm of pain, sorrow and loss. I'll stop asking you questions about the Matunga Residence Complex. Enough of the toxic brew boiling in their couldron! Instead, tell me about good days and happy occasions we celebrated together. What is your earliest memory of visiting my home in Worli? Is it full of happy memories? Or was I mean and nasty to you?

My diary says you graduated in December 1972 convocation with great honours. Tell me about the graduation and what you did after.

Ayush, do remember that I love you. How deep and sincere it is, I'd rather keep to myself, given our circumstances, but I hope you feel it all the same. For a change, I'm sending you a joke to bring a smile to your face. Either Sheila Bhagwandas or Neena Shupeck had forwarded this joke to me. Tell me what you think.

Mrin

P.S. What you said about your wife warms my heart.

WRONG E-MAIL ADDRESS

A Michigan couple decided to go to Florida to thaw out during an icy winter. They planned to stay at the same hotel where they spent their honeymoon years earlier. Because of hectic schedules, it was difficult to coordinate their travel schedules. So, the husband left Michigan and flew to Florida on Thursday, with his wife flying down the following day.

The husband checked into the hotel. There was a computer in his room, so he decided to send an email to his wife. However, he accidentally left out one letter in her email address, and without realizing his error, sent the email.

Meanwhile, somewhere in Texas, a widow had just returned home from her husband's funeral. He was a minister who was called home to glory following a heart attack. The widow decided to check her email expecting messages from relatives and friends. After reading the first message, she screamed and fainted.

The widow's son rushed into the room, found his mother on the floor, and saw the computer screen which read:

To: My Loving Wife

Subject: I've Arrived

Date: October 16, 2005

I know you're surprised to hear from me. They have computers here now, and you're allowed to send emails to your loved ones. I've just arrived and have been checked in. I've seen that everything has been prepared for your arrival tomorrow. Looking forward to seeing you then!!!! Hope your journey is as uneventful as mine was.

P.S. Sure is hot down here!!

"Dad is going through an emotional wringer. Maybe we should do something to help him feel better…," said Anya.

"You know, I was batting for Mom and not for Dad; on the other hand, you've been for both of them. In my rush to judgment I became his prosecutor, judge and jury. I feel awful for that. What can we do? We can arrange their meeting, but that would almost kill Mom and if we ask for her permission, she may go nuts. If at all she said yes, it would be very torturous experience for her. Best we could do is to write letters, exchange pictures," said Zara.

"That's interference, meddling. Dad would be immensely insulted. Let me give you some ideas how Mom and Dad would feel…slap in the face, contempt, disgrace, shame and dishonour…Make your choice, Zara."

The pair sat in silence for a while, until Anya spoke again, "Let some time pass. Perhaps we can create right conditions for an accidental chance meeting. Or maybe, *we* could visit her with our family albums and stuff to show her what we are doing. It will be a different perspective."

"That's a better idea. At least she would know more about us; more importantly we'll learn a lot more about her life. That's what we are going to do," said Zara. "And Mom would remain unhurt and in the dark. But we will have to carry Dad's secret to our graves."

They remained seated and calm for long time thinking about their Dad and Mrin and what their lives could have been. "I know for a fact that after a severe disappointment, a loss or crying, I seem to have some kind of awareness that helps me connect to my peaceful core."

"Zara, any heartfelt loss drives you to introspection, clarity and some higher value. Sadness and helplessness help us mature."

From: Ayush@*****.com

To: Mrin@****.com

Subject: Knock, knock.

Mrin,

Oh my God! That joke is indeed funny; seriously funny. I couldn't stop laughing for a long time. I do remember you girls used to talk about the comedy of errors quite a bit in your classes!

I thank you for relenting and switching from the cauldron of Matunga Residence to fewer painful memories. I say "less" because even treasured memories underline the fact of our separation, and leave me with the thought of what could have been!

Coming back to what you asked about me visiting your residence in Worli, let me recall for you, my first visit to your apartment. It was sometime in late February of 1972, a month after our tryst at Kirti Manubhai Doongursee College. That was the day when you made me see the heavens and promised to get a ransom in your trousseau to save me from the world. What a day that was!

I could see an 'all safe' signal with the kitchen light on. Your parents had gone to attend a wedding and were returning home late in the evening. Your eight-year-old sister Nayan had gone to play with her neighbourhood friends. You called me to your kitchen and suddenly pinning me against the wall, began kissing me. But a young lad, standing in his balcony in the building across from yours, saw this drama of passion about to unfold, and called his brother and his friends to witness it. His loud voice alerted you and before we knew it, we were in your bedroom where again, you pushed me on the bed, lay on top and began kissing me.

You looked up and said raunchily, "I'm hiding something. Find it before it's too late!" The body knows the genetic code of the expected behaviour in a romantic situation.

A few months earlier, you had explained John Donne's metaphysical poem whose title eludes me, but nonetheless, it described a lover who was an explorer of his lady love's body, his globe. With your encouragement, I became your avid explorer and found lands that I had merely imagined, but hadn't come close to imagine the glorious and sumptuousness of the riches of those lands! I said quietly, "John Donne, Thank you!!"

Shocked by my words, you exclaimed, "What?"

I explained. We both laughed.

"Ayush, instead of economics, finance, currency and interest rates, you should have majored in English or French Lit," you said rubbing your nose against mine.

"Silly girl, why would I do that when I've you to tutor me in everything delicious?" And we both laughed.

However, we were soon interrupted and separated by a knock at the door. The nosy neighbour frequented your apartment, under various excuses, to see that all the boundaries of decorum had been observed. You explained to your neighbour, "*Kaki*, Ayush and I were neighbours before we moved here. Our parents are very good friends too. Plus, we both have some classes together. *Kaki*, this boy's a *genius*." You said the last thing to reinstate the fact that geniuses don't do funny stuff and don't need to be so thoroughly supervised. Well, it worked. She didn't come back once she heard of my credentials. She, in fact, left looking pretty impressed. These were things that only you and you alone could do! However, you were thoroughly disappointed and a little angry at the woman for having interrupted our amorous, intimate dance.

You sat next to me, leaned your head on my left shoulder and gently kissed me. Then you said, "You know Ayush; I would like us to go someplace absolutely beautiful, serene, rustic and private, at least for one night, if not longer. Can we, please?"

"Mrin, I think we can do it in two- or three-weeks' time in March. What do you think of Matheran Hill Station? It's not too far, and neither is it too near. We go there on weekdays to avoid the crowds!"

Pleased, you touched my face and smiled. "Let's do it. You fix everything."

There was raging sexual storm in your body. Every part of your skin was red-hot warm, electrified and overly charged and had goose-bumps. Your sexual circuitry now fully loaded, you wanted to be touched, caressed, stroked and massaged. Whatever I gave; you returned doubly. We had known about the intimacies, had felt its immense urge and that day in late February when we were about to surrender ourselves to it completely, the arrival of younger sister doused the raging fires, and we returned from the brink frustrated. Even so, we were truly happy that we were together even in our frustrations.

Mrin, this is how my first visit to Worli went down. It was delicious, exciting, and heavenly. The fun part was climbing the mountain and reaching the precipice. I think of that day with so much love and affection. I hope you also think of that day with the same reverence as I do.

Even now, after the lapse of 40-plus years, in the silence of dark nights, I have dreams of the image of you jumping on me and kissing me as on that day in February. I remember the image of your face when you said what you would include in your trousseau. And I reminisce about of your images from other occasions, including Matheran when your luminous and alluring face would kiss and your fingers would caress, comfort and soothe me and make my heart dance with the euphonious rhythms of passion and pleasure.

Mrin, of course I do love you as well. You're a gorgeous woman.

You were so then, and I believe you are more so now. You were undoubtedly wonderful to me, but not much comfort came from my family to you. Sometimes such situations as ours make one wonder if there is a rhyme, reason or perversion that runs the lives of people. Mrin, have no doubts. You were magnificent to me. I hope this answer and settles the issue forever.

Next, you asked me about my graduation at the Bombay University Convocation in December of 1972, but a lot of water had flown under the bridge before that event. You came to my graduation, but sat far in the crowds with your friends and didn't wait to meet or to even congratulate me. You wanted to be there, wanted to be with me in my celebrations, but somehow you couldn't bring yourself to wait. Even today, I wonder what could have been your reasons for not seeing me then, and thereafter as frequently. For me, the ceremony has remained incomplete and not celebrated.

However, my economics work, in addition to projects at the Bajaj Institute, earned me *'summa cum laude'* and a prestigious job at the Reserve Bank of India. My career and life were launched. No matter where I went, and who I went with, I felt your absence and incomplete without you.

We met a few times after that. There was longing and an incredible sense of disappointment and forlornness that you had accepted grudgingly. You were not tired of me. Your eyes and quick steps to hug me spoke of love. You did not loathe me; you were civil, extraordinarily so, and deeply respectful. We still held hands; I put my hands around your waist, and you at the same time brushed against me; now our kisses were different. You would look at me with searching eyes, as if asking me what went wrong, where we erred. It hurts me deeply that nothing good came from my family to you. There's a lot here for you to recall, assess, and ponder and perhaps to weep with me.

Mrin, I need to go now. I love you and I miss you, really miss you.

Regards,

Ayush

"You know, Anya, this woman Mrin always takes charge of the situation and guides Dad. Personally, I've come to think that she's fantastic and wish that I had a friend like her," said Zara.

"Me too. I think she is not your typical Indian woman of the sixties. Perhaps at present, Indian women are different with better education, more information, high-paying jobs and greater freedom with on-line technology. However, because she had the freedom, knowledge and personal drive, she did then what most of us are able to do currently. No question in my mind."

"Even in their separation, Dad had no idea why it occurred, but had some inkling that she was not sharing something with him. He doesn't know what he could have done wrong. In their relationship, he follows whatever she wants. She's the guiding principle."

"If these two didn't know, I can venture a guess that Mom and aunt Sona certainly know. Grandpa and Grandma are gone. Her brother or her parents, if they're alive, would know," said Anya.

"Here's the next mail. Maybe it'll hold some clues."

From: Mrin@****.com

To: Ayush@*****.com

Subject: Knock, knock.

My dear Ayu,

My diary agrees with your description of your first visit to my apartment. I now understand why I disliked that nosy neighbour. I was yearning so much for your physical presence in my life that I tended to forget what my parents expected me to do.

According to my diary, one of my friends asked me if my parents' emissary met your parents. I told her, "No need to do that. I just stole Ayu from them." At your arrival in my life, my friends were excited, happy and they began to compliment and congratulate me. However, I also had written on the same page that Simi and Megh both looked at me with pity or anger for not seeing you after the convocation.

I used to call you Ayush, but my friends called you Ayu. It just dawned on me that Ayu sounds more logical and endearing than Ayush. When I say 'Ayu', 'you' and 'I' seem conjoined, rolled up, one, united. That's what we both wanted, which sadly, wasn't destined to be. We wanted to be one, as in one of John Donne's themes, "two bodies, and one soul." You had reacquainted me with his metaphysical poems when you had become an explorer of me. Yes, forever from this day forwards you shall be my Ayu. According to my diary, the neighbour did give a detailed report embellished and elaborated with the number and times of her arrivals and departures. It was easy to tell my parents about you and the Matunga folks. They had a high regard for your family, and therefore, for you as a prospect for me.

I was proud of your awards, the Gold Medal and the granting of the *"Suma Cum Laude"* at the convocation. Tears were rolling down my cheeks with happiness. Inside, I was thrilled that I was your friend and lover. I felt proud that I had seen, touched and savoured your beautiful and glorious nakedness and you, mine. My lips and fingers had kissed and caressed the skin that no one had seen.

However, in my heart, there was anxiety about what the future held for us, and my place in your sweet life. I was praying that no matter what happened to me or what my place in your life might be, that your life would be filled with happiness and glory. I'm so sorry now that I didn't wait long enough to felicitate you. Right away, Lulu Divecha, Simi Shah and Meg Dalal all three reprimanded me for not staying and seeing you there.

I think we did go to Matheran for a night, and I believe Meg was my cover, wasn't she? I'm trying to decipher my stupid diaries. You need to be my painter again, Ayu. Do your photographic wonder for me on this trip.

My diary says within months or so after you joined, the Reserve Bank nominated you for a job with the International Monetary Fund. Am I right? I wrote to you from South Carolina, but you never answered!

Coming back to my parents, they expressed a desire to see you once the exam results were out. I know you came home to meet them. Perhaps you can explain and describe the most critical aspect of the meeting you had with them. And please, do so without mincing any words. Save nothing. Tell it all.

Ayu, many aspects of my life are coming together thanks to you. My jumbled and chaotic life of the past is gaining structure, shape and form.

Yours,

Mrin

One day you'll see me

All decked in the finest colour

Adorned in the brightest reds and pinks

My hands sparkle with red henna

My body lustrously exfoliated

Waiting in the rose-petal strewn bridal bed,

The chamber filled with seductive scents

And lyrics of mischief and playfulness

You'll look at me all demure and shy

Caress my soft skin with your seductive fingers

Arouse me; turn me into a raging river

And slowly undo each layer of the bridal wear

To find my beauty beneath the adornments

And see the raging river overcome her mighty ocean

"Mrin's friends were smart to figure out the symbolic meaning of Dad's shortened name. How romantic is his name, made just for his lover" said Zara.

"Or, wife…You know, I'd taken his name for granted and didn't see the mystical beauty and symmetry until Mrin's email brought it to our attention. Come to think of it, Prof. Lulu Divecha did say all her friends except one called Dad by his abbreviated name. Now we know who the one was who didn't call him Ayu," said Anya.

"Like our Mom, she still calls him Ayush most of the time."

"Looking at Mrin's friends, there was a good following for Dad and I am sure there must have been a large number of broken hearts. Mrin does have trustworthy friends," said Anya. "Such people tend to attract people with the same characteristics."

"*Suma Cum Laude* is a huge honour, isn't it, Anya? He has never made a big fuss about that, or for that matter anything he has done in his life…truly a grounded man."

"That's normal for him, but even Mom has never made a big ado about his education and accomplishments."

"I recall that grandma often saying those who have it do not show off. That's great counsel," said Zara.

"Now any time soon we should hear of Matheran where John Donne ought to rule the day's proceedings," said Anya.

"And the night too," said Zara.

"I am touched by the poem…erotic and sensual, revealing the state of her mind."

"Me too, but the poem describes a bridal bed…things she imagined and celebrated in her mind. I'm keen to know more," said Zara. "Let's read on."

From: Ayush@*****.com

 To: Mrin@****.com

Subject: Knock, knock.

Dearest Mrin,

The three questions that you have- Matheran, IMF, and meeting with your parents, cover a time period of little over one year, March 1972 to July 1973. Why doesn't your diary follow a chronological sequence? Perhaps your diary is in the same shape as your recall is. I will explain what happened at the Reserve Bank of India quickly and then explain about 'our' meeting with your parents. Perhaps the Matheran will have to wait until the next email.

My RBI job started even before the results were out. Anil Kansara, a close friend of my father, was a high official with RBI headquarters in Bombay, and he thought I would be an asset for the RBI. He convinced me to apply for an IAS job, which I did and, as you might know, I went through the process and got the job.

Mr. Kansara's nurturing and mentoring brought me to the attention of the Indian Finance Minister T. T. Krishnamachari. Soon, I was seconded to a job with the IMF, and that July 1973 appointment took me to Trinidad and Tobago where I spent almost four years.

When I returned sometime in January 1972, your mother said, reluctantly and sadly, that you were in the USA. However, she would not give your address or phone number. She was moving in with your brother in Hong Kong. Had we known, it would have been so easy to meet and re-connect our lives, and begin our journey anew.

Mrin, did you write letters from the USA? I didn't even know that you were gone there! Imagine, while I was still working in Bombay! I never received any letters from you! I wonder who intercepted them! Sona had already gone to her in-law's home. Was it my father? Was it Somi? Was it your dad or your brother? My father passed away some thirty years ago, so there's no way I could question him about this intrigue, or worse the conspiracy. If that is the case, I wonder how many connived… who would hold a grudge of such gargantuan proportions to deny us even the basic privilege of mail and messages? I fail to understand. Why? Why?

However, tell me now why, where, and how long you were in the States. Even though, we kept on seeing, albeit infrequently, until December 1972, I made many attempts to see you in 1973, but to no avail. I tried to contact you at Somaiya College, but to my complete surprise, I discovered that you were not teaching there anymore. I didn't visit your apartment because your parents, particularly your mother, were not only so distant and disinterested, but they were also visibly annoyed to see me. I sent my friend's girl, Saguna to give you my messages. At her insistence, you came to see me for the last time sometimes in March 1973, a year to date in 1972, we had, for the first time, made love in Matheran.

Let me now give the details of on 'our' meeting with your parents. The meeting took place about a month after Sona's wedding in early June, which you and your parents attended. I will mince no words and tell it as I saw and understood it. We may not like it, but so be it.

We were all disappointed that you didn't graduate with first-class honours, but your parents were thoroughly grim and glum. They thought it lowered your chances for a high achieving groom. Your mother was miserable that you got a poor B in two papers that you took with me. I wondered why they were looking at other prospective matches when I was there for you. They had come to a conclusion that my influence had brought you down to an overall 'honours with second class' grade. It wasn't an inferior grade, but it undoubtedly was a lousy grade for a girl of your ability. We all felt bad, but I didn't want you to feel bad. You were still going to get a lecturereship at Somaiya College after all!

So, when we met in June, we talked about your results… what went wrong, what you'll do, and how to deal with your parents' disappointment. I asked you how soon we could be married, with or without our parental support. I asked you because if your parents accused me rightfully for my role in your 'second class' results, then we would own up and say, 'Yes; we are in love. We goofed up. Now let's talk about what we can do.'

You were against my suggestion. You said, 'no owning up.'

I asked, "So no confession of romance?"

You were firm, "No confession of any sort."

I pleaded, "Mrin, just think. This is our golden chance. This has to be dealt with sooner or later, why not now? I got everything, including a fabulous job. What would they have against us or me?"

"I will not give you any reasons. Even so, no confessions; no talk of love or marriage."

Again, my failure to be assertive doomed us in here too. Had I spoken up, I know you would have forgiven me subsequently, but we could have led a life of togetherness that we miss so sorely. However, it's neither here nor there but a mere speculation.

When we all gathered at your home, it was an incredibly cold meeting. Your mother wouldn't even look at me, let alone talk. I was a pariah. Nobody offered me a glass of water, or a cup of tea… traditional marks of welcoming guests in your home.

Your father bluntly said, "Mr. Ayush, you're responsible for Mrin's poor grade. How do you plead?"

Your father addressed me in a cold officious manner for the first time. I knew he meant to create distance and detachment, but nonetheless, it hurt.

"Not guilty, Sir." I used to call him Uncle, but subconsciously I too created a sense of detachment by calling him 'sir.'

"Are you two in love?" He asked me without wasting any time. I looked at you, Mrin.

"Sir, it's not a question you should ask me. Mrin, May I ask you to answer your father's question."

You fidgeted with your handkerchief, took a long-time to gather your thoughts and then slowly and deliberately said, "We are close friends. We trust each other, but as far as love is concerned, we are not there yet. We need more time."

At that point, my eyes were teary, my throat all choked up at the denial, deferment or rejection of the most beautiful relationship of my life. This was the mountain we had to climb, but we did not. We just took the easy route of doing nothing, and hoping conflicts would sort out themselves sooner or later which they did, but not in our favour.

Despite my supposed intelligence, I lack that assertive quality that would force me to come out with a booming voice, strong arguments and draw a line in the sand and claim rightfully what was mine. I could have interrupted you, corrected you, but I didn't. I failed to climb the mountain too.

My vow to make you happy no matter what, regardless of how big a loss I would incur forbade me to deny you the choice you made after I had given you the reasons and arguments before. We both chose not to see the bigger picture. One lapse in judgment and the whole life to pay for it!

Your father said, "You are friends. That's fine. Friends come, and friends go. Mrinal, your friendship with Mr. Ayush is not good, and we do not encourage its continuation. It ends here and today." And then looking at me, he commanded, "Mr. Ayush, you presently know what our wishes are. We don't like your father, and now we don't like you either. You're not welcome in this home. Please leave us alone and in particular, Mrin. You may now leave."

He summarily dismissed me from their presence, and I was expelled from the paradise I had found for the past three years. I was left a pauper. You were sobbing and telling your father to stop making those rude comments. Your mother was pulling you to your bedroom, but you kept on fighting and struggling. At that point, your father slapped you and told me to 'get out of here.'

Suddenly, you stopped sobbing, sobered up and said in a dignified voice, "Ayu, leave in dignity. I shall speak to you soon. Don't worry. The price for this indignity is only one life."

I was amazed at your quiet and strong attitude but now when I think of it, I curse myself for the steps that I didn't take at that point.

I went to the Worli Police Station to complain about the abuse to you, but they kicked me out too, accusing me of causing trouble to the family. They took my address and ordered me not to go even near your apartment, or I would be charged with causing a nuisance.

Mrin, that was 'our' meeting with your parents in which nothing was discussed, no give-and-take took place, only orders were given. Mrin, I still don't understand; why did your father say that he didn't like my father? What did my father do? When I asked my father about that after a few days, he expressed his surprise, even bewilderment, and said, 'I've no idea why he would say such a thing, especially when they had a great time at Sona's wedding.'

Despite his denials and pretence of innocence, I have a gnawing suspicion that he had something to do with it. I do remember my Dad having an engrossing conversation with you and Somi at the wedding. Mrin, can you recall or check your diary to figure out what he said to you? If you can, we can solve the puzzle to determine what went wrong even though it's late in our life to be of any value, but we will have some consolation that we didn't need to have been separated.

Mrin, I feel tired just recalling those painful seconds ticking away in my psyche. However, I do find inner strength from the belief that our kin conspired against us and ended what could have been a happy life. But they were not able to "end" the relationship.

 Some relationships are like trees. Once they take root, they nourish themselves. Despite the distance and absence, deep relationships keep on renewing themselves. Ours is one of them. Death will knock on our doors and end our lease on this mortal coil, but our relationship will live, as long as one of us is alive, and keeps on nourishing this tree. So, if I go first, please remember to keep me in your heart, and as you do now, keep on recalling the glorious moments of our three years together. That would nourish this tree of love and friendship.

Mrin, I've always loved you. In the passage of these years, our friendship has stood the test of time. It has neither dimmed in my heart, nor has it stopped nourishing my soul. Tell me how much you remember about the meeting and its after-effects and our subsequent rendezvous.

One of these days, you better open up to me about your medical condition. I think I have got a pretty good idea what's happening to you, but I need to hear from you first.

Take care

Forever,

Your Ayu

Anya said loudly, "Oh my God!"

"Shhh…you are too loud. Mom can hear us," said Zara in a whisper.

"How near and yet so far! Dad was in Trinidad and Mrin in South Carolina…only a short flight away! If only one of them knew!"

"Zara, destiny wrought havoc here!"

"I can understand Mrin's parents didn't want to tell Mrin about Dad's job in the Caribbean, but why did no one in our family care to inform him of Mrin's whereabouts in South Carolina? The more I think about this, the more revulsion I feel for those responsible for this planned and deliberate neglect and omission against Dad," said Zara.

However, their anger was levied against the Mrin woman's parents and all Indian parents in general. "What's wrong with us that second class with honours isn't good enough? How many lives get ruined because our parents have unreasonable expectations, and they never come to grips with our honours class? Do we prefer our children to become only doctors, engineers, stock market analysts, business managers? Doesn't the world need masons, plumbers, store managers or bus drivers?" Anya vented.

"I think we have successfully created children whose lives are driven by stress," said Zara.

"On the other hand, I really don't ever want their story to end. If I can, I will tell my kids about their grandpa's deep and abiding love for a woman who knew how to give and shine in his life. If I have daughters, I'll encourage them to be Mrin-filled," said Zara.

"I feel sad that Dad is getting tired just thinking and recalling the unhappy events of his life," said Anya.

"To be honest, I'm also drained reading, talking and rethinking about these exchanges," said Zara. "These emails keep on shadowing me, following me as if I am an offender. They are suspecting me and challenging the inner core of ethics…"

Just then, there was a knock on Zara's door.

"Mom?" Zara asked as Somi opened the door and saw her slap shut the screen panel of Ayu's laptop with a bang.

"What are the two of you doing at this time of the night, shouting 'Oh God'? Are you in trouble?"

Zara looked at Anya for a way out and decided to bluff it out. "No, just girl talk… about relationships and trust and love…"

"Were you looking for answers to those issues on the Internet?" Somi asked, incredulous.

"Well, it's a start…to be honest; I am having some trouble with Shaan…"

"I think you're going through the adjustment period. You need more time and space. Perhaps he needs them too," Somi said.

"Thanks, Mom. Problem solved."

Somi said nothing, and an uneasy calm prevailed. However, in their hearts, the girls knew their mother had kept peace and dignity with her calmness without asking any further questions.

Chapter Ten

Celebration

Next morning Somi served breakfast of Mexican omelettes with eggs, parsley, salsa, Monterey jack cheese and chopped green pepper with toasts lathered with cream cheese, along with orange juice and coffee. It was topped with a helping of fruit such as papaya, mango, avocado, pineapple, and Asadero cheese.

Anya set the table for three. Zara turned the radio on listening to CBC station. Somi promptly switched to one of the Indian stations. Zara poured coffee and orange juice.

Taking a bite of the omelette, Zara joked, "I'm glad we're in Mexico… but where are the Mariachi singers?" Anya fiddled with her iPhone and Hispanic music filled the room.

In middle of breakfast, Somi suddenly blurted out, "Oh my God!" recalling a date with her friends, which she had completely forgotten in the company of her daughters.

"Girls, I'm sorry for leaving right now. Promise you that I will make up for it. Friends…they're important."

"But Mom, why don't you call friends and tell them you're with us. You know kids always trump friends. Come on Mom, call them. We had a whole day planned, starting with some poetry reading at a Harbourfront gathering."

"Who's reading?"

"Margaret Atwood, for sure," said Anya tempting her with rolling of the eyes. "How can you not choose Margaret Atwood over friends?"

Anya made a gesture of desperation with eyes rolling and hands flailing.

"I never stood my friends up, and I don't intend to do it now, Margaret will understand. Tell her so."

She gathered her overnight bag, running to her room, returned, hugged and kissed the girls and walked out, dialling her friends for being late. Though they were disappointed at their mother's abrupt exit, Anya and Zara were happy and much relieved that the last night's conversation had not been brought up and was hopefully forgotten, never to come up again.

In the evening, the sisters met around seven and went window-shopping at Eaton Center Mall, which was packed with locals and tourists. When they settled into a restaurant for dinner, the topic of last night's emails was finally brought up.

"I still have chills thinking about when Mom walked in on us…"

"I feel wretched. The ironic part is that we are doing this out of concern for her," said Zara.

"Yes, exactly. Oh, by the way, everything is fixed for our trip to St Maarten next week."

"That should compensate for our guilt…," Zara said in a low voice.

"I wonder from where this ethical reaction and feeling of guilt come from. Is it ourselves, or is it due to correct upbringing?" They both laughed at the self-observation.

They were home a little past nine and took their habitual seats on the sofa and began to read what Mrin had to say.

From: Mrin@****.com

To: Ayush@*****.com

Subject: Knock, knock.

My dear Ayu,

Reading your last email, I too feel depressed and sad. I feel horrid for putting you through hell, and even more horrible that I didn't walk with you in those days of fire and brimstone. I beg your forgiveness for not climbing the mountain. In retrospect, it would have been a lot easier to climb, much less painful and more comfortable for us. I erred. I failed you and your belief in me, and we paid for it lifelong!

The world writes lyrics in honour of love, but the world often doesn't let love succeed. Love's success comes only after its demise. Only then does the world realize the loss of beautiful lives and what they could have been. Only after the death of lovers, the powers-to-be, condemn the atrocities of injustice inflicted as unfair and undeserved, but refuse to accept their responsibilities, their doing and their heartless vindictiveness. The blame is ascribed to something indefinable called 'life.' It is life's flaw and fault, Ayu, so they say. How unkind is this life that with such denials, it leaves behind bloody welts that we cannot see, but neither do the welts forget the pain of the lightest, softest silk brushing gently against them. I wonder, till today, why it happened to us…so undeservedly.

Now I will try to answer some of your questions as you're perhaps working on our rendezvous in Matheran.

Unknown to me, my father secured me a two-or-three-year college teaching appointment through an educational consultant. He was convinced that getting me out of your eyesight, from your city would do wonders for me. He kept me in the dark until the last minute of the final interview on the phone with Winthrop University in Rock Hill in South Carolina. It was under a Rockefeller Foundation grant that allowed foreign scholars to work in the USA for educational and cultural purposes. He said that if I didn't like it, I could return home without any problem. It seemed the interview was a formality, as they wanted someone very badly. That was sometime at the end of March 1973, and I was gone by early April to teach spring and summer semesters.

I came to see you at your home the day after my interview. On my way up, I met the funny twin sisters. I think they were Rhim Jhim and Jhil Mill. Unusual names, yes; and their clothing had even more panache. I remember them playfully telling me, "Hey girl, don't go up there...So have you picked the date of your departure...? Remember to leave Ayush for us...No matter what you do, don't go upstairs. Let us warn you that death awaits there for you. If you're smart, run, run as fast as you can and as far as you can. But don't die upstairs."

Did they mean that my departure to the USA was a step to my death? I was stunned with this experience because this was a déjà vu. I had the same experience with these girls, saying the identical things when I came to apologize to you after the shameful meeting with my parents.

"Will leave;

Will go;

Will have no choice;

We heave; we heave; up she goes Has no poise.

Will leave; Will go,

She has no choice."

When I went upstairs, your mother welcomed and hugged me, closing the kitchen door for privacy. She said quietly and quickly said in my ears, 'Leave Ayush.' Before she could tell me more, the door flung open, and your father strode in and bluntly thundered, 'Mrin, you need to leave right now. Your parents don't want to see Ayush, and I don't want you to see him either. Your father told you that Ayush was a forbidden fruit for you and I agree with him."

Before I forget, let me add that I have often asked myself how your father knew the exact conversation you and I had heard at my home when you were interrogated and then summarily dismissed.

Going back to that event, I could see he was angry, but I don't see why. I felt it was a fake anger as his heart wasn't in it. I believe your mom sought to confide about us, but your Dad made it certain that she didn't say it, and I didn't hear it. They had no idea that I was seeing you at the Reserve Bank, although only occasionally, as I also had started to teach at SIES College in Sion where I had irregular hours. I made more attempts to contact you, but later about them.

You asked me if I remember my conversation with your father at Sona's wedding. I looked at my diary for details, but don't have much. My diary scribble says:

We all had great fun at Sona's wedding. Everything was fabulous. Music, dancing, clothes, colours, food, laughter…everything was there. A's father tried to tell me something, but it was too noisy, and I couldn't hear him completely. He talked about stars and how they cross their paths. Somi was there too; I need to ask her what he was saying so seriously. A number of girls were going gaga over A. They wanted to talk, touch and dance with him. However, A made sure that I was his new world. Dad likes A so much.

Despite the good feelings in my home, I'm surprised that our relationship fell apart in a short time. I've asked myself a thousand questions or more to determine what I did, or my parents did to deserve a sudden ouster of my presence from your life, and I am yet to find a convincing answer. I hope we can unravel this mystery together, Ayu.

Yours,

Mrin

This tale shall not end

On every cross road I befriend

Thy shadow, a relic of my past

Thy name appears as a landmark

Helps me find my moorings

You know well the path I must take

And thou shalt be there for me forever.

This tale shalt not end

On every path and each turn

Straight or twisted

Thy memories fill the air

And as I inhale, they fill my lungs

You're there in my blood

Infused and enlivened

This tale shall not end.

No matter what I do and say

Thou walkest with me at heart's choosing

Sing me melodies of our happy love

Thou makest me cry, sob and moan

But when I turn to talk to you

Let me talk for the rest of my life

The nights we climbed the mountains in toy trains

Stayed in the ravishing gardens of joy

Thou shalt choose to be silent

Put finger on thy lips forbidding me to speak.

Wrapping me in the finery of thy mystique

This tale shall not end.

"Poor grandma, she was caught between the rock and the hard place. She knew something, and perhaps wanted to warn Mrin before Grandpa spoke to her. What could that have been?"

"We've no answers; and without them our post mortem is going nowhere," said Anya

"I'm shocked Mrin's father, just like our grandfather, was equally an autocrat. He didn't seem to care what she wanted. He just wanted her out of Dad's sight across the oceans half a sun away in a far away land…" said Zara.

"It was a cruel punishment. He was devious to shuffle her off to America in such haste," said Anya, while she thought about how the wheels of destiny had moved so quickly against Mrin - her job was applied for; interview taken; visa arrived, and she was gone! In all this, not even a meeting between the valentines!

"We believe that wheels of justice move slowly, inexorably slow. But in her case, they rushed too fast as if there was no tomorrow… Grandpa talked at aunt Sona's wedding to Mom and Mrin both. Perhaps we should speak with Mom about this without seeming to be nosy. She does know something, according to Mrin's diary," Zara suggested.

 "Mom *and* grandpa keep showing up," said Anya.

"It's true; I can't wait to read the next email…" Zara's tone was meditative and eager, "So much of my perspective on Mrin has changed in the last few days through these emails. Parts of me wish they had 'Mrin' in them!" And with that she smiled wide and clicked to the next message.

From: Ayush@*****.com

To: Mrin@****.com

Subject: Knock, knock.

My dear Mrin

I'm horrified that you went through a lot to contact me before leaving, and they all failed. An inconsolable rage is brewing in me; I fear I may do much damage to someone. I'm betrayed and heartbroken that my own, instead of helping, simply chose to banish you, and punish both of us. Yes, despite all that grief of banishment, I want you to ignore the hurt for the time being and experience the luxuriant silken sojourn we pirated from the autocrats of our lives to see first hand what mindfulness and consciousness is all about when two lovers elevate their oneness.

Now, the red-letter days of our lives that were formed by our love and shaped by your mindfulness. It was a rendezvous, a secret tryst between the sweethearts. It didn't have the approvals and blessings of others, but it was propelled by our own hearts and deepest desires. We were ready to abandon all rules, and seek our own path. Every detail that I'm going to give comes from the multiple slow replays of the rich experiences, abundant surrendering, and yielding encompassing a little more than sixty hours.

Megh Dalal was your cover for our rendezvous that started in the morning of Wednesday March 23 until Friday afternoon on March 25. You told your parents that you were going to Matheran with some friends who would board the Karjat bound train at Dadar, but you and Megh would board the train at the VT station. To foolproof the plan, she told her family the same story, and she spent two nights at Sukhada Solkar's home in Colaba. When your father came to drop you off at the VT station, he met Megh, who was waiting for you while I was sitting in another part of the train to meet you both at the next station. My thanks to Megh and Sukhada wherever they are now!

We reached Karjat. From there we boarded a narrow-gauge train, to Neral for two hours at a slow speed on a winding road peopled with sellers, hustlers, kids and monkeys. The leisurely train journey was precursor to the experiences best enjoyed when there's no rush to get anywhere soon.

You were intensely excited. You were holding my hand lovingly, looking at me wistfully and humming a happy tune that was tinged with doubt and fear. I remember it was a song from the movie *Hum Raahi*. You looked at me, touched my face gently with the palm of your hand and sang softly, under your breath:

Mujhko apne gale laga lo aye mere humraahi Tum ko kya batlaau main ke tumse kitna pyaar hai

Mujhko apne gale laga lo aye mere humraahi Tum ko kya batlaau main ke tumse kitna pyaar hai

Other travellers saw our happiness and excitement, but left us to our own. You stroked my hand; on my palm, your finger scribbled the Greek letter Theta with a circle and a connecting line inside. I didn't know how to respond to your singing, your gentle touch or your love-dripping stares. Your mood, slow pace of the plodding train and the abundant greenery outside on the hills had made us calm, all our worries faded away into the landscape.

We were staying at Woodlands Resort cottage. The municipal laws forbid the motor traffic in Matheran to retain its rustic ambience, verdant glory, and slow pace of living. Leaving the fast blur of Bombay behind, we began to see every detail, and instead of a whir, we watched the glacial pace of the scenery glide by us. As we walked, you hung onto my left arm with both your hands. I wanted this scene, this feeling of the sensual warmth, our hot skin touching and your radiant face glued on me, to last forever.

We hired a horse buggy to take us to our resort. After a quick registration and payment, we were escorted to our cottage that included one bedroom, living room, bathroom and porch. Outside the cottage, we had a beautiful garden with patio chairs, tall trees, red soil amid the pristine and enthralling beauty that had hushed the city clamour and nestled us into the *"Dolce vita"* and perfect harmony. Standing in the porch, Mrin, you extended your arms and melted into my embrace where you stayed folded for some time and kissed me briefly. You were awakened by soft and cool breezes strumming on the ancient trees in a chorus of rustling branches and leaves. The breeze brought the sensuous fragrance of lavender to us, and that launched you to search the source… and found to your exhilaration, gentle velvety whorls of purple lavender. You kissed me, picked some spikes of lavenders and asked me to place them in your hair, just above your ears.

It was barely five, and the day was still young. We sat on a rocking love seat on the porch to take in the atmosphere, much like the serene and engrossing way we sat in the Romeo Corner next to Kirti College. You played with my hands; you kissed my palm and then bit it hard. "Ouch!" I exclaimed playfully, but you were somewhere else. Then you kissed me on the mouth but at the same time your one hand lightly caressed the inside of my right thigh giving me cascading ripples of tingling sensations.

The resort was not full, but considering it was Wednesday, one would say there were more people than there should have been. Most of the guests were middle-aged people who had settled into their lives, but were enjoying the fruits of the life's harvest. Some of the older folks were eyeing us happily, and I was sure before we left, they would befriend us.

We walked back to the train station, looked in the stores and their merchandise and decided to buy peanut, cashew and sesame brittles cooked with jaggery. We spent the evening doing nothing except dawdling and holding hands. Intimacy was in our mind, but it had not yet overpowered every limb in our body, nor was the hot blood running our common sense wildly restless. For a young couple, I think we were showing remarkable restraint. Instead of shuttering ourselves in our suite, tearing up each other's clothing and clawing and devouring each other, we stayed calm, civil and orderly.

Going back to the station made me feel that perhaps you were having second thoughts about coming to the hills and what we would end up doing. "Mrin, are you sure you're ready for this?"

You stopped, turned around and placed your finger on my lips, "Ayush, yes, I'm ready for this. You've never pushed me into doing anything that I didn't want to. This was my idea, and please don't put seeds of doubt in me. My heart was ready a long time ago. My body doesn't repudiate you."

"Even then, anytime we need to cut short…"

"Don't even talk about cutting short, Ayush. These hours in the hills are mine, my lifeline," you said kissing me.

We went back to the resort around sevenish. It was dark now; lamps were lit everywhere. Someone had lit a jasmine candle stick and someone was chanting an evening prayer. I was speaking with a man at the information desk about things to do in Matheran, and I saw you were speaking with the receptionist. After dinner, we both leisurely walked to our cottage along the lighted path, with our hands around the waists. So far, it was a perfect day that was promising even a better amorous night.

We entered the cottage, bolted the door and then suddenly you pushed me on the bed and jumped on me lathering my lips and face with your smooches. Laughing aloud you said, "That's not the way to give a kiss that leads to your business," stressing the word business. Then, from nowhere, you cooed, "The whole day you've been imagining ways to get me disrobed. Now go ahead, Mister. Let me see what you got!"

Now Mrin, I don't wish to give every detail of our intimacy. I have an innate anxiety that someone on the Internet would not respect our privacy, honour and integrity and leak what's personally sacrosanct. I've treasured those cherished hours, and I'm not prepared to divulge to others for their perverted sense of pleasure. I don't want anyone telling my sweet daughters that their father was lewd and immoral and offend Somi. I hope that it's okay with you. Nonetheless, I'll tell you unique habits of your character to light a spark in your psyche, awakening the half-asleep memory to create an avalanche of recollections to deluge your being.

Let me confess that in this exciting journey, I was like a tourist who had an overall idea about the adventure, but lacked the specific knowledge and skills to continue the celebration until arriving at the destination. Fortunately, you taught me how to cease being a tourist and become a local.

At that point you removed a little booklet from your bag and handed to me. "Ayush, I've a little something for you read...it's on the yoga called Kundalini...some people call it sex yoga. Despite my forthrightness I feel a little awkward to talk about this right now."

I quietly read for fifteen minutes and discovered a beautiful concept that even the profane subject of sexuality could be filled with energy of spirituality. Once I finished reading, you said seriously, "we were about to enter a realm, ruled by a heartless sorceress who could impose weights of gravity on anxious lovers, strangulating them, making them crash against their will."

"I understand."

"Let's do a breathing exercise, you follow me and echo my breathing until our breathing is synchronized; keep in mind that you'll follow me and control the breathing." They practised it a while and once Mrin was convinced he understood it and mastered it and kept on their conversation until everything was normal.

"Ayu, are you calm now in every way…your body, mind and breathing? If yes, close your eyes and imagine and practice this… vividly…see the whole picture that I'm going to describe to you. This is serious and you need to focus and be with me one hundred percent, synchronized, step-by-step. We've never talked about these things before and I feel a little stressed doing this…"

Then you explained how sensual touching awakens the skin, which ripples through the nerves and energises the brain completing its circuitry. At this critical point, you emphasised, the soulmates must show discipline in their breathing, tempo, rhythm and visualization.

"Is this all clear to you?"

"Yes."

You asked me to breathe, fully synchronized with yours. You insisted that I get my cues from you and not allow my body derail me. You said to consider how the great Ulysses did not surrender to the enchanting music and charms of the dangerous Sirens, and advised me to avoid the shipwreck at any cost.

When you lose focus and control, you will see, instead of me, the magical temptress, the Siren…she is hypnotic, she can mesmerize you… she's astoundingly seductive, her eyes are full of longing. ..Don't rush into her embrace; if you do, she will suck your lungs out, collapsing you. You must assume the Zen like breathing of complete calm. Remember that. Complete calm…Any questions?"

"Yes, how do I slay the Siren?"

"Keep your poise, control your breathing, slow down a bit, sync your energies, bond with me, feel the energy rise from the spine, let it rise upward…You see me now…Do you see me now? Are you ready, Ayush?"

Opening my eyes, looking quiet and serene, breathing quietly, I said, "Yes, I am ready."

We stayed up the whole night, talking about ourselves, our futures and exploring our intimacy, sensuality and ecstasy. What you taught me that night has remained in good stead for me.

When you thought I was likely to forget your advice and loose my way, you said, "Ayush, we are not an express train. Ours is a jalopy going at a slow speed, visiting every village, conversing with every stranger, tasting a fresh delicacy at every unknown stop. Our time has a new dimension. Our day has a lot more than twenty-four hours; our minutes have additional seconds than sixty. So much so we want to say, 'I want a second' of everything. Time is not our enemy. It's a slow burn love; you churn, and you keep on churning."

Mrin, that night you tutored me to be a great lover and, even a better man.

"Ayush, the calmer, more rhythmic and relaxed breathing removes selfishness, increases emotional pleasure, encourages love for the other and creates a sense of timelessness. Your conscious breathing will give you control over body responses. Instead of your body, you'll run the show. Always include Kundalini with it, you'll unleash mystical powers that will enhance you physically and spiritually. You'll be a master slayer of the sorceress."

Mrin, you made me see the entire range, the whole range of pleasing experiences. It's not one place, one part, one organ that yields the bounty of physical love and inner joy.

"It's the union of two people, and many intensified sensory experiences, raised to a higher level, Ayush."

It was almost morning; we hadn't slept much, but neither of us was sleepy. However, I saw you doing some yoga exercise that had a mixture of breathing, stretching, chanting, and meditative postures. I could see even now how flexible your torso was that each limb was so limber and elastic that you could easily be a contortionist! In a pose, you were lying on your stomach; your legs were arched backward and pointing up your hands arched backward grabbing your toes. Then you rocked your body making it a circle.

You explained the Kundalini yoga was all about awakening a coiled up snake lying at the bottom of the spine. Once the serpent awakens, it travels sequentially from the base, to navel, stomach, heart, neck, forehead and the brain and then returns to its base. Once this cycle is completed without interruption, one can feel the power emanating from the process. The energies of glandular and nervous systems create an awakening in the spinal fluid which eventually spreads like ripples to other areas. This corresponds to the uncoiling of the serpent. I was impressed that you, a young woman in her early twenties, were not going to accept the sexual play as a secondary sideshow, but merge it into a spiritual exercise with healthy benefits.

I remember so vividly one of the reasons you gave me for your learning Kundalini. I'm still shocked by it, but equally awed. You said, "When it comes to physical happiness of every kind, I must know the quality of consideration I was going to receive; nothing less would do."

I was awed because I had never read or heard a woman ever say what she was going to do to improve the quality of her intimate joy. I hope somebody outstanding in your life appreciated your remarkable knowledge.

Then the phone rang, and you said to the reception desk to leave the stuff right on the front porch table and just knock on the door. I asked what was going on. You said you had asked for room service and a picnic pack for the lunch. That morning, after we showered, you wore American style stirrup pants, pink button-down shirt, and a colourful scarf and Mary Jane shoes. We were out of the cottage by eleven with our picnic pack, hired a horse buggy to take us to Charlotte Lake to enjoy its rich luxuriant beauty. It was much enhanced by crisp refreshing air that teased your face, and played with your beautiful hair.

There were other young couples, but there were also some young families, which seriously restricted the public display of affections. We could see, not too far from here, Echo Point and Louisa Point on the right and Pisarnath Temple on the left. We were sitting on a blanket, under the shade of an ancient sprawling oak with thick lush foliage. I fell asleep with my head upon your lap. You sang some beautiful songs with your heart totally into them. Other picnickers enjoyed your singing, and they came to our tree, and we all played a musical singing game, *antakshari*, for almost an hour. One of the older men, a guest at our resort, asked you, "Newlyweds, children?"

Before I could answer, you said, "No, uncle. We are married for two years."

"Nice... an arranged marriage, is it?"

I was stupefied. I was wondering what yarn you were going to weave to mesmerize them with and cast your spell to draw them in your world. They were curious now to hear your story.

"Uncle, we are from Jaisalmer. We both were maybe ten years old, and childhood friends. My family was attending a wedding at Ayush's family Haveli where people were celebrating."

"Then? Tell us more."

"So, our grandmothers are sitting together, exchanging gossip and reminiscing about the good old times. Ayush and I, and some other kids were playing right in front of them in a huge courtyard in the middle of the Haveli. My grandmother said to his, looking at me, "I think she'll be a woman pretty soon. We will have to find a suitable Brahmin boy for her."

Mrin, you know how to have dramatic pauses, and then you surveyed the inquisitive gathering to see the impact of your words and dropping the evocative words. You cleared your throat and pointing at me said, "Ayush's grandmother said if you are looking for a good match, it's not really hard to find. One is playing right in front of us."

"Oh Lord of the Universe! Wonders never cease!" exclaimed the old man.

You were gratified with the response of the people.

"Then?"

"Well, my grandmother said, "Do you want to ask your son, or do you want to exchange the silver coin?"

His grandmother said, "Well, I'm going to give you a silver coin first, and then I will inform my son. Do you want to ask your son if this arrangement is okay with him?"

"No, my promise is enough," said my grandmother.

However, she didn't have a coin on her, so she called my father, asked for a coin, and then she broke the happy news. My father was elated, soon his father was called in, was given the news; they embraced.

The Haveli got the news. Drums came to life; firecrackers burst; the singers came out, and sweets were exchanged. Our grandmothers danced; others joined in and everyone started to sing folk songs, and then, we both were carted away to separate places to hide us from each other. Nevertheless, at our grandmothers' insistence, we were allowed to play together again and resume our childhood affair."

Mrin, our wedding never came to be. But there is this consolation that at least in the eyes of those afternoon tourists, we were wedded and that at least in imagination our marriage had lasted at least a few years. It's a heavenly memory for me.

A young girl said, "I can't believe it. I thought such things happened only in movies. Can I touch you? Are you real?"

Mrin, everyone wanted to talk to you; nobody bothered to ask me about anything. You spun a magical myth that connected to their heartstrings, and you tapped into their desire for a similar happenchance occurring in their own destinies. Your narrative was magnified with its pauses, details, and cultural references and nuances. There was resonance as you brought myth, magic, chivalry and romance into the drab city culture that seems to be the antithesis of what your imagined story stood for. We came to the Lake as a couple, but left it with a lot of friends. We went back to the resort, had a cup of tea and some snacks, thanked the reception desk for a lovely picnic basket and returned to our cottage. I grabbed you in my embrace, kissing your mouth with passion and purpose. We fell asleep in each other's arms.

We had a couple of hours of sleep and when I woke up, I felt your warm body furling into me with your hand on my cheek, the face resting against my chest and one knee settled on my thigh. Then we stirred, looked at each other. You kissed me on my chest and whispered, "I'm so happy that we came here. Ayu."

You talked about how you relished the tangy, zesty taste of my sweat and how musky my body smelled. I remember it because it was the only time, I had heard how I smelled and tasted.

Fully awake now, you said, "So what do you think of me? Too forward? Vampish? Outrageously aggressive? Too strong for my own good? I hope you are not one of those men who can't stand a strong woman."

"Mrin, you are God's gift to me that I will always cherish. Your knowledge and abilities make me whole, not threaten me. We had a wonderful time here, we discovered just how compatible we are. I can hardly wait to start our family."

You laughed and said, "No, don't worry. We made no babies here. I'm on the pill for this rendezvous in Matheran and will stay on it until we are wedded."

You were your own arbiter, not at anyone's mercy. I liked it so much.

After dinner and talking with some curious guests who were charmed by your tale of Jaisalmer Haveli and child marriages, we returned to our cottage recharged and seduced by your own glamorous charm. I gathered spikes of purple lavender, scattered them on our bed and sensuality descended and overpowered our minds and bodies.

We both agreed that as soon as Sona's wedding was over in June and our post graduation done and jobs secured, we would start planning for our life together with marriage or without it. Let there be a scandal if need be. And with that decision, we both slipped into a wonderful slumber. We woke up well rested, calm and satisfied; it seemed our purpose of coming here was fulfilled.

"You smell like a woman with lavender oils on your chest. Even your armpits smell so nice, Ayu Vyas," you said with your head on my chest.

I went back to sleep. You stayed up. Soon, you woke me up.

When I slipped out of my sweet sleep, I saw you again doing your yoga exercises, immensely absorbed; nothing seemed to bother, distract, take away from the yoga regime.

We bathed, got dressed, had our breakfast, and now we were ready to return home. At the station, you bought peanut and sesame brittles. One of the guests from the Resort took me aside and said in a conspiratorial tone as if he was giving me secrets that needed to be protected with my life, "Keep her happy. Never lose her."

I said, "Uncle, I will remember your advice." And then I walked away as I did not find it necessary to ask him to explain what he meant. However, I did find out about the myth once we drifted apart. Husbands and lovers who wrong their wives, or abandon or betray their lovers, are haunted by the floating images of women, roaming the woods and seeking their revenge.

At the train station, startled, you realized something that needed to be done. You called a buggy, grabbed my hand and pulled me to the buggy and asked the man to take us back to the resort.

"Mrin, what did we forget?"

"Just follow me," you said.

You got your camera out, took me to our cottage, and took a picture of the memory filled haven. Later, you took my picture alone. Next, you made me take your picture, unaccompanied. We were done.

"This is where I gave you the gift that I could give only once to the man I love," you said.

Mrin, that's how we spent sixty hours together doing what young paramours do, but without clawing into each other's flesh or tearing up each other's clothes. We returned, not bruised and battered but rested, loved and happy. Thanks to John Donne I learnt to be an explorer, and even more thankfully to you, I ceased to be tourist and became a local, a slayer of the sorceress. Above all, I learnt to enjoy the slowness of jalopies.

You've left me a bundle of memories that are still good for another fifty years. When I reach the end of my life, I hope I have your name on my lips and the memory of Matheran in my eyes. If God is merciful, that's what should happen.

Mrin, I love you more than my words say. I must add here something that I found in a book left by Somi in the family room written by Anais Nin that's so reflective of you. Nin wrote, "Life shrinks or expands in proportion to one's courage." Yes, you showed the character, gumption and courage in your life. No wonder you live a full life, fully expanded. I have often expressed my love for you, but I need to show my huge respect and appreciation for the kind of woman you had been to me…

This turned out to be a marathon email. I hope it helps you to remember the stellar days and nights of our lives.

Yours forever.

Ayush

Zara burst out, "Anya, my God, she is a goddess! An absolute goddess!"

"Yes, an incredible woman! I'm dying to meet her!"

"I'm so happy that Dad quoted Anais Nin from Mom's copy…I do recall how they both wanted us to take an elective in Women's Studies at a Radcliffe summer session," said Anya.

As they were talking, Zara googled Nin and another quote by her came up on the screen. "The day came when the risk to remain tight in a bud was more painful than the risk it took to blossom."

"Anya, this the one I vividly remember from that summer session. Time comes in every person' s life to be decisive and proactive, to take a leap of faith to grow, mature and take a step forward despite the lack of experience and the risk of failure notwithstanding."

"Zara, come to think of it we wondered then why we were directed to Radcliffe experience. Now we know Mom played a role and Dad played a role. I'm sure Mrin is not too far behind for her part."

Anya stepped up to her little library, and not finding what she was looking for returned to her seat.

"Zara, I thought of finding a quote to explain a relationship that doesn't blossom, that it doesn't get a chance to understand or explain why it didn't and why it was miscarried. Their story is like they fell off the cliff and nobody heard or knew about it. No spin, no gloss, no eulogy and no memorial." Anya was moved by her own words to misty eyes. "It pains my heart."

Zara moved next to Anya and placed her arm around her shoulder. They sat quietly for a while, until Zara spoke, "I think I'm dazzled by her magical, seductive and alluring style. She knows the esoteric yoga of Kundalini. Nevertheless, for a celibate, she has an astounding knowledge, her needs and how to fulfill them! Could a woman like this be a threat to men?"

"She is fabulous. How many women go through lives without ever knowing what creates happiness and personal satisfaction?"

"Yeah," said Zara looking sideways.

"Zara, can I ask you a frank question?"

"Sure."

"Would you blame Dad now, if he were to say to Mom that he doesn't love her?"

"Oh my God, Anya, did you have to ask this question?"

"Please tell me."

"No, I wouldn't blame Dad at all. She was actively involved in hurting their affair. She wasn't there for him. Now, that's my first impression, my first opinion."

"You always hedge when it comes to Mom, don't you? Anyway, what happens to such powerful, imaginative and creative women?" Anya wanted to know.

'Is this, your personal question or a generic question?"

"I'm nothing like her, but I would like to be like her. Zara, let's find out about the Kundalini classes that we both can attend while you're in Toronto"

Zara added, "Yes, when we visit Bombay, we will see Kirti College and other venues, and definitely this resort in Matheran."

Anya said, "Zara, let me make a confession. If I were a man, I would find it inexorably difficult to live with another woman after seeing all the galaxies in heavenly cosmos with a woman like Mrin. How did Dad manage?"

"Oh, don't explore this angle, Anya," pleaded Zara putting a finger on her closed lips.

"Let's see what our mentor has to ask now," said Anya.

From: Mrin@****.com

To: Ayush@*****.com

Subject: Knock, knock.

Dear Ayu, My lover Ayu:

I'm so thrilled to receive this email, awakening dormant emotions and sensations, and bringing blushes of happy embarrassment to my face. My dry skin is all of sudden, lustrous and oily from just reading your account. I'm a young again! Intimacy with you is pictorially a blur, but I cherish even the blurriness. It blurs, but doesn't dim for it burns brightly in my blood. After you, intimacy was a mandatory chore, a price tag for the title of being someone's wife; however, short-lived it turned out to be.

Your email brings to life our train trip to the Hills. I was so much longing to cuddle up with you. Nevertheless, your quality of staying aloof, in asking less made me remain restrained too. I felt as if you were testing who had the most control and poise in dealing with internal fire. Your coolness was enough to make me enjoy your companionship; the world of beauty was fanning my inner fire, and soothing my feverish self, outside.

You made me see and feel the difference in the air between Bombay and the Hills. And you made me see it all in slow motion and in colour too! I now know a photograph that was so special to me, but slipped out of my memory as to why; it was taken as a souvenir of our gorgeous trip. I was wondering why I was in the habit of kissing that picture every day! Picture of our cottage!! I still kiss that picture, Ayu, for it is like kissing you and the memory of our two nights in each other's embrace in a lavender-strewn bed!

One of the virtues that drew me to you was your humanness and unpretentiousness. You were always detached, but never arrogant. You spoke less, but this was by no means less communicative. However, above all your willingness to learn from others was the most cherished quality. Despite your intellectual prowess, you never considered others less intelligent to be unworthy of your tutoring. You were also a fast learner. You learned well the virtues of jalopies and slow trains, and there is no better place to learn this than the hills of Matheran. Our climb to the top was on a slow-moving toy train.

After you were untraceable, I wound up with someone who turned out to be thoroughly detestable. I told him everything about you; yes, everything, including the hills of Matheran, but not Kundalini.

During one of the nights in the first month after the wedding when I started to show him, he got up, put his pants on back, spat on me, called me "a nymphomaniac, a slut, a whore…all rolled into one" and walked out! I still can't understand why he called me a whore!

I've got a little box of goodies that I'm certain came from you. I call this box Life's Treasures. It includes stirrup pants, a necklace, a perfume bottle and lipsticks, among a few other things. Any recollections?

Ayu, I won't be able to receive or write emails for the next few days as I need some medical attention. Meantime, you take care of yourself, my lover. I'm going to miss you a lot.

I love you, Ayu, and shall do so for ever.

Yours,

Mrin

I lifted my veil a little today

Soon I shall reveal myself

Without a blush or eyes cast downward

He will see my majesty, my glory.

Let him be the discoverer

Of all my contours and folds

That lay unseen and untouched

Let his fingers and lips

Light fire in my flesh that dips

So, let him indulge and savour my yielding

Plant together our seedling.

Let his kisses quench my thirst

And douse fire and fever first.

Let him unleash an avalanche

Of passion, lust, love and sweet pain

Let him nibble, nuzzle and tickle

I submit to his whisper with a gasp

I'm all yours, only yours.

All I'm is yours, pull me closer

Make love and take me as yours

I lifted my veil today

So, take me Ayu, and make me yours

"I must admit that despite my earlier revulsion for Mrin and character assassination of Dad, I am happy that I went through the heartache the last few testing days."

"I know what you mean, Zara. In their own ways, our parents don't ever stop helping us to see, understand and grow."

"I feel sorry about all the fights we had earlier. But now I understand you see things lot sooner, earlier than I do. I can't cut through the noise, but you do so readily… When you said a few days ago sisterhood has its privileges, I didn't get its core, but I now grasp the full impact of its intent. As far as they are concerned, I am convinced that not only did Mrin take Dad to the heavenly altitudes, but left behind in his soul, heart and mind the essence of good."

"Zara, among us siblings, you're the bulwark. When you thought Mom was vulnerable, you stood your guard, protective and loyal."

 Zara smiled, happy that the bond between her and her sister felt stronger than ever. "Well…." She said, "Shall we read on?"

From: Ayush@*****.com

To: Mrin@****.com

Subject: Knock, knock.

Dear Mrin:

I'm so sorry to hear about the first-month marital disaster. I know you revel in your honesty. But disclosures and transparency of personal nature should come only when you've a decent idea how they would be received. However, it was a long time ago; I m pretty sure.

I'm not allowed to ask questions about your present life. However, you said you were going to be away for medical attention. I pray everything is well with you and yours.

I do remember your treasure box, and I was pleased that you gave it my name. You used to save souvenirs, mementos and knick-knacks to remember events, places and people who either impressed you or left *"an indentation on my soul."* Then every few months, you would go through your cherished treasures and discard those whose indentations were mended.

The things you listed came from me. You remember my close friend Kundan? People used to bring imported stuff to him to sell. Most of the stuff came either from Indians living in Africa or in the Middle East, particularly, the city of Aden. When he once got the thinnest possible necklace, he told me that I could have one. I liked what I saw. I said I want two of them. So, you got one with a small Om pendant. Now, the Om pendant caused a little flutter in the heart of Om Prakash Jain, who thought the pendant was to celebrate and immortalize your love and devotion for him.

You told me once that you would like to own a bottle of Chanel 5. I remember my folly when I asked you if it were okay if I got Chanel 1, 2, 3 or 4. You laughed your heart out. You mocked me, "Mr. Well-informed if you can get all those numbers in the Chanel, please buy them for your sweetheart." You then explained to me the importance of Chanel 5. So, when Kundan had Chanel 5, I just bought it and gave it to you in a handmade package that said, "Channel 1-2-4" We had a good laugh about the numbers! What was unusual about our relationship was that with you, life was fun, living was joy, and there were no problems too large to handle. But I digress…

Once he had an extensive collection of Max Factor lipsticks, and I had no idea which colours you preferred even though I loved looking at your lips, kissing them and grazing my fingers across their soft surface. Then we saw a beautiful woman, your age, walk by his storefront. We asked her to come inside and help us select lipsticks. She asked questions about you, and then she picked some colours. I bought all of them for you. I sent them to the Somaiya College with some students who were in the senior year.

I gave you one more gift, and you don't seem to have any recollection of it. I must add you never asked for this gift either. The idea came to me from nowhere that I must buy this and send it to you *soon*. It was a beautiful sari that I had seen in a store in Port of Spain in Trinidad. The store was owned by a Gujarati Sindhi family, originally from Karachi but settled in Bombay after the Partition, now doing business on the Caribbean island. The owner's wife helped me select it, a beautiful Gharchola sari, crisscrossed with woven gold squares. It was full of brilliant reds overall, but littered with shades of mustard, jade green, peach and old rose. That was the only thing I ever mailed to your address in November of 1971. I'm surprised that you didn't mention it. I hope you got it. I wanted to see you in that sari so much! If you've got a picture of you in that Gharchola, please send it to me. I must confess that at that time. I didn't know that the Gharchola sari is also worn by brides at their nuptials. I hope that no one was offended by the gift.

Well, my wife just got invited by my daughters Anya and Zara for a weeklong bonding trip to St. Maarten, so I will be home alone reminiscing about you and our days together. I will recall every minute of our love, our lust, our laughter and our oasis where I return every night for restful reminiscences and then face the searing heat of the relentless sun of this life.

Yours forever,

Ayu

"My God! That was fast. Dad just wrote an email to Mrin as we finished telling Mom about our yet-to-happen trip this morning. Come to think about it, didn't we talk about the trip last week with mom, Anya."

"Dad has a pretty good idea what he would do when we are gone. I'm surprised that Dad didn't gift her books or anything like that, which is more in sync with her character. His gifts are really what women enjoy receiving for their personal preening and pleasure," said Anya.

"Do you ever remember Dad giving anything personal to Mom?"

"None that I can recall, Anya"

"Hey, Zara. On another note, you know we leave in five days for our trip with Mom. Don't pack too many things…" said Anya before she began to list all the essentials.

Interrupting Anya, Zara said, "Hey loser, I've taken holidays in the Caribbean before, for your information. If I do forget something, which always happens, there are stores there too. Let the islanders make some money off us."

"Okay, boss, your call. But I'll remind Mom of these things too!"

Zara immediately called their mother to talk about packing. Zara heard her Dad talking in the background. When he came on the phone, she asked him, "Hey, Dad, you're missing out on fun. Why don't you go with us?"

"Zara, it's pretty hot and humid at this time of the year on the island. Maybe some other time, some other place, you girls have a ton of fun. Drink some margaritas on my behalf too. And above all, see to it that Somi does not get drunk!"

They all laughed.

Chapter Eleven

Bonding in St. Maarten

Somi, Anya and Zara arrived in St. Maarten for a week's holiday. They had chosen a posh two-bedroom condo with a mini kitchen, and a balcony overlooking the blue ocean writing peaceful music on the restless surfing waters. No matter where you looked, you surveyed the magnificence of the azure ocean below and fluffy white clouds above.

"Anya, this is good. Are we staying here the whole week?"

"Yes, Mom, we'll stay here, but we'll have lots to do. We'll go island-hopping for a couple of days, visit Anguila, St. Bart's, perhaps Saba. We'll eat out, go shopping. Oh, yeah, there are a lot of Indian stores and restaurants. We'll have fun," said Anya.

"Anya, you know this place well. Been here before?" Zara wanted to know.

"Yeah, I've been here a couple of times with friends."

The sisters exchanged a knowing glance.

"That's all we're going to do?" Somi wanted to know.

"No, Mom, we're going to court-martial you here for being a wonderful mom. We're going to bond, talk, listen to music, dance, and savour our friendship. That's what we'll do," said Anya hugging Somi tightly. Somi smiled; she liked it.

They sat in the balcony, equipped with white wicker furniture, and potted plants filled with narcissus, lavender and lilacs, enjoying the bottle of complimentary wine. The breeze, bouncing off the flamboyant trees, brushed their cheeks and hair. Somi walked to the lilacs and plucked a cluster, then to the lavenders and picked a spike, brushed them both against her eyelids, and kissed them, whispering, "to my best friend with fragrance like no other." Anya and Zara had always liked this softer side of their mother.

"This reminds me of *dada*'s house in Mumbai. Mom, we visited our grandparents often, but we didn't really know them. Our information is sketchy. Kids growing up in India don't need to hear from anyone as they see everything unfolding, with their engagement and participation. Here, our lives are too personal and private, rather detached and distant. So, we have always been curious. Tell us, what was the Vyas household like, Mom?"

She told them that their grandfather was a scholarly Brahmin who had devoted his life to tutoring, giving sermons on Hindu culture and religious texts, as well as performing small rituals and preparing and reading horoscopes. She added that he was a brilliant palmist and an even better astrologer.

"I was drawn to him for palmistry and astrology," Somi confessed. "Fortunately, he agreed to teach and mentor me."

"Or was it because you wanted to be very near, in the same space with your childhood crush?" Zara coughed suggestively.

Ignoring her daughter's suggestive remark, Somi continued, "Grandpa and Ma lived with their two children in a comfortable, but not particularly spacious, apartment in Matunga. The residential complex, that included four buildings, was large enough to keep him well occupied. *Hawans* were needed for all the significant events in the complex including childbirth, naming ceremonies and children's first days at school. He blessed young men and women when they got jobs, or received promotions. He was there when a new bride arrived, or when a car was purchased. He attended engagement and wedding ceremonies, New Year's Laxmi Pooja, Satyanarayan worship, which occurred at every full moon …these are some of the auspicious and happy events that kept him busy. There were also death rituals like cremation services, which he only performed for close relatives. Such a massive reverence and following Grandpa had that it was unthinkable to call upon another scholar to perform any ceremonies and rituals. If someone got into some prestigious program, Grandpa had to be the first to give his blessing. People would bow, bringing various gifts, but always a box of best Bombay *mithai* if there was any celebration going on in the Matunga Residence. Unless he took a piece first, the celebrants didn't get to eat anything."

"That's awesome," Anya said quietly, a little star struck.

"Eventually, your Grandpa became a family elder whose counsel and approval were considered necessary and sacrosanct. This power influence was not sought; it was earned over time, purely based on his wisdom and successes. He had a record of successful blessings and their result.

Now, to your Grandma. She was a loving and caring woman. She was smart, but like your Dad, not given to loudness and empty talk. Don't worry though, Aunt Sona did the talking for everyone!" Somi laughed and then continued, "Grandma was an incredible cook. The family was a vegetarian, and her repertoire was astounding. She would sometimes cook three different kinds of meals so that the grandparents and both the children had food they cherished eating. She was an early riser; bathed as soon as possible so she could do the temple rituals. In the mornings, Grandpa's clients would come to pay their respects or to have some work done, and your Grandma would serve freshly brewed tea. She was a warm, loving woman who kept the household together and running."

"Just like you, Mom."

Somi blushed at the high compliment.

"Your Dad was academically brilliant, endowed with giftedness and a photographic memory. He's a soft-spoken man, but nonetheless, a grand speaker when he chooses. He's not given to anger or loud complaints. Despite all his brilliance, he is not assertive. He understood the Brahminic code, 'remain calm, give counsel, but do not participate in enforcement of the counsel.' Detachment was his watchword. Grandpa was pleased with your Dad. He was very concerned about who your Dad was going to wed. Let me confess that I have the inside information." Somi smiled at the voluntary confession.

"Like what?"

"None of your beeswax, girls!" Somi said with laughter.

She continued, "Your aunt Sona was about three years younger than your Dad. Sona could have been really smart had she chosen to be so. Unfortunately, neither of the grandparents encouraged her to be scholarly and shine. She was allowed to be fanciful, gossipy and a social butterfly, just like me, back then. Her antics of gossip and chattiness were considered cute, and treated with smiles and indulgence, like mine were."

"But we have never seen you unnecessarily chatty or chummy even with your own friends. It seems you either didn't have that habit, or perhaps it was just an exaggerated impression of..." Zara trailed off.

"I think you're right. I am more like your Dad, circumspect and silent. Perhaps living with him, I've changed…Anyhow; Sona enjoyed seeing Bollywood movies because of their tear-jerker plots, inane jokes and pretty foreign shooting locales. We enjoyed Bollywood music and songs that had pleasing lyrics. We would not only sing those songs but analyze the words of those lyrics to see beauty, symmetry and poetic inventiveness in the structure."

However, Aunt Sona knew the influence and the power her father carried. She was the arbiter of taste and social acceptability for the younger set. If she liked you, then you had a happy life in the residential complex. If she didn't, there was no worse enemy. Without her support, your life could be a real hell.' She had her own retinue of busy bees, and I was one of them. Sona and I were the leaders of the younger set in that neighbourhood. Our word was the final authority."

"Mom, you were a mini-mafia there, weren't you?" Zara said with laughter.

"Your Dad and Aunt were so unlike each other. One sought no influence; the other relished it. One thrived in the academic environment; the other showed no desire. One disliked gossipy cliques; the other nourished them. One was self-effacing; the other was a self-promoter. One was unsure about his father's motivations; the other was a blind adherent. One was secretive and almost reclusive; the other was open and gregarious. I must say they were from two different worlds."

"So, Mom, tell us about the boys who liked you… any secret crushes?" Anya said with a wink of confidentiality.

Somi blushed. "Oh, my girls! You know so little of your parents! I followed no boys. There were some who liked me, but when Aunt Sona got the whiff of it, she made those boys scram. The truth was, your Aunt Sona liked me so much that she didn't want anyone for your Dad but me. Fortunately, their dad agreed with her."

"Oh, our aunt was one determined match-maker. It seems she always got what she wanted. Anyway, who were those boys our illustrious aunt repulsed?"

"They were the same age as your Dad. However, to be honest, nobody could light a candle to Ayush. I married my sweetheart. He was the only one in my eyes and heart," said Somi with much tenderness and pleasure. "Your Dad had a huge following and I was not at all on his radar. There were girls everywhere seeking him out - in school, in the residence complex, in the neighbourhood, colleges and the Reserve Bank of India, as well as International Monetary Fund offices."

"He was a hot, hot hunk. A Casanova?" Zara joked.

"Nobody is going to say that our Dad was a habitual Casanova," said Anya.

"No, he was not a 'player' as you girls would characterize it. He was always decent. Girls were awed by his looks, behaviour, speech and mind. Above all, his detachment and aloofness were the main attractions. I think young women like to chase someone who doesn't want to be pursued. The longer he remained aloof, the larger the throng became. At the IMF meetings, there would be more female than male staff attendees because of Ayush."

"Didn't our illustrious aunt shut them out?"

"Anya, yes, she chased female lovers away whenever she could."

"Tell us who they were Who did you and Sona chase away?" Zara was curious to know.

"Well, we chased away Mandy and Lyric. We managed to save Dad from Avani and Mrin with some help from Grandpa. Rhim and Jhil were never really a threat, they were just a pitiful nuisance."

At the mention of Mrin's name, both sisters stole discreet glances at each other. They had not expected their mother to divulge so much information so easily, and now that she herself had brought up the topic of Mrin, the girls decided to prod a little further.

"Mom, among all these girls, which one, would you say had the best chance?"

"Oh, without any question, it had to be Mrin. She was exceptional. Despite all that I've said about these girls being a threat, I liked Mrin very much." Somi nodded earnestly.

"Why were the girls with irregular names just a nuisance and not a real threat to Dad and you?" Anya wanted to know.

"Those girls came from a talented, but crazy, bohemian family. They all had double names, to start with. Their dad's name was Niranjan, but he added 'Alakh' to precede it. So, everyone called him Alakh Niranjan. His wife's name was Barakha, but hers was preceded by 'Bahar' to her name. Thus, she was called Barakha Bahar, and she became a 'Monsoon Beauty'."

"That's cute. Didn't such names become problematic in getting good jobs?" "No. They were self-employed entertainers of Gujarati literature, history and mythology. They danced, narrated stories and did things that buskers do. The act was full of slapstick and risqué materials. It's called *Bhavai* in Gujarati. They did *diaro* too, which is a form of 'no holds bar' comedy revues. Because of their work, these girls were exposed to adult stuff early in their lives. They were good at what they were doing, and made a decent living at it."

"They were shameless. They seemed to get their thrills in seeing boys embarrassed. They harangued other girls who were eyeing Ayush. The poor girls had to deal with them as well as us. With Rhim and Jhil, you didn't argue. If you said something, you were in deep trouble. Aunt Sona and I were defenceless against the twins. They gave you back more than you dished out."

The girls decided to take a break from reminiscing and explore the island. Dressed in the Caribbean whites and colourful summer tops, they drove twenty minutes to reach the French capital, Marigot. They went to window-shopping and loved the quality of the European merchandise on sale, but disliked their 'European' prices. They sauntered into the upscale store, Manek. Somi and the girls went to the perfumery section and, after spending some time among the fragrances, Somi chose the classic Chanel No.5.

Somi confided, "Your Dad's friend Mrin was very fond of this fragrance."

"Mom, how did *you* know that?" Zara wanted to know, stealing a glance at her sister, knowing full well that she too was thinking about the email they'd read just recently. But Somi pretended not to hear the question, and the girls ignored it, as well.

They walked languidly, peering into little boutiques with their designer and quaint goods. At a street corner, the eclectic rhythm of reggae and blues drew them into a plant filled, open-air bar dressed in the vibrant Caribbean colours. They decided to rest their feet and have drinks. Somi ordered a mango flavoured *pina colada*, and the girls went for the island's home-brewed beer, Carib.

"I wish Dad were here! We could have asked him about his

girlfriends," said Anya provocatively.

"No. I don't want you girls ever to talk to your Dad about his girlfriends. Please don't cross that line. I beg you… in fact, I forbid you." Somi spoke with such force that both girls were surprised.

"Okay. We'll ask you then. We don't know much exclusive stuff about two people we love so dearly. We want to know." Then Zara added to lighten the mood, "I want to know all the juicy parts, in particular, Mom, okay!"

"Shame on you Zara that you want to know about the juicy parts. He's our Dad, for God's sake!"

"Dream on!" Somi smirked at Anya and Zara. They all laughed, and the air of joviality and amiability returned as they drove back to Maho Beach Resort.

The Caribbean evening was crisp, comfortable, something to savour. They changed into elegant evening dresses, after a short rest, afternoon tea and sandwiches. The Resort was a vast complex with a golf club, shopping promenades, a casino, restaurants, Vegas-style shows, on-going dancing and beaches. Evenings at the Maho Beach were memorable as the afternoon heat subsided and the sea breeze cooled the warm sands.

After dinner, Somi, Zara and Anya enjoyed an evening stroll. The air felt good, and they found a lovely bench for the three of them, overlooking the sea. While sitting there, they saw planes land at the Princess Juliana International Airport.

Zara picked up the thread of their earlier discussions, "You know Mom, when we went to school, if you didn't like somebody, you would start gossiping, start mean rumors, and if you really wanted to be nasty, you wrote gross stuff in the rest rooms. Did Aunt Sona and you do the same nastiness?"

"Yeah, we did nearly the same stuff but our culture gave a little edge to it. Back home, kids believed the stuff you said or wrote, and they would tell their parents and other elders about these things. So, you got the needed results sooner."

"Besides, the presence of Aunt Sona's name in the rumor mongering would add weight too," Anya joked. "So, what did Aunt Sona do to dump Avani?"

"Oh girls, why do you want to know all these things? I feel bad enough remembering the things we used to do as children, let alone narrate them to you girls. To be honest, I now have a lot of sympathy for poor Avani for putting her through torture at that early stage in her life. Our main instrument of torture was innuendoes. Then we would raid her circle of friends and deplete its strength. At any competitive shows, when Avani appeared on the stage, we tried to sabotage her performance. We vandalized her posters. I know, I know we were ferocious, ugly and ruthless, but we were immature kids at the time…"

Somi's recollections corroborated what the sisters had read in their Dad's emails. They wondered if somehow, she was also reading his secret emails to Mrin, as the descriptions were near identical. They decided to remain quiet about this for now.

"You shouldn't feel that bad Mom, you guys were not any different than kids in Toronto. Here, we have cat fights where the girls use the foulest language, pull hair, kick butts and spit in their enemy's food. One of the worst things some girls do is to steal or seduce the other girls' men and then dump them as damaged goods. You can't match us!" Zara said, and they all laughed at the supposed innocence of the young.

"I pray you girls didn't do any of this nastiness," said Somi.

"Did grandpa know about Avani and Dad?" Anya wanted to know.

"He learnt about it from overhearing our strategically dropped conversation. We would show up when grandpa was reading something, and we would start talking about Avani, and we would always end our feud with "What does Ayush see in this short, ugly, pock-marked Avani, *yar*?"

"So how long did this Avani saga continue?" Zara asked

"I think Ayu spoke with grandpa about our behaviour, and then he went to her home, saw her parents and apologized to her and the family."

"Did Dad say this to you?" Zara asked.

"You girls are too nosy," retorted Somi with mock sullenness.

"Sorry, Mom, we're curious about the family. You guys appear to have had a lot of fun," said Zara manipulatively.

They were walking down the Maho Resort promenade, window shopping at the European stores, and seeing young and old all swaying to the bubbly Caribbean calypso music that keeps your feet tapping, and heart pumping. The dread-locked Rasta singer's sultry rhythms stirred many dancers, no less the sexily clad youthful women in his audience. His lyrics were rhythmic, alliterative and laced with rich sexual overtones. Once Somi recognized the double entendres and sexually charged body movements of the singer, she lost interest in the music. They returned to their rooms, talked about their next day's trip to the island of Anguila and Somi headed to bed.

Not yet sleepy, Anya changed into pajamas, poured herself a glass of wine, plucked some lilacs and plopped on the wicker sofa on the balcony and meditated on where her own life was going. Inhaling the bouquet of lilac, she recalled her days of bliss as well as later feelings of abandonment, and heartbreak. She found herself wanting a life of spellbound love, much like her father had shared with Mrin, for however short duration. Sighing deeply, she wondered if she would ever find such a love, whether it even existed nowadays. Tears rolled down her cheeks, and her soft sniffles brought Zara out onto the balcony.

"What's going on, sis?" Zara whispered.

"Nothing, Zara, I'm just thinking about life and love... what I wouldn't give to have a quarter of the love that Dad has. Is it too much to ask?"

"I want that too," said Zara.

"But you are married. You have a husband." said Anya.

"That makes it even worse…We'll talk some other time," Zara whispered.

Both drank their Pinot Grigio, sitting there meditatively, and contemplated the choices life had offered each of them. Eventually, Zara said, "Let's go to bed."

"By the way, before we came here, did Shaan call you?"

"Yeah, he did. As a matter of fact, he called Mom and Dad a couple of times. He didn't know I was with you."

"Good."

The next morning following breakfast, they drove to Marigot, parked their car and joined a small queue to board a ferry to Anguila, which boasted of thirty-three fabulous white sandy beaches.

"So, this is a small island, smaller than St. Maarten." Anya explained, "Anguila is only about sixteen miles long. It's shaped like an eel; that's what the word Anguila means, I think. Now tell me, are we going parasailing or not? I'm going, no matter what," she said, determined.

"While you two go parasailing; I'll go horseback riding on the beach," declared Somi.

They spent a couple of hours on the beach, taking pictures, laughing and giggling.

"This is paradise," said Somi stretching and enjoying the sun. "Thank you, girls!"

When the sun was bright and harsh, they found refuge in a shack-like a restaurant right on the beach. There was a shade, a live steel band, revelers, beer, and divine food. *Such beauty, such company, such atmosphere! Life doesn't get better than this,* thought Somi. Anya reminded them that the last ferry left at six for St. Maarten, the

French side of the island.

A silence descended upon the table as they ate their dinner. Then suddenly, Anya began a relentless line of questioning, surprising Somi, "Mom, what do you remember about Aunt Sona's wedding? Did a lot of people attend? Who was there? Did you and Avani and Mrin and all of Dad's rejected girlfriends behave and get along? How much did grandpa, and grandma enjoy the wedding even though they were busy looking after details and attending to people? Did our Dad have lots of fun with the Bombay beauties? Did you ask our Nani and Nana to have a similar wedding or better when your time came?"

"My dear, so many questions! Where is all this coming from today?" Somi asked, curious. The sisters looked at her shrugged, eager to know the answers and so Somi gave in. She explained her parents were different people, in principles and values. They didn't believe in the dowry system, nor did they believe in extravagant and ostentatious ceremonies. They believed in modest living and high thinking. Life for them was a straight and narrow path without complications and strife. "My wedding was a simple one, strictly for close family members. Ayu was happy with that arrangement."

She turned to her oldest and said, "So, do you have any more questions, Anya?

Anya reddened at the jab, and so laughing Somi continued to tell them about her sister-in-law's wedding, "Sona's wedding, perhaps a few hundred people attended right from the Matunga complex. Then Grandpa's large number of friends, clients and well-wishers were present too. Everyone dined in the complex hall where we had three days and nights of fun.

The first night we had *mehndi*. Every female was dressed in traditional, colourful and beautifully designed *Chania choli* dresses. Men wore *lehngas* and *jubbahs*. It was like a Diwali celebration in June. The *Mehndi* or henna is the essence of love and romance in weddings. Brides get the most elaborate designs on both hands and feet. Brides' friends and family members also get henna designs on their hands. We served delicious snacks like *bhel, kachoris, dhokla* followed by *raas Garba* dance."

"That must have been so much fun. I love the Garba," burst in Zara.

"Anya, remember that Diwali where we bumped into each other because our skirts were swirling, and we forgot to go in reverse order…" said Zara.

"We bumped into each other because we had no practice. Our eyes, hands and feet were not coordinated." With that, they all laughed at their own clumsy weaknesses as well as enthusiasm.

"Despite the lack of practice, you girls were once very good at these dances, you know. All four of you girls should go to India to attend the festival of *Dusshera* that lasts for ten days, enjoy these dances and…" Somi said with a wink, "hook-up with great-looking guys. I'll go with you!"

"Ma, what happened to your admonition that *'looks are here today and gone tomorrow, but the character is forever?'*" Zara asked.

"Forget it, Mom. We can go to New Jersey, Chicago or even Toronto for *Dusshera* festivals if we want to. You are not arranging any of our marriages," said Anya playfully. "Let's go on with your recollections, please."

"Then we had the *sangeet* party, in which both the bride and grooms' families celebrate by singing, and dancing with horse play composed into the lyrics of the songs we sang late into the evening. For example, at Sona's wedding, the women of the groom's family in innocent fun, teased our family members by making fun of their appearance, clothes, or some personality trait, and we countered with similar repartee. We all had a fabulous time. The music and dancing were followed by dinner that included fried *puris,* two vegetables, lentils, *Pulav, kachoris,* various chutneys and mango smoothie, all of it so delicious that I can still remember the tastes and smells!"

"Zara, do you remember the *Grih Pooja* performed the day before your wedding? Well, with this prayer, we offer thanks to the family deities for blessing us with the occasion, as well as for seeking protection for the family from bad luck, misfortune and the evil eye."

"Then off course, on the morning of the wedding day, we had *Haldi*…"

"What's that and what's it used for?" Anya asked.

"My dear Anya, *Haldi* is turmeric, the yellow powder used in all our Indian cooking as well as the skin-cleansing ceremony during weddings. All our female friends and family members placed turmeric paste on Sona's face, hands and feet as the music played on. Turmeric paste mixed with rose water is the most effective skin cleanser there is. After a while, Aunt Sona bathed in milk to exfoliate her skin to remove any blemishes. Once the bathing was complete, her skin was glowing."

"So…were the other girls like Avani and those twins invited? Or the perfume woman?"

"Anya, no, Avani wasn't there. Rhim and Jhil were there with their self-assured delusion about their nuptials to your Dad. You wondered sometimes on which planet these two lived!" Somi laughed, "And of course, the perfume woman and her parents were there. They really had a great time…"

"Who is this perfume woman, Mom?" Zara interrupted her heart beating fast as all the dots were slowly being connected.

"You are not really listening, are you? She is the one who liked the Chanel No.5 perfume. Mrin, she is the perfume woman. Your Dad used to fawn all over her like you wouldn't believe! A lot of girls wanted to speak to your Dad, find any excuse to touch his hand or shoulder, but he had eyes only for her."

"The perfume woman, I like that description," Zara smiled romantically.

"Mom, you didn't like Mrin much, did you? As you say, Dad only had eyes for her…"

"Girls, to be honest, I didn't like her that much until the wedding festivities. She spoke to Sona and me very sweetly and politely, as if we had never offended her. She helped Sona and me to dress in colour-coordinated *Ghaghara choli* with tastefully matched jewellery and stylish hairdos. I remember, that evening, she said, 'You know, you two are very pretty young ladies, like actresses.' And that was it, her tone was pure and it was evident she carried no malice in her heart. It was as though she barely remembered how mean we had been to her initially."

"This is really great of you, Mom, to be able to confess like this. It takes an enormous amount of character and maturity," said Zara.

"Well, my dear, so many years have passed this sense, one is able to view the experience objectively. Even then, I felt sad that Sona was so was mean to her, but Mrin gave me her address and asked me to visit her. As a matter of fact, we even went to some movies together in a theatre not too far from her home in Worli, which was quite impressive. It was huge, beautifully decorated with Rajasthani, Gujarati and Madrasi art and artefacts. They also had beautiful *Sankheda* furniture that looked classy and royal. Eventually, we became such good friends that she even wrote me letters from America when she moved for work. I knew my friendship with Mrin was going to blossom despite Ayu."

"Mom, did you ever meet her parents at the wedding celebrations?" Zara asked.

"Yes, I did. Mrin, her dad, grandpa and I had a little chat at Sona's reception."

"What did you talk about?" Anya asked innocently.

"Grandpa talked about the stars, alignments of planets and horoscopes. My mind was somewhere else at that wedding, and I could tell that Mrin's mind was on *your* Dad because of the whimsical and lost look she had on her face. Besides, the music was too loud to hear anything."

"And Mom, did you answer Mrin when she wrote to you from America?" Zara asked.

"Yes, I did. We exchanged letters once in a while and more so after she went to teach in South Carolina."

"Did she not ask you to say hi to Dad?"

"Yes, she did, always. I think I even passed on the messages to your Dad," said Somi looking at the ground, fumbling with the ends of her shirt. "I don't know exactly what occurred between them, but it seemed as they'd had a falling out over something."

"Did they have a fight? Why did you think that?"

Somi was at a loss for words for a while, and then she finally spoke again, "Since your Dad didn't write I thought they perhaps had some kind of disagreement. That's all."

"Well, Mom, I'm sure it must have made Dad very happy to know that you and the perfume woman exchanged letters with each other," said Anya.

"I hope he's never forgotten that…," said Zara and before she could finish, Somi cut in.

"I forbid you to ask your Dad anything about the perfume woman. There is no need, whatsoever to let him know, or remind him that she and I wrote letters. It's a private matter. Case closed!"

Somi's tone was so firm that Anya and Zara were startled by its sudden vehemence laced with angry authority.

"Why are you so upset, Mom? We don't care about anybody other than our family; you know that, don't you? We're just a little curious because Dad has always been overly reserved, and it's fascinating to discover all these juicy tidbits about his youth. So come on, Mom, spill the beans. What kind of stuff did you two write about? Girl stuff? Or Dad?" Anya cajoled adroitly.

Somi's looked around anxiously, evidently flustered with her outburst and then returning to her normal tone, she divulged the very facts that her daughters had craved to unearth. Somi now spoke more honestly than she had in the entire trip, "Well, I was curious about America. Also, I was kind of envious that we were the same age, but she had a better education than I'd had. Not to mention the man I loved and adored, loved *her*...." She stopped in the mid sentence, as if a weight had been caught in her throat. Seconds later she recovered and continued, "... she lived and worked as a single woman in a land endowed with riches and individual freedoms. You could see that I was kind of awed and jealous of her. However, despite my jealousy and envy, I have a lot of respect for her for the way she treated me with dignity and kindness."

Somi sighed sadly, careful not to meet her daughter's gaze.

"But Mom, *you* got Dad. She didn't. Dad chose *you*." Zara said.

"That's true, but your Dad didn't jump at the first chance he got to marry me. As a matter of fact, he ignored me for a long time. You know his aloofness, his distance and detachment. It really hurt me then, and even more now." Somi's softened tone surprised even her.

"Yeah, you were jealous. So what? It's natural. No big deal, Mom. It happens. But you didn't hurt her, did you? You said so yourself, you were friends." Anya asked.

"Look, girls. I really don't feel like talking anymore," Somi said quietly.

They understood and probed no further. "No problem, Mom." Said Zara, "How about some more horseback riding?"

"No, you girls go parasailing. I'll stay here and keep an eye on you and our stuff."

She watched her two girls, but her mind had traveled back in time and she re-lived the scenes she had just described. *Her life had at no time been perfect; events rarely happened according to her choosing or planning. In those critical years, at an impressionable age as a young adolescent, she had to keep her emotions, dreams and even fantasies in check. She never had the luxury of love and attention from the one she so much admired, fantasized and loved so intensely. Unfortunately, she received commiseration and glances of pity from others who knew of her secret love. That hurt even more. She didn't want anyone's sympathy or pity; all she wanted was the passionate love from the man she loved dearly. She would have been happy with some kind of recognition, some gesture that showed he noticed her, that he liked her. That would have made her heart flutter.*

She knew this exclusion had always gnawed at her, and she felt inferior, lacking the qualities her idol didn't find sufficient for him. She wanted to know what she could do to win the affection and attention from Ayu even after all these years that they had been together. She almost wanted a mad, licentious and torrid kind of love, but all she had received had been a perfunctory, almost clinical, medicinal dose of such love. How often she looked at mirrors wondering what glamour, what enchantment her face lacked that Ayush didn't stare at her, didn't rush to kiss her, didn't hold her face in his hands and say something rapturous, lifting her spirits so high that her heart would palpitate so hard that it would want to burst! Often, she had asked Ayu how she could be closer to him, but his reluctant answer accompanied by clucks had always been, "We're close. I love you. I am married to you." However, she wanted more closeness, the closeness of John Donne's "two bodies, one soul," one that she knew Mrin had celebrated with him most repeatedly, and without her asking.*

"What are you daydreaming about, Mom?" Anya asked, waking her up from the reverie of questions and longing. They had returned from their parasailing. With a dismissive hand, she gestured that it was nothing and wiped her eyes with a Kleenex.

They seemed to have had enough excitement for the day, so they decided to return around four, and were back at Marigot dock a little before six. They walked down the pier, listened to the Parisian and patois French of the Europeans and the locals, and then drove to the Maho Beach Resort. At their condo, they bathed, freshened up, looked out at the undulating ocean and felt good. Both the sisters held each of their mother's hands unconsciously and lightly swung them. The girls had decided that they were not going to broach the topic of their mother's jealousy towards the perfume woman, at least for a while.

They went back to their well-trodden path of the Maho promenade and the sea. Their walk was interspersed with the memories of Somi's parents, their influence on her and Bollywood movies. They talked about the high quality of education in Bombay generally, but Bombay University, in particular.

"Mom, where did you and Dad go to have fun in Bombay?" Anya asked

"Oh, we didn't go anywhere special, really. I can't say there was one place that was ours that we frequented. We went on social outings to visit someone, meet someone, buy something, and or escort someone who had something to do. Our meetings before our marriage were more mundane chores, and not of our choosing," said Somi. Her voice revealed a bit of regret and disappointment that she had missed out on the fun part of dating. Anya and Zara both were sad to discover that.

"Mom, did you ever go to Dad's bank in Bombay?" Zara asked.

"No. I didn't go there, nor did he take me there because there was no need to do so... He had worked there long before we were married. Often your grandpa used to have visitors from the Reserve Bank of India, who would bring salary checks or some mail for your Dad when he was visiting New Delhi on business."

"What kind of mail would Dad get from the bank?"

"Oh, all kinds. For example, once Mrin was told not to visit the Vyas household, she would leave letters for Dad at the bank, which the bank would duly send to your grandpa."

"Then the grandpa would give Mrin's mail to Dad, right?"

"Are you kidding, Anya? Grandpa didn't give any mail to Dad. Since he didn't know that something had come for him in the first place, he didn't miss anything," explained Somi.

"Wouldn't Mrin ask Dad whenever she saw him about the missing letters?"

"I don't know if she asked or not. I'm sure she must have. But what could your Dad say? He never got them, and he is not the kind of man who gets angry and seeks answers to his questions."

"Obviously the fact that someone wrote those letters, and expected, and deserved to receive replies from the recipient didn't bother Grandpa," remarked Anya.

"That was awfully mean of grandpa!" Zara said.

"Well, grandpa thought he was protecting his son from something evil."

"He thought that Mrin was evil?" Zara asked incredulously.

"Not that she was evil, but that she could bring evil onto your Dad. I can't explain the difference, but that's what he believed," said Somi.

"Do you believe in people bringing evil on others?" Zara asked their mother.

"Yes, I do. I have seen many examples of that happening," reiterated Somi.

"Since grandpa didn't give Mrin's letters that came from the bank to Dad, I think he also didn't give Dad the letters that she wrote from the US, right?"

"I think you're correct, Zara," responded Somi.

"I remember, once when Ayu was in Bombay working at the bank, but perhaps he was not at his desk, Mrin even went to see him. Your Dad's co-worker told her that he was out for the day. At his insistence, she left a note for him, but the note was duly sent to grandpa instead."

"Mom, I'm confident you would, at no time, do anything like this to anybody. Did you ever read Mrin's letters from the US that grandpa kept?

"No, I never did, though I was so very tempted, Zara. Once I thought I would open one letter, read it, and write a reply and mail it to your Dad as my own letter." She remembered that she had so much wanted to write love letters to him. Now she was sad that she had never followed her desire. Somi's sighs were filled with past regrets.

Anya looked at the ground and slowly said, "There's no need to talk about this to Dad; nor do we want Dad to know that Mrin wrote letters to you in Matunga from South Carolina, right Mom?"

Somi liked this vote of conspiratorial confidence.

"What did Dad do to those people working at the bank that they would lie, steal his mail and pass it on to grandpa? How did grandpa have such power over them?" Zara wanted to know.

"Some Kapadia guy from the bank was grandpa's client. So, this Kapadia took it upon himself to safeguard grandpa's assets," said Somi.

"Wow! Grandpa had a long reach!

"Mom, grandpa was your mentor, and you audited some of his clients. Was he any good?"

Somi coughed, took a sip from her water bottle and continued, "Yes; he was a fabulous astrologer and palmist, Zara. He used to have clients starting at seven-thirty in the morning. After bathing and morning chores, I would sit with grandpa for learning. Once, a man came to seek his counsel. Grandpa introduced me, and asked him if it was okay for me to audit as I was learning the trade."

"So, what was the man's problem?"

"The visitor confided that some astrologer he had met had told him of his imminent demise and asked him to look after his financial and other family matters urgently. Obviously, the visitor was very upset."

"Grandpa closed his eyes and was rapt in his meditative silence. The man was worried, but I hushed him and whispered 'just wait'. A few more seconds elapsed, and then the calmer grandpa said, 'Kalyanji, I want you to come back on Thursday exactly at seven thirty-five, not a minute sooner or later.'

Grandma brought tea and a light snack for the man and tea for me and grandpa. They talked about his business and how well he was doing, again thanks to grandpa's advice.

On the Thursday morning at the appointed time, the man arrived. He was made to wait a few seconds at the front entrance. As soon as grandpa said, 'Come, Kalyanji,' the man entered, Grandma brought tea and snacks for him.

Grandpa said, 'Kalyanji, yesterday I made your astrological chart and studied it carefully. No matter what I tell you, I just cannot take away your fear of death planted in your mind. So, listen carefully. He gives you six months to settle your affairs. I give you at least another twelve years and perhaps more. However, I cannot destroy your doubts and fear; what I can save you from are the foolish decisions you are about to make.

'First, your major concern is your daughter's future. After you consult with her and your wife, look for an appropriate match. Then perform the official engagement ceremony with pomp and style. Inform the groom and his family of the supposed impending tragedy. Request them that if your fear comes to pass, it is your strong desire that the marriage should proceed as planned.

'Secondly, you have a successful business. Don't sell it off at a give-away price the way you're planning to do right now. Put the word out that you are looking for a good manager to run your business for now, and that should you pass away before a certain date, you would sell your business to him at the predetermined price. If you outlive the supposed tragedy, you will offer him a minority partnership of your choosing.

'In this way, you will have a guaranteed sale of your business and the engagement of your daughter.

'Thirdly, take a short-term life insurance of the amount you can afford so that your family is fully protected.

'In this way, you will have sufficient insurance to protect your family, and you will have adequate leeway to continue your life, should you be as lucky as I am saying you're going to be!'"

"So what happened to the man?"

"Anya, seven months later, the man arrived early in the morning with a truck load of gifts for grandpa and his family. However, this time, he brought his wife and daughter with him as well, to thank him for his wise counsel. The man kept returning to him as often as he could with gratitude. He even gave gifts to you girls too, on one of your Bombay visits.

"Yes, grandpa was a fabulous Brahmin. No doubts about his abilities," concluded Somi.

"Mom, how good did you become in astrology and palmistry? Maybe you can read my palm…" said Anya.

"No, I can't read your palm as you're my fam…," she stopped in mid sentence as she realized that grandpa had read and interpreted Ayu as well as Sona's horoscopes. The girls felt something was amiss so silenced themselves, amidst their mother's apparent conflict as they sensed it was bound to come up again when they discussed palmistry and astrology.

"But Anya, I had been looking at the horoscope that your grandpa had made for you soon after your birth. To my understanding, this is the year of your wedding bells," said Somi.

"Why do you think so?"

"Because Venus aligns with Mars, and the Moon is in the seventh house for you."

Both sisters raised their eyebrows in confusion, so Somi explained, "The Moon in the seventh house indicates the passion and love. All the planets seem to be in the converging orbit. So, get ready to be surprised."

"Thanks," said Anya, smiling.

"Is anyone missing Indian food, by any chance?" Somi asked to break the silence, waiting to hear agreement from both the girls.

Anya suggested, "Well, I know a fabulous *Dhaba* style Indian restaurant called Anand here in town. It's owned by man called Ram Kishanji, has excellent food, good service and a home atmosphere. It has no pretensions of any kind, but it's conscious of its quality. He is a straight-forward gentleman from Haryana who has been helpful to newly arrived Indians living on the island. I cannot comment on the other places."

"Anya you're like a walking encyclopaedia of the island and the region. Are you sure you've been here only a couple of times?"

"Oh, shut up Zara," said Anya affectionately teasing.

"Well, what do you say …shall we go there tomorrow evening? We can spend some time window shopping on the Front Street of Phillipsburg; enjoy the music at the Wathey Square where the cruise travelers' shop, and then we go to Anand?"

Somi agreed, "That's the plan, then."

They went to *Le Jardin*, in the Nettle Bay, Sandy Ground area to enjoy the Creole cuisine that evening. They thought it was one of the prettiest restaurants with its lush, beautiful garden and a log fire inside.

"So, what are we doing tomorrow, Captain?" Somi inquired.

"Tomorrow from Phillipsburg, we will catch a catamaran to visit St. Barts in the morning. We should have a light breakfast, so we don't throw up in the rough sea. Did you know that St Barts is an entirely French Island? We plan to be back in Phillipsburg by four, window shop, and catch the music and then, dinner," suggested Anya.

"What do you mean by entirely French Island?" Somi asked inquisitively.

"Well, most islands have activities and choices that are American as well as those that are not, but on this island, there are no casinos. You can't gamble. So no American or any other mafia or vice industry is present on this island. Secondly, Americans love to golf, but there are no golf clubs here, only tennis clubs. Thirdly, unlike in America, this French island has clothing optional beaches. Is it one hundred percent French? You bet it is," said Anya.

They had a pleasant sail on the catamaran, which, although not full, carried convivial guests just like them who came from France, the Netherlands, Columbia, Mexico and Canada. Many were returning visitors who had not had enough of St.Barts. Anya asked a woman in her late twenties, "What are must-do and must-see on St. Barts?"

The young woman said, "You should go to a beautiful art gallery *'Galerie Asie'* that has excellent art and religious pieces from Asia, especially from Tibet. The gallery has Tibetan ritual artifacts, old sculptures and some Japanese tansus."

Anya complimented the young woman, "That's an excellent suggestion. You're our type of tourist. Any other recommendations?"

The young woman continued, "There is a unique museum "The Inter Oceans Museum" which houses enormous numbers of seashells collected from all over the world. It's just a short cab ride to Corossol. Gustavia, the capital of the island, has an impressive collection of boutique stores and merchandise, the best France could offer, so go crazy. If you see celebrities, it's uncool here to pester them for autographs. And yeah, a bar, as soon as you are there, you just can't miss this place with charm, gargantuan outside patio with shade parasols and reasonable prices for beer. And the food is great too!"

Anya knew that they would enjoy all the suggestions the young woman had made to her.

When they reached Gustavia, Somi immediately walked along the beach, ran to the ocean, scooped it up in her palms. Then to the world she announced, "and just like a river, I run to my ocean." Anya and Zara both clicked their camera shutters simultaneously and looked at each other fully convinced that their Mom was reading their father and Mrin's exchanges.

Zara quietly said to Anya, "Three strikes, and you're out!"

"Mom, that's a beautiful expression. Is there a latent poet in you that wants to come out?"

Somi blushed and said, "Oh, it's from a poem a friend of mine wrote a long time ago."

"Do you know Mom, why rivers run to oceans?"

"Zara, I have no idea. You tell me, sweetheart!"

'The oceans asked rivers, 'why do you all rush like you're insanely in love?' The rivers said, 'We rush crazily because we want to make you as sweet as we are,' Isn't that cute?"

"Wonderful, I must remember this," said Somi.

They enjoyed their day trip to St. Barts and brought with them souvenirs from the sea, small paintings by the local artists and some jewellery pieces made by the island craftspeople for Bijli and Anoushka. In the evening, they returned to their resort. They had a good but tiring day. They had a great time in Phillipsburg and saw the last tender carrying cruisers to their massive ships. As they were approaching the Front Street, someone yelled out Anya's name, and the three of them turned around to see an Indian man walk towards them with a smiling greeting. He hugged Anya first, and then shook hands with the other two women. Anya did the introductions. The gentleman was Akhil, who owned a colour business called Antillean Gems right on the Wathey Square.

"Lavanya, you haven't visited us this year at all. We miss seeing you. By the way, I have good news to share with you. We've another daughter, and guess what, we decided to call her Lovenya!"

"That's very cute, even more beautiful than mine!" said Anya, touched by the gesture.

They talked for a while; Akhil invited them for drinks and took them to his store. Akhil and Anya talked briefly in private. Inside, Zara and Somi looked cursorily at the jewellery in the display cases. Anya liked a beautiful bracelet of tantalizing Tanzanite stones.

Akhil got it out and said, "Take this with you, enjoy wearing it, and when you return to the island next year just bring it back and forget about everything else."

Somi couldn't believe that there were people like Akhil around. However, he corrected, "No, there are not too many people like Anya.

I want her to meet a friend of mine in Boston, but she won't listen to me. At least go, see, and talk with the guy," he said insistently.

"Tell you what, Aki, I'll certainly think seriously about it. I'll call you in the next couple of weeks for sure. You talk to your pal as well and see if it's okay with him."

With that and the beautiful bracelet, Anya, Zara and Somi left Akhil's store.

Zara said, "Sis, this is amazing! That someone could trust you like this! Especially since he's known you only as a visitor to the island. You know a lot of people here."

"Yes, I do. There's another gentleman here who is like a father to me. They all call him Harry, but I call him Hargovind Uncle. He owns a store in the Amsterdam House over there," she said pointing to her right. "Hargovind Uncle's store sells the finest table cloths. I walked by his store earlier, but he wasn't there."

They walked to Anand Dhaba, and as soon as Ram Kishan saw Anya enter, he came forward with an effusive welcome and said, "Anya, Anya, I haven't seen you for a whole year. Come in, my dear, how is everything?"

He made them comfortable, insisted that they have wine or beer of their choice. When they found out that the restaurant was open until ten, they asked Ram Kishan if they could go to their resort, freshen up and return in a while.

He replied, "There are no set hours for you at my restaurant. You come here in the middle of the night, and we'll open to serve you. Have no worry. Go to Maho, get rested, change and please, arrive. I'll wait for you."

Zara and Somi were impressed by the service that they were getting because of Anya.

When they returned, as usual, the restaurant was full of local clientele, mostly local Sindhi business owners and families, their staff and visitors of Indian origin who had come to the island. Anya explained that the island was a major draw for Indian families who sent their kids to study medicine on nearby islands. St. Maarten is the leading international hub and an island providing a variety of Indian groceries. They enjoyed extra crispy stuffed *parathas*, spinach and cheese, vegetables, *kadhhi* and yogurt. They had wanted simple but delicious food, but this was cooked with extra servings of care and love.

Somi, scooping up spinach and cheese with a bite-size piece of paratha, remarked, "Anya, tell me what have you done for some of these people who are bending backwards to welcome you!"

"Mom, you both have taught us that if you do a good deed, never talk about it," replied Anya.

"Anya, what we meant is that you should not gloat repeatedly about a good deed to draw attention to yourself seeking recognition and praise. Anyway, I'm curious. You're telling me because I'm asking you. That's allowed."

"Well, I brought a team of lawyers here a little over a year ago to work on complicated, property transactions, spread over more than half a dozen countries. One of them was Holland. I decided instead of going to Holland, to come to St. Maarten, a Dutch island with Dutch attorneys, working here to accomplish the tasks. My superiors thought it was a superb idea. So I was in Phillipsburg, shopping, and ran into Akhil while visiting his store. In a casual conversation when asked, he said that he wasn't looking forward to doing business here because of the inconsiderate and market-blind landlords. When I pressed, he said his landlord was giving him a very short-term lease. He wondered how any businesses could improve their stores if they didn't know their future with the landlord who demanded unpredictable rents.

I asked him the identity of his landlord. I was pleased, as his property was going to be in our deal that I was working on. I asked him about the kind of lease he would like to have, and the rent that would be acceptable to him. To my surprise, Akhil was more than a reasonable businessman. I didn't tell him anything at that time about what I did.

I went back to Oyster Pond at Philip Izzard's villa overlooking Captain Oliver's Marina where we were staying for about ten days. I drafted a memo and faxed it to the manager of the property, requesting her assistance for a few of our 'reputable assets who rented our properties in other prestigious locales. I asked her to send her proposals to me for an approval. Before the day was over, she had sent me her proposal that included thirty-year lease, with capped rents with inflationary adjustments every fifth year.

In the evening, when I went to Wathey Square with my friends for a drink, I saw Akhil. I asked him if he would like to see the new deal. He couldn't believe his eyes and his luck that was the result of an accidental meeting and a chance conversation. I did a similar deal for Uncle Harry too. And, well, that's that!"

"That was God's work that you did. I'm proud of your good work," said Zara.

"You must have saved them a lot of money," said Somi, impressed.

They finished their meal and just as they were about to leave, Ram Kishan, the owner, walked up and said, "Please, come again and bring your friends with you."

Zara understood what the reminder meant for Anya.

Chapter Twelve

Matrimonial Interviews and Rebellion

After dinner, they drove back to the Maho, opened another bottle of Pinot Grigio, changed into pajamas, and got comfortable on wicker sofas and the love seat. It was a pleasurable day; especially as it had given them a chance to bond and enjoy some old friends Anya had made. Somi felt happy that she could share experiences of their Dad's life and his family with her daughters. In fact, she was elated too, that the ambiance of the Caribbean had provided a great backdrop to peek into her past, which was not separate from Ayu's, except for the affairs of his heart and his longing. Part of her was also relieved that feelings that had remained unspoken and unexplored for years, had finally spilled out, and it left her feeling lighter.

"Mom, did grandpa ever place a matrimonial ad for our Dad?" Anya wanted to know.

"No, he didn't, but Mrin's parents did."

Anya thought if well-educated families couldn't find suitable matches for their sons or daughters in their own community, it would be natural for them to seek proposals from outside. She had learned from her other Indian friends in Canada, and the USA that this was how some families found proper matrimonial matches from suitable families with education, higher reach and wealth when their kids didn't find appropriate matches.

Somi said, "I had become a close friend of Mrin's after Sona's wedding. We grew even closer after Ayu and Mrin's parents had some argument, and he was told not to show up at their home. She told me her parents were hell-bent on doing whatever they could do to keep her mind off your Dad. One of the things they did was exactly what Anya talked about. They placed a matrimonial ad in Times of India, Jan Shakti, and the Mumbai Samachar that they were looking for a suitable groom for their daughter, in her early twenties, who was a college professor."

"Was Mrin angry and disgusted? I know I'd be!" exclaimed the ever-feisty Zara.

"Oh, yes, Zara, she was. However, you don't know Mrin. She's like your Dad, they both were like two peas in a pod in this; she also knew how to keep her cool, but make no mistake that her mind was busy and dealing with the situation"

"Did they get a good response to their ads?"

"They did, Anya. Mrin's parents prepared the list of the candidates for Mrin and gave it to her. They were happy that some eligible prospects had shown up for this proposal. They couldn't hide their excitement, although they wanted that to be her choice, her interview, and her selection process."

"Then what happened?"

"Mrin said to her mother, 'You've already gone through all the trouble anyway, and now you have a list. Why don't *you* just interview them too?' Her mother was angry that her daughter wasn't being cooperative. She asked Mrin, 'Tell me how you want to continue with the selection.' Mrin said, 'I'll interview them in a restaurant or a park or some public place where I am not alone with them. I may even ask one of my friends to help me select the best candidate.'"

"So, she was ready to accept one of the prospects," said Zara.

"No. That was just a ploy. She told me that all she was doing was selecting the best prospect. That didn't mean she was going to marry him. However, she yielded a bit. It was that simple for her."

"So, Mom, did she tell you about her interviews of any of the prospects?"

"Mrin, Megh, Simi and I had a lot fun talking about these interviews...."

"Who are Megh and Simi? You never talked about them before...," Anya asked, though she remembered both the names from their Dad's emails.

Somi told them Megh and Simi both came from extremely rich families. Megh's family was Mumbai's leading brokerage trading house and Simi's family was in the pharmaceutical business with subsidiaries in Africa, Asia and South America. The two girls were Mrin's classmates and also knew Ayush well. They were close to her, true confidantes.

Anya and Zara were intrigued that their mother had rarely mentioned these names. Since Simi and Megh were Mrin's friends, their curiosity was further piqued. The sisters learned that after their father left for Trinidad, the four girls- their mother included- had all become strong friends.

"Okay, Mom, so tell us about these interviews," said Zara.

"Well, she showed me the matrimonial responses; it was obvious some were written by other family members. But remember, don't tell your Dad about it. He didn't know even then that I knew about these things."

She picked up her glass of wine, had a sip, and then she continued. "She conducted the first interview at the Gateway of India, right across from the Taj Hotel. She said his name was Anand...."

And so began the first interview,

"Anand, it's so nice to meet with you. Please tell me about you, first."

"Shouldn't I be asking you questions?" a perplexed Anand asked.

"No, not at all, you don't ask me questions first. We placed the ad; you responded. It's just like an employment interview. You don't ask your boss questions first, do you? I'll give you some time at the end. If that's not acceptable, you may leave now."

Anand didn't walk out. Mrin asked him about his age, education, family, what each person did, their home, his income, how much he had saved, and his prospects for advancement. The guy was sweating as no woman had ever grilled him with such sharp and pointed personal questions. Even so, despite his new doubts and fears, the young man persisted with the interview. She was too beautiful for him to give up on her; he had his own fantasies.

Somi confided that he was not healthy looking; he was short, stubby and poorly dressed. By far the worst candidate.

"Anand, let's talk about your knowledge," she continued.

Anand gave all the answers on his undergrad, post-grad and professional training. He went on and on to impress Mrin. In his heart, he was certain he was going to bag this woman.

Out of the blue Mrin asked, "I'm sure you've detailed information on carnal knowledge?" and she looked directly into his eyes to gauge to what extent he would bluff his way through.

"Yes, I do. I've taken a couple of classes at the final year level in Economics. My friends think I'm pretty good at it and so does my boss, who happens to be a woman, Miss Mhatre," he said. There was an aura of confidence and pride in his demeanour now.

"That's really good to know. So, tell me Anand, if I choose to marry you, where would we live? Do you have a home that would allow us privacy, as well as comfort?"

"We would live with my family, jointly. It's a joint family," said Anand, fumbling in his answer.

"I'm sure we'll have a room all to ourselves for privacy that we'll need for our carnality," inquired Mrin.

"What is carnality?" He wanted to know. He knew his bluff was called and began to perspire profusely.

"Well, once we're married; we would indulge in intimate pleasures… Right?"

He smiled shyly and muttered, "Yes."

"That's what carnality is. I thought you knew and your boss Miss Mhatre knew too."

The guy was profusely sweating at the words 'intimate pleasure', and he was now a total wreck. He fumbled for words, "No; we won't have a room all to ourselves. We'll have to make some arrangements."

He ventured, "If your parents don't mind, we could live with them. I don't mind being a live-in son-in-law."

Mrin knew now the truth was out. The life in Bombay is tough where it's easy making money, but difficult to find a permanent house that's not in the rundown buildings.

"So, Anand, your idea of getting married is to get a wife, who can provide intimate pleasure, bring home a good income, give you status and keep meals ready when you arrive, or provide for your friends, or your family, or even cousins from your village. You're not looking for a life partner, Anand. You're really looking for an 'excellent deal', or as we say in Bombay, a 'good offer'. Is that it?" Mrin asked him.

Somi laughed, remembering all the little details.

"Mom, Mrin's so smart and aggressive and speaks her mind. I don't know how Dad would have dealt with her," said Anya.

"That's immaterial now. However, your Dad was different. She loved him. With him on her side, she would have lived in a minuscule area and called herself the queen of that dominion."

Anya and Zara were impressed that in a singular unguarded moment, their mother revealed her honest opinion of Mrin.

"Then Mrin said, "Anand, when you came, you wanted to ask me questions. Now, I'll give you five minutes to ask me anything your heart desires. Ask away!"

"Madam, no questions at all. If you don't mind, may I leave?"

Somi laughed again, To which, she replied, "It was a pleasure to meet with you. You taught me a thing or two. God speed!"

Before she could finish it, Anand had sprung out of the starting gate to save his skin. That evening Anand's dad called her dad and said angrily, "Sir, we didn't send our well-educated son your daughter to insult him. There is nothing wrong with being a live-in son-in-law. My son offered to be one so your daughter doesn't have to leave you. That was his motivation for which your professor daughter insulted my son and my family. What do you think of yourself? Your daughter thinks that interviewing for one's marriage is like testing people on their vocabulary. Come down from the heights if you want your daughter married off!"

Mrin said the offended father wanted to go on and on, but her dad disconnected the phone.

"That's really funny. How many interviews did Mrin conduct that you remember them so vividly?"

"She talked to ten prospects. Not all were well educated even though the ad had asked for a good education. Even so, their heart wasn't in the right place. Mrin could read their minds without even talking to them. She was that good. Do you want to hear more?"

"Yes, please mom, go ahead. We've the whole night in front of us. We've a few more bottles of Pinot Grigio. Let me open another bottle, Anya," said Zara.

"A day later Mrin interviewed another guy at the Oberoi Hotel at Nariman Point. The guy was dressed nattily, and perhaps thought he was heading to be a model or a Bollywood actor. He walked up to her with a cigarette dangling from his lips, shook her hand and sat down telling her to take a seat as well."

"Please, would you take the cigarette out of your mouth, and extinguish it. I honestly don't like cigarette smoke," said Mrin firmly and politely.

The guy was stunned that his Elvis Presley hairdo and style were failures.

Mrin said, "I'm sorry I didn't get your name. However, I like the Elvis hair. You must be spending much of your time on hair. I sometimes have a bad hair day. Do you too?"

"I'm Kiran. Yes, I do spend a lot of time and money on my hair. There's no point in living if you can't live in style!"

"Oh, Kiran I love your philosophy that fabulous hair's a sign of a good life. That's quite deep thinking. Which school of philosophy did you subscribe to for the higher consciousness?"

"I do a lot of reading of novels and, of course, we buy old issues of Playboy magazines from the roadside sellers in Flora Fountain for serious articles. Have you read any of those articles?"

"No, I've not reached that level of consciousness yet. If you say that there're serious articles in it, I'll take your word for it."

Mrin asked him the same questions about his age, education, family and so on.

He attended a college in Ahmedabad, but quit the college as he found it boring. He thought his teachers were pedantic and were always talking about education, excellence and examinations. He thought they didn't know how to have fun. Nevertheless, everyone, including the professors liked his Elvis hair.

On the strength of his hair, he wanted to be an actor. He spent time hanging around studios so directors, actors or producers might see him and change his life. He was the eldest among four siblings; his father ran a small shop, selling household stuff. As far as savings were concerned, he hadn't banked anything yet. He felt that he was too young to save and in his line of work, his time to save would come later. His major expense was the care of his hair. He had come to Bombay a year ago and was living with someone from his village.

"So, Kiran, where do you sleep at night?"

"We sleep on the terrace of the building with other men. It's nice and cool and lots of fun."

"Well, Kiran. I honestly don't know what to tell you. I don't know if I should be sarcastic, or not. Without much education, you have the nerve to aspire to marry a college professor whose ilk you think is pedantic and who only talks about excellence."

"But you're as beautiful as I am. We'll look great walking together. The world will be jealous of us, believe me."

"Kiran, go. This interview's over," said Mrin.

She now realized why a lot of Indian families preferred to check prospective families out; where and how they lived, and what others had to say about them.

"And of course, to match their horoscopes too," added Somi, and continued that such halfwits existed here in Canada too.

"Do you still want to hear more about the interviews?"

"Yes, mom, these stories reveal something about Bombay, its men and their reasons for getting married. It could bring respectable housing, progressive jobs, decent money, and better connections with the larger world or even get other siblings married. Please, go on," said Zara.

"After a lapse of a couple of days, she interviewed another one at the Jehangir Art Gallery at Kala Ghoda right across from the museum and Elphinstone College, your Dad's college. This candidate introduced himself to Mrin with hands held together and head slightly bowed, saying, 'Namaste; I'm Aniruddh. I'm pleased to be here with you.' He asked Mrin if she would like to drink something, a cold drink, tea or coffee. Then he went to the self-service counter for two cups of coffee. He said he came from a small family of four, including his parents. He had a post-graduate degree in architecture, had a respectable job with a fitting salary and financial benefits at a great firm in South Bombay, regional vernacular for our downtown. He had saved a reasonable amount of money deposited in a local bank, earning an above-average rate of interest, and after he had saved enough, his dad would recommend blue-chip, dividend-paying stocks.

"Aniruddh, do you have this money and stocks in your own account or in your parents' account?"

"It's in my name and my personal account. My parents want me to save as much money as possible so that before, or as soon as I get married, I'm able to get my own home. My parents wanted me to have my own account from the first day I got some money at Diwali, or the New Year or as a birthday gift ever since I was a baby."

"I see, understand and enjoy your pride in this. Good parents make smart kids, who make good spouses," said Mrin.

"Let me ask you, a big question, Aniruddh. What would you say and do if you discovered that your fiancé had once a boyfriend?"

"In life those eventualities do happen. It's the nature of human beings to have flaws and blemishes. If she renounced him, then I've no problem with her past, but it would have to be a clean and permanent break," said the young suitor.

"What would you say to her if she had a sexual relationship with her boyfriend?"

"Well, Mrinal, I honestly can't give you an answer to that. I need to think about it. Perhaps seek some counsel from a trustworthy friend or even speak with my parents," he added.

"Why do you suggest talking to parents?"

"I am fully aware that times have changed, but I want to know if my parents and I have changed or not. If my prospective fiancé tells me everything, and I accept her past, then it's my responsibility to see that no harm ever comes to her: verbal, physical and emotional, from me and my family. I can vouch for myself. But parents? I need to speak to them, not for my sake, but for her sake. If any harm comes to her, I would never forgive myself, and my life would end there."

"Aniruddh, you're a one-of-a-kind gem. Your parents have done a fantastic job raising you, but you've been a terrific recipient in developing your thinking and responses. I can also understand why you would build beautiful homes."

Anya and Zara both realized this man was an exception in recognizing things happened in life, and that times have changed and that all stakeholders in relationships needed to be informed and work together. They wanted to know what Mrin did to let this guy go.

She said, "Aniruddh, you're a reasonable man, a true designer of perfect homes. You deserve to hear the truth, but I'll tell you if only you can keep my secret."

"I promise so help me God!"

"Look, I am going steady with a wonderful man, just like you. We're very much involved. As our horoscopes don't match, my parents are opposed to it. Hence my parents have set up these interviews. Earlier, I met idiots; it was easy to dump them. However, you're different."

He stood up and said, "Mrinal, say no more and worry not. I'll tell my parents that you're too beautiful for me. I don't want to live a life suspecting my wife having illicit affairs. Is that fine with you?"

"You know how to respect me even when you're about to dump me. What a man!"

Zara thought the excuse the last suitor used was beyond belief and showed his internal fortitude and strength of character. "Mom, did Dad ever rebel against his parents and raise hell in the household?"

"Zara, oh, yes, he did; he tried. However, it's not in his nature to be immersed in a problem and make it bigger than it really is. You know what I am saying?"

"Yeah, you're saying Dad never blows anything out of proportion."

"Good; that's it. He tried. You ignore him, and the problem disappears. It never gets exaggerated. He confronted his dad, even threatened to leave the family home, but before he could deliver on his threat, he got a call from the Finance Ministry in New Delhi that he was needed there immediately. He was out of sight. Probably, that had a lot of influence on both the families' decisions."

"But he didn't do anything bad; did he?"

Somi recalled that whenever Ayu was in Bombay, he started bringing Muslim and gay friends to his home just to annoy his parents. In this battle, poor grandma got punished for nothing.

"Did he do anything specific?"

"Oh yeah, Zara, he certainly did, but he never anticipated that Grandpa would take direct and pre-emptive action. One day he returned home from the Bank with a Muslim friend, who had brought with him an amulet from the shrine of a Sufi saint in Ajmer. In front of his dad's presence, Ayu tied it on his left upper arm, which he could have done before he arrived home. He didn't have to bring his Muslim friend home to show it off, but he did both just to let his family know that he was his own man.

"His family did nothing. They were never against knowing about other cultures, traditions and practices of other faiths. As a matter of fact, many Brahmin families encouraged their children to know these realities and Grandpa was highly talented in Persian, Pali and Ardhmagdhi, the languages of Iran, as well as of Jain and Buddhist scriptures."

"Then one day, Ayu brought home a book titled 'Islam for Uninitiated.' Not only did he clearly display it, but he read and discussed the contents with his mother and me! I asked him, "Ayush, what are you up to in this Islam book mess?"

"Mom, why did he read the book to you? Was he seeing you then?"

"No, we were not dating then, Zara, nor was I on his radar yet. He read to me simply because I was there. He needed a warm bodied sucker, and I was it," said Somi laughing.

"He used you. That is unlike of him," said Anya.

"He said, 'Somi, I like what I see in this book. I feel the religion of Islam is much misunderstood. I'll consider its principles and practices. If I like them, then I'll become a part-time Islamist.'

"So, you are the chosen one to fix the issue of misunderstood Islam!"

I said. Somi said she was amused by Ayu's convenient practice of being a 'part time Islamist' and let him know what she thought of the fence-sitters.

I asked him, "Isn't it like some men, who say that they are part-time virgins? They enjoy sex on the sly, but are not married yet?"

"What did Dad say to that zinger?"

"He didn't like it, Anya. I think it hit home. I felt guilty after that for my outburst."

"Wow, Mom. Good for you," said Zara.

However, still his family did nothing.

"I was shocked, immeasurably, that an outstanding and immensely respected Brahmin's son was thinking about converting to Islam! I gasped for breath. I couldn't sleep for two nights. I was scared about what would happen in the Vyas household. I said to myself that I must be a crazy woman to secretly love a man, who was about to denounce the faith of his parents and ancestors, some of whom would have given their lives for the protection of their Hindu belief, and their faith which they had been practicing for centuries.

I was having my doubts in Ayu's wisdom for the first time in my life, but I was equally bitter that he would do it to annoy his parents, so they would ease up on his demands for Mrin! I was forced to re-examine my own dreams and aspirations as they were turning into nightmares. Had he converted to Islam; I would not have married him despite my huge crush. My parents would have objected strongly. I thought he was losing his marbles. I couldn't believe it."

"I can't believe it either," responded Anya.

"However, it seemed that his mother and father hadn't taken any offense at their son's outlandish behaviour. That changed one day when Ayu's Muslim friend showed up with a beautifully woven prayer mat for his dear friend. They were both practicing the correct pronunciation of some Arabic words from the Quran, looking west to Holy Mecca."

"What did they do? I mean grandma and grandpa?"

"Grandma was devastated, Zara. She was crying her heart out. For the first time in many years, I saw their door closed so that no neighbours could hear of their sorrow, shame and humiliation at the hand of their son, their pride and joy. That day, Grandma spoke to Ayu always softly and lovingly. She begged him, 'Ayu, tell me what I failed to provide to you as a mother that you do this to me. I know well that I am not your target, but as an innocent bystander, I will be killed by the shrapnel. I don't know what your father has told you that he would do, but this offense against history, culture, ancestors and against your mother is sure to bring me to the brink. I don't know if I'll break or survive. Nor do I want you to find out what the final score will be. It's a path that's going to wound people, especially you.'"

"What a woman! She spoke well; our grandma did," said Zara. "What did Dad say and do after that?"

"During the next few days grandma fell sick, Anya. She was taken to Nanavati Hospital, a hospital frequented by rich and influential Gujaratis of the city. The doctors found that she had become anaemic. She complained of shortness of breath and once, she passed out as she was speaking. After a detailed examination, she was put on intravenous feeding, and ordered to have complete and worry-free bed rest. Because of Grandpa's reputation, she was getting the best medical treatment.

When Ayu went to see her in the hospital, I was there too. Grandma wanted a sip of water. Ayu stepped forward to give her the water. However, grandma told me, 'Somi, my child, you give me some water please.' Ayu had the glass in his hand, and he jovially said, 'Ma, I am still a Brahmin,' But grandma didn't want water from him. She insisted that I give her the glass of water saying to him, 'But I know your intentions and your heart are sullied.'

Ayu was thoroughly distressed at his own mother refusing to accept a sip of water from him. It stunned him."

"That certainly was strong," commented Zara.

Somi said, "Zara, you don't yet know what strong is. Just be patient. As if that was not enough, in the next few minutes, grandpa entered the hospital room with a friend, carrying a bag in his hand. According to the arrangements he had made with nurses, everyone except the family and grandpa's friend were evacuated. He gestured for me to remain...Then they closed the door. Grandpa introduced his friend as Attorney Taraporewala, a Parsee gentleman, and asked him to speak."

"Why would grandpa bring his lawyer there into the hospital when someone was sick?"

Mr. Taraporewala addressed Ayu, "Ayush, there are problems within the family, and the way and the speed at which these problems are escalating; they are getting out of hand. Your parents don't want the problems to reach the stage where it would be simply impossible for you to retrace your steps."

The attorney took a sip of water and continued, "However, being the good son that you are, instead of disobeying your parents and walking out, you have taken a route of utter independence that is detestable to the family, their culture, history and heritage. You have made your intentions known that you may become a part-time Islamist, whatever that means."

Ayu looked visibly perturbed. He was fidgeting, but still he did not know the step his family was taking to remedy the situation. He had to wait for the second shoe to drop.

Mr. Taraporewala cleared his throat, looked at grandma and continued, "As the legal representatives of the family, we've determined the value of the family assets, including investments, the present residence in Matunga, gold and diamond jewellery in the family and furnishings that the family owns. According to your parents, their needs will be met by half the value of these assets."

Somi said, "To say Ayu was shocked would be an understatement. This was definitely out of his league. He had no idea how to handle it, or how to react or respond."

Bespectacled Mr. Taraporewala surveyed the audience, drank a sip of water, cleared his throat and peered through the lower part of his bifocals and continued, "Your parents have authorized us to issue you a check for the other half of the assets in the amount of Rs 520,000. Please advise us if you would like to dispute this and if so, would you please provide the name and address of your attorney. As soon as this legal necessity is done, and terms and conditions are amicably agreed upon with you, your parents will leave the city of Bombay and move to a location where they are not known and recognized by their name."

Ayu then had the first glimpse of what his parents were doing. He was shaking his head in disbelief that it had come down to this so quickly. He was upset, severely.

Mr. Taraporewala added, "Their first condition is that you'll never contact them by letter, phone, by third-party or in person. Second, if you so desire, and if your new faith demands a change in your identity, then you do that as soon as possible to sever the present relationship. Finally, these details about the arrangement must be kept in confidence until our clients, your parents, abandon the city. Do you have questions, Ayush?"

"Holy crap, that was big time. It must have been worse than a hurricane!" Anya commented.

"What did Dad say to this onslaught?"

"He was as stunned as you are right now, Zara. He was speechless that his bluff had been called. They wouldn't throw him out of the house penniless. They would give him half of what they owned. They would let him choose his faith. They encouraged him to change his name. They wanted to sever the relationship, a complete discontinuance."

"I knew that our grandparents were loving and just, but I didn't know that they were this tough, this quick, this direct and this forthright. So, they didn't waste any time negotiating with Dad or trying to justify why their religion was better. They bet the whole farm, didn't they?"

"They were never going to say that their faith was superior, Zara. They were really enlightened people, who knew that every belief system, to its adherents and followers was an exceptional tradition, and the people who follow it needed no evidence that theirs is an admirable allegiance. There should be no debate as to which theology is unrivalled," Somi said.

Somi continued, "Hinduism doesn't practice conversion from other faiths. Hindus believe you're born a Hindu, and you die a Hindu."

"Instead of this extreme measure, why didn't they punish him with something?"

"Anya, he was a grown man. If you punish, expel, disown, or incarcerate a person, then you're inflicting those punishments to him because he has hurt your dignity. These folks didn't believe in honour punishment, honour expulsion or honour anything. To them, it would be the anti-thesis of esteem. They were saying to him, you go your way; we go our way, and we hope that our paths don't cross again. It was that simple!"

"So, how did the situation end?"

Somi said, "Zara, your Dad was all choked up and was incoherent… He was emotionally moved by the hugeness of the hurt that caused his parents to resort to that. He said to his father that he was a proud Brahmin just like him. He would die a Brahmin, no less. He told his mother that he would refuse to eat and drink anything until his mother took water from him first. Then, as if on a cue, she asked for water, and I fetched a glass and gave to it to Ayu. The drama lingered long but ended precipitously."

"Did it end there or did the discussion continue for a while over this drama?"

"It died, but Grandpa wanted Ayu to know that he couldn't choose a different faith and have his ties with his family too. They told him that the rejection of their theology was a rejection of their relationship. They were what they were because of their belief, practices and rituals. They knew that Ayu was doing this to put pressure on the family to allow his marriage to Mrin, but before anything further could happen, Mrin had already left for America. In all this, I was caught in between. I had asked Grandpa one day if I should stay out of the family strife and secrets so that their dignity could be maintained."

"What did he say?"

"Anya, he said that I was his witness and a recorder of the events. I had to be present there regardless of dignity. Then he corrected himself and said 'because of the dignity,'" concluded Somi.

"Mom, that's a high honour and a responsibility," said Zara, throwing her a kiss as she filled her glass with more wine.

"Whatever happened to Dad's Muslim, and gay friends?"

"They never showed up again. Your Dad's character helped him align his life to the family requirements of his conduct," explained Somi. "By the way, what time is it, Zara?"

"It's only midnight, mom. Let me pour you all a little more Pinot.

"How did Mrin manage to avoid marrying one of the ten guys she interviewed?"

Somi explained how her parents pestered her to pick any one of those guys, marry and get it over with. At that demand, Mrin was depressed. Megh, Simi and she tried their best to lift her out of her funk. She was distressed because it made no difference to her parents whom she picked. At that point, she thought she was no more a daughter to be loved, pampered and safeguarded, but a burden that needed to be offloaded.

Eventually, she told her mother that she would perform an act of charity and would be willing to marry Trilok if they helped him get a divorce from his opportunist wife. She said, "I can't seem to save my life, but at least I could save his."

"Mom, I don't think you told us the tale of this Trilok guy…," reminded Anya.

"I think mom is either very sleepy or truly tipsy," said Zara.

Somi briefly narrated the story of Trilok, who was trapped by a girl and her family into a marriage, just to secure his apartment by accusing him of spousal abuse. Disgusted, Trilok left his apartment without a fight and without the divorce. Mrin felt immensely sad for him.

"So Mrin says she would marry him if her parents help secure his divorce from the hustler he married. Mom, this is truly an act of charity…," said Zara.

"When Mrin's parents heard it, they knew it was fruitless to force her to marry. They relented." Somi was feeling a little lightheaded as the Pinot was coming into play. Anya and Zara also felt it was time to turn in.

"Mom, I know you're tipsy, but I must ask you a couple of questions…," said Anya.

"Ask away."

"Did you sit on any of the interviews?"

"No, I didn't sit as such, Zara. However, Megh and I sat not too far from Mrin to hear most of the interviews. Except for one, they all were losers. Let's go to sleep."

"Who is this Megh? Did she live where you, and Dad did?"

"You already forgot? I told you Megh was Mrin's close friend, a real confidante. She was also, just like Mrin, a beautiful girl with a lot of sass and attitude. Our friendship grew once Mrin moved to the States."

"Where are Megh and Simi now?"

"I don't know, Anya. I lost touch with them after I got married."

"You feel like getting in touch with them?"

"Zara, my heart wishes, but my mind objects…"

"That's kind of strange, Mom. Why are you so conflicted? Did you have an argument with her?"

But Somi didn't answer. When Zara looked her way, she saw her mother had fallen asleep.

Chapter Thirteen

Return Home

Over the next two days, they rested, ate, talked and shopped. They went to the Butterfly Farm, visited Pinel Island, and saw people of all ages, in various states of nudity at the Orient Beach. They visited an eclectic art gallery at the Oyster Pond, and to her delight, an old acquaintance Philippe Izard called for Anya. She introduced him to her mother and sister. They talked about his family in Guadalupe where she and a friend on a previous trip had sailed on his yacht to visit his wife Michelin and their daughter Yvette.

The week went by too quickly. Somi was happy that it was a friendly island where you were not a customer or client, but a friend, truly remembered and appreciated. She was inwardly smiling that she had a chance to reminisce, savour her past and enjoy the company of her grown daughters. She wished it had happened earlier.

"Anya and Zara, you've really made me happy by coming here. We should do this more often…"

Hearing the compliments and wishes for the future, Zara felt ill at ease. She couldn't forget the motivation behind the trip. She felt pity for her mother, but she returned her smile instinctively.

They reached Toronto where eager Ayu was waiting at the airport to receive his family. They exchanged their customary greetings; he could see the happiness and excitement on Somi's face. That alone was enough to make him hum a pleasant tune as he was driving home along the highway. On their way, they talked about their trip, various memories, shopping and how they missed their other two sisters and Ayu.

Zara said, "Dad, you and mom should visit the islands again."

Ayu said, "Yes, I would love to go back to Trinidad and Tobago. I had visited most of the islands before we got married. I thought you guys knew that. Don't you remember those slides that I used to show you?"

"Dad, we know that. But we are talking about you two going there together. Understood?"

The rest of the ride home was spent with Anya and Zara recalling details of the frequent slide shows they were subjected to for their geography, history and economic lessons.

Later, that night when their Dad had gone to his bedroom with an unfinished crossword puzzle, the women stayed in the family room, chatting about family matters and reminiscing about the childhood lives in Italy. After a while, Somi disappeared, and returned with copies of a poem.

A stranger turned and looked at me searchingly

My eyes first averted.

Then, our eyes locked… as if forever.

His glance glazed with adoration

Beckoned me to him

And I unaware, eyes transfixed, as if in a trance

Rushed like a river to her ocean.

Her face was beaming with pride. "What do you think?"

They were shocked that their mother had handed them the same poem they had read in a Mrin email. Too stunned to say anything, Zara fumbled with her words, "Oh my Go…."

Swiftly Anya intervened, "God, it's a beautiful poem. Mom, did you write it?"

"No. Don't you remember in St. Barts, I said something beautiful and you girls loved it? And then I told you that a friend had penned it down?"

"Mom, it's a poem of new beginnings. It celebrates an unconscious acceptance of love. I think it speaks of destiny, kismet and 'what is meant to be'. Your friend started something beautiful, but she feels a lack of control over her life as it relates to 'the stranger.' Do you know whether the relationship flourished or not?"

"I really don't know, Anya. Perhaps there's an element of kismet or lack of control. But I really couldn't say it's an imagined and artificial construct, or personal and autobiographical."

"Where is your friend now?"

Somi shrugged, and said that they'd lost contact many years ago, and she had no idea how she could re-connect with her.

"How did you come to have it? Did your friend send it along with a letter? I would love to read more of her poems, Mom," said Zara.

"No, it was in a pile of old letters from my youthful days. I think I have more poems from her somewhere in the house. If I find them, I'll let you have them."

"Ma, why do you want to save old letters or poems? I don't understand," said Zara.

"That's my past. I want to remain connected, tethered to it."

"But that's past, gone. We are your future…" said Zara.

"Yes, you are my present, and I enjoy it as much as I can; I also know you lead me into the future. Even so, it is the past that keeps me rooted, reminds me of the promises I made and tells me if the road ahead is fraught with dangers. You have your own lives to live. I don't want to become a nuisance or pest by taking up your time and space. Anyway, what are you girls doing tomorrow?"

"Mom, I'll go home early tomorrow morning to prepare for Monday. I'm going to be really busy for the next few days as I've to get caught up with the work that piled up over the holiday. What are your plans, Zara?"

"I think I'll go with Anya for a few days. I'm thinking of taking some yoga classes downtown; so, if I get in, I'll stay with Anya for a week or more. That will give us a chance to spend time with Bijli too."

"Okay, I'm going to mosey on to my chamber in the Vyas resort now and enjoy their sumptuous comforts and leisure," said Zara with a dramatic flair.

"Okay, Zara, pull me out of this lovely sofa so that we both can mosey together. Good night, Mom."

The two sisters went to their rooms, closed their doors, but reconnected by opening their shared bathroom doors. Zara asked, "What do you think is going on here?"

"Zara, my guess is as good as yours. I think maybe she copied the email poem. We'll possibly never know the truth. Give me Dad's computer, so I can check my emails."

"Yeah, you know Mom is not really as simple as she makes herself out to be. I mean, this trip to the islands showed us that first hand. She can be as complex and layered as an onion!" said Anya.

Anya signed in to her email and was happy to find a message from Prof. Divecha. She opened it and read out that the professor would see them in her office at Osgoode Hall between four and six any day of the next couple of weeks. She also indicated that knowing well how busy Anya was, she would not mind if Anya called the day she was visiting her. Both sisters were happy that she had written without a reminder and was so flexible.

"I'm sure that the fact that she knows Dad from her college days has something to do with it," Anya said.

Zara said, "On Monday when you're at the office, I'll look into yoga classes we both can attend downtown. Until then, I've some doubts about these emails; I need to do some research. Don't ask me anything. I will tell you once I'm done researching."

"By the way, Anya, those sniffles, those tears, that 'quarter of love'… what's going on?"

"Zara, we'll talk at my condo. Not here. I know you've something to tell me too."

On Sunday morning, the girls slept in. After their early cup of tea, a light breakfast and peek at the newspaper, Ayu and Somi went out for their habitual hour-long walk. Zara heard the alarm chime as their parents opened and closed the door. She quietly walked out of her room and entered the sanctuary that her mom used for personal and spiritual purposes. She had a small shrine there with pictures, icons and worship necessities. Earlier, she lit a lamp and a jasmine-scented incense stick. Zara opened a couple of closets and searched for something, although she had no idea what she was looking for. She knew that as soon as she found it, she would know if that was what she was looking for or not. She looked under her mom's old saris and elaborate outfits wrapped in muslin, and at the bottom of the shelf, she saw what looked like journals with yellowing covers. This is it, she thought.

Before she could even pick up a book and open a page, the sound of the security system warned her that one of the doors had opened and shut. She replaced things as they had been and tiptoed out of the sanctuary and hustled back to the comfort of her bedroom. Her heart was pounding with the fear of being caught trespassing. Zara considered various scenarios of the morning's discovery. As soon as she heard Anya waking up, she called out to her and described what she had discovered.

"Look, Zara, you don't know for sure what's in those books in Mom's closet. Those books could be *her* diaries, or some anthology of Bollywood lyrics that she's so fond of. Don't rush to conclusions. We'll pursue this some other time. Seriously, what a mess our lives are turning out to be! Once upon a time I craved a life of excitement, but sometimes excitement brings turmoil and unexpected consequences. It's a curse. Now I yearn for a sedate life full of innocuous routines… maybe we should have never read so far into those messages, Zara.

It's opened up a whole new can of worms."

For a while the sisters talked about how difficult it was for them to consider the flaws in their parents' lives, especially matters related to marital integrity and sexual fidelity. The conversation dwindled as they both retreated into their own thoughts, literally jumping in fright when they heard a knock on the door. They had barely heard their parents come back from their walk.

"Anyone ready for breakfast, girls?" A voice came from the other side of the door.

"Mom, come inside. We're just waking up. What happened, you're back so soon from your walk?"

"Yes, I had an upset stomach, Zara. But I'm better now. Come, come down to the kitchen," she called.

They had a Gujarati breakfast of fried *khari puri*, bell peppers sautéed with spices and chickpea flour, potatoes with puréed tomato, garlic chutney and *masala chai*. This was their Dad's favourite breakfast menu, which he got only when the girls came home. Along with the delicious breakfast, Somi and Ayu savoured conversation about their four kids: their childhoods, their careers and now their prospective weddings. Zara was the only one who was married out of the four.

"Look, Anya, it's about time that you seriously consider getting married. I can't wait any longer…" said Ayu.

"Dad, don't get entangled in these frays. Arranged marriages are all fake; it's all about adjusting and accommodation."

"Anya, that's how *all* marriages are. Accommodations and adjustments are other words that describe life. We do that everywhere," said Somi.

"I'm not talking about arranging anyone's marriage here. Fix it yourself, but do so."

"Don't get exasperated Ayu, she *is* getting married this year."

"If mom can control the weather, she sure can manage your marriage," joked Zara.

"Instead of getting cutely sarcastic, why don't you ask for the reasons, my dear?"

"Okay, Sage Somi why do you think my sister is heading to the wedding altar?" Somi closed her eyes and sat in a meditative pose for a few seconds.

"Anya, this repeat explanation is for the people with a long-term memory problem. Presently, for you, Jupiter is transiting Aries, and you were born with Venus in Aries. Furthermore, Jupiter is casting its aspect on the 7th house, the house known of marriages, contracts and unions. For you, Moon is in harmony with Venus, Mars and Jupiter. Nothing can get better than this. That's why I think this is your year for marriage."

"We'll see, Mom," said Anya, brushing off the topic.

Somi didn't show it, but was disappointed with their 'nothing' response.

Later, as the girls prepared to depart, Zara turned around and said, "Dad, I forgot to pick up your laptop. Do you mind if I use it for a few more days?"

"Whatever your heart desires, and stay young forever. Why don't you keep it with you until you leave here? I will use the other computer." Ayu said and went inside to get his laptop from Anya's bedroom.

Zara and Anya were at the Lakeshore condo within an hour. Anya unpacked, went through her snail mail and suggested Zara to check the emails, asking, "Did Dad receive any more mail from Mrin?"

Zara was just thinking about the same thing. "No more mail from the perfume woman," said Zara, looking at the computer screen. Then remembering the Kundalini yoga, she googled to check if any classes were offered in the downtown studios.,' On Harbord Street, classes are offered from beginners to advanced levels, including prenatal and private sessions.' The schedule suited the sisters. "I will call someone at the yoga center and discuss whether someone would come to our condo to teach us," said Zara.

As they settled into a day of quiet nothingness with no emails to fill their hours, Anya felt that she should bring up what she had truly wanted to ask her sister for days now." "So, what's going on in your life?"

Zara sighed loudly, giving in. "Well, it appears that I have to sacrifice more, accept more compromises, ask fewer questions, receive fewer benefits and show more thanks. I'm tired of giving, Anya."

"Shaan doesn't seem to appreciate what he's got."

"I've to stand in line, but I'm the last one to be served with whatever crumbs are left. And the worst is that he can't seem to forget his old love, who dumped him unceremoniously."

"Oh?"

"Yes, and he speaks of her all the time."

"That's not good at all. Maybe you should speak with his ex first…to find out what happened" said Anya.

"I know. However, I never thought of doing that, although it may come to that. Maybe I should do it now, rather than later. What do you say?"

"What would you do now? What could you do now?" Anya's tone revealed incredulously.

"Well, I have his ex-girl friend's phone number. She knows me a bit." Zara said sheepishly, "I'll speak to her, ask her if she's still interested in Shaan. I'll tell her point-blank, without anger that if she is, then one day without telling him, I'll drive him to her condo and say, 'Go, there she is. This is over,' That's what I'll do."

"If that's what really feels right to you, then yes, perhaps you should. It's always better to be honest and upfront."

Zara got her cell phone out, dialled a number and waited.

"Hello," said the voice on the other line.

"Hi, Logan what's up?"

"I'm fine Zara. Thanks. What's new with you? How is the old dog doing?"

"Yes, he…he's fine. Logan, I need to ask you a huge favor. If you can't or don't want to talk, I understand."

"Go ahead. Shoot!"

"Look, Logan, Shaan and I have been married for almost two years, but he can't seem to get you out of his head. I think he has some unresolved issues. I know you'll agree with me that in a marriage, three's a huge crowd, unless we want it that way."

Logan started to laugh.

She said, "Zara. Threesome! It's a great idea, but not with Shaan. I was just joking… you have my complete sympathy. I thank you for taking this guy off my hands. I've no idea what's with some men that they can't love the woman they're with. It's always the other woman who's a lot better, including the one they left behind. You tell me how I can help, girl, and I'll do exactly as you want."

"Okay, that takes a load off my chest. Next time when he has a temper tantrum and tells me indirectly how much he misses you; I'm going to bring him to your doorstep, and perhaps you can read him the law that you don't crap where you live."

"Zara, I have no problem. Just bring the stuff to clean his poop off the floor," Logan laughed.

"Thanks, what else is going on in the jungle? Are there any lions roaring out there in your neck of the woods?"

"Yes, I'm seeing a phenomenal mature man. He's been around; seen a lot. His wife died of cancer not too long ago. He is incredible. Even though he's the one who needs to be looked after, he makes sure that I come first in his life, and he knows about Shaan," said Logan appreciatively.

"It's nice to hear there are still some decent men around. Take care, talk to you soon," said Zara concluding the call. Then she looked at Anya expectantly.

"I'm proud of you, Zara. I wish I could take things as in control as you can. Really go for what I want. I'm starting to wonder more and more what's wrong with me. I'm at a loss to say why certain things are happening to me…"

"Such as…?"

Anya sat quietly looking at the ceiling, meditative and reflective. Zara could hear Anya's deep breathing and see her chest heave. She looked at Zara for a moment and then diverted her eyes as they began to tear up. She quickly stood up and walked up to the balcony, overlooking the lake. Zara could hear her almost inaudible sobs. She walked up to Anya and held her from behind first and then Anya turned and was in her sister's embrace.

She remained there locked in her sibling's comforting clasp. The tears subsided; her breathing became steady and whispered, "Thanks, sis."

"I came across men, educated and professional, who used me, abused me, and left me feeling guilty, ashamed and worthless. It happened twice. More of the same old crap."

Anya continued, "I knew an American attorney who visited Toronto a lot, almost regularly. I was at a bar, frequented by the law type. I used to go there regularly with my colleagues. It was not that I was alone. This guy, talking to some of my friends, found out my name and where I worked and what I did. He knew well that my firm, Shipton Arnott and Smith Barristers and Solicitors, represented all kinds of clients on joint ventures, mergers, acquisitions and international trade issues. Our clients are all over the world.

He sent me flowers with a card saying, 'Secret Admirer wishes you a great day!' I was astonished that there was a furtive admirer. I was all warm and fuzzy, excited and charged, hoping to see this enigmatic admirer for the first time. The following week he sent me a box of imported chocolates with a card saying, 'Just can't wait to surprise you….secret admirer.' I thought, well. I was about to see this under the wraps admirer in person who is doing everything right. On

Monday of the third week, he sent me beautiful pajamas made of the richest silk, imported from France, with a card saying, 'I really can't wait to see you.'

The following week when Monday came around, nothing happened, and I was full of anticipation as to what I would receive from this secret admirer, and more importantly when I would see him, but nothing came on Monday. Then Tuesday brought dozen red roses with a teddy bear, and a card saying, 'I'm hurting inside to see you.'"

Zara interrupted, "You know Anya, and this phony mutt was playing you even without being there. You're all worked up. You could hardly wait to jump into bed. Right?"

"Zara, you are so right! To make the long story short, we became close friends, were intimate, and I went to Italy, Baja and St. Maarten with him. He knew everything about me, my firm, and our business, including forthcoming prospects, as well as those I was working on. I knew singularly little about him, except that he worked for a small American firm.

As time passed by, our visits became infrequent and so did the emails, texting and phone calls. One fine Monday morning, my team of attorneys from Shipton Arnott and Smith took their seats to discuss terms and conditions and other business issues for a joint venture between a Canadian and a Chinese company. Guess who was representing the Chinese?

That bastard! I glared at him throughout and he then had the audacity to send me a note, saying 'There is nothing personal here. It's strictly business, Counsellor.' I was livid. He seduced me, used me, abused me and then abandoned me. I can't forgive him, but neither do I forgive myself for being played for a fool. And this man is an attorney who has had lessons in ethics!"

"Anya, lawyers and ethics don't go together. We know you're an exception. Who did he work for?"

Anya retrieved a business card from the bedroom and handed it to Zara. "Let me see if we can do something here," said Zara, looking at the business card.

"Zara, I'm still devastated. I'm afraid to date. I can tell you a few more such stories, but that would be punishing you. I must be stupid that I didn't learn my lessons from these predatory bastards."

Zara listened quietly and then said, "You know what, forget about him for now. Give me the number of your friend in St. Maarten, Aki. Let me ask him if he spoke to his friend or not."

Zara called Akhil and firstly, thanked him for his warm reception of their family. "Akhil, you said that one of your friends would be a good match for Anya. Are you sure that my sister will not get hurt? You can vouch for his character and the family?"

Akhil indicated that he was sure that Anuraag would never cheat, play dirty games or be selfish. He was unquestionably a gentleman, a man of his word. He was not spoiled by success or money. "Zara, I'm going to call him right now and tell him more about Anya. I will order him to call her tomorrow evening!"

"Anya, we should expect that call from Anuraag tomorrow, around this time. Let's take a break, a really long break. Get out, have a beer or two, get some fresh air."

On returning home, Zara asked, "Let's look at our inspiration, our goddess. What can we learn from her?"

"Anya, I don't want you to think about what I can learn from Mrin, when I couldn't learn from up close, fraud masters. So, let's make a list of five things we like about her that we would like to be blessed with."

After a lapse of a few minutes, the girls were ready with their list.

"I worship her love and respect for herself. She is more comfortable in her skin; she doesn't want to be anybody else," said Zara.

"Zara, you're good. Such people don't seem to have issues of low self-esteem and jealousy. They're happy with whoever they're with and whatever they have. I like her overall attitude of being nice.

Never once did we hear Dad complain about her arrogance, pride or nastiness. She was always kind and courteous to him."

"Anya, Mrin was fair and cordial to even to her arch enemies like Mom and Aunt Sona. When Sona was getting married, Mrin was there to help them look good. She praised them when all they had done was to put her down. She became friends with Mom who had tried to put a hex on her. She is too generous and admirable, unduly good. Anya."

"Considerate people never have to feel guilty, or lose sleep. I, at no time, saw anyone anywhere saying that she was easily disturbed or perturbed. She has that sense of equilibrium, poise and inner confidence."

"Only that kind of internal poise can give you a love for Kundalini and the desire to turn hot sexuality to a higher-level spirituality. The funny thing is she was not even initiated into sex before she met Dad. She already worked out a system to improve, enhance and enrich herself. What a woman! " said Anya.

"I agree. I think she doesn't want to change anybody according to her tastes or preferences. She has this unique quality to accept others as they are."

"Knowing well that Dad is distant and aloof, she didn't try to change him to impress her friends."

"Zara, and her humor! She comes up with cute repartees when you least expect it."

"But her humor is not mean-spirited. I think it rubbed off on Dad. How often have seen Dad come up with surprising twists that would calm all down? In our household, Dad's humour that has kept the peace sanity and respect," said Zara.

"True, his humor has saved us from many fights. However, I also like Mrin's nobility of character, the principles she lives by, her skills and talents. It's not one quality, but a series of interdependent strengths, creating the whole delicious enchilada," said Anya.

"You know, we should meet her soon, spend time with her. I don't know how we'll tell her we know about her, but I'd really like to personally thank her for what she has done for me, for us."

"Zara, your feelings towards her humble me."

"Anya, remember how Dad used to make us sit in the front seat on long drives to educate us about how we can become successful in life. I think our list is coming from those Socratic lessons with Dad."

"I like your notion of humility. Dad would say that's the first step. Remember he used to say 'there is always someone better than you are'," said Anya.

"The world is not going to change. The transformation we seek has to come from within us by looking at people like Mrin and others we admire. If someone is drawn to me, it means I'm doing well. I must keep on doing whatever I'm doing. If someone is repelled, I must have caused it. Right away, I must cease doing what I did. Once I consciously know and accept it, I now need to find out how I can change my thinking, my demeanour, my responses, and my body language. This consciousness is what we need," Zara said.

"Zara, that was fabulous. Now we know what we need to do."

They wondered, despite these common sense values, why men and women fail to grasp them. They felt virtues listed in do-it-yourself manuals were just words on paper. When those ideals become incarnate in life-or-death conflicts, then only the common person recognizes the value, and the prototype for the correct conduct.

"Yes, we have seen Mrin's response to many conflicts. Despite being a fallible woman, she does her best not just for self but for the principles by which one can live with self-respect and dignity," said Anya.

"You nailed it, Anya!"

On Monday, Anya returned home from her office late in the afternoon to find Zara lounging on the couch. As she was getting a glass of water, her cell rang., It was Akhil from St. Maarten telling her that his friend Anuraag was on a week-long business trip overseas, and as soon as he returned home, he would call her and even visit Toronto to meet her. Akhil added that Anuraag would make his own accommodation arrangements, close enough to where Anya lived, so they could easily meet.

After that unexpected call, Zara contacted the yoga center and enrolled them both for ten private sessions at Anya's condo. Her thoughts then drifted to Prof Divecha. She wondered what all they would discover when they met her at her office this week.

Chapter Fourteen

Somi's Interrogation

On Tuesday night, the girls called their mother to know whether she'd like come over the following evening for dinner, to which Somi more than happily agreed. But secretly, the girls had another motive, to clarify some of the questions that their mother had raised of her history during their trip to the Caribbean.

Somi spent some time on the Tuesday morning preparing food that both the girls liked, and that afternoon she arrived at five o'clock to spend the night with her three daughters. She walked from the Union Station to Anya's condo, barely making it to cover from the sudden rain. For dinner, the three ate spinach cooked with cubes of cheese, rice pilaf, lentils, yogurt salad, mango pickles and naan their mom brought.

"Such a shame that Bijli couldn't join us. That child works too much!" said Somi, "But girls, I must thank you again for the trip, it was such a perfect gift."

"Mom, I'm still curious about some of the things we talked about during the St. Maarten trip," remarked Zara.

There was a brief silence between the sisters, but Somi failed to notice the tension in the atmosphere, so Zara continued, "Mom, remember we were talking about the perfume woman and Dad, then you made us swear never to ask questions about them. 'Case Closed', you had said. Then you also mentioned that you were a little jealous of her because she received a better education, had a better lover, had even more freedom, and a job in the USA. Jealous, yet awed by her. Remember that Mom?"

"Yes, of course I do. But I want to know why we are still talking about *her*," Somi asked quizzically.

"No, Mom, we are not talking about her. We are talking about *you*. We don't care about her. She's not our mother; you are," was Zara's impassioned response, a bit loud.

Anya added, "Zara, don't raise your voice. Mom, we said you got Dad; she didn't. Dad chose you."

Anya continued, "Do you remember what you said then?"

"Yes, I do. I said your Dad didn't jump at the first chance, he got to marry me. If you want to know, he just ignored me for a long time. You know his remoteness, his indifference and nonchalance. It hurt me then, and now, even more after all that I have done…" Her voice trailed off.

"Mom what do you mean by 'after all that I have done'?"

"Forget it. I misspoke. I've just made everything worse," said Somi apologetically.

Zara hesitated, debating on whether she should say something or not. She knew their mom was concealing something, but she decided to defer the issue for now. Instead, she talked about herself, and by extension, Somi.

"Mom, like I told you in St. Maarten, jealousy is an absolutely natural human phenomenon. To be honest, I used to feel jealous of Anya so much for her smarts, her looks, her grades, and her friends. I have learnt to overcome these feelings of low self-esteem by talking about it, even with Anya herself. Perhaps, you need to find out if you really, truly are jealous of the perfume woman, or our Dad."

There was a stunned silence. The precision of Zara's words sliced through Somi's miasma of smugness and self-righteousness. "I beg your pardon?"

"Mom, are you jealous of the perfume woman or our Dad?" Zara repeated.

"Why would I want to be jealous of him? He is my life. I live *for* him," Somi said meekly.

"I just wondered if you have a vendetta against Dad for not noticing you, first, loving you, proposing to you, first, and enjoying dating you, first," elaborated Anya softly. "And Mom, always remember, you live first for *you*, not for Dad."

Somi remained silent mulling what her response should be and, in the meantime, Zara spoke, "We know how much you want yourself and everything yours to be number one. Our second-class grades were not good enough for you. You haven't yet forgiven me for not becoming a Wall Street trader or banker. You haven't forgiven Bijli for becoming a social activist. I am glad Anou came along and became a big name in NASA and erased your shame over Bijli and me. Mom, it sounds like your life is rivalry, and it is a nasty rivalry!"

"I am sorry that you think this way. I am never ashamed of anyone of you, including Bijli. Yes, I do wish that she has a regular career, but you girls have always made me proud."

"When you lived in Matunga, with the help of Aunt Sona, you could pull off your rivalry stunts in a cinch. You had a powerful ally in her, since she was skilled in dealing with competitions. You left the Matunga address, but the Matunga home didn't leave you. It lives and thrives in your mind. This need to be number-one, this need to be perfect, this need to be in command, being a control freak has made you less of a wife, and mother than you ever cared to imagine!

"If you knew that your rivalry makes our lives a hell, that we are forced to seek medical and psychiatric help, I wonder what you would do. If you don't recognize your jealousy of Dad, if you don't recognize your competitive nature, you must be delusional," Zara concluded, looking directly into Somi's eyes with emotions bordering on deep resentment and humiliation.

There was palpable anger in the room. They could hear thunder and lightning outside on the lake, and a downpour lashed on their condo glass panes from all directions. The heavens crackled; lightning tore up the sky, and an ocean of water came down thoroughly blocking their view over the lake and beyond.

Somi had known it well that in every family, actions of one afflicted person altered lives and circumstances of others in an immeasurable way. Not only were there sever reactions for every action, but there were also destructive side effects of unintended consequences. She had known her daughters were sensitive in domestic peace and harmony, sibling teasing and sarcastic ribbing, notwithstanding. Despite this knowledge she was at a loss to comprehend the issues of jealousy, rivalry and competition that these daughters were talking about and accusing her with. As a mature and loving mother, she decided to plead mea culpa and take the high ground. By doing this, she hoped to re-establish peace and seek then her own solutions.

She didn't think much; she let her internals respond to deal with pain that her daughters suffered. "I'm sorry that I caused so much grief for you. Even though I can't fully visualise my dubious actions, but this is not the time to quibble. As always, your emotional well-being is so important that I'm prepared to do anything you girls want me to do."

She stood up, touched Zara's cheek with her right palm, and said, I'm sad and pained for causing this."

Lightning outside thundered, and almost blew up the sky with power and intensity. "What do you propose I do?" Somi asked, yielding to her maternal instincts.

"Mom, you need to begin looking at your life and perhaps writing down all the events you have experienced that may smack of your jealousy and low self-esteem," suggested Anya.

"Are you saying I have a low self-esteem?" Somi asked the girls indignantly.

"It appears so, Mom. Those two, jealousy and low self-esteem are twin sisters. Once you own up to them, then maybe take some counselling along with Dad."

"Why do I need him there?"

"Because you have some issues, and he is part of the solution. If he knows, he will be on your side. You know he is one man you can trust," said Anya gently.

"What are other issues?" Somi asked them meekly, dreading a long list of self-improvement habits.

"They will have to wait for a while," said Zara, softening.

"You girls scare me! I will do what you suggest, and I will do so in the company of your Dad."

On that note, the sky having cleared up, they came out on the balcony to look at the promenade and the lake. They felt relieved that some good might arise from this confrontation. They knew the cleansing and purging had started with the reading of the emails, a week in the Caribbean, counselling for their mother and now a prospective meeting with Dr. Lulu Divecha.

Somi asked the girls when they would visit home again. They agreed that they would be home with Bijli on Friday evening.

Chapter Fifteen

Two Sisters meet Prof. Divecha

Wednesday couldn't come soon enough for Anya and Zara.

When her secretary informed Prof. Divecha that her two o'clock appointment had arrived, she came out of her office effusively as if she were meeting old family friends after a long separation. "Welcome, girls. How are you and how is my old friend, Ayush Vyas?"

"Oh, he's fine, doing crossword puzzles, reading the *Economist, New York Times*, other boring magazines and solving other nations' trade and currency issues. Professor, this is my sister Zara. And Zara, you already know about Professor Divecha."

"Oh, Anya I feel very happy whenever I see you. Still as beautiful and poised as ever!"

Anya blushed at the unexpected compliment.

"You both remind me of a friend I once had. She too, was lovely and graceful. Anyway...come, come." She whisked them both into her office.

"Professor, I am so honoured and happy to meet with you, especially since you were once our Dad's classmate," said Zara.

"Your Dad is a proverbial 'one in a million', guy. I had only two seminars with him every week, but some of us wished that he were in all of our classes. His knowledge, eloquence, and argument presentation were exceptional."

Prof. Divecha recalled their dad's seminar on Beauty for its originality and imagination. He hypothesized that beauty by its nature is short lived; it can't exist longer than a glance. He said 'love at first glance' is an excellent first attempt at its definition. At the second and each subsequent glance, the beauty of the original object diminishes. The haunting beauty of the Bollywood actrss Nargis, Elizabeth Taylor, Marilyn Monroe or Sophia Loren is never topped by another viewing. The picture of Mona Lisa's famous smile is no different. The beauty of the Taj Mahal lies again in the first sight. Subsequently, it remains a grand vision of architectural wonder, but not as beautiful as the first sighting of it.

Then suddenly, she stopped and smiled, "Oh my girls I must be boring you, aren't I?"

"No, you're not. As a matter of fact, we are thrilled because we often take our Dad for granted. For us, he's no scholar, just a Dad. He never speaks of those concepts to us. For us, he is an economist, a banker. What you're saying throws a new light on him," said Zara.

"Well spoken, my child." She continued, 'Ayu said the true character of beauty is its fleeting nature. It can't exist longer than a glimpse, a moment. Familiarity diminishes the value of beauty,' He said. 'Granted that for some, this glimpse, this moment lasts for a day or longer because for them, time ceases to exist, or they seem to have overcome the dimension of time.'"

The girls were simply amazed at the ideas their Dad had presented.

"He was a marvel to have around. He didn't say much, didn't dispute anything even when he found something laughable. In spite of praise, which he received often, he didn't get carried away and strut his stuff, saying 'look at me.'"

After a lapse of initial conversation of reminiscences, she asked, "Anyway, girls, tell me what can I do for you?"

"Prof. Divecha, could you please, tell us about one of your classmates, Mrin?"

Momentarily, the question startled the Professor as it came from nowhere, but she didn't show her surprise. "That's.... that's the friend, I said you two reminded me of…"

"You mean that we look like her?"

"Yes, Anya, not completely, but mostly, yes. Some of my friends would describe you two as her nieces or cousins, if not daughters. There's a striking resemblance."

Professor Divecha was unsure if she should divulge more or remain circumspect. She felt that in terms of age, she was like a mother or an aunt. Mothers and aunts must remain protective of their daughters and nieces. "I am not sure how much to tell you about her."

"Whatever you can tell us without offending Mrin and your own sensitivities…" said Anya.

In a calm voice, she recalled that Mrin and Ayu were made for each other. They started out as friends and neighbours, and soon they became a couple. They both were similar in their intellect, interests and views on life. Mrin, thought Prof. Divecha, was truly a beautiful woman. She could have competed in beauty pageants with the best and come out a queen. She was tall and graceful. Clothes, no matter how cheap, always looked fabulous on her. Nevertheless, she rarely owned anything that lacked class. Clothes, colour, shoes and other accessories…nothing was ever mismatched. She was an accomplished athlete with a wonderful sense of humour and a style befitting a queen.

Professor Divecha paused and looked at the girls, waiting for any questions. Because of how acquainted the sisters had become with Mrin, none of this seemed surprising. So rather than being angry or upset at her being described as their father's true love, they revelled in the details of a woman they'd come to admire.

"She sounds too good to be true!" Anya said.

"But she was true, absolutely true and real, palpably real."

"Was she your friend?"

'Her world was full of friends, Anya. Nevertheless, yes, I was her friend. Her best friend was Megh Dalal."

"When did you last see them together?"

Professor Divecha recalled that she had seen them last at Ayu's graduation in December of 1972. Scratching her head, she added that she and other friends wanted to hang around to greet and congratulate Ayu on his achievements. She felt it was odd that Mrin was not keen to hang around and left. Flippantly she had said, 'Divecha, the pleasure of being his lover is that I can see him anytime I want. I'll leave him now for you all!'

"Zara, I knew something was wrong, and so did Megh," said Prof. Divecha.

"Did you also know her professionally?"

"Yes. Anya, I was a lecturer at Sophia College, and she was at Somaiya. We both taught at reputable colleges, I must say.

"I must tell you about this little anecdote even though it didn't come true. You know most of our classmates were girls from well-to-do families, and all of them liked or loved Ayu. Every one of us was enamoured with Ayu Vyas. Smart… handsome…tall and well-spoken… his shield from all of us was his distance and aloofness. I think it was one of the last few weeks before graduation when he was sitting with us, and of course, Mrin, Mrs. Alvarez said on behalf of us all, 'Ayu, we have a suggestion for your second child.'

Prof. Divecha stopped, as Zara and Anya both leaned forward to listen intently, "She said that he must name his second child as per our suggestion…"

"Why not the first?"

"People in both the families want that right. So, the first child's name is the family prerogative. However, we can take a chance with the second child's name."

Zara couldn't take this loquacious academic's verbosity any more. "Aunty Divecha, please proceed with the story. It's killing me!" She begged.

At that point, Prof. Divecha became Aunty Divecha, a term of respect Indians accord to someone who earns it through kindness, generosity and selflessness. She laughed and continued, "So, Mrs. Alvarez said to Ayu, 'Like you, your second child should have a name that means aloof, untouched and unsullied…Niraj… '

Zara's jaw dropped with amazement. "Is there anything more, Aunty Divecha?" Zara's eyes were filled tears and anticipation, which puzzled Prof. Divecha.

"Yes, there's little more to it, Zara. However, your Dad and Mrin both excused themselves. When they came back, they were holding hands and smiling, and Mrin said, 'Well, ladies, we have accepted your proposal. But yours is a boy's name, and Ayu's father has told me that I will have all girls. So, I am going to change it slightly to Nirjara.'"

Before aunty Divecha could complete her story, Zara was sobbing and giggling, tears of joy rolling down her cheeks and Anya hugging her. "Prof. Divecha, meet my sister Nirjara, aka Zara."

Zara hugged Aunty Divecha for a long time, "Aunty, you have no idea how great I feel. I am reborn of knowing how my name came to be."

"Oh, my dear, I feel so privileged that we came up with this name that was beautifully enhanced by an equally graceful couple. We didn't know the meaning of Nirjara then, and we asked one of them to explain it to us. It was Mrin who said, 'Nirjara is one who never gets old, and remains forever young.'…..Just like Mrin…," said Prof. Divecha.

"Dad's forever-young-Zara'…" gasped Anya.

Zara felt a little awkward that the woman, whom she *once* hated as a potential home-wrecker, didn't give her birth, but certainly gave her an identity that would last her a lifetime. Zara knew life was full of surprises, ironies and lessons. "Aunty, thanks for this. Now I know my name is not a ritual of astrological divination, but from a deep and abiding love story. I feel good that a lot of thinking went into my name ceremony. *Grazie mille*."

"Aunty, when did you last meet Mrin?"

"Oh, we met during the summer of 1971, Anya. Nevertheless, please tell me who did Ayu marry?"

"Another childhood friend," Anya said, with a smile. "Aunty, where is Mrin *now*?"

Prof. Divecha was taken back. She slightly recoiled as the words just slipped out "Zara, you don't know?"

They both said at the same time, "No. What is it that we don't know?"

It seemed to the sisters that aunty Divecha was regretting the revelation of this information. Her contorted face showed her own revulsion for divulging the information. They knew she didn't mean to reveal it, but the flow of her recollections brought it out unconsciously. "I am sorry that I blurted all this out. You see, once things begin to pour out, it's difficult to stop them. But I should have known better. You need to promise me that this will remain a secret, and Ayu will never come to know this."

They nodded their heads in agreement, two pairs of wide eyes looking at the professor.

"I'm deeply sorry to say this, girls, but Mrin died. She was killed in a head-on-collision."

Zara's eyes were misty and voice barely audible. "And Dad doesn't know?"

Anya leaned on a nearby desk and dropped her head, "and I'm so sad and angry...ashamed and embarrassed...," said Anya, sorrowful and began to weep and as if this tragedy was unfolding in front of their eyes. Professor Divecha held the sisters in a tight hug and kissed their foreheads to comfort them.

"I barely knew her and I am so shaken up. I can't believe that Dad doesn't know, can't imagine what it would do to him..." said Zara, but she wondered where the emails under Mrin's name were coming from. The mere thought of her suspicions made her sick in the stomach,

"Thank God Ayu doesn't know and please keep it that way too," said Prof. Divecha.

"He missed out on his right to grieve the passing of his lover. What crime did the poor man commit for this exclusion? This is worse than not getting his woman…twice punished…" said Anya.

There was calmness suffused with sadness and helplessness. No one said a word.

"When did it happen, aunty?" Zara wanted to know.

"I think it happened a long time ago in 1971, sometimes in November."

They were shocked that it happened a long time ago, eons ago. Anya looked at Zara, sad and bewildered. She mused over how things that happened a long time ago were still working their way to conclusion.

"The weird thing is a group of six or seven people was going to Baroda to see a prospective groom for Mrin. In that collision, three people died including Mrin, her father and an older gentleman whose last name also happened to be Vyas."

"And then?"

"When the newspapers reported this calamity, a shroud of shock and sadness blanketed the city colleges as most of us were now college lecturers or tutors. However, the papers failed to give the ages of the victims, and we all presumed that Ayush also perished in that tragedy. Thinking that two of them had died together drained all energy from us until we got the full details that Ayush was not in that collision. Since the troupe was on a wedding mission, obviously Ayu wouldn't be there. It was a huge funeral. I do have some pictures if you girls would like to see."

"Yes, I am glad that you foresaw the need of your album," said Anya. Prof. Divecha straight away went to a page that had lots of pictures of Mrin and her friends, including Ayush. Anya grazed her finger over Mrin's angular oval face and endearing, mischievous smile!

Zara looked into her piercing eyes. She felt her perfect set of white teeth were nicely set as if an orthodontist had worked on them. Her hair looked like Farrah Fawcett's feathered hair. It spoke of her free nature. "In most pictures, she always carries flowers, often lilacs or lavender, in her hair. Let's see what else we got here," said Zara.

"Women adorning their hair is a common practice. Most women use jasmine to adorn their hair. Mrin wanted to be unique with lilacs or lavenders."

"So beautiful! Ripped out in the prime of her life! There is no justice..." said Anya.

They flipped a few pages and saw a lot of people dressed in the white of mourning with sombre faces. Recognizing one of the faces, "That's my Mom," screamed Anya. It showed Somi in a white sari, so perfectly draped hugging her lithe torso as if she were lifted from a store show window.

"Well, I am glad I showed you the album. This way, another puzzle got solved!" said Prof. Divecha.

"What do you mean by puzzle, aunty?"

"Zara, I always wondered who that Mrin look-alike young woman of my age, our age was. She played an important role in the preparation of last rites."

"Aunty, I didn't say it but when I saw Mrin's and my mom's pictures, I felt weird inside. I couldn't figure out which one was Mrin and which one was mom..." said Anya.

Aunty Divecha explained that despite their striking similarities, how different the two women were. Mrin walked as if she owned the world and Somi, as if, the presiding officer of the world affairs. Despite the sad situation, Somi looked sombre, but in command. The woman carried an enormous load of pain, grief and loss with dignity. I'd thought she must be Mrin's cousin," said Aunty Divecha.

Silence ruled as they again compared their pictures. Their height, forehead, eyes, nose, necks and cheekbones were so similar. "What did my Mom do?" asked Anya finally.

"I'll explain in a bit. However, I did learn later that Mrin, your mom, Simi Shah and Megh became great friends after we all graduated."

Aunty Divecha recalled that the family was in immense emotional turmoil, and they had no idea what they needed to do. Fortunately, Ayu's Dad showed up. Mrin's mom, stunned and directionless, was much appreciative that an experienced man was now in command. He made someone in the family responsible for calling all the close relatives and friends to attend the cremation as well as tenth, eleventh- and thirteenth-day ceremonies. Someone was asked to prepare a newspaper announcement with specific details of the mourning rituals. He organized Mrin's as well as her dad's cremation. They had to wait for a little longer to receive her dad's body as the mortuary had to prepare it for the cremation. He organized and performed the last rites for both in the Hindu section of the Mahalaxmi Cremation Grounds.

"Ayu's dad asked your mom- and this we found out from gossip and listening to the continuing conversation- that she should help prepare Mrin's body for the cremation," said aunty Divecha.

"Were bodies intact or mangled in the crash?"

"Anya, because of the severe impact, one of Mrin's ribs came undone, punctured her heart and then her inside collapsed. Other than that, her body remained unharmed. I took a picture of her lying in state."

"It must have been a very painful task for mom to prepare Mrin's body. Mom was her age then. Even older people would be traumatized. I sincerely pray that Mom is not left with residual trauma after that experience," said Anya.

"Your mom cleaned and bathed Mrin's body and put the finest clothes on her. She wanted to put on a bridal sari. There was a Gujarati Gharchola sari that had come from somebody that day or a day before, and it was laying down a table inside the house. With the Gharchola sari on, Mrin looked like a ravishing bride, stunningly beautiful. Then your mom adorned Mrin with a bunch of lilacs and lavenders, her favourite colour, including that thin necklace with Om pendant Ayu had gifted her."

"Aunty, when did you know about that necklace with Om?"

"We knew as soon as Ayu gave it to her, Anya. We all liked it."

"Aunty, now let me solve a puzzle for *you*. That Gharchola sari my Mom put on Mrin came from our Dad, who had sent it from Trinidad where he had an IMF posting. I know that was the last gift that our Dad ever gave to Mrin," said Anya.

"Ayu couldn't have picked a better time. It seems he had some uncanny foreknowledge of the impending tragedy. It's ironic that what should have been bridal wear turned out to be a funeral shroud. Nevertheless, it's fitting the gift came from Ayu," said Aunty Divecha.

"I wonder if our mom knew where that Gharchola sari had come from!" Zara said aloud.

"I think I may have misspoken; I have a feeling that she didn't know it for a long time, but it's likely she knows it *now*," said Anya.

"It seems her body was decorated with roses, jasmines and marigolds," added Anya looking at Mrin's cremation picture.

"Yes, your Grandpa also applied the ash and sandalwood paste on her forehead as Mrin's family worshiped Shiva. He put a few drops of water from the holy Ganges in her mouth for her soul to gain liberation from the bondage, the cycle of rebirth. I saw Grandpa put some Holy basil leaves on the right side of the dead body. Her head was pointing south but looking skyward," aunty Divecha said outlining in sufficient detail the Hindu rites of cremation.

Aunty Divecha then recalled that women are not encouraged to attend the cremation *ghat*, but some of them insisted on being near Mrin as her physical body was consumed by religious pyre, the fire of liberation. The pyre was surrounded by a huge throng of people. All her college students were there. After the pyre had gone silent and the body now changed to ash, your Grandpa and her family member collected the ashes in a jar to immerse it later in the holy Ganges. Then according to the Hindu practice, there was a barber to shave off the head hair of the males within the family.

"Then even though he was not a close family member, Ayu's dad sat down on the ground to get his hair shaved off. I overheard him saying, 'She was my daughter too' with tears in his eyes. He continued, 'It wasn't meant to be. You can't fight the divine plan. I knew it; so did her parents.'"

"What did he mean by 'I knew it; so did her parents?'"

"It seems that he had a sense that she was going to die, that's what it means, Zara," answered Anya.

"What did he mean when he told that her parents knew too?"

"Zara, perhaps it has to do with a belief in destiny, karma, stars… who knows?" "Yes, nevertheless, there is more to it. Perhaps Mom knows…" Zara said in a conspiratorial tone to Anya.

Professor Divecha saw Anya fidget in her seat and looked agitated. "Is there anything else, Anya, you don't look good?"

"No. Aunty I am fine, but was wondering if I could ask a huge favour?"

"Ask away Anya," said Prof Divecha.

"Would you mind emailing me a picture of Mrin taken during the happier times?"

"Of course, my dear! You will have it when you go home, and open your mail."

"Thanks a million, Aunty. I promise to stay in touch with you. It's about time that we had a dinner together and talk about those days during the life in the Maximum City," said Anya.

"I'd like nothing better," said aunty Divecha. She saw them leave in silence, withdrawn and eyes wet.

Chapter Sixteen

Good News

It was early afternoon, but after what they had just heard, Anya and Zara were certain that they wanted to retire for the day. But they got home to a ringing phone.

"Hi, may I speak with Anya, please. I am Anuraag in Boston, Akhil's friend."

Anya's eye widened as she tried to mouth to Zara who it was. Clearing her throat, she spoke into the phone, "Hi, Anuraag. Nice of you to call so promptly. This is Anya."

"Anya, Akhil talks so highly of you. He is a jeweller blessed with a keen eye for rare gems… he is hardly ever wrong in his judgment… Yeah; I work with Goldman Sachs… at the international currency office…yeah, I like it here, but it's still *work*…just a part of life, and no more… with this business, I hardly get time to get out and see new people…"

"Join the club, Anuraag. So, I understand you're coming to Toronto to meet me," she said teasingly.

"Anya, I first thought I would see you next weekend, but I just got the word that there's a meeting in Toronto tomorrow for which I volunteered. I believe you're not too far from the Financial Center. I will be staying at the Westin Harbour Castle Hotel, which is also quite close."

"It's in my backyard…within walking distance… So, when do you arrive?"

"I am about to board the flight. In about less than three hours, around sevenish I will be at the Westin."

The visitor knew that Anya and Zara would meet him in the lobby of his hotel. Zara heard the conversation and was pleased with the way Anya handled it. Though the earlier events of the day still lingered in her mind, she was glad they had a distraction for the evening. She walked across the room to the dining table and fetched the newspaper. She flipped pages to find the daily horoscopes. She looked for her sister's reading and said, "Anya, here we go. It says: 'Romance, relationships, beauty, and happiness are accentuated for you now. A new romantic liaison is in the offing. Your friendly manner will shine, radiate warmth and draw people to your aura. Let yourself go. Ask someone you trust for the counsel."

"Zara, I'm not the one to count my chickens before they are hatched."

"Remember what Mom said about you marrying this year?"

Anya raised her eyebrows at her sister.

"What I'm saying is the universe is unfolding as Mom had predicted," said Zara.

"Despite that I don't want to jinx myself. I have been there and getting disappointed. So let me bide my time. Yes, I feel positively about this man coming here, no more, no less."

"You're right. We won't jump the gun. Wait and experience what life brings, but I know in my heart what Mom said."

Zara went to the borrowed laptop to check one of the queries she had sent to one of her colleagues in the Justice office, in Washington. She looked excited as there was a response to her request.

"Anya, about that ethically-challenged attorney in the States, the gift bearing Lothario… do you want me to bring him to his knees?"

"Yes…"

"You told your boss what he did and how he sabotaged your deal, right?"

"Yes…"

"Consider it done. The Justice is already investigating his firm and *now* him… you may have to give testimony…Let your boss know about the possibility."

"I am not a vengeful person, but this man needs to be stopped."

"Understood…"

Three hours couldn't pass quickly enough. Anya was excited at the sudden turn of events. She told herself to calm down and remain in control and stay focused on the present, and not the future. She reminded herself to keep the image of Mrin in her mind. Think about her. What would Mrin do…think what Mrin would do and how she would do it. With these thoughts, serenity returned to her mind. She stopped being fidgety shredding her napkin to pieces. She didn't want Zara to sense her excitement and expectations. She thought the less said the better. Mrin, hold my hand, stay with me, and take me there, she whispered to herself.

Anya and Zara walked along Lakeshore Boulevard. After a couple of rounds of walk down the boulevard, they entered the Westin lounge and walked to the bar, ordered glasses of red wine and sat in the front lounge. As Anya looked at her wristwatch for the umpteenth time to calculate once more expected time of arrival for Anuraag, a man walked up to them unnoticed and said, "I presume you're Anya and Zara. I'm Anur."

Startled, the sisters looked up and the sight of a tallish man dressed in khaki pants and a pastel blue shirt, carrying an attaché case impressed and excited them. He looked more like a GQ model than a Wall Street banker, sporting short, spiked gelled hair and a day's old stubble. Anya loved his dimples, dark eyebrows, high cheekbones and symmetrical lips… she liked this man… stylish and contemporary, 'right now' kind of man. "Wow," she muttered to herself.

"Aren't you a tad early?"

"Yeah, I flew upon the wings of anticipation…"

"It's a great flight known for its roller-coaster ride," said Zara.

"I'm glad you arrived sooner," said Anya.

"Girls, have you had dinner yet?"

"Yes, we have sort of eaten, but you?"

"No, I haven't. I am sort of hungry. Since you already have…"

Look, Anuraag, Anya's condo is right there, and we have a mom-cooked meal sitting there   waiting, " said Zara pointing at condo building

"Zara, nothing beats mother-cooked meals. Shall we go, Anya?" He put his hand on her back. Anya liked it, but Zara momentarily flinched.

Anya couldn't believe things were moving so quickly. There was anxiety, but also happiness. She liked this man the first sight, but she loved more how he carried himself in front of strangers. Not that he acted with too much familiarity or jocularity, but as if he felt no strangeness. More importantly, she didn't feel strange with him either. He talked to them as if he'd known them all his life. He sent right vibes. She felt it would be fun to have him at least as a friend, a real friend, if nothing more. Zara could sense Anya's internal happiness, and soon she felt happy too. However, both the sisters reminded themselves to slow down, focus on the present, and take one step at a time.

Once they were inside the condo, Anuraag took his loafers and socks off without asking, behaving as naturally as one could. Anya liked it so much. That's what she did too. He did it as if he were in his private place. He acted *here* as if he was in *his* place, with *his* own people. He walked to the fridge, poured himself a glass of apple juice and sauntered to the balcony overlooking the lake.

Zara's gaze followed him out and instinctually she disapproved what this likeable man did. To her, this was an invasion of personal space. In a flash, she remembered Robert Frost's poem how good fences make good neighbours. The fridge is like your bathroom or bedroom or purse. You know what is there and how it looks, but others may not like what's in your fridge. They may judge you, she thought, your life or your character on the basis of what you have in the fridge. On the other hand, Anya didn't think twice of it. Zara flinched a bit and wondered if Anuraag came from a single child family who had not learned lessons in boundaries.

"This is majestic," said Anuraag, looking at the Lake. "No wonder people keep on returning to Toronto."

Whether he was aware or not, Anya and Zara were watching every move he made. Every word he said was parsed in their understanding of young males' prowling gestures. Every smile was scrutinized to see if it smacked of dishonest sub-text. Zara studied where his eyes lingered and where they stopped…on Anya's face, eyes, lips, hips or angular curves. She monitored if his conversation and eye movements were in sync or not. If his mind was busy examining her, then he would stumble in his conversation.

Looking at the photos on the wall, he asked, "Who are these gorgeous looking young people, Anya?"

"We bought these pictures, frame and all, at a flea market. They're a couple of models, and we present them as our parents to all the strangers we like to impress," said Anya laughing.

"Great answer, sister, but where is this stranger you want to impress?"

They all laughed with this friendly banter.

Anya knew right away that Zara had picked up her vibes so correctly. She acknowledged it with a wink.

"You are not going to believe this…, but I know these models," said Anuraag with the furrowed brow.

"Dare you to name them," said Anya.

"I double dare you to say a thing or two about them," said Zara.

It was a jovial atmosphere. Anya prayed that it not dissipated.

Anuraag pressed his furrowed forehead as if he was recollecting the thoughts. He understood in his heart that he would need to be circumspect. He needed to speak with his mom *first* to let her know the identity of the woman, and her parentage. He recognized she would be happy. However, he must keep her cabal intact. He was meeting this beautiful woman whom he loved at first sight. He was finding it extremely difficult to restrain his spirits. Nevertheless, you never fathom how life might turn out; he thought. He didn't want to jinx himself. He didn't say a word. He knew that, despite his wish to remain a bit distant; his heart was determined to assert its independence.

"We're waiting…," said Zara.

"Okay, Anya, I already gave you a clue on the phone as to what I do for a living. I'm clairvoyant, and I saw these pictures when I spoke with you."

"Wise guy, fewer words and more substance," said Anya.

Anuraag was impressed by Anya's disarming style of conversation. There was no veneer of enforced correct manners; she was a natural, 'what you see is what you get' kind of woman. Her mannerism was neither distant nor prying. Her gait, hand and facial gestures, smiles, shining eyes all indicated a deep familiarity. He loved it. He felt at home. Please God don't let this end.

"The man is Dr. Ayush Vyas…Rhode's scholar, London School of Economics, Oxford University, Harvard's doctorate and the IMF."

The girls were stunned and speechless.

 "If Dr. Vyas is your dad, I must bow before his picture."

"Yes, go ahead. Do your duty and bow," said Zara, smiling and mocking his deferential attitude.

"I have attended his lectures and seminars. He is my guru. I follow his writings earnestly because I want to make money, lots of it. About the lady there, I presume she's Mrs. Vyas, your mother. I could be wrong, but I think I've seen her picture someplace I don't know where." Then looking at them, he said, "Great DNA, girls."

"So, you don't know her?"

He thought for several seconds, and his eyes lit up.

"Yes…let me lie to you, Zara, and say I don't know her."

Zara thought that was a cryptic answer, nonetheless, according to her gut feelings, an interesting answer. She felt in due course she would discover more of its intent.

"So, confess that you're not clairvoyant then," said Zara.

"I do…," said he and they all laughed.

"It's amazing how you meet complete strangers, and happily feel you have never been disconnected, or away," said Anya, who was opening the lids of food containers at the kitchen island.

He was happy that she spoke what was in her heart and mind without playing games. He walked up to her, standing only inches apart, looked at her eyes and said, "Now, confess that you're a clairvoyant, knowing my thoughts and feelings. I feel so at home here."

"Here goes Mr. Space Invader, again," muttered Zara, seeing Anuraag standing barely inches away from Anya's face.

Their eyes remained locked for a few more seconds. Zara thought he was about to kiss her and the way Anya leaned slightly forward she was certainly going to join him.

"If you guys have done enough staring, then perhaps we can warm up the food," said Zara. Anuraag and Anya blushed and tried to walk away, but ended colliding. Zara could see the goose bumps on her arms.

The food from home was warmed and served on three plates even though the girls had had their dinner. They enjoyed it, relished the conversation and cherished the company. Around midnight, Anuraag said he should leave, even though he didn't want to.

The sisters walked him to the Westin, and as they were leaving him, he turned and said, "At this point we are supposed to shake hands and wish good nights, or hug, kiss and wish sweet dreams. So, tell me your choice…"

"Mr. Anuraag, you know your way around women, don't you?" Anya giggled like a schoolgirl and offered him her right cheek.

As he was boarding the elevator, he waved and said, "Anya, I will call you."

As soon as he was out of sight, the sisters stared at each in their disbelief that such a gorgeous man had simply walked into Anya's life. He was smart looking, late twenties or early thirties and slightly taller than most Indian men. He showed a good sense of humour and above all, he behaved as if he belonged there and treated them as if they had always belonged to him.

"A genuine Kobe beefsteak," said Zara with wide-open eyes. She touched Anya's face, ears, and arms.

"Hey, your face and ears are red and warm. I see the goose bumps on your arm. Not good signs, sis. I think you're coming down with something!" Zara said with a mocking gesture.

Anya was giggly. She sat down on a bench on the curb with knots in her stomach, but continued to giggle until she rolled down with happiness. Her eyes were wide and luminous.

"You're in love!"

"Yes, on the very first sight! I want to bite every bit of the Kobe beefsteak, Zara. Get him here, right now!" Anya screamed with exaggerated hand gestures.

"My sister is in love… Grow up, Anya."

"I love his lips. They are meant for kissing. I want to kiss them, Zara." Anya screamed.

"Earlier I thought you both almost just did that…slow down my lover sister. Take your foot off the gas peddle and just cruise. He'll come to you."

Anya hugged her, and they both felt exhilarated. They wondered when they should inform their parents about the man, but agreed that it was too soon. They knew he had to speak first.

"Anya, I know you're not the one to count your Kobe steaks before they're perfectly grilled."

Anya laughed with frolicking steps!

Back in his suite, he called his mother.

"I was waiting for your call, Anur. Tell me all about the girl. What is she like? What does she look like? I'm dying to know."

"Slow down with your questions, mom. She's gorgeous, very smart, terrific sense of humour, great manners and an excellent lawyer. But..."

"What is *but* doing here?"

'She's the eldest daughter of …now listen carefully…Ayu and Somi Vyas."

After a prolonged silence, his mother mumbled prophetically, "Miracles are about to happen…promises made in jest are going to be kept after all!"

"Yes, Mom?" Anuraag said, unaware of exactly what promises were made to be fulfilled.

"Did you tell her anything?"

"No, you told me so many stories of your best friends, college friends. I know you women have a compact. I won't break it. I like her. Truly, I could even love her, if truth be told. I really hope she likes me and accepts my proposal. She's hot, thinks on her feet and comes up with answers that show how comfortable she is with herself and with *me*. She's the one, Mom. Akhil was right! And I pray that you love her too, Mom!"

"My liking or loving is immaterial. Your and her liking seals the deal. That makes a happy mother. And if she accepts you, then it would reawaken my old friendship with Ayu and Somi"

"I'm surprised that no other man scooped her up a long time ago.

I'm spending tomorrow evening with her."

"That's wonderful. Surprise her with something beautiful. Do what my mentor would do. If you two like each other, then I'll call Somi first and Ayu second. My best wishes and blessings are with you. Make me proud, son."

Anuraag couldn't wait, and as if on an auto-pilot, he called Anya right after.

"Zara, it's Kobe's cell," said Anya giving him a pet name.

"Are you guys home already?"

"Yeah, we are!"

"Thanks for a wonderful evening. I enjoyed it immensely…haven't had such an evening for years…Is it okay to do lunch with you tomorrow? Please don't say no…find a way to do it, please"

Anya could imagine him on his knees and begging her to accept his lunch date. She loved the idea. Her parents taught her well how to be gracious and less politically correct in a situation like this. "Anuraag, you're clairvoyant after all. I was going to ask you for lunch too, but you beat me to it. Yes, we'll do lunch. Remember it's your treat!"

"No, I'm in your town, should be your treat… But I'll try to find some loose change to pay for it, and if I am short, I know I can trust you to cover me. Good night!"

Anya and Zara sat quietly for some time. No one said a word. Their faces showed smiles and contentment. Anya hadn't felt this happy for a long time. This man was different in every respect. He didn't boast about his education, job or family. To her, he seemed to have his act together. The man didn't show signs of spiritual corruption, mental fatigue or physical discomfort. He looked to be in great shape, athletic and quick, agile and alert, funny and friendly. When he talked, his eyes connected with hers; they hid nothing from her and played no games either. She mumbled, "Thanks for holding my hand, Mrin."

"Anya, what did you just say?"

"Earlier, I had prayed that Mrin hold my hand, guide me and take me there. And she did. I trust her. But it looks like I'll have to kiss good-bye to sleep…my eyes do not want to see anyone but Kobe. Zara, I can't figure it out how quickly he has taken over me; I'm already this…captivated and hypnotized. "

"Anya, you're under Mrin's spell. I'm so happy for you."

"She gives me my name and holds your hand…those are our gifts…," said Anya.

"From the woman who could have been our mother," said Zara.

"If I can spill my guts, Zara, I sense she is with me."

 "Be happy then. I am for all of us."

On Tuesday afternoon, a little before lunch, Anuraag called Anya and reminded her of the date. He offered to take a rain check if she was too busy although, but in his heart, he wished she could drop everything and be with him.

"The world waits in line when Anuraag comes to town. And in my world, he never stands in line." Unknown to him, she puckered up her lips in a kissing gesture as she concluded the call.

They agreed to meet at Soup Nutsy on Bay Street in the financial district. As soon as Anuraag saw Anya walk up, he instinctually kissed her on the cheek. They ordered lunch.

"Your Gazpacho looks great."

He took a spoonful and held it out for her. Delicately, smiling, she accepted and tasted what he had ordered. "Yummy!" said Anya.

He gave her second and third spoonful. Then in jest he said, "Okay, get your own soup."

They both laughed.

"Anur, you're so deliciously funny."

"Thanks for turning me into a food item."

Anya caressed his upper arm and looked at him with adoration. She was glad that the place was noisy as no one could overhear their conversation. They talked mostly about their families. Anya learned that his mother was a professor of English Literature at Boston College. He was the only child of his divorced mother. He went to The Penn State as an undergrad and then Wharton for an MBA. He had been employed at Goldman Sachs for the past three years and enjoyed his work.

"How do you know Akhil?"

"I know him from our college days in Philadelphia. My home was practically his second home. My mom thinks of him as her son."

"And what did he tell you about me?"

"All foul, filthy disagreeable stuff. He really doesn't like you."

Anya smacked him lightly on his arm. "Come on!" she laughed, "Okay, so tell me, when did you folks move to Boston?"

"No, we never left Boston. Only I left for a few years to go to Philly for college. Anyway, enough about me, tell me about you." His hand inched closer to hers, "I understand that you are a merger and acquisition attorney…What are you acquiring now?"

"Well, I am working on a sizeable deal right now. But my lips are sealed. Since you are a Goldman guy, I will have to be circumspect as to what I reveal to you."

"Say no more, I fully understand. I should have known better."

"In a way I am so glad that you asked this question, and we now understand our legal obligations. I don't want you to go to jail and nor do I want to be disbarred."

Anuraag was about to be sullen, but Anya's last sentence shook him up and realized what Anya was all about. "Thanks for thinking for both of us…I know you got my back."

After lunch, Anya promised that she would meet him at the Eaton Centre in the evening where he could buy some gifts for his mother. She'd finish work and walk right over.

They both parted, but Anya turned around and shouted, "Anuraag…" He came back, leaned and stood inches from her, and she craned her neck into his face and kissed him on his right cheek, saying, "See you soon." Her eyes sparkled, and his face turned red.

As a parting shot, she said, "Can't wait to see you later, Kobe."

"What did you say?"

Anya ignored his question and walked away with a chuckle.

In the evening, in an upscale perfumery shop in Eaton Center, Anuraag bought two bottles of Chanel Number Five. He said, "My mom's favourite fragrance…one for her and one for you, Anya. I hope you like it."

Anya couldn't believe the uncanny coincidence. "Yeah, I love it too. My mom bought one of these when we were visiting St. Maarten. Thanks, Anur."

Once the shopping was done; they went to the Westin lounge for a drink. They continued talking about their lives, families, experiences, jobs and what they would like to see happen in their lives.

"Anur, do you have questions for me?"

"Like what?"

"I don't know. My personal life?"

"My mother taught me that good men never ask their women about their past affairs or indiscretions."

"That is great advice. Hats off to your mom! I think I've heard it before too." She noticed the use of 'their' in front of 'women.' She wondered if he revealed his innermost thoughts unawares. At that point, Anuraag asked her if she had her own questions or her family's questions.

"None at all. I like who you are, what you are. Nevertheless, you go ahead with your questions…"

"I have a pretty good idea, but tell me what kind of person you are, and what values, ideals you live by."

Anya thought that it was vague and broad but nonetheless, crucial.

She said she was a decent person, felt comfortable in her skin, and didn't want to be like anybody else. She was happy as she was. She believed she had an inner strength, that she was an inclusive person. And she didn't like people who wished to change others into their image.

"Did I turn you off with the last one?"

"No, you didn't. You are just like me. I am responsible for my life; you're in command of yours. That's the way it should remain. When I marry, that's the assurance my spouse will have. Not that I'm in a hurry, I don't know when that moment will come, but whenever it is…" his voice trailed.

"I certainly hope that your day arrives sooner than you think." She teased, looking closely at his face and more at the lips and eyes. She couldn't tell him yet, but she loved his soft, full and symmetrical lips. She recalled what Mrin's friends had said about her Dad's lips. With that thought, she smiled.

Anuraag stood up suddenly and Anya's eyes followed him, apprehensive about his next move. He got down on his one knee, and said, "That all depends on you. Anya, will you please marry me?"

Happily, astounded, Anya put the right hand on her mouth and holding his hands with her left hand raised him and said Mrin's poetic verse, "I accept thee as thou art. I'll bring in my trousseau …"

"Don't bring any riches in your dowry. Just reveal my own to me. My mother is allergic to receiving a dowry. Just bring a lot of laughter, plenty of open-mindedness, and a heavy dose of inquisitiveness. Come just as you are."

"Come here," she laughed and kissed him on his mouth. Not a passionate kiss, just one of acceptance.

People in the lounge saw the unfolding romantic drama, and they all stood up, and cheered them. Camera lights went off of people taking their pictures on their cell phones.

Anuraag said to the bartender, "This round is on me," and gave him his suite number.

They thanked the anonymous well-wishers and moved to his suite. Events were moving at whirlwind speed. She didn't know whether to cry or to laugh. She was dizzy; she was giddy; she was buzzed; she was delirious. She wasn't sure what was going to transpire once they reached his suite. Literate in dating and mating rituals, she knew she would have to either join the dance, or break her leg to sit out the evening.

Before they entered the suite, she had inhaled the gorgeous aromas of oregano, thyme and garlic and heard the sizzle of butter and cream. The door opened; flashlights went off; a Videographer was busy taking a movie, inside a master chef was preparing a sumptuous meal and there was a table set for two. What all had Anuraag been planning, she thought, amusedly. Champagne, an Italian meal cooked by one of the best chefs at the Westin, and the piano music all added to the glamorous surprise that Anya had never expected or imagined.

Thirty minutes later her cell rang, and she came back to earth from the heavenly feeling of extreme happiness. "It's Zara."

"Let me talk to her," said Anuraag.

'Where in the world are you, Zara? We need you here as a witness to a crime being committed."

"Have you gone nuts, Anuraag? What's going on? What crime you are talking about? What are you doing with my sister's cell, more importantly, is she safe?"

"Come right now to my suite. She's safe, and we're waiting for you."

Anya giggled and was touched by her sister's aggressive concern.

"That's awesome to include Zara," said Anya.

"She is family. Our family," he added, "We both need her, especially if we're going to convince your parents. Now, if they approve, I'll have three sisters whom I've missed all my life growing up in a single-parent home."

When Zara entered, she was happily amazed with what she saw in the suite. Immediately the chef's assistant brought a chair, plates and the cutlery for the third guest and first offered her a glass of champagne and then served her the meal.

"What kind of craziness is going on here," demanded Zara as she sat down at the dining table, smiling. Anuraag explained each step of the day, including their lunch and his intuition that this was the best day of his life. Zara could see the happiness on her sister's face, and considered herself fortunate that she could be a part of their day. After the celebration, three of them sat wondering and absorbing the sudden and swift happiness of the day. However, suddenly, Zara was serious.

"Anuraag, I have questions for you. May I see you, in private?"

"Okay, Zara…" and he led her to the next room.

Once inside his room, she asked him where they were going to live after their wedding. Sensing a potential relocation problem arising, Anuraag said, "If Anya can't move to Boston, then, I'll move wherever I need to, to be with her. I am not wedded to my job, and I know there are plenty of opportunities here as well."

"I approve of this marriage," said Zara, "Now you tell her what you told me to make it official, Anuraag. Now get the woman right here, and make her see the stars in the heavens…make her hear those bells…those gongs…Go, you've my permission. Go, Kobe…Wait… wait, I'll send her here…"

Anya entered the bedroom at her sister's bidding and lurched into Anuraag's embrace. "Oh, Anur, you made me so happy."

Before he could say anything, Zara saw that Anya's lips had found Anuraag's and they both remained enclosed in each other's arms for a long time.

She closed the door behind her.

After a while, the couple came out looking extremely happy.

"Anuraag, talking about your proposal, are you always like this? This decisive and this extreme?"

"Yes, Zara, I'm so when I'm clear on what I want. Once I know, I'm this instinctual. My mother taught me this. She said calculated moves are for accountants and strategists, not for sweethearts and currency traders… you will be happy to meet her."

"So, when?"

"Anya, next Saturday evening my Mom will call yours first, and then to your dad. Until then, this is our secret."

"What's her name?" Zara wanted to know.

"Megh…" said Anuraag.

"A very pretty name. My mom had a friend by that name too," said Anya.

Anuraag knew exactly what she was talking about, but he remained silent.

"But a kind of popular name among Indian girls," said Zara. The girls understood well what Anuraag was doing. He was following the protocol of Indian weddings. First, the groom's parents make a proposal and treat the bride's parents with respect and dignity. The rest follows the auspicious first step of the exchange of gifts and sweets.

Around midnight, Anuraag suggested that they could call it a night.

"Why do you always terminate my sister's beautiful evenings exactly at midnight?" Zara joked, "She kissed you, and you can't turn into a frog, now or ever. So, enjoy her company."

They all laughed at the suggestion of his mythological transformation. He escorted the girls to their condo, kissed them good-bye and said, "Anya, I'm going back to Boston tomorrow but I'll call you in the evening."

He returned to his suite and described to his mother what he had done.

"So, now tell me how does she look?"

"I told you last night. Even so, I don't mind telling you a thousand-time. Mom, she is tall, gorgeous, with sparkling eyes, thoroughly poised, funny. She reminds me of your friend."

"I love you, son. You found her! You've made a perfect choice. You make me proud."

"Thanks Mom. I'm flying back tomorrow morning and will see you for dinner after work."

Megh Dalal was extremely happy. She hadn't been this pleased for a long time. She was excited that her son had found the woman he could spend his life with. However, more than that, she was ecstatic about the pedigree of the woman. She didn't come as a question, or a blank slate. Megh knew her whole history.

Thinking about Anuraag and Anya, Megh lapsed into the world of memories, her favourite place, and she breathed a deep sigh of complete happiness. She recalled how she had first met Mrin, Simi and later, Somi. Megh, Mrin, and Simi attended the same residential school in the hills of Shimla. They attended the same college, St. Xavier's College in South Mumbai. Megh's family owned one of the oldest brokerage houses of Mumbai Stock Exchange. Theirs was as old as the stock exchange, making them old money. Simi Shah also came from the same business environment. Her family was in pharmaceuticals with factories in Asia, Africa and South America. Mrin's family was rich too, but nowhere near the other two. On the other hand, Somi was from a middle-class working family. The girls never let her ever feel that she didn't belong there, or was loved less, or respected not as much.

Somi's parents worked as librarians at The Asiatic Society of Mumbai on Mint Road. Her father was a curator of rare books written in Persian, Pali, Sanskrit and Prakrit; her mother, a researcher at the library. Somi developed her taste for reading from her parents; she felt her family led a slow pace life, unlike her friends and their families. Yet, Mrin, Simi and Megh thought highly of Somi's parents.

Mrin had said, "Our parents have wealth for themselves. What Som's parents are doing is for the nation." Somi liked how Mrin thought.

Megh remembered how Mrin and Somi both were similar and yet different. They both looked beautiful regardless of what they wore. Somi adorned her hair with jasmine strung together. However, Mrin wore either lilacs or lavender, but never jasmine. Somi wore a tightly wrapped sari around her graceful and slender body and looked like the famed Air India hostesses. She was always becoming and elegant, but less flamboyant. She was well informed, but less chatty. She was funny, but not hysterical. On the other hand, Mrin was the life of the group, and not an addendum to the group. She saw humour everywhere, but not always the awaiting lessons of life. She reminisced how they teased Mrin and how she gave it back to them with laughter. There never was envy or jealousy among them even though they all lusted for the same man.

She remembered after seeing the wedding pictures of Ayush's sister, how differently Mrin and Somi had felt. Mrin talked about her own awaiting marriage with Ayu with enthusiasm. Somi was down in the dumps.

'Who will marry me? My family doesn't have much to give except rare books,' said Somi.

'Why don't you marry Ayu too and raise his kids? Like in the olden days… princesses took their best girlfriends to their palaces after their royal weddings,' said Simi.

'What am I going to do in the palace then?' Mrin asked.

'You just look beautiful and rule, have fun with Ayu and let Somi bear the kids,' said Simi with a wink.

'You look like Mrin anyway, Somi. He may not even know the difference at night," Megh laughed.

She remembered they all laughed at their silliness. Sometimes they got lewd in their imagination, but it was all in jest. Somi used to remind them that they didn't need anything else other than their friendship to make them insanely tipsy.

She recalled Somi saying, 'I will be pleased to raise your kids, any of you.'

'And so, whose daughter is my son going to marry?' Megh had asked.

'Mine,' said Mrin.

'Or Mrin look-a-like's,' said Somi, laughing.

'Do you girls think of anything other than having kids?' Simi asked.

'You think about kids; I think about sex,' said Mrin.

"Exactly, that's what I said, Mrin. You have sex and Somi will have the kids," said Simi.

"I like it, but how are you going to do that?"

"Simple…Mrin. It's called 'switcheroo'…" said Megh.

"It's settled then, Somi. Be prepared for the switcheroo. You have the kids," decreed Mrin.

"You, ignoramuses, do you know that to have those kids, he'll have to sleep with me?"

"Well… I am okay as long as you two don't enjoy it and don't make a habit of it; it is fine by me. Did you hear, Somi?"

"Mrin, you're such a killjoy," said Simi.

They felt there was nothing better than elixir of friendship.

"Yes, God wanted to create a new heaven and He made a circle of true friends," said Somi.

"How do we know we are true friends?"

"Megh, you go through a series of tests…God tests you to know the depth of your friendship," said Somi.

"What happens if you fail?"

"What happens if you fail?" Megh asked.

They all stared at Somi.

"You fail; you go to hell. If you're a true friend, God names the biggest star in the galaxy after you," said Somi.

"So, there's no heaven for a good friend, right Somi?" Mrin asked.

"No, there is a heaven, but the path to this friendship heaven goes through the gates of Hell," said Somi.

"I thought they were in opposite ends…," said Megh.

"For saints and sinners, yes, that's the way it is. However, for friends, for true friends there's a special dispensation," said Somi.

Megh realized no one challenged the statements Somi made. They accepted her statements as sacred truths.

Megh thought about those innocent days, those days of friendship and laughter until that day, when Mrin got a teaching job at Winthrop University in Rock Hill, South Carolina. She was the life, the soul of the group. When they came to see her off at the Santa Cruz International Airport in Bombay, they watched their soul, their joy fly away. Their teasing conversation of sensuality and sexuality went underground with their dreams, diaries, letters and personal world of fantasies.

They still met, went to see movies, ate out, talked over the phone and even sometimes wrote philosophical letters and lyrical poems to one another. Yet, with her departure, the imagination and creativity abandoned the group; they were less enthusiastic, as if their spirit had left them.

The joy of friendship returned for a time being when Mrin came back home for good. Again, Megh, Somi and Simi reassembled with the infusion of Mrin to their lives. Sunny days were back once again, and they continued as if she had never left them. However, they were wrong. It got worse. They wondered why she had to return, if all she was going to do was to die in search of a spouse. . . The onslaught from the reality of death impacted their psyches deeply as if they were short-changed, as if their limb were severed, as if sleep abandoned them forever, and henceforth, they could dream no more. Their hearts recoiled, became silent and withdrew into a cave for a long wintry coma.

Megh recalled how morose they were after Mrin's cremation. For thirteen days that seemed like eternity, they lived in purgatory; every aspect of their soul in turmoil. She remembered Simi crying her heart out and demanding why *she* had come to Bombay to die. She was hysterical and out of control. Eventually, Somi walked up to her, rubbed her back, massaged her shoulders, touched her hair and cheek, and said quietly, "Because she wanted to die among her sisters."

That answer settled the issue. Megh was thankful that, in one short sentence, Somi had decided the question for them for all-time to come. She realized that it is devastating when a loved one dies near you, but that's the way it should be. Dying where no one knows you is certainly dying like a dog. Nobody wants to die like that, and nobody deserves it either. Megh thought perhaps Mrin had a premonition of her death, and wanted to die among family and friends. She wanted the final exit with nobody else, but friends.

She got her album out, and looked back at those pages to bring the nostalgic and painful days to life. A few weeks after Mrin's death, Megh recalled, Somi phoned the other two for a 'meeting'. The word 'meeting' stunned Megh. Friends meet, date, party and rendezvous; but businessmen have meetings. She sensed something serious was up. Simi and Megh met Somi at the Marine Drive promenade where they both lived.

Megh would never forget the meeting. Every detail was etched on her mind, including the weather and how even the breeze had brushed against her cheeks, stinging them. When they saw Somi come out of the cab, instead of soft and beautiful, she looked hideous and horrid. Instead of clean and brightly colourful, her clothes were grunge, mismatched, crumpled and wrinkled. Instead of smooth and lustrous, her skin was dry and scaly. Her shoes were frayed and frazzled. Her usual confidence was absent. Her face looked frowzy and uncared for. Signs of severe neglect of personal well-being were everywhere. Her eyes were withdrawn and sightless, cast downward, as if she looked, but saw nothing. Her generally shimmering long hair was now without the traditional jasmine ribbon. She walked up to them and stood in front of them.

'I'm not going to see you anymore, nor am I going to write,' said Somi.

Megh remembered how much she was struck by that terse, matter-of-fact declaration. There was no emotion, just the downcast eyes without any tears. There was no introductory explanation, no pleasantries. There was no anecdote or a segway into what she wanted to say. She didn't care to make it easy to understand and feel. She just opened her mouth and got it over with. No questions asked or answered. Megh and Simi could sense signs of emotional and psychic wounds.

Megh remembered Somi asking, 'Can I go now?'

Two small and unassuming sentences and the case closed. She was terse and laconic but always full of substance and purpose.

'No, you can't go now. We're going to Simi's home. We've questions for you,' said Megh.

Somi didn't fight, made no fuss and walked like a zombie behind her friends without saying much. Simi kept an eye on her, in case she missed a step. Simi wanted to be there to help if Somi did stumble. Megh recalled that then she had told, "Sim, Somi never stumbles. She's a tightrope Walker."

Once they were inside Simi's home, the three girls went into her bedroom. 'What have we done to deserve this abandonment from you?' Simi asked.

'You've done nothing. It's me, this is *my* moral dilemma. We've taken an oath of secrecy, but I live in *that* neighbourhood. Someday, sometime I'll run into *him* if I'm not married in a far-off place, and I know I won't be able to look into his eyes and tell him 'I don't know anything' if I continue to remain friends with you. I love him, but he doesn't love me. It should be easier to lie to him, but I cannot lie. My heart still yearns for him. So please forgive me and please release me from this friendship so that I may be true to myself and to the man that I love.'

Simi wanted to know if seeing them would lessen her pain. Somi's face remained unchanged as she answered, 'I'm not worried about the pain. I don't want it reduced. Nevertheless, seeing you both would remind me of our glorious days of happiness and joy and innocence. That's what I'm apprehensive; it reminding me of what was possible…what we once had. I feel I'm afraid to be too happy, knowing Mrin won't. Ever.'

Simi asked, "So that's it?"

"No, I didn't say that. I will never forget *you* two and *her*. Just pray that I don't break."

Megh asked her, "…and our friendship down the drain?"

"Some friendships are born, cultivated and nurtured in hearts… Hearts are horribly funny, dangerously so. We have no control over them. You two, *her* and *him* are squatters in my heart *now*…no matter what I do, I am unable to evict you from there… You chatter…noisy clatter at oddest hours in my dreams and sleepless nights, make me a restless insomniac. You all hold me like a prisoner. See, what you've done to me…I love you…and that's been the biggest error of life…"

Somi remained quiet, digesting and thinking of her own words. Megh recalled that they too remained distressed to hear her last words that Somi was a prisoner, a hostage.

"Love is a sword that carves you up with million gashes that never heal and the bleeding goes on forever… Please let me go," Somi said.

Megh remembered that they remained silent for a long time, holding Somi's hands, digesting what she said about love. Megh recalled her and Simi's eyes teared up and sensed for the first-time unyielding weight of love on their hearts. As Somi stirred perhaps to stand up, Simi, pointing at the bathroom door, ordered her, "Get in there. I can't let you leave my home looking like this."

Somi got a scrub down, received a set of clean underwear, salwar kameez, and a polished pair of shoes. Megh dried her hair and put rouge on cheeks, lipstick and eye-liner for her. Simi put moisturizer on her hands, arms, elbows and feet.

"There. Now you look beautiful, Som. You helped us to remember her and understand what all this meant." Simi's trembling voice was soaked with immense loss that they were about to experience again with her departure. Then Somi looked at them with tears rolling down her cheeks, stirred and turned. They hugged her and Megh said to her, "Remember, you promised your daughter to my son… I'll hold you to it."

Megh recalled those were her last spoken words to Somi.

Somi stood up, hugged and kissed them and began to leave.

However, Simi had the last word. "Som, she dies and now you walk out. We don't get out of this hell and put a closure on her until you come back. Don't ever forget that we will wait for you…"

With that memory of sweet pain and hurtful laughter among friends, Megh wiped tears rolling down her cheeks and said to herself, "Life is a merry-go-round," and closed the album after kissing Somi's picture and holding it in her embrace.

Chapter Seventeen

Mother and Son

Anuraag flew directly to his office in Boston, spent the day working on currency trades in the unfolding financial crisis in the post-sub prime housing bubble. He felt that if the American problem escalated, the Asian and European economies would be severely affected. Taking a break from his work, he looked out the window and sighed.

"I wish I were near Anya…," he said it aloud.

"What did you say, Anur?" Jesse Boothe asked, occupying the next trading desk.

"I was just talking to myself about my girl…" he said unconsciously, busy looking at the terminal and executing his trades.

"Here I thought you had no time to date. Your first date in three years, Anur…" said Amber Hamacher.

"Amber, I feel this is a keeper. I'm in love."

The whole day his mind was engrossed with the images of Anya… her moist eyes when he knelt to propose, her luminous, infectious laughter. He saw these scenes repeatedly and found them enriching. He was looking forward to sharing his thoughts, feelings and dreams with his mother, and later with Anya. His mother treated him as a friend, a confidante. He knew she had a terrific life as a young woman before her short-lived marriage. He was amazed how often she talked about her post-grad college friends, and how often *even now* she would go back to her albums of black-and-white and sepia pictures. He had heard her saying, "Anur; it was Edenic, joyful, full of romance and so elegant! Oh, those were the days!"

With those words, she would lapse into nostalgia, and paint pictures of a grand life in leisurely moving sequences, inhabited by dreams, soft fluttering breezes, unhurried walks on Nariman Road and Marine Drive promenades, and aimless traveling by buses, going nowhere, just enjoying the rides, wearing jasmines or lilacs in the hair, talking and holding hands. He felt when she talked like that she was in the land of old dreams, much cherished and never forgotten. He knew that was her safe and favourite place.

He knew that was how he became more than a son to her. He became a friend, confidante. However, he knew the converse of it was true, as well. She became his friend. She taught him to imagine, reminisce, yearn and pine. She awakened in him poetry and lyricism; she tutored him in beauty and philosophy; she inculcated in him friendship and trust. Despite his career's demands, with her help, he taught himself to slow down, savour, meditate and reflect. Reflecting on this, his mother had put it so succinctly, "Even the most devastating hurricanes, have in the center, the eye, peace and serenity." She nurtured his spontaneity and generosity. He knew her mantra was, 'pleasure and happiness come from yielding, imparting and giving.' At first, he failed to see how giving could be an experience of pleasure. Nevertheless, he discovered she was right. His experience with Anya was testimony to his mother's philosophy. He knew he could tell her his innermost secrets, his worst fears and the most-favoured desires.

He had known the names of Mrin, Ayu, Lulu, Nikhil, Somi, Simi, Mrs. Alvarez, Damo, and Vishwanath, whenever the albums were opened. They were all great friends; they all were generous in giving. Among all these names, Ayu, Mrin and Somi were the most luminous. Every time she spoke about herself, she was somehow speaking about those three. It seemed to him his own memories were filled with their presence too. They became an integral part of his psyche.

He was at his mother's home by seven. Standing at the front door, he smelled the air, knowing that she would have cooked his favourite dishes. The smell of a home food brought back memories of Anya's apartment where he had enjoyed a mom-cooked meal and rich conversation suffused with laughter, gentle teasing and the eye-filling beauty of Anya. He stood there with his eyes closed to ring the doorbell, but Megh Dalal opened the door before it even rang.

"You're lost in thought already! Thinking about her?"

"I was just reminiscing and yearning…"

"Oh, Anur I'm so eagerly waiting for you to tell me everything. Today, dinner can wait a little longer. First tell me about Anya and Nirjara."

He narrated the details of the last two days, the best days of his life. She kissed him on his cheek and said, "I'm so happy that you found her on your own."

"Mom, I was pining and yearning, but I didn't know what I was looking for, what I was pining for, who I was yearning for until she arrived. In a flash, I knew she was the one. It was settled so quickly."

"Tell me about her…"

"Ma, here are her pictures…" Anuraag gave her his iPhone, and then he gave her an envelope, saying, "and some more snaps."

She went through a series of photographs of Anuraag's marriage proposal to Anya.

"She's tall like her father. Look at her eyes, piercing eyes with bright blue irises, so alive, like pools of sparkling, shimmering water. That smile is extremely captivating and friendly. An angular oval face… perfect set of teeth… I love her, Anur."

"Who does she remind you of?"

"Of course, Mrin. Her eyes and smile are all Mrin. Her face is Mrin and Somi. But I do see many overlays of Ayu and Somi in Anya."

"And she's not even dressed for the occasion. We both had business to attend to during the day. I brought her to my suite straight from a shopping center. If she had her make-up on, I am sure...,"

"She would win any beauty pageant. Right?" They both happily laughed.

"Mom, it's dangerous that you could read my mind." He hugged her.

"Tell me more about her..."

"Akhil was not exaggerating about her. She is flawless in her thinking, values and judgment. She has the clarity of a quality diamond. If one looks at her physique, one can tell she's nicely put together. She's all proportion and perfection. She's not shallow or pointedly sharp. She's a princess-cut."

"Are you courting a woman or buying a diamond here?"

"She's a diamond, Mom, no denying that." They both smiled.

While she was getting food to the table, Anuraag fetched his mother's album and went to Ayush's picture that adorned Anya's wall. "Who gave you this photograph?"

"When Mrin and Ayu were going to their rendezvous in Matheran, they wanted me to cover for Mrin. This is from that day. That's his and this is hers," said Megh showing another picture of Mrin.

"Ma, how did you feel helping them?"

"The value of what I did wasn't obvious to me right then. Some may have considered it lewd and unconventional, but I thought it to be aphrodisiac and adventurous. But now, since I know what happened to their lives, I think I did God's work."

"Does Anya's mom know this?"

"First, none of your beeswax. Second, you're funny. Until a couple of days ago, you could easily say the name Somi, but now she is the mother of your fiancé, so she becomes Anya's mother..."

They both laughed at the gentle teasing. "So, you're happy," said Anuraag.

"Yes, that I am, but more than that, this opportunity has changed my whole life. What I've been telling you, to be a giver, has come from that experience. I am sure Ayu has never forgotten those sixty-odd hours in her embrace. In that time, he learned and acquired gifts that continue to nurture and nourish him. Anuraag, your mother did well."

Seeing Nirjara's photograph, Megh said, "She's equally a beautiful, strong personality. I must tell you someday how she got her name. She's taken, right?"

"Yes, she is. They're about to move to Washington D.C. There are two more after Nirjara; Anoushka is working for NASA and Bijli a rabble-rouser."

"I love rabble-rousers."

"Why?"

"They are destiny's long arms…mischief makers. God works through them… I may want to talk to Anoushka…"

"Why?"

"Get her cell number from Anya. I'll tell you later."

Anuraag turned the pages of his mother's album. Pointing to various pictures, he was full of questions.

"Ma, how do you rate Anya's mom among your friends?"

"It is unfair to rate friends. Mrin was certainly the soul, the spirit, the sky of the group. She was pure energy. Exactly opposite was Somi, the earth or *Chi*. Somi represented confidence, gravity and stability. Pure energy is good if one knows how to control and use it. If one doesn't, then the ferocious energy will burn you, destroy you. I loved Mrin and still do, but have come to recognize the beauty of Somi's character. Thanks to her, Ayu was saved from destruction."

"Rock solid, ethical, self-reliant, focused and independent thinker… she is the one who knows the value of waiting."

"She married Ayu, but did she ever show jealousy of Mrin?"

"She never felt jealousy for Mrin and if she did, she hid it well. Knowing what I know of her reactions before and after Mrin's death, I can bet the woman is beyond self-destructive jealousy."

"What did she do?"

"You had to be there to understand it, my son." She said and changed the topic to more current events. "So, what are our plans? How do we take this forward?"

"Well, that's your job now. I said to Anya that you would call them on Saturday and talk to her mom and dad."

"That's fine. But we've to think of the wedding date, place, invitation cards, guest list, our rituals and celebrations, duration of the celebrations. Then we've to visit India to shop for bridal clothes, shoes, colour, and accessories. Are we having guests coming from other parts of the world? There are so many details to look after."

Anuraag quietly stood and listened to his mother's to-do list. He knew among Indians, weddings were huge affairs, and if you were not careful, they took over your lives. "Ma, we'll hire a wedding planner to coordinate everything, including the arrival of overseas guests. What say you? On second thought, just talk to Anya's mom and we'll take it from there. I'm going, ma."

"Oh wait, I have a present for you," she said handing him a box, "and be sure to share this with Anya!"

Promising that he would, he kissed her goodbye and walked out.

Alone and happy, Megh walked up to her phone directory and called her childhood friend. Megh and Simi talked for a long time about the imminent engagement of her son. Megh earlier told her of Anuraag attending Ayu's workshop in New York City. Simi listened carefully. "I am happy for Anuraag. God bless him for he is about to bring home our lost paradise. This engagement is great for *all* of us."

"Yes, I haven't cried out of happiness for ages. I will cry joyous tears in her presence, Simi."

"In her company, even tragedies became comprehensible and tears took us to sweet understanding. Anuraag is our bridge to the heaven of friendship," said Simi. "The woman is…like no other… a true trapeze artist who can walk across the globe on a tightrope without tottering."

"Yes…and at last, the dots are being connected…,

"I can't believe how God's mysterious ways work. In such a wide, very wide world, Anuraag attends Ayu's seminar; Akhil in St. Maarten meets with Anya; Akhil thinks of the possible match, and Anuraag finds Anya, they fall in love. Wonders don't cease to exist. This was meant to happen, I just know it," said Megh.

The friends hung up that evening feeling happy and light, with the possibility of a long-lost friendship being renewed and the world having come full circle. Meanwhile, Anuraag went home and called Anya. She answered it on the first ring, eager to know what he told his mother, her feelings, opinions and questions. He answered, explaining everything in detail.

"Tell me what you two sisters were talking about."

"Oh, it was about a prediction that our mother made. So, you were saying your mom giving you something…"

"Mother gave me a set of books and asked me to share them with you. Let me open the bag…. Oh, Oh, my God…You're not going to believe this…I feel a little embarrassed…Two of them by Jan Kennedy. Her first book is titled 'Sex, Pleasure and Power', and the second one is called 'Tales of the Sex Snake'…"

"Kudos for your mother." Anya said, her voice alive with details of Mrin's emails, "My yoga coach recommended those books too. They're about Kundalini yoga."

Anuraag was happy that Anya made no snide comment about the gift, or his mother. He was pleased that she found it to be a nourishing gift. Anya was touched that here was another woman who encouraged her son to read books for self-improvement and empowerment for the happiness of his spouse. She felt a little sad that her own mother would never consider a gift of such books.

Conversation between Anuraag and Anya went on for a while. Zara pretended to be engrossed in a People magazine, but she could overhear, despite the low voice, "Anuraag, I saw you last night, and I'm already missing you. I want to be near you… so near there is no room for even a sliver of light to pass…I want to be in your arms, your warm embrace. Come here, Anuraag."

At that point, she saw Zara's eyes turn to her, see her giggle and smother the air around her in kisses. Anya hung up the phone finally and threw a pillow at her sister. "Don't forget we have a Kundalini coach coming to my home on Monday, Miss Zara."

"I'm *Mrs.* Zara for your info."

Chapter Eighteen

Death in the Family

On Friday evening, when the three daughters arrived, the house stirred itself out of its inertia; activities, laughter and music brought the joys of life to every corner. Ayu was happy to see the rambunctious excitement and joy. He always hoped that his daughters would be wonderful women, but also always carry an element of mindfulness and discernment that once one woman showed him. He became nostalgic and prayed in his heart that she was happy wherever and with whoever she was. "Bless my daughters with your indomitable spirit, Mrin." He mumbled,

They dined, joked, sang, argued and reminisced. Anya said, "You know Dad, we should invite Prof. Divecha for dinner here. She misses you. I saw her as I was crossing at the corner of Yonge and Dundas Streets a couple of days before Zara arrived from the States."

"Please think before you do anything… impetuous," said an insecure Somi in a sharp tone.

Ayu responded, "I would like that. Would be nice to see someone from the old days again, she knows so much about my life and friends in Bombay. Anyway, So, tell me girls about your lives. Are they unfolding as they should be?"

None of them bothered to respond to his question. They knew a fatherly lecture was in the offing. Out of the blue then, he added, "Anya, there's an aura of immense happiness on your face, and on your younger sister's, mischief. Is there something you need to share with us?"

"Which one are you talking about?"

Anya was happy that Bij had changed the subject. She didn't want to be found out. She needed her secret to last until the weekend was over. However, she was so glad that her Dad noticed her 'immense happiness.'

"Bij, the elder one," said Ayu. Silence ruled the dining room again. Ayu returned to his 'lecture'.

"Let me tell you something about life. It is not predictable. There is no app, formula or paradigm to guide you. So, what do we do? If we come across decent people, we allow such people to nourish our lives. If they turn out to be bad, walk away without regret and thank them for teaching you a lesson. But make sure that you are strong inside. Recognize that you've internal strength. When you have a question, go to your inner recesses to find your answer. Life is not predictable, but you have a very reliable compass inside that can lead you in the right direction,"

"Dad, how long is this going to take? Can you can spill it a little faster?"

"There you again Bij with your brazenness," said Zara.

Ayu felt his inspirational articulation had deserted him. He knew that his advice was true, but felt its expression trite and clichéd. He decided to terminate his fatherly discourse. "Yes, okay Bij is right. You've heard this hundred times. I don't know why I am always giving you the same speech."

"See, he's a reasonable Dad. Now, thank me for saving you," said Bijli.

Eventually, Ayu retired with a book and a couple of magazines to read in bed.

"Mom, you should show Bijli that poem your friend wrote. She will love it," suggested Zara.

"Well, I've some more poems from that friend. I'll get them," said Somi exiting to her sanctuary. She brought a few poems and gave the first one to Bijli. Zara and Anya noticed a few poems that were not in the emails; however, most were. They were too stunned to say anything.

"Anya, put a lid on your happiness. You're smiling too much," whispered Zara in her ear.

"I heard that, Zara. Is it me, or some guy who put this goofy smile on her face?"

"No, it's definitely you, my dear Bij," said Anya, pinching her sister's cheek.

"Find a man, Anya. You're wasting away," said Bijli.

"Can I have one of yours, then?"

With that comment, Bijli was certain everything was normal in the household. However, she had to have the last word. She lamented, "Why do I bother to come here and get insulted by people who know so little?"

Anya and Zara didn't laugh, just said, "Ha, ha."

Somi handed a couple of sheets of hand-written poems to Zara.

Looking at one of the poems, Zara said, "Mama Mia...."

Before she could finish saying what she started, Anya interrupted, "God, these are exquisite poems of unrequited love. It seems your friend started something beautiful, but she feels sad the relationship did not flourish, did not continue or came to nothing. Even then, she kept her word and promise to herself. Am I right, mom?"

Anya knew in heart that these must have a high value for her mother. She also felt that maybe her mother missed the friend who wrote the poems, which could be a possible reason why these poems turn up every few days.

"Anya, I don't know. Perhaps, there are sadness, disappointment and sorrow. Nevertheless, you never know if they are imagined and an artificial construct, or personal and autobiographical."

"Where is your friend now?"

Zara and Anya felt that this was *deja vu* all over again, but they decided to continue the drama of feigned amnesia.

"Zara, I have no idea," Somi said with some sadness.

"How did you come to own these? Didn't your friend keep them?"

"Bij, whenever she wrote to me in Bombay, along with the letter came some poems. That's how I got them. I thought you would like them," said Somi.

"Mom, we are not poetry buffs. You know that. We don't appreciate the finer beauties of life," said Bijli dolefully. She was miffed that her insults either didn't register, or they were masterfully ignored.

Anya and Zara couldn't believe their mother was still pulling the same-old stunts. They wondered if their little 'issue' discussion had fallen on deaf ears. They knew that it was going to take some more time and effort for her bad habits to die or change. They said their *Buena sera's* and retired to their bedrooms. Somi thought that was too early for the young girls to go to bed. Before she mused further, Anya answered her mental question.

"Long week, Mom," said Anya.

"Mom, don't trust these daughters. They are devious and up to some mischief," said Bijli.

The girls checked their emails, the news and sport scores, and then they waited quietly, knowing well Anuraag's call should come anytime.

As if on cue, Anya's cell rang. "Hi, Anur, I was waiting for the night to come."

"Me too. I savour this hour in the evenings when I can hear your voice."

Zara kept on mimicking, teasing and harassing her sister. Anya shot a glance her way, exclaiming into the phone, "Anur, wait a minute. I need to get rid of this pesky little sister… I think she's gone."

Conversation between the soulmates went on for a while. Anuraag told her about his conversation with his mother and how excited and happy she was.

"Tonight, Dad also noticed my 'immense happiness.' I'm so glad that he did."

"The heart doesn't know how to keep secrets, Anya"

"Absolutely…do me a favour and call St. Maarten and let Akhil know our status. Tell that I'll call him soon."

"I will do that with pleasure… my mother will call your parents tomorrow afternoon… same time tomorrow, Anya, but meantime I want to sleep, but sleep is staying miles away."

'Anur, perhaps you don't know that the sleep is an enemy of lovers."

"Now I know and shall enjoy my sleeplessness," said Anuraag and with that they ended their hour-long conversation.

In the morning, when Zara heard the security chimes go off, signaling her parents' morning walk, she went straight to her Mom's sanctuary and looked inside Somi's old clothing closet, rummaging through carefully to where she had found the books earlier. She got the whole set out, quickly glanced over the writing, and knew in an instant that it wasn't her mother's. She read some of the writing. She found dehydrated lilacs and lavenders, every few pages, may be used as page markers.

"Bingo. These are the perfume woman's diaries!" There were nine books of varying colours with yellowing paper coming apart from their spines. Zara looked for the last number of the sequence, found it and peered inside for the final entry. It was in November 1971. She got her camera out and snapped pictures of the diary pages. She carried some of the books to her room and continued to take as many pictures as possible, considering various scenarios of the morning discovery.As soon as she sensed Anya's waking up, she called out for her to join her.

"Don't say a word, Nirjara. Let me see the image of my lover come to my mind first." Anya said dramatically, "Let me kiss him, embrace him, and feel his warmth… Ah, yes, now I'm awake. Talk to me."

Zara rolled her eyes and gestured towards the diaries on the bed. She held up the one in which Mrin had written her final entry. It was not cryptic, not coded, not embellished. It was a simple attempt to archive carefully each emotion she was experiencing.

Nov 20, 1971

Today is Saturday and I am about to take a step that will bring me sadness and disappointment. Ayu is still incomparable despite my prospective fiancé's education, wealth and success. Anything that happens to me is not of my choosing. Like me, someone out there is going to wonder what I was and what I became.

I want Ayu to know that I am not abandoning him. That I will never do. Despite my efforts, I just can't reach him. So many tries have failed. As Ayu's dad would say, all the stars in heavens have aligned their powers against me.

It is early in the morning. My house is still asleep. I have this desire to write my diary before I go to Baroda with my parents and another couple that thankfully is also a Vyas.

I am going to be 'shown', and I will see what kind of man will be my husband. With Ayu, I had no fear, nor any shame, only happiness. However, with some other, there will be no love. Only a lump of flesh with my name attached to it, doling out its dutiful response.

On this road to Baroda, when folks in our car will sing some happy tunes and indulge in joyful talks of celebrations, I shall think of Ayu and in slow motion relive and savour every moment of my history with him. I shall think of my daily walks to the bus stations at the Flora Fountain or Electric House in the evening. I shall think about the gorgeous Saturday Jan 22, the February day he visited my home for the first time, and repeatedly I will think about those sixty hours in Matheran and the fun I had at his sister Sona's wedding. Those days, I will relive in mind's eyes today and every day of life.

If he cares about me, if he ever gets hold of these diaries, I would like Ayu to re-live those days and keep me alive in his mind and heart. Don't let my memories die.

I love you, Ayu.

Anya and Zara read the final diary entry repeatedly and felt that Mrin had a sense of foreboding and fateful finality. They remained quiet, prayed in their hearts and minds for her soul even though her death had occurred a long-time ago. Neither could figure out the riddle of the diaries even though they both had some suspicions, which they didn't want to speak about just yet.

Finding no new Mrin messages on Dad's computer, Zara looked at one of the emails from her and did the reverse search to discover its origin. Once she found out the address of the Internet service provider, she went back to her Dad's email to do the identical reverse search to determine his Internet service provide. As her gut feeling had prepared her, she confirmed that Mrin's as well as her Dad's emails originated from the *same* source. Anya watched this unfolding drama with a little shame, disgust and embarrassment.

"But what can you do when it's one of your parents?" Anya wondered.

"She has Mrin's diaries. She could read what Mrin and Dad did. I think she acquired a phony email address in Mrin's name, took selections from her diaries, and used them in her emails to elicit information from Dad to figure out what had happened and got into Dad's head. That's what she did," Zara said in a low voice.

"And all her life, she hid the horrendous news of her death…. He never learned of what happened to Mrin. She didn't even let him grieve. What kind of mother do we have?"

"Anya, all these years, Mom lived wondering what her husband thought, felt and imagined about his lover. She could not see the whole picture by just reading her diaries."

"But whatever was in the diaries propelled her to see their love from her, Mrin's view," said Anya.

"She wanted to know what Dad thought, what he saw, what he did, and how he felt. It was *his* view, and *his* view alone that mattered to her; Mrin's was incidental. It was important for her to see and feel what *his* world was like when Mrin was around," said Zara.

"Zara, that's what Mom longed for and that's what she got in the end. Now she has the whole picture."

"I can't imagine Mom lived all these years planning how she could find out the intimacies between Dad and Mrin. Mom's perhaps jealous and angry that his passion for her isn't as compelling as it is for Mrin," said Zara.

Anya hummed and said, "I think our Mom, instead of being a lover like Mrin, is happy to be a voyeur and indulge in self-pity. This way, she can elevate her bad habits and guilt to sacrifices she made for her husband and his four girls."

"Why did you say '*his*' daughters?"

"Then her sacrifices, imagined or real, become more substantial," explained Anya.

"But you know, I am simply astounded at Mom's ability to get into Mrin's character and write some of those emails in which she was severely critical of her own indiscretions and character flaws to learn what transpired in Dad's life and what went on in *his* head. I think Mom has a talent. She camouflaged well; hid her identity and got Dad talking. A very smart woman! Conniving but smart," said Zara deliberately.

"But she's our mother," said Anya with a sense of generosity and forgiveness.

"Yeah, we cannot change that. Let me put these books in the right spot."

Zara returned to her bed in a few seconds as the security chimes announced the return of Ayu and Somi to the house. Life, too, returned with them. Everyone gathered in around the kitchen and the Saturday newspapers. To everyone's surprise, while sipping *masala chai*, Anya said to Somi, "Mom, I want to see you for a few minutes to arrange a surprise. So, let me know when you've time. It's just the two of us."

When ready, she gestured to Anya to sneak upstairs in her sanctuary. Somi couldn't hide her excitement for a surprise.

"I see a ravishing smile on your face. So, what's cooking, Anya?"

Anya ignored Ayu's question, but smiled at him nonetheless.

"Mom, remember I said to Dad that I ran into Dr. Divecha on Friday afternoon? When I saw her, I invited her for coffee?"

"But when I asked you what you two talked about, you said she didn't talk about any one person. So, what did you really talk about?"

"We talked a little about Mumbai and Dad's school…"

Cutting her short, Somi pointedly asked, "Tell me, did you and Prof Divecha talk about Dad and his friends?"

"Yeah, that's what I wanted to tell you. We also talked about Mrin. Dr. Divecha said you were present at Mrin's cremation. She said you prepared her body for her final rites and cremation."

Anya could see her mother's face displaying a wide range of emotions of alarm, fear and terror. They both remained still; no one moved an inch. Time seemed to have frozen. Her face was downright ashen. Anya couldn't stand the longest stare of her life. Somi's eyes were fixed on Anya and despite her wish she couldn't avert it. Anya couldn't bear the silent staring, limp arms, slightly hunched back, quiet introspection and vacuous eyes. Nevertheless, she carried on. It seemed like a battle of stares and she wished that it ended soon.

"I thought before Zara heads for Washington, maybe we meet with Dr. Divecha. That would make Dad happy. We'll learn about Dad's college life, his mischief and his friends. So, tell me what's the best day for this? Where do we meet? What cuisine do we have? I think this will be a surprise for all of us," Anya said in a tone that she would employ in legal courts…to the point, enunciated clearly, all questions arranged in a row and ending with a punch that contained understated irony.

"Mom, you're absolutely quiet. What's the matter?"

"I'll let you know," was the curt, lifeless answer Somi gave and walked out. She came down in the kitchen where other two daughters and Ayu were talking. Somi puttered around, mechanically doing this and that without speech or emotion. Anya noticed that her mom, despite acting like an automaton, was in deep thought as if trying to recall some minute detail to see a bigger picture, not in its parts but its wholeness. Anya kept a close eye on her mother, watching every gesture including her moving lips as if in debate with herself to convince of certain path. She saw her sit, immediately stand up and walk around the kitchen island. Then she saw her raise hands looking skyward as if praying. Then she sat down and again stood up and opened the kitchen pantry. Anya noticed that other two siblings too observed the errant behaviour of their mother.

Somi announced, "I think I'm not feeling well. I'd better rest for a while. Don't disturb me, please," and she quickly walked upstairs to her bedroom and closed the doors, which she rarely did. She turned her laptop on and checked mail and then she retrieved a saved document, read it a few times, made some changes, added something more to finesse it and finally copied and pasted it and sent it as a mail. Then she stayed in her bed lying there and thinking about her life and what it was and what it was not.

As was her habit she always thought and reminisced about Mrin, Megh and Simi… that's where she went when her soul needed affirmation of love and friendship. She smiled as she became aware that the life-draining hike was almost over. She was feeling happier that Ayu was getting better everyday in his affections and relationship; she still needed her stories from the youthful friendship to fill the gap of intimacy and friendly chatter that Ayu was not comfortable with.

She recalled the day she travelled to Mrin first and then met Megh Dalal and Simi Shah at Mrin's condo in Worli. Somi had had mixed feelings about Mrin, whom she had known since her childhood, but never had time to develop friendship with. Somi had always been away for her middle and high school education in a private girls' school in the hills. When she returned to Bombay for college, Mrin's family had moved to a different neighbourhood.

A few weeks before Sona's wedding, Somi saw Mrin walk up to her, Somi was first happy and astonished, but was soon dismayed when she understood that the visitor was with Ayush, her own secret crush since childhood. However, Somi maintained the facade of cordiality while Ayush talked to Sona and his mom. In those brief moments, Mrin gave her phone number and home address and invited her to visit her in Worli.

A few days before Sona's wedding, Somi walked out of her apartment and as if automatically, called Mrin from a public phone and then boarded a bus going to Worli. Somi was a little uneasy as she didn't care much for Mrin earlier, and now, she was on her way to meet her. She thought wonders never cease. She considered how she was going to like her when her secret crush loved *her*. Momentarily, she was thrilled at confronting her worst nightmare head-on. There was a strange feeling inside her stomach; bile almost jumped through her esophagus and kissed the back of her mouth. Her face contorted and she muttered, 'yuck!' Tiny beads of perspiration, hung on the forehead and above her lips, refused to be dried up. The heartbeat went up a bit too. She was aware of those body responses. She closed her eyes, whispered a brief mantra, and she was calm. Somi was always in control of life's situations. She didn't like things getting out of hand.

It was a thirty-minute ride, and she wished it lasted longer to reach Mrin's beautiful home that she had visited before. Once she reached there, Mrin greeted her warmly, hugging and kissing.

"Let's go to my bedroom. A couple of my friends are coming here too, and then we will go out," said Mrin.

"Who are coming, Mrin?"

"They are school and college friends, Megh and Simi. You'll like them."

Mrin said she was so looking forward to attending Sona's wedding festivities and enjoy three days of delicious food, fast dances and music. "And of course, there will be great-looking boys too," said Somi, surprised that she could prick into her rival's soul.

"Yes, Mrin, we will see all the girls going nuts over Ayush Vyas."

That was one thing Somi didn't like...Ayush in the middle of so many single hustling girls.

"Yeah, those shameless girls would chatter with him, touch his hand, shoulder and even would dare to dance with him!"

But Mrin suffered from no fears that Somi dreaded.

"Hey Mrin, yes, that's how it's going to turn out." She smiled, but there was an element of hesitation, uncertainty.

Interrupting their conversation, the doorbell rang and Mrin opened the door to two beautiful women in their early twenties. Somi was introduced to Megh and Simi.

"Is Somi your cousin, Mrin?"

"No, she isn't, but she could pass for one; but anyway, she is our adversary...my opponent. Like us, she loves Ayush too."

"And there are a lot more than four of us. Our apartment building is full of those evil vixens," said Somi, laughing and exaggerating.

They liked Somi's silliness. Newness of friendship didn't affect her reactions. She was spontaneous and eccentric.

"Somi, if you don't leave Ayu for Mrin, you are forewarned... she will have to kill you," said Megh.

"Megh, I'm prepared to die, but will never ever relinquish my Ayush. I cannot live without him," said Somi over-dramatizing around the bedroom like a Bollywood actress in distress.

"Oh, woe is you!" Simi said reciprocating Somi's emoting.

"Are you always this deranged?"

"No, Simi, love makes me so…"

"How come *he* doesn't know?" Mrin asked Somi with mock seriousness.

"Mrin, don't you know that it's a secret?" She spoke with a soft whisper.

The girls convulsed with laughter. Mrin's mom brought snacks and coffee for the girls and sat down with them. With an adult in attendance, the buffoonery and balderdash disappeared.

"I feel awful that I enter and all the laughter dies," said Mrin's mom ruefully.

"Aunty, you know Mrin has a strict rule that we have to leave the common sense and logic at the threshold… now we have this new lunatic, just released, from your old neighbourhood," said Megh.

"Oh, my Somi is no lunatic. She has a good head on her shoulders. I've known her since she was a little girl."

Somi liked Megh and Simi instantly. She didn't know anything about their social status and wealth. They saw her crazy liveliness and also quick wit and glimpses into a probing mind. They were sure that behind the façade of fun and frolic, there was a serious person hiding in Somi. If she was a friend of Mrin, she would never be a dolt, a duffer or a drag.

"Hey Somi, I've heard you're a good palm reader," said Mrin.

"Who told you?"

"You can guess, Somi."

"Oh, it has to be my lover…Okay, let me see your palms."

At Somi's request the girls readily showed their palms. She held each girl's palm in her hand and studied it briefly. Then she examined her palm as well.

"Okay, pretender, tell us what does each of us is looking for in Ayush Vyas?"

Mrin's question created suspense for everyone and they awaited her answer with a real sense of anticipation. There was complete silence.

"I am looking for love," said Somi with seriousness. "And I know what it means."

"What does it mean?"

"Megh, I am prepared to put in years of waiting, standing guard, sacrificing."

"What do you get in return?"

"Simi, I get a lot of pain and tears and a load of questions, whether life is just and fair. And as a bonus, if I've to die, I will do so for my love."

"Oh, my God is that what love is?"

"Yes, it is and more."

The girls considered the profound truth behind the statement. In a rush to find love, they knew we all searched for romantic love without anticipating the cruel grind of daily life and its realities. Mrin coughed to break the silence that Somi's reply created.

"Okay, Somi, tell me what is Simi looking for in Ayush?"

Here Somi waited and waited as if interminably.

"Somi?"

"I don't want to offend my friends, so maybe I should tell lies, or claim the Fifth Amendment."

They realized that behind the sudden retreat of zaniness, there lurked a thinker for whom every sentence was a gold nugget.

"No, tell me what's in your heart," demanded Simi.

"You want a trophy husband who will love you as a reward."

"That's how my parents think," said Simi in a monotone.

"Somi, that was very profound. Tell me what am I looking for in Ayu?"

"Megh, you just want a thorough-bred donor to fulfil your destiny as a woman."

Megh was shocked by the divination. She knew how often she had fantasized and formed a family portrait in her mind…she, her husband and a child. In that fantasy, she spent more time with her child and less and less with her husband.

There was absolute seriousness in the room as future and the inner motives were laid bare before them.

"And what am *I* looking for in Ayush?" Mrin asked in a humble voice as if kneeling before a deity. There was no sass, nor was there any humour, but there was a slight tribulation in her voice, perhaps of fear or doubt.

"Mrin, you want to show him the heavens first, rouse his spirit second and live in his musky embrace for ever."

"Will I live in his embrace for ever?"

"Not in his embrace, but for sure you shall live in his mind and soul, as long as he lives."

"We declare you shall be called Sage Somi whenever we come to the inner sanctum," said Megh.

"No sage, simple Somi without titles. Mrin, how do you know of my love for Ayush?"

"It's your eyes that hide nothing. When I speak of him, your ears are red, and they perk up instantly. You know how it works, Somi."

"This love is causing me plenty of heartaches if truth be told," said Somi.

"Don't lose sleep over it. I know it's easier said than done," said Mrin.

"As you said it's easier said than done," replied Simi, "Sometimes love makes matters worse. If marriages were legal and contractual arrangements, then you can walk away and limit your pain," explained Somi.

"I read it somewhere that it's our destiny to love one person, marry another one, and be meant for an entirely different person," explained Mrin.

"No wonder they say life's journey…long one at that…to meet with all these three characters," said Simi.

There was silence.

"Instead of falling in love when we are immature, we should fall in love later in life when the heart knows what is true, what is lasting and what has roots," said Mrin.

"That's what happens if you persist, fight personal conflict and stay in the team…yes love does happen."

The girls were happy that, as usual, Mrin had succinctly defined the life's issues…

Somi always broke down at this flashback of her prescience. Bijli's scream downstairs woke Somi up, refreshed and rested, from the flashback. She felt happy thinking about Megh and Simi as her eyes welled up. She walked to her little shrine in her office and prayed, "God keep my friends safe and make our paths cross again."

After some time, she came down to their den where the family was seated. She joined them, but her mind was somewhere else, not sullen or distressed. She sat there reclined with eyes closed. Meanwhile, Anya texted Zara, not wanting anyone else to know or hear... She noticed her mom looked better than she appeared when she went up.

Anya went over and hugged her. "I love you, Ma."

Somi wiped her eyes with a napkin and smiled, mussing Anya's hair.

"Mi *scusi*, I'll be right back, Ma," said Zara.

She went to her room and looked at her Dad's computer if there were any Mrin messages. And, just as she had predicted, there was an unread one!

From: Mrin@****.com

To: Ayush@*****.com

Subject: Knock, knock.

Ayush:

There is no need to introduce myself, as it is irrelevant for you to know my identity. Let me assure you I am a close confidante of Mrin.

As you are fully aware, Mrin was receiving medical treatment for a terminal illness. Her life is over, but she will live forever in our hearts and memories. You may perhaps want to publish a book of her poems. A parcel that's coming your way could be your source. You could contact your common friends who might want to contribute to her legacy.

She has left a message that whenever you miss her, she is as close as your memory and imagination are to you. She would like you to see on your mind's screen, your significant events with her, and keep her memory alive. She took a rich legacy of your love and memories to her death. Even though, she had doubts in God's existence, she prayed that she was not too far from you in her succeeding incarnation, or that she relives her following incarnation in one of your daughters' families.

I am sending a parcel of books Mrin wanted you to have. The parcel will arrive by a roundabout route of friends taking them from point-to-point until they arrive at your door. Do what you will with them. I have made a couple of suggestions earlier. I'm sure your deep love for her will outshine the suggestions I have made.

I'm deeply grieved to be a messenger of this news. However, I had known for a long time that one day, if I didn't go first, it would be my duty to inform you of this terrible news.

I'm attaching the final closing poem Mrin told me to send you with this announcement.

Take care, Ayush.

A Well Wisher

I pick some dreams from thy blood
I pull colours from the rainbow
Make my heart write thy name
The sun comes out 'n' erases thy name.
I'm so crestfallen.

At the beach against the setting sun
I write thy name on washed, wet sand
With my fingers that know all the contours
Of thy sinews, bones and muscles

Playful toddlers walk over it 'n' erase thy name.
I write thy name again with more panache
The sudsy surf erases thy name with a slosh
I'm so crestfallen.

All summer long I write thy name
On flower beds my heart nourishes
Butterflies of vivid beauty come to embellish it
Summer breeze soothes thy name off sultry heat.
Strong autumn winds, laced with morning frost, erase thy name.
I'm so crestfallen.

I gather early fall's snowflakes
Each one unique like you
Write thy name on snowflakes
On my patio with a quill from my favorite yew
The sunrays come out to play with thy name

In their playful mischief, they erase thy name

I'm so crestfallen.

The sun, the ocean and the wind

All conspire against my dream

I shall write no more thy name

Where others come to play with malice or mischief

It's etched on my aching heart and my dreams,

On my restless nights of endless sleep

If I be allowed, let thy name be on my tombstone

"She loved Ayu and lived Ayu-filled"

"Anya, I need to go to a drugstore," said Zara coming down the stairs and scooping Anya up. Before Zara could finish, both the sisters were out of the house. Zara continued, "Yes, Mrin's dead. No info on how or when. It's a very dignified and respectful email."

"Is it from Mrin, or Mrin's address?"

"It's from her address, but written by an anonymous friend, well wisher, Anya."

"Gist?"

"Died of terminal illness and she arranging to send Mrin's diaries to Dad…dignified and sensitive."

"Zara, you know we have a problem. Mrin passed away a long time ago and the final email perhaps makes it a recent event."

"That's our cabal, our secret. Prof. Divecha is the one who will hold the secret together. She is sworn to secrecy and has done remarkably well."

"Yes, she could have told you in round about ways a lot earlier if she wanted to. But her respect for Dad and Mrin is so lofty that she will maintain her dignified silence," said Zara.

"Then this classified detail remains in a lock box."

"Anya, your pro-active strategy worked. It made Mom re-act and put a closure to it."

Anya smiled and touched Zara's left arm, but her face remained sad, rather calm and sad that the turmoil of the past few days was coming to an end. She was happy that it was all over and wondered if it was worthwhile going through emotional turmoil. She had her doubts, but all of a sudden, she realized that they would never have known of their mother's character, inner conflicts and their father's luminous love affair if they hadn't pried in the email saga.

When we're back at home you should read it. It's a lovely letter with another Mrin poem that's equally beautiful and reflective," said Zara.

"No, Nirjara. We'll not read anymore… emails or her diaries. You also need to erase all those diary entries from your camera chip," said Anya. "No, Anya. No. This last email you need to read. It absolves Mom of many evil deeds. She's suggesting to Dad how Mrin should be remembered. You got to read it," said Zara.

"Alright, I'll read just the last email, and no more," answered Anya with consideration.

"We have to leave Dad and Mrin their privacy, dignity. Anything more will be a voyeuristic intrusion. Look at how deep we've gotten ourselves into it already. We want none of it except for the last concession I made," said Anya with conviction."

Zara wanted to talk about Anuraag, and she knew her sister needed to understand some issues because of Mrin's news. Zara was concerned that the news of Mrin's death was going to have a huge impact in their home, especially on their Dad. She was ready to continue the façade that Mrin's death happened only recently. And this pretence would allow him to grieve over her passing and put a closure on this chapter of his life.

She wasn't sure if the home would go into the mourning rituals or not as Mrin was not an immediate family member. She was more concerned about how Anya would handle the situation; more importantly how the family would receive her good news. It would be unwholesome for her to talk about love, engagement and marriage when their Dad was going through huge pain of loss. She knew it would be painful for him as well as Anya.

"Anya, I'm concerned about you. Mrin's death is going to trump Anuraag's news. You have a problem."

"Yes, I do. I have left my destiny in *her* hands, Mrin's hands and I feel quite safe and serene. I am unsure how my happy news is going to be impacted by the Mrin news. Perhaps this may not be bad news."

"Dad is going to be torn…" said Zara

"If that is the case, he will have to make a choice. I'll respect the choice he makes and will do so with regard, understanding and love… I know he has always taken the right decision for us… he loves me… I have a good idea what his choice will be… Zara, I have no qualms."

They remained silent for a while.

"Zara, I do have grief and pain in my heart that their affair didn't pan out, and that she died so young in life. But I also have the immense joy at the arrival of Anuraag in my life; the kind of joy that Dad felt when he saw her in Mumbai and recently when her emails started arriving. Perhaps this is how we become ourselves, and not clones of others."

Zara was pleased with Anya's answer. She saw maturity, wisdom and life in it. Zara didn't say anything, but her hand touched Anya's cheek with tenderness. "I guess we have no choice… life makes room for all kinds of news… we decide not what is good for us, but what is good for the people we love… Let's go back home."

When they returned, there was absolute quiet, almost funereal quiet around the house.

"What's the matter, you folks are so glum?"

"Zara, Dad got an email. Someone very close passed away.... I think in the family. Dad's upstairs in his office," Bijli confided.

"And mom?"

"In her room," Bijli said.They could hear his office door open, and out came the dour, grim and sorrowful looking tall man clad in the white clothes of mourning.

"Zara, could you please, drive me to my barbershop?"

Zara picked up her sister's keys and along came Anya with Ayu leading the pack.

They said nothing, just squeezed each other's hand. Ayu asked his barber to give him a complete tonsure. The barber saw the sad face and decided to remain cautious and keep his inane chatter to himself.

"Dad, you feel okay?" Anya asked once they were out of the barbershop.

"I'm fine but immensely sad, Anya," as he said it, he lost control over his emotions and began to choke up. "I feel very lost...but I'll be fine."

Anya requested Zara to drive around until Ayush felt better. When silence pervaded in the car, she blurted out the one truth they had hid from him for weeks.

"Dad, we know about Mrin. Aunty Divecha told us about her and you. You're not alone...We're with you..., but we can't be in your heart unless you allow us to be there."

Ayush was not shocked. He just looked at his daughters with sadness, "Who else knows?"

"Just the two of us. And it will stay that way too," said Zara.

"Dad, we love you. We love Mrin too. Aunty Divecha said Mrin was a fabulous woman. We're sorry that it came to naught," said Anya.

"You know Anya; you're something else!" Ayu said.

"What do you mean, Dad?"

"The word Anya means 'something else' in Indian languages. You shortened your name to a beautiful meaning on your own. Nirjara is 'forever young', and you are 'something else'. Instead of championing your mother's cause, you're praising the woman I loved so deeply. Now, that makes you 'something else.' Doesn't it?"

Zara stopped her car in a parking lot overlooking the Lake in Port Credit.

"Life is strange. Alive one day, gone the next! We exchanged emails not too long ago. Now she is gone," said Ayu again choking up.

"It is immaterial that a person we love dies this week, or died five years ago, or thirty years earlier…," said Zara.

"It is significant how long this person inhabited your mind and soul, days and nights; and how long, in our case, Mrin dazzled your personal and private life and the memories she has left behind to light your path and *now ours*," said Anya.

"Dad, which one of us two is like Mrin?"

"I have seen nothing but Mrin in you two… I look at you, and she's there… you two speak, and she's there. But I must see in you, not Mrin or Somi, but your unique beings. My battle has been to remind myself that, and see you two as you are, not anybody else."

"Thanks," said Anya as she kissed her Dad on his left cheek.

"Nirjara, I don't know if Prof. Divecha told you how you got your name or not…"

"Yeah, I love the name your friends gave, and I'm thrilled that Mrin explained the meaning of the name. She didn't give me birth, but she's given me an identity that I'll never relinquish as I'll be called again Nirjara and not Zara."

"Dad, what's next?"

Perplexed, Ayu asked, "What do you mean?"

"Are you going to banish the memory of this exceptional woman to a personal island existing in your imagination and heart where you can visit and speak to her in the monologues of solitude?" Anya asked touching Ayu's hand.

"Or?" Ayu asked looking at her.

"You let us travel with you on this journey so that we can help you see…"

"I thank you, Anya for this. But I think it's your mother who should be on this journey with me. Even though, I now have much sorrow and grief, I'm used to it for some time. Mrin's death has saddened me beyond words. At the same time, I was expecting it awhile. It helps me to put the closure on that chapter of life."

"So, that's it…? Book closed?" Anya asked with a bit of complaint in her voice.

"No, that's not it. I was actually thinking of writing a book about her life, something to chronicle the spirit she had. In the last few months, she's come back into my life, sent me emails, awakened my most precious feelings and rejuvenated my life. Because of her, I looked into my psyche, my memories and my judgments to re-live those beautiful three years. I now have an account of my relationship. However, there're a lot of holes in my recollections…" Ayu drifted off as his line of thought was disconnected.

"You've got an asset in Mom for this," said Zara.

"That's what I intend to do. I'll open up to her, and I hope she does too."

"Perhaps she's waiting for it, Dad. You will be happily surprised at how useful she can be," said Anya.

"You must have millions of questions about your life, Mrin's life. Perhaps Mom can help you connect all the dots. You have your truth and maybe Mrin's reality. And you recognize there are other points of view, as well. Now it's your job to bring all those certainties together, and Mom can help you see and more importantly understand the whole picture," said Zara, taking her father and sister's hands and walking towards the lake.

"Nirjara and Anya, you're my daughters, but today you become my friends, friends who comforted me when I was grieving. More importantly, you passed no judgments, nor cast any smears. Mrin would have been proud to have you as her daughters, like your Mom is. Let's go home and comfort the others, girls," said Ayu with a slight smile upon his face

The girls thought their Dad, with no hair, still looked handsome.

"Dad, since we are more like friends, can I ask you something?"

"Sure, proceed, Madame Attorney," he said with a chuckle.

"Between Mrin and Mom…"

"Mrin and your Mom are fabulous, incomparable women… one is my past and the other is my present, who gave me future and four exceptional daughters."

"What's in the offing for the incomparable present?"

"She gets the life that her deep love for me has earned, Zara. My love and romancing and reliving our lives with no cares and concerns…"

"Dad, don't just put her on the pedestal for worship and then forget her…give her what you intended to gift Mrin."

"Zara, in those few words you've said a lot. Even though she deserves to be on the golden pedestal, her place is beside me, in my heart, my eyes and my arms. I should have pursued her more vigorously when she was distant and aloof…I feel awful…I must seek counselling, if not therapy. I love her and always have. I intend to make the task-oriented sombre serious woman"

"The laughing, serenading and the whimsical woman in love?" Zara suggested.

"Exactly! You stole my words, Zara. More than that, I need to loosen up too…"

They laughed, momentarily forgetting that there was a death in the family.

"Dad, you need to be the laughing, serenading and whimsical man in love if you want to change her…"

"Her changing begins with my own new *avatar*."

"Dad, why is Mom so stand-offish with you?"

"Anya, that question I have been asking myself for years. When we got married, I was so looking forward to a rich life with her…"

"But?"

"The more I tried to get closer, the more distant she became. I asked her if she had someone else in her life, or if I was not the right man for her…I offered to release her…But now, I don't intend to give up…in the last few months, I have seen a pronounced change in her behaviour…she's kind of relaxed, more forth-coming…even singing."

Placing their arms around their Dad's waist, Zara and Anya walked back to the parked car.

After reaching home, Ayu took his post-death ritual bath first, and then asked his daughters to do the same. Somi was not surprised to see a clean-shaven head as she had expected gestures of renunciation from him at the passing of his beloved. She noticed he didn't ask her to bathe, which pricked her, but she accepted the exclusion stoically. She, however, was the last one to perform the ritual bathing. She was gratified with Ayu's responses to the sad news. Feeling Mrin's presence, Somi turned around and whispered, *"Do you see Mrin, he has never forgotten you?"*

"Som, I'm happy that you bathed as well," said Ayu and then hugged her tightly for a whole minute long.

At first Somi was hesitant and even surprised. But soon, she gave in and hugged him back, relishing his embrace.

"Guys, cut it out; there's death in the family, and we're sitting right here. And there are children present," reminded Zara. She smiled mischievously.

"That should have been my line, and as usual, you stole it," said Bijli.

"You snooze; you lose," retorted Zara.

"When we say something you like, you accuse us of stealing it. When we say something that you don't, you snicker at us for our stupidity. We can't win with you, Bij, can we?"

The girls, including Bijli, laughed.

Somi and Ayu smiled, Zara's comment bringing a feeling that life must go on.

Somi threw away all the sweets she had prepared. She knew the house would be in an official state of mourning for the next thirteen days. They were not allowed to enter the family shrine during this period. Cooking and the kitchen would be forbidden too. She must call a couple of her close friends to look after all the personal requirements during the period. She knew that they would not use salt for the next three days, and would touch as few things as possible to avoid contamination.

Bright lights were dimmed to provide minimum illumination. All TVs were turned off and so were the radios, iPods. A DVD of spiritual songs intoned so the departing soul could leave without much tugging at her soul. Ayu joined the singing of the DVD songs to create an atmosphere of meditation. Somi lit an oil lamp which would be kept alive for the duration and a few rose incense sticks, and then she joined Ayu in incantation of the spiritual songs. Anya, Zara and Bijli also joined them. Crying and loud demonstrations of sorrow were discouraged to allow Mrin's spirit leave this cycle of birth and reincarnation. This ceremony of a safe and quick passage ended when Ayu stood up.

"What happens for the next thirteen days?"

"Bij, we'll continue with what we've done tonight. We seek peaceful thoughts and practice renunciation as much as possible. Perhaps Dad and I will sleep on the floor," said Somi.

"I will sleep on the floor too."

"Me too, Nirjara," said Anya.

Ayu and Somi exchanged a look of agreement with a smile.

Ayu noticed the inquisitive expressions on the girls' faces. He explained that, on the eleventh and twelfth day, a priest would conduct rituals of peace in their home. On the thirteenth day, the mourning period would end with a ritual granting the departed soul the status of an ancestral elder in the family. The family would promise that the late soul would be remembered at least twice every year: the anniversary day and the month devoted to ancestors. On those days, a Brahmin would be given a meal and a small gift.

"Wow. It's amazing how much we value the dead," said Bijli.

"Come to think of it, we stand on the shoulders of the dead," said Zara.

"What do you mean?"

"Bij, our births are made possible by our ancestors. We wouldn't be here without them," explained Somi.

"Dad, are we talking about *samskaras*?"

"Yes, *samskaras* are rites of passage ceremonies celebrating significant events during the life of an individual and this is one of them," answered Ayu.

There was a long silence in the room. The three sisters were awed by the homage Hindus pay to their ancestors. The girls felt the ritual reminded them that they were a link in the long chain that went back to the beginning of their culture and civilization.

In the evening as Anya was expecting, Anuraag called her, and he noticed right away that her voice lacked the exuberance of anticipation.

"What's wrong, Anya?"

"We have sad news today…a death in the family. Dad is hurting, but still, standing tall…"

Without going over the details, Anya told him it was an old friend from Mumbai, and how sad her Dad and the family were.

"Maybe we should delay…"

"I'm really conflicted," said Anya. "I want it to go on…we need some elder's counsel."

"Tell you what; I'm going to pass it by Mom. I'll ask her to speak with you, regardless."

"I like that. I can't tell my own mother. It will be really comforting if yours steps in."

"Consider it done. I love you. We'll talk tomorrow."

"*Mi piaci tanto,* Anur."

Chapter Nineteen

Rebirth

The next morning Zara and Somi, seated on the swing in the backyard, talked about life, death and rebirth.

"Mom, do you believe in reincarnation?"

"Yes."

"I wish…," Zara caught herself saying something she thought her mother might object to.

"I hope Mrin is reincarnated in this family. I would love to have a little Mrin running around here…," Somi said wistfully, stealing the words from Zara's mouth.

Zara was astonished and pleased that her mother had echoed her inner thought so intuitively and quickly. Zara realized that her affection for her was returning after a lapse of a few weeks. She felt right away that her mother's jealousy couldn't be that deep.

"What impeded Dad's love affair with Avani, and his wedding with Mrin?"

"Zara, I'll tell you something, which must remain between us."

"No, Mom, I have to tell Anya," protested Zara, "and please from this day on, call me Nirjara."

"Okay, Anya's fine. Nevertheless, exclude the little ones."

She waited for a while to form her thoughts and create a sequential narrative. She recalled that Ayu's dad was never against his son seeing, loving or marrying Avani, his teenage dream. However, Aunt

Sona and she didn't like Avani and carried a vendetta against her. When Grandpa got the news, he went to see Avani and her parents with his apologies. Then he offered to make horoscopes for everyone in the family. He didn't tell her parents, but his objective was to see if her horoscope made Ayu's a strong one. Somi stopped momentarily.

"Armed with this information, he examined all the charts, but particularly Avani's. It was a mortally dangerous chart for the man who was going to marry her."

"How dangerous?"

"The man Avani would marry would die within three years of marrying unless his horoscope was stronger than hers.

"A low twenty-two points in the seventh house, the house of marriages, agreements, treaties and partnerships, and twenty-one points in the eighth house, the house of crisis, change and death among other factors, pointed to a strong possibility of the short span of married life, not exceeding three years.

"This is one of the primary reasons we Indians prefer matching the horoscopes. You want to marry someone with the right horoscope, to make you stronger and not weaker."

"How do you know this?"

Somi explained that she had learned the art of horoscope and astrology from Ayu's dad. According to her, he was a revered teacher, and he found her to be a keen student too. She became very skilled at reading and interpreting charts and assisted him for a while. However, once she found out that Ayu was against this pseudo-science, she decided to step back to please her heart-throb.

"Mom, you like making sacrifices I can tell. Okay. Then what happened to Mrin?"

Somi was happy to hear the comment Zara made about her giving and nurturing character. She coughed; sipped the orange juice she had brought out with her and continued the story of Mrin's horoscope. Both sets of parents had presumed the horoscopes of

Ayu, and Mrin would converge and be compatible. However, the charts had to be looked at with care. When Ayu's dad went to Mrin's home to invite them to Sona's wedding, he had asked for details to make a horoscope should it be necessary. Somi recalled it was the most agonizing period in the Vyas household.

"Were you not in the picture then?"

"No, I wasn't even though my heart longed for it. He was my secret crush."

 Then what happened to Mrin's horoscope?"

Somi recalled those agonizing days in the Vyas household. Ayu's dad was convinced it was not a good chart for the longevity of Mrin's life. He felt that he could have erred in his interpretations. He consulted other scholars, but they all came to the same conclusion. Because he could not bring himself to give the catastrophic news to Mrin's family, he asked them to get the natal horoscope with progressions for Mrin.

"What did the charts say?"

"It was worse than Avani's. In Mrin's case, she would die either before or soon after her wedding. She had a weak Saturn transiting to the eighth house invoking negative influences. It is the house of crisis and death. Saturn signifies lifespan. For Mrin, Mars and *Ketu* both were in her eighth house suggesting severe threats to life. The prediction was full of dire consequences of death and dismemberment. Her sudden departure to the US was an early outcome of this planetary convergence."

 "Nothing could save her?"

"Grandpa looked at Ayu's horoscope to check if his horoscope could save her. It was impossible," said teary-eyed Somi.

"So, Dad couldn't continue his relationship with Avani because if he had, he would be dead. He couldn't marry Mrin because she was going to die. Is that it?"

"There is a little more to it. Then Grandpa looked at *my* chart, next, Ayu's chart."

Somi recalled that, at one stage, Ayu's dad had thought of letting him marry Mrin. He knew there was no recourse against the destiny. Whatever was willed would happen. He knew death came to one and all, but when it came to one of your own, it hurt deeply. He rationalized that if Mrin passed away after the marriage, Ayu would be emotionally handicapped, but at least he would be able to continue his life.

"But what happened then?"

Somi explained that Ayu's dad discovered to his horror as well as relief that Ayu's chart allowed only one marriage. Likewise, her own chart also permitted simply one marriage, but didn't include passionate and mad love that Mrin and Ayu celebrated in their youthful days. Somi was told it would come, but come later in life.

"But the relief for grandpa came from my physical presence and my love for Ayu."

"Who made your chart?"

"Ayu's dad, grandpa did. However, he did say that I would have an abiding love later in my life."

"So, what did Grandpa and Grandma do?"

Somi recalled there was a huge argument. Grandma wanted Ayu and Mrin to know about the impending harm predicted by the charts. He was against informing them of the imminent danger. He thought doing so was to invite the unavoidable to happen prematurely. He felt that had Mrin and Ayush known, they would have rushed to the nearest temple and got married.

"He said, 'I love these kids. They're not sacrificial lambs.' Oh, there were arguments! They really loved Mrin! Grandpa went to Mrin's home and suggested a way out of the conundrum. They were petrified, but became abusive when he recommended co-habitation.

Mrin's parents accused Ayu's dad of everything in the book. They said he was a cheapskate, who spent all his money on his daughter's wedding. He was a selfish, immoral man to recommend such a thing for another man's daughter."

"Mom, Socrates said it the best, 'Those whom the gods wish to destroy they first make mad...'"

"No, it was Euripides," nodded Somi. She seemed tired. She took a deep breath.

There was an extended period of silence. Somi's mind was in turmoil. Zara could see that recalling of these events was painful for her mother. Zara took her Mom's hand in her own, patting it.

"No matter what Grandpa said, nothing was acceptable to them, unless there was a wedding," said Zara.

"Oh, my dear Zara, you've no idea how much pain we went through, including Mrin's parents. I think now that it was one of the worst periods of my life. We really can't blame her parents for rejecting the co-habitation. They saw that this arrangement gave all the benefits to Ayu and nothing to Mrin."

"Yes, shame and embarrassment for Mrin."

"Destiny…" said Somi.

"Yes, Destiny is more potent than God. God doesn't carry a hammer; God doesn't do anything bad. God just outsources the dirty work to Destiny. Mom, you were friends with Mrin. Did you say anything to help her decide?"

"What could have I said, Zara? I was then an inexperienced young woman! I didn't know how to fight God's will or for that matter, Destiny's heavy-handed resolution.

"Really, Mrin wasn't a problem, nor was the cohabiting. It would make no difference to their lives. She was a playful and naughty girl. I don't mean it in a bad way."

"What do you mean?"

"'Som, I can give you all the juicy details about Ayu.' Then she would tease me and laugh, telling me, 'You're dying to know. I know you're burning with love and lust for him… tell me which girl isn't?'"

Zara enjoyed Somi's mimicking of Mrin's gestures and speech pattern.

'Mrin, stop farting around. For God's sake be serious and deal with the issue,' I said.

'She said, "Som, having sex and living together are entirely two different realities. My parents would rather see me dead than see me living with Ayu without a marriage. It's that simple, Som,' recalled Somi with sadness.

Zara continued patting Somi's hand.

"You're truly sad and emotionally moved *now*, but were you so *then*?"

"Oh, my God, Zara, how do you come up with *such* questions? You're determined to see me bare my soul."

"No, Mom, don't worry… I know it is painful. I thought since you had a crush on Dad…,"

"Yes, I did err a few times. Ayu's dad corrected me two or three times. I am truly sorry for those feelings *then*, Zara."

Zara stood up, hugged Somi and kissed her. They both sat quietly for a while, and then Somi pointed out to Zara a single red cardinal staring from a landing pole without making its habitual 'chip, chip' sounds.

"It's been staring for a long time."

"Perhaps it's looking for its mom, or its Mrin. Tell me more about Mrin, please."

"She promised that she would tell me everything about Ayu, including all that personal juicy stuff," said Somi.

"Please, don't tell me any of those lurid details, Mom. However, did she?"

"She told me some, but not everything. Mrin, Megh, Simi and I were planning a trip to Matheran to enjoy her favourite rendezvous resort," said Somi ruefully.

"What's so special about this place?"

"That's where she gave herself in abundance to your Dad."

"Doesn't that gnaw at your innards?"

"No, why should it? I am so pleased that they had their amorous time together…At least Ayu has something to cherish…I am glad that poor Mrin had a glimpse of exquisite happiness, and then she passed…,"

"Did you guys visit that resort?"

"No, we never got a chance."

"Tell you what Mom, we should go on a trip to India, and visit this place as homage to her memory."

"That's a fabulous suggestion. I would like to do that with you and Anya. Thanks so much for saying this…"

Zara remained quiet as Somi was overcome by the generous invitation from her daughter. Once she regained her composure, Somi smiled and took Zara's hand to her lips.

"On second thought, perhaps you and Dad should go together…," said Anya.

'That too is a great idea… really a better idea. It could be a therapy for him…"

"What did grandpa mean at Mrin's crematorium grounds when he said, 'It wasn't meant to be? You can't fight the divine plan. I knew it; so, did her parents,' asked Zara.

"He meant that we have no recourse against God'splan," said Somi. At that point, Zara felt an urge to talk more about preparations for cremation. "Mom, you prepared her body for the cremation alone, or…?"

"Men are not allowed to prepare a woman's body. Grandpa looked at me purposefully, and understanding his look, I agreed to do the last act of love for my friend. Then Megh and Simi Shah also assisted me. I love Megh; she's a true friend."

"What kind of sari…"

"Megh and Simi wanted her to go looking like a bride…That's what I was thinking too, but I had no courage to say it…"

"How did she look?"

"She was exquisite and resplendent in a Gharchola sari I found sitting on the coffee table…"

"I am sure her family placed it there."

"No, it had recently come by mail…I looked at the postal stamp… it had come from Trinidad. I knew it must have come from her lover, your Dad. I was utterly moved…I thought I was going to be crushed under the weight of emotions…of gratitude, the weight of the whole world was on my heart. I cried and so did Megh and Simi…I was inconsolable and proud of the magnificent act of love that God prompted Ayu to do for her…Even in her death, in the gift of the unintended funeral shroud, we saw God's presence in His kindness…I was deeply heartbroken and forlorn…but happy and thankful…

Megh gently slapped me and said, 'snap out of it *right now*; we all will cry later. You have love's labour to finish.' That was the most excruciating day of our life. It is horrible to cremate your friend and is horrendous to prepare her body for the cremation when you so admire what her lover did…"

But Dad didn't mean to send it as a funeral shroud, did he?"

"No, the poor man had sent it as a gift, but it ended up for the funeral."

Somi was moved by the recollection of the preparations for cremation. Right then Anya came outside to join them.

"What's going on?"

"We're putting the pieces of the puzzle together, Anya."

"Mom, you need to tell Dad about the horoscopes of Avani and Mrin sometime," said Zara.

"What about the horoscopes?"

"In short, Anya, according to their horoscopes, Dad would have died in about three years had he married Avani. He couldn't marry Mrin because her horoscope meant she would die before or soon after their wedding. Her parents would not allow them to live together without a marriage."

"Yes, I'll tell your Dad about the horoscopes when the right time comes. I hope it comes soon enough. I need to unburden myself and lead a peaceful life. How did you girls know so many things about Mrin and Dad?"

"Mom, we learnt everything by asking you questions and more questions. Yes, we had a little more info from Aunty Divecha, but you were our primary source. Mom, that's what we both do for a living, knowing the facts, digging for the facts and putting the facts in sequence and perspective. Right, Nirjara?"

Looking sideways in discomfort, Anya ignored Zara's question. Anya and Zara both again felt the pangs of guilt, and hoped they would find a way out of this personal ordeal of injustice, suspicions and gross unfairness to their mother.

"Yeah, Mom, do you know what happened to Mrin's...." Zara caught herself. She didn't want to reveal her sleuthing and snooping into her Dad's computer.

"You were saying...," asked Somi.

"Whatever happened to Mrin's and your friendship?" Zara said as she recovered from the *faux pas*. She knew it was an illogical question, but that's best she could do. "Mrin, Megh, Simi and I became close friends, like you two sisters, after Aunt Sona's wedding. We went out together. I visited them at their homes. We wrote letters to one another.

"Even now I think about Mrin often and with love. I miss her. She treated me like a sister, a profoundly close sister. Never a day goes by that I don't think about her and my life without her.

"I was jealous of her in the beginning before we became friends, but I liked her as a friend beyond words. Perhaps you are right that I was jealous of Ayu because his life was so much filled by Mrin that there was no room left for me. On the other hand, in Mrin's life, there was room for me, Megh and Simi. He was exclusive; she was inclusive. Although I was jealous of him, I was extremely proud of him as Mrin's lover. I have some comfort that if anything ever happened to me, he would never stand by as an onlooker."

At that point, Somi was overtaken by emotions, and she began to sob. The more the daughters tried to comfort, the more she began to wail. Anya held her mother in an embrace.

A period of silence prevailed as each daughter understood the depth of their mother's love for Mrin. They were almost in tears when she said, "Mrin was the best human being I have ever come across or heard or read about."

The girls continued listening to their mother with affection. Zara was moved by the revelations. She wondered how one could develop a friendship lasting a lifetime despite the rivalry to win one person's heart. She wondered if awareness of jealousy cleansed the dross in one's heart and soul.

"Did her passing change your life?"

"That's what I'm talking about. It took time, but eventually her death made me a different person. I'm not sure if I'm a better person."

At the same time, Anya wondered if her mother was a class in itself in terms of character. She smiled as she found a new mentor who could teach and guide her through the maze of relationships in which many lose their way and, disheartened, they give up finding the way out of the labyrinth.

"Yes, Mom, please go on," said Anya.

"When I visited her home once, she showed me her diaries, and so I knew where she had kept them."

"Talking about Mrin, tell me why did her mom not say anything to Dad about her accident? Dad must have tried to see her?"

"Your Dad visited them a few times before she passed away. Because of their attitude, feigned or real, your Dad decided against going to see Mrin's family. They never got a chance to see each other privately.

"After the accident, Mrin's mom realized what your grandpa had been saying all along. But then it was too late."

"On the thirteenth day after cremating Mrin and her dad, Grandpa told her mom, 'this news would kill Ayush if he ever comes to know about the tragedy. I'm going to do my best to hide this tragic news from him. Can I count on you? We couldn't save Mrin, can we now save Ayush?"

'*Bhai*, I'll do anything to protect Ayu. I'll never tell him what happened to her. You know how much Mrin, her dad and I loved him. Now I've to live with two tragedies; I don't want a third one. I'm planning to move in with my son in Australia. So, I'll never see Ayush again. You have no idea how dearly we loved Ayush,' said Mrin's mom.

"Were her college friends there too?"

"Yes, there were some friends who regularly visited Vasundhara aunty for a while. However, that day was a special day, the thirteenth day. So, a good number of college friends were there, and they heard this conversation between grandpa and the aunty."

"Then?"

"Megh looked at her friends and speaking for all of them, said, 'we also make a compact that we'll never reveal this tragedy to Ayu.' They all put their hands on their hearts and said, 'so we swear.' Anya, your Professor Divecha was there, and she said the same thing."

"Did you?"

"Yes, I did, Anya." Somi again broke down, but this time these tears were different. There was an element of release, catharsis. She was not weighed down; her spirits seem to lift her.

"I have been paying my whole life for that promise."

"How so?"

"I'll never tell. Respect that wish, please."

"Do you regret the promise?"

"No, you should never regret the promises you make to your friends. However, I do wonder at times how my life would have turned out, had I not…"

Anya and Zara knew there must be a good reason, most likely painful that she wanted to keep it to herself. However, Anya wondered if the vow of secrecy was necessary in the first place. Life and death are both natural events, and she thought all human beings are hardwired to deal with the most savage pain. Zara too believed the vow of silence, and secrecy was overdone. She thought that, in the throes of a severely felt tragedy, people commit grievous errors of judgments to protect the affected loved ones, and this was one of them.

"Mom, I don't mean to pry into your personal pain, but I would do anything to make it lighter and better for you. I just wonder if you ever had any second thoughts about the vow of secrecy…," asked Anya.

"Yes, I did as soon as Ayu agreed to marry me. Others had the same vow, but they didn't live with Ayu. I did."

"It must have been very painful…," said Zara.

"You have no idea! I was frightened to be in his presence even though my heart lusted to be near him. I was in constant fear that he might just ask me if I knew anything about Mrin. I would not even look at his face for fear of being discovered. The closer I was to him, the more scared I was of being asked about her. No matter what I did to be busy, the fear shadowed me, and I did not enjoy the early years of marital bliss. I wasted that opportunity of bringing him closer to me. It may even seem that I pushed him away… It was difficult until Anya came and changed all that, and soon you followed, Nirjara.

Life pushed Mrin into the back of my mind. Those first three years of marriage were filled with fear and uncertainty."

"So, we helped you to deal with the vow," said Zara.

"Yes, you two filled up my mental space that fear had occupied and Ayu's mind that perhaps Mrin had…"

Anya and Zara mulled over how life manages its affairs.

"But by no means, the fear left me entirely; it had now become an anxiety and a reminder of what I still had to do…"

"What did you still have left…?"

"To keep her memory burning bright in Ayu's heart, that's what."

Zara and Anya knew this was the most critical part of their mother's life. It needed to be treated with soft hands, deepest respect and genuine gratitude.

"Oh Mom, you don't give up that easily. Do you?"

"No one should. A promise is a debt…if people accept your promise; they do so because of your character. If you want your character untarnished, you better keep the promise you make."

The girls remained silent trying to understand the de-layering of their mother's character. With each layer removed, they began to see the luminous character of their mother. They learnt that if promises are made, they need to be kept. A broken promise signifies a character in disrepair.

Somi explained how she continued to see Mrin's mother until she left for Melbourne. In one of the last meetings with her, she gave Somi a pile of diaries with a note from Mrin. The note urged Somi either to give the diaries to Ayu, or do something to keep his love for her alive.

"Were you and Dad married then?"

"No, we weren't yet. It was possible that Mrin never thought your Dad would marry me. Perhaps, that's why she gave me the diaries and the task of keeping her memories burning bright," said Somi.

"My God… that must have been very difficult for you. It's burdensome for any woman to keep the memory of her husband's ex alive. Really, your goal's exactly the opposite. You must have gone through a lot, Mom," said Nirjara.

With those appreciative words, Somi again lost control over her emotions. Anya and Zara both hugged and comforted her, but when they saw their Dad come out the patio door, asking if everything was okay, Anya waved him off.

Ayu stayed indoors fully aware that his wife was going through, perhaps, Mrin related trauma, and that his daughters were helping her overcome its after-effects. Along with Somi, Anya also began to tear up. Seeing her breakdown, Somi got out of the gloomy mood, and began to comfort the daughter in pain.

"I'm so sorry for that stupid, clueless, moronic question, Mom. Obviously, you've gone through a lot, and still do. Such wounds don't heal," said Zara.

"Nor do I want it to heal. It helps me remember her," Somi said, sobbing and sniffling.

"But it is difficult…," said Zara.

"Yes, it is onerous and difficult. When you love your husband as well as his former lover, who was a great friend to you, you have twice the responsibility. Love is never a burden, but I did feel the immense weight of the double love. It didn't crush me, but it made me so protective of Ayu. Loyalty to both husband and friendship is equally sacrosanct. I did my best. To do one without the other would be unforgivably selfish and callous," said Somi.

"Mom, we are learning from you that love is neither a burden, nor is it ever so light. When it matures and grows like a tree, love has its density. That's when it acquires humility, gentleness and understanding. It empowers us to withstand pain and make sacrifices for the ones we love," said Anya.

Zara looked at her sister, smiling with happiness.

"Anya, you spoke just like *her*, like Mrin…," said Somi kissing her daughter.

"Mom, you said I spoke like Mrin, but I know from a reliable source that, in your younger days, you looked a lot like Mrin. However, you never said it…"

"Yes, people said that I looked like her. Some even mistook me for her. Even so, I didn't want to be her, or anybody else. I just wanted to be myself. See, your Dad loved her, and I'm sure looking at me, he must have noticed the similarities. He didn't love me then, and despite the similarities with his lover, my face didn't evoke love for me in his heart. It's her character, her personality, her mind he loved. Our insides were different."

"Yes, you love a person and not a face," said Anya.

"Perhaps, your face reminded him of Mrin," said Zara.

"I'm happy if my face reminded him of her and made him peaceful and pleased. To be honest, I have often wished that my face reminds him of her, and recently those wishes have come true. Enchanted, he comes into my arms under the magic of her face."

"Did you ever wonder what God was doing to you for giving you a face like hers?"

"Anya, yes, that question I have asked often. I wondered how my husband could ever love me if my face reminded him of the 'missing' lover…but my love and affection for Mrin were never diminished. It was not her fault that I had a face so akin to hers. What was a gift for her turned out to be the cross I had to carry…"

Somi took a sip of orange juice and looked at a robin perching not too far from where they were seated.

"So, Mom going back to your fears and anxiety and debt, you were saying something about keeping her memory going…" asked Anya.

"When Mrin left her diaries for me for safekeeping and keeping her memory alive in Ayu's heart, the poor woman had no idea that my fate would bring us at the crossroads where our destinies intersected, and collided. Had she known or had the slightest inclination of Ayu's likely arrival in my life, she would *never* have given me this enormous responsibility. I am sure of that. Once Zara was married, I started worrying about my promise every day…"

"Mom, when did you promise her to do this?"

"Zara, I misspoke, I never promised her. When I read her note left in the diaries, I promised myself that this was my debt to her."

"Then…," asked Zara.

"I started to read her dairies for the *first*-time… and saw her deep love…I understood his desires. For the first time through her diaries, I re-lived as Mrin what my heart had ached for… I analyzed her poems… and made a list of the songs she had sung for him…I learnt the lyrics of those songs …made them part of my mind and soul… Once, I sang one of those and found Ayu at the door, listening… then asking me every few days to sing for him…I knew the dam was breached…"

"Wow, Mom…"

She continued how one-day Ayu asked her to sing those songs again to him, and staring at Somi, he broke down. Feeling his pain, she rushed to him, held him in her embrace for a long-time. Once he had calmed down, she reminded him that she was with him, and she would always be there to comfort him. And after that, she sang as often as she could to nourish his memories of his lover.

"Did he ever talk to you about Mrin and his love?"

"No, Anya. Not yet. I will let him speak only if it makes him feel better for himself and her. I want no confessions from him…"

"What kind of songs were they?" said Anya.

To their surprise, Somi began to sing in a soft tone,

Tera mera pyaar amar, phir kyon mujhako lagata hai dar

Mere jivan saathi bata, kyon dil dhadake rah-rah kar

Tera mera pyaar amar, phir kyon mujhako lagata hai dar

Mere jivan saathi bata, kyon dil dhadake rah-rah kar [1]

"Which Bollywood movie is it from?" Anya wanted to know.

"From Ashli Naqli."

Zara wanted to know how she felt singing that song for her husband, but Somi stayed calm but lost in her reverie. *She imagined how transformed she was instantly, and saw that he too was different… changed. She rarely felt the honest expression of belonging from her husband all these years. She was married to him, but she had remained distant, but that lyric changed everything. He melted like a wax candle in her embrace. What was once a fortified citadel, had now surrendered to the power and grace of love, patience and friendship. She knew then that he belonged to her, and he was hers.*

"How did you feel when Dad was listening to your singing?"

"Anya, when I sing for *him*, I sense internal transformation. I am, then, Mrin-filled. Her spirit, her charisma takes over my personality. I feel liberated, unburdened. I don't mind telling you one thing if… if you don't think ill of me…"

The daughters prompted her to go on, "Well, when I sing to Ayu" she began, "I feel her ethereal presence. Soft breeze swirls around the room and Ayu says, 'It feels good and airy here. I smell lilacs here.' And I know right away that *she* has entered the room. I sense her presence. I think she is bringing a huge transformation in our lives…"

"Did you two ever talk about Mrin?"

"No, we never did. But I have a feeling, we soon will. I have so much to tell him about *her* and *me*…I really want to speak about her for my sake, my friendship's sake… "

Anya and Zara smiled and said, "Ma, you're so right. How do you feel talking like this… to us?"

"My time in purgatory is over…"

They remained silent.

"When did he *first* ask you to sing?"

"It was on the twenty-second January of this year."

"Why do you remember the date?"

"Because it was the first request, and then I figured out why he chose that day. That date was significant to them. That's when they had kissed as a man and a woman for the first time and declared their love."

"How do you know?"

"She told me…"

"What else did you do…" asked Anya.

"That's when I began to write emails to him under Mrin's name," she confessed.

Anya and Zara were speechless. The perceptions turned upside-down. What they had thought to be true was not so any more. They were mesmerized with new knowledge and their fresh understanding of their mother's character and involvement. They thought she was voyeuristic and jealous, conniving and manipulative, vengeful and small-minded. She wasn't any of them, not even close. They were disappointed in themselves; they had never known what their mother really was, and they regretted their judgment.

Zara put her arms around her shoulder. "You're an amazing woman. There is no one like you out there, Mom. I'm sorry, really, really remorseful for being loud and rude with you earlier." She was almost ready to confess, but realized that it would take away attention from their mother. It was her time, her day to show her inner character, strength and abiding love.

"Sweethearts, I wasn't going to say anything about this, but you asked me questions, and you deserve a truthful answer. I thought that if I wrote to him as her, it would bring him back to life. He would become the Ayu he was, the man I once fell in love with. He would be full of song and happiness, even if it were because of the memories of *her*. Memories that I had given to him. "

Silence reigned briefly as Zara and Anya digested their mother's revelations. In their hearts, they felt guilt and shame. They wondered how and when they would confess to their mother about their snooping and huge error in judgment. They knew their time would come.

"Nirjara, Anya I need you to promise me that this will remain between us. You'll not reveal this to anyone. I don't want Ayu to feel any guilt or pity or sympathy for me over my role in this. I didn't do it for anything other than my love for him and my friendship with Mrin."

The girls simultaneously said, "We promise, Mom. However, doesn't Dad need to know what you did?"

"No, no one needs to know. I didn't do it for people to know, or to win thanks or any medals. It was my war, and I want nothing changed. If he knows…, then my life, my sacrifices are wasted… I don't want Ayu to feel any pity for me. Because in this, I don't deserve pity and pity is what he would give me.

"If Ayu is to feel anything for me, then that shouldn't come from what I did for him. It should come from his heart, from his love for me, not as a reaction, or a reward."

"Our lips are sealed, but he may not feel pity. He may feel something else, something beautiful," said Zara.

"But that's taking a chance. As I said I want no rewards, and for sure, I want no thanks… and nothing will come unless he feels he mistreated me. That above all, I don't want *ever* to happen. He has never mistreated me…

"One more thing, girls, this last issue about the gift of the diaries perhaps raises a question in your mind why I never revealed to Ayu about my deep friendship and exchange of letters with Mrin."

"No, Mom, it's not that important," said Anya.

"But you need to know. Ayu's parents had massive faith in me. His dad had told me that it grieved him that my life would pass in caring for Ayu and his family without receiving deep and abiding love from him until *later* in life.

"If I had told Ayu about Mrin's whereabouts in South Carolina, he would have flown there at once to see her. That would have reactivated their desire to be married and thereby unleash the astrological onslaught on both the families.

"That would have left him to live a life of solitude without a family of his own. To protect him, I had to keep these secrets which I hope you now understand. I did what I had to. There was no one except Grandpa to guide me."

"Mom, you turned out to be a magnificent witness and recorder of events," said Zara.

"And a rock-solid keeper of faith and the secrets of the family... we can't thank you enough," said Anya with a kiss.

They looked at the squirrels scampering around and chasing one another on a maple tree. Starlings, goldfinches, and cardinals were helping themselves at various bird feeders. Corinthian chimes, full of lightness and with the resonance of liturgical music, were making the late-summer morning air serene and soul enriching. Right then a radiance of cardinals was about to alight on the resting pole. Somi saw Ayu closing the patio door behind him, and before he could reach her, Somi waved at the birds.

"Hush, you birds. My lover's here, shoo," she said to the radiance. The birds flew away. Zara and Anya both smiled at the playfulness their mother seemed to have acquired or came to life within her. She walked around the lilac tree, culled some purplish flowers and put them in Anya and Zara's hair first and then in hers and later sat with her daughters on the swing. Ayu walked up to Zara and Anya and sat between the two and then looked at them softly saying 'my forever young and something else' daughters.

"Lilacs look fabulous in your hair, girls. I feel happy to see you look like this." "It's Mom's gift to us, Dad," said Anya.

Intuitively, the girls left their parents alone. Zara and Anya were half-way to the door, and they stopped in their tracks as Somi began to speak.

"Anya, call Aunty Divecha for a dinner here whenever it's convenient for her and you, sisters. Your Dad and I are comfortable with any evening," Somi said with contentment. She looked at Ayu for a tacit nod of acceptance. He smiled back, nodding.

As the girls were nearing the back entrance, they could hear Somi saying, "I've sinned against you, and beg for your forgiveness, Ayu."

The girls lingered near the door.

"Then you're on a path to sainthood, Som, and I wish you to lead me there too," said Ayu.

"It would be just crazy if we both were anointed with sainthood at the same time, Ayu."

"You talk more and more like Bijli, you know, Somi?" Ayu said with a happy grin and a twinkle in his eyes.

"But I must say with lilacs in your hair, you look whimsical and wild."

"I did that before too, Ayu."

"But today I don't know why, but you look different, very different, endearing and exceptional."

"What do you mean?"

"You remind me of a woman I knew once; beautiful and endearing, caring and smart."

Somi had never ever heard Ayu speak about another woman with such affection. She sensed the dam that breached earlier was about to run over. She stared at his eyes, moved closer to him and staring at his symmetrical and curved lips, her hand on his shoulder. She said nothing just gazed with craned neck. He leaned and kissed her and she was folded in his tight embrace. She sensed his right hand pushed her back into him… She knew it was a different kind of kiss, not like the ones given out of habit or the ones given to avoid any questions. Even the hug was different, she felt electricity, sensuality and she felt as if she was melting, like a young bride.

"Som, I don't know if you knew Mrin," whispered Ayu in her ears.

"Yes, I knew her and she was my friend too..."

Ayu sounded surprised, almost shouting, blurted out, "Were you?"

Then she took Ayu to the garden of lilacs and lavenders and placed a plucked lavender in his hair and said, "Pray here looking at the lavender and lilacs. You will be happy."

He followed her instruction with closed eyes, folded hands and bowed head.

"Ayu, I need to write an obituary for the death in the family, Ayu."

With a gentle smile, he put his arms around her. They stood in a close embrace longer than the girls had ever seen their parents before. He said softly in her ears, "I will never let you go out of my embrace," and kissed her. She looked at his face, but not his eyes, and smiled.

The chimes hung from the maple tree came to life, and serenading the family, birds and squirrels as the gust of wind swirled around in the backyard and swooped over the neighbours' garden.

Somi entered her private sanctuary and stood in front of the deities she worshipped. There were also the pictures of her and Ayu's parents who had passed away. Even though it wasn't the time to worship, she lit a candle, stood with folded hands and head bowed. She muttered looking at Ayush's dad's picture, *"Bapuji, your blessings are coming true. Continue to bless us all."* Then she came down. And she went back to the backyard, humming one of Ayu's songs.

Inside the house, as three sisters were digesting the events of the morning, phone rang.

Bijli saw Anya answer the phone, her eyes and ears glued on the eldest sister.

"Hello, no, I'm her daughter Anya. Excuse me; I'll give the phone to her. May I know who is calling?"

Anya learnt the identity of the caller and before she could say anything further or hand the phone to her mother, the caller said, "Anya, don't give the phone to your mother yet. Wait a while. I want to speak with you."

"Yes...?" said Anya.

However, when questions were asked, she fumbled and tripped on words, began to perspire and turned red. She looked embarrassed at her incompetence and lack of composure.

Bijli couldn't hold back her comments and a loud laugh any longer.

"Zara, it's definitely a man's call. Look, how giggly and uncoordinated she is, either tongue-tied or tripping on her own words."

"Maybe you should instruct her on the art...."

"Don't be cute, Zara, it doesn't look good on you...Anya; you need to get out more often than just visiting Mom and Dad," she shouted.

"It's Kobe; I think, Bij," said Zara.

Anya left the room, calmed down and said, "I'm sorry to make a fool of myself. Here I am, now fully composed."

"So, what happened there?"

"My sisters are teasing me about Kobe...I mean Anuraag," she flustered.

"Your sisters know, but your parents don't?"

"Only one sister knows, but yes, my parents don't know yet..."

"Please, tell me if you like Anuraag."

"Yes, I think I might even love him. To be honest, I can't sleep, sometimes I can't even breathe."

Megh thought in her mind that Anya revealed what was in her heart exactly the way Mrin used to... honest and direct, no games, no shame, just pure truth. Megh thought Anya got her characteristics from Mrin as well as Somi.

"That you must do… breathe, inhale, exhale…"

At that point, Megh talked about the conversation with Anuraag regarding the death in the family. She was happy in her heart that eventually had finally come out in the open, they had closure on the issue.

"Anya, what I'm trying to say is that I should speak to your parents as planned. In a way, it is preferred that you get the sad news first because good news always trumps the bad news. This news about Anuraag's engagement with you will change everything in your dad's heart and mind. Believe me. I know some things that you don't, but soon you will too."

"Thanks for the counsel. You're right and that's what we'll do…So, what more do you want to know?"

"I heard what I wanted to hear. When you and I are together, we will talk and see where we can take this relationship."

"I would love to do that. Is there anything else you would like me to do?"

"Yes, my dear, there's something I like you to do. I would like to invite a close friend when we come to see your folks. Her name is Lulu Divecha."

"Oh yes, I know her. She was my prof at Osgoode, my law school," said Anya. "Great. Please invite her and tell her there's a surprise for her. Don't tell her we are coming."

"My pleasure…"

"Anya, one more favour…let Anoushka know that I will speak with her in a day or two. Please give her cell number to Anur."

Anya thought it was strange they wanted to speak to her sister, who had not been in the picture at all. Crinkling her eyebrows together, she asked, "Well, yes I suppose I will share her name with him. But is it something that *I* can do?"

"No, actually, we would like to know how we can get a star named after our dear friend."

"Oh" Anya was touched, "I understand, of course." She smiled.

"Now if I may speak with your mother, my dear friend Somi!"

"Oh my God…." Finally, Anya connected all the dots. "Megh. You're Megh. The Megh Dalal she was talking about? How small is this world? And you two were close friends, you said?"

"Yes. We started out as acquaintances, but soon became very close. And if Somi is your friend, you never need another friend in life. I want a star named after her, my best friend with whom I haven't spoken for years, but never forgotten."

"If you want to know in the last few weeks, she has spoken about you, Simi aunty and Mrin aunty so much…"

Megh was moved by the last revelation. She felt proud and reverential for her friend whose character continued to dazzle her. "Love you Anya. Your mother keeps on mesmerizing me."

Anya took the phone outside where Somi and Ayu were seated.

"A call from a friend called Megh Dalal," said Anya quietly to Somi.

"Boy, your face is radiant, happy and blushing. What's going on, Anya? Look at you…all these goose bumps…," asked Ayu. Somi, on the other hand, was confused but took the phone.

Embarrassed, Anya ran away like a girl whose secrets were found out.

Somi, making faces as if she was talking to the other person in face to face, said, "Is that my favourite loser? What have I done to hear from you after so many years?"

"Yes, you're a bigger loser than I am. You know I'm planning to make you the biggest loser ever," said Megh.

"You didn't succeed in the past and nor do you have a chance now," said Somi.

This chatter, banter went on for a while. Anya, Zara and Bij could see that they must be childhood friends resuming their competitive spirits from where they had left off before.

"Megh, you're going to live a hundred years and more. I was talking to my girls Anya and Nirjara today, and your name came up so often."

"I hope you didn't say anything mean about me. If you did, I will make Anya pay," she said with laughter.

Somi missed the clue that Megh had dropped. "So, Megh what's going on?"

"Som, you're still clueless, aren't you? Listen…"

Somi listened to the revelations quietly. However, soon, her face changed and displayed varying degrees of happiness in an ascending order… smile, happiness, elation, ebullience and rapture. She got excited as the conversation went on for more than thirty minutes.

"Last time I spoke with you Som, you had said you were afraid to be happy. Are you still?"

"Megh, today after a long, very long time none of us is a loser. I am joyous, positively jubilant and not afraid of happiness. A new chapter begins in my life today, Megh. We both have in our lives what we lacked before. God has placed the gold from the Spanish galleons and the treasury of *Kuber* in our laps, Megh. Are we lucky or what?"

"When we last met, you said love is a sword that bleeds you a hundred times or more…"

"Megh, yes that blood turned out to be the blood of life…I bled, but I was never drained…from somewhere it kept on coming …from the memories that you sisters left behind…from visiting me in my dreams and living in my poems…blood had its source…"

"Thanks again Mrin for giving me the right perspective…"

"What did you just call me?"

"Yes, you heard it right. However, let's not debate this now. Pease, tell me when the last time you opened up about *her* with others was?"

"Anya and Nirjara have made me talk about *her* in the last few weeks. In dribs and drabs, I opened up, and they finished digging the whole story a little before your phone came today. And when you see them, you can fill in the gaps for them. I am out of the salt mines. I was trapped in an endless labyrinth, feeling asphyxiated and claustrophobic… I can now breathe and live again… I've missed you and Simi so much, Megh."

"I talked with her too. You have no idea how much we missed you. Don't worry; Simi is coming with me and Anuraag when we see you in the next few days."

"Megh, I must have done something right in my previous life to have friends like you, Simi and *her*. I love you and here's your heart throb."

"You still love *her after* what you've gone through…?"

"Not less, but more…Every time I stand in front of the lilac trees, *she* talks to me… Here's Ayu."

"So you built a garden of lilacs in *her* memory…"

"Yes, I did…and lavenders too. My own a little spring and summer shrine…"

"Does Ayu know why you have the lilac garden?"

"He doesn't need to. It's for me and *her*."

Somi gave the phone to Ayu and told who the caller was and went to find Anya and Zara.

"You two sisters kept *this* from me! Such huge news that I have been planning and dreaming ever since you were a little girl, and you kept it from *me*? Brats! Ingrates!"

Anya and Zara scrambled around the shrubs, jumped over the flower beds, but Somi caught up with them and as Anya fell on the ground giggling, Somi climbed on her stomach, pinched her reddish cheeks and said, "Never hide something this beautiful from your mother."

Then she kissed Anya, hugged her, and pinched her cheeks one more time, making faces of extreme happiness. Bijli walked to Anya and kissed first on her cheeks and said, "Congratulations, Anya. You are one sneaky sister! However, because of you, now the pressure is going to be on Anu and me to get married. Hate you for that!"

"Hey, Bij, thanks. You know how to give compliments.'

"Anu should have no problems with the NASA tag. And you have a large retinue of admirers, so you should be fine too, and somebody, please make a call to Anoushka," said Anya.

"I will do that," said Bijli.

Ayu narrated the happy mayhem to Megh, who was ecstatic to hear that the celebrations had already begun. Anya, Zara and Somi went inside the house. Everyone's faces reflected happiness.

 "Mom…" Anya said, "When we were in the Caribbean, you fell asleep talking about Megh aunty and Simi aunty. Remember?"

"I don't recall, but I do have a hazy impression that I was kind of too happy that evening…"

"The word is…drunk," said Zara and they all laughed.

"Zara, did you say Somi was drunk? Wonders never cease. Why was I not there when that happened? Do you have it on your iPhone? If you do, YouTube, here we come," said Bijli.

They all ignored Bijli's irreverent remarks, but laughed and simultaneously pinched her cheeks. .

"Mom, I'll take you bar hopping…"

 "Dream on, Bijli."

"It doesn't look good for your image, Bij. People may think you have a court-appointed chaperone to monitor your behaviour…" said Zara as she smacked her shoulder with teasing and love.

"Yes, after Mrin, Megh and Simi are my next best friends. Anya, if Megh is any indication, then Anuraag has to be even better. You will shine with them. However, we'll talk more about her later. Girls, go and see what's going on in the backyard. I will be out soon."

They saw Ayu was still on the phone.

"Ayu let me spring a huge, but happy surprise on you. Somi already knows, but you got to hear from me first. My son wants to marry your daughter, Anya. So, I'm bringing the *Baraat*. I want a big wedding."

"We want nothing less. We will be ready for the *Baraat*, your wedding party. By the way, did Anuraag ever tell you that I met him six months ago in New York? I was so happy to meet with him."

"He told me everything and wished that he had another chance to sit with you."

"I'm so happy, Megh, but…"

"Don't mind *her* absence. As a matter of fact, *she* is not absent at all. I have seen the photographs of Anya and Nirjara, who are the living embodiments of Mrin. And Somi is no less, believe me."

"That certainly has been a blessing."

"Ayu, you've been a lucky man with a flawless lover and a faultless wife. Who can beat those odds? However, I do hope you are a perfect hubby for Somi. That's how you can re-pay her who never stops giving gifts."

"I am going to exceed everyone's expectations, I tell you."

The conversation between Ayu and Megh went on for a long-time. The girls heard many names, picked up on their stories of youthful days, but the name they heard the most was that of Mrin. Ayu seemed happy to talk about her with unadulterated joy with a friend who knew them both intimately.

"I didn't know you were friends with Somi."

"Ayu, I'm glad you didn't know…Somi thinks she must have done something right in her last life to have friends like me and Simi. However, in reality, Simi and I consider to be blessed to be her friend."

"And I found out only seconds earlier that Somi was a friend of Mrin too!"

"Well, that's great news for you to understand what had transpired earlier…Any time now you'll receive a parcel of photographs and a DVD of Anuraag's proposal to Anya. Enjoy it. We're coming down in two weekends as soon as the thirteenth day ceremony is over to fix the wedding details. We will bring all the *mithais* you love. I can't believe how life has come full circle, Ayu. Some things are just meant to be!"

Outside, a FedEx deliveryman rang the doorbell.

9 789354 585883